PRAISE FOR JOEL C. ROSENBERG

"Joel Rosenberg has an uncanny talent for focusing his storytelling on real-world hot spots just as they are heating up. He has done it again in *The Kremlin Conspiracy*."

PORTER GOSS, *former director of the Central Intelligence Agency*

"Marcus Ryker rocks! Breakneck action, political brinksmanship, authentic scenarios, and sharply defined characters make Joel C. Rosenberg's *Kremlin Conspiracy* a full-throttle and frightening ride through tomorrow's headlines."

BRIGADIER GENERAL (U.S. ARMY, RETIRED) A. J. TATA, *national bestselling author of Direct Fire*

"Joel C. Rosenberg writes taut, intelligent thrillers that are as timely as they are well-written. Pairing a fast-paced plot with an impressive understanding of the inner workings in the corridors of power of the Russian government, *The Kremlin Conspiracy* is a stellar novel of riveting action and political intrigue."

MARK GREANEY, *#1 New York Times bestselling author of Agent in Place*

"*The Kremlin Conspiracy* is my first Joel C. Rosenberg novel, and I am absolutely blown away by how good this guy is. The story moves at a blistering pace, it's crackling with tension, and you won't put it down until you reach the end. Guaranteed. Simply masterful."

SEAN PARNELL, *New York Times bestselling author of Outlaw Platoon*

"If there were a *Forbes* 400 list of great current novelists, Joel Rosenberg would be among the top ten. . . . One of the most entertaining and intriguing authors of international political thrillers in the country. . . . His novels are un-put-downable."

STEVE FORBES, *editor in chief, Forbes magazine*

"One of my favorite things: An incredible thriller—it's called *The Third Target* by Joel C. Rosenberg. . . . He's amazing. . . . He writes the greatest thrillers set in the Middle East, with so much knowledge of that part of the world. . . . Fabulous! I've read every book he's ever written!"

KATHIE LEE GIFFORD, *NBC's Today*

"Fascinating and compelling . . . way too close to reality for a novel."

MIKE HUCKABEE, *former Arkansas governor*

"[Joel Rosenberg] understands the grave dangers posed by Iran and Syria, and he's been a bold and courageous voice for true peace and security in the Middle East."

DANNY AYALON, *former Israeli deputy foreign minister*

"Joel has a particularly clear understanding of what is going on in today's Iran and Syria and the grave threat these two countries pose to the rest of the world."

REZA KAHLILI, *former CIA operative in Iran and bestselling author of* A Time to Betray: The Astonishing Double Life of a CIA Agent inside the Revolutionary Guards of Iran

"Joel Rosenberg is unsurpassed as the writer of fiction thrillers! Sometimes I have to remind myself to breathe as I read one of his novels because I find myself holding my breath in suspense as I turn the pages."

ANNE GRAHAM LOTZ, *author and speaker*

"Joel paints an eerie, terrifying, page-turning picture of a worst-case scenario coming to pass. You have to read [*Damascus Countdown*], and then pray it never happens."

RICK SANTORUM, *former U.S. senator*

THE KREMLIN CONSPIRACY

JOEL C.
ROSENBERG

THE
KREMLIN
CONSPIRACY

Tyndale House Publishers, Inc.
Carol Stream, Illinois

Visit Tyndale online at www.tyndale.com.

Visit Joel C. Rosenberg's website at www.joelrosenberg.com.

TYNDALE and Tyndale's quill logo are registered trademarks of Tyndale House Publishers, Inc.

The Kremlin Conspiracy

Designed by Dean H. Renninger

For information about special discounts for bulk purchases, please contact Tyndale House Publishers at csresponse@tyndale.com or call 1-800-323-9400.

Library of Congress Cataloging-in-Publication Data

Names: Rosenberg, Joel C., date- author.
Title: The Kremlin conspiracy / Joel C. Rosenberg.
Description: Carol Stream, Illinois : Tyndale House Publishers, Inc., [2018]
Identifiers: LCCN 2017047720 | ISBN 9781496406170 (hc)
Subjects: | GSAFD: Suspense fiction.
Classification: LCC PS3618.O832 K74 2018 | DDC 813/.6—dc23 LC record available at https://lccn.loc.gov/2017047720
ISBN 978-1-4964-0630-9 (International Trade Paper Edition)

Printed in the United States of America

24	23	22	21	20	19	18
7	6	5	4	3	2	1

To my paternal grandparents and great-grandparents, who took unimaginable risks to escape from Czarist Russia in the early 1900s, and in so doing gave me and my family a chance to be born and raised in freedom.

CAST OF CHARACTERS

Americans

Marcus Ryker—*former U.S. Secret Service agent; former U.S. Marine*

Marjorie Ryker—*Marcus's mother*

Elena Ryker—*Marcus's wife*

Lars Ryker—*Marcus and Elena's son*

Javier Garcia—*Elena's father*

Nick Vinetti—*deputy chief of mission, U.S. Embassy, Moscow; former U.S. Marine*

Robert Dayton—*U.S. senator (D-Iowa), member of the Senate Intelligence Committee*

Peter Hwang—*aide to Senator Robert Dayton and former U.S. Marine*

William "Sarge" McDermott—*deputy national security advisor; former U.S. Marine*

Annie Stewart—*senior foreign policy advisor to Senator Robert Dayton*

Andrew Clarke—*president of the United States*

Cal Foster—*U.S. secretary of defense*

Richard Stephens—*director of the Central Intelligence Agency*

Tyler Reed—*ambassador, U.S. Embassy, Moscow*

Jennifer Morris—*CIA station chief, Moscow*

Carter Emerson—*pastor, Lincoln Park Baptist Church, Washington, D.C.*

Russians

Aleksandr Ivanovich Luganov—*president of Russia; former prime minister; former head of the Russian Federal Security Service (FSB)*

Yulia Luganova—*wife of the president*

Oleg Kraskin—*senior aide and son-in-law to President Luganov*

Marina Kraskin—*Oleg's wife; daughter of the president*

Boris Zakharov—*chief of staff to President Luganov*

Mikhail Petrovsky—*minister of defense*

Dmitri Nimkov—*head of FSB*

Nikolay Kropatkin—*deputy director of FSB*

Pavel Kovalev—*chief of the president's security detail*

Katya Slatsky—*Olympic figure skater*

Vasily Malenchenko—*journalist*

Galina Polonskaya—*journalist*

"Be polite, be professional,
but have a plan to kill everybody you meet."
GENERAL JAMES MATTIS,
U.S. MARINES

"The idea that safety can be purchased by throwing a
small state to the wolves is a fatal delusion."
WINSTON CHURCHILL

PART

ONE

Louisa Sherbatov had just turned six, but she would never turn seven.

The whirling dervish had fallen asleep on the couch just before midnight, still wearing her new magenta dress, still wearing the matching ribbon in her blonde tresses, having finally crashed after a sugar high. Snuggled up next to her mother, she looked so peaceful, so content as she hugged her favorite stuffed bear. The two lay surrounded by the dolls and books and sweaters and other gifts Louisa had received from her aunts and uncles and grandparents and cousins as well as her friends from the elementary school just down the block at the end of Guryanova Street.

Strewn about the room were string and tape and wads of brightly colored wrapping paper. The kitchen sink was stacked high with dirty plates and cups and silverware. The dining room table was still littered with empty bottles of wine and vodka and scraps of leftover birthday pie—strawberry, Louisa's favorite.

The flat was a mess. But the guests were gone, and honestly her father, Feodor, couldn't have cared less. His little girl, the only child he and Irina had been able to bear after more than a decade and four heartbreaking miscarriages, was happy. Her friends were happy. Their families were happy. They were happy. Everything else could wait.

Feodor stared down at the two most precious people in his life and longed to reschedule this trip. He had loved planning the party with them both, had loved helping shop for the food, had loved helping Irina and her mother make all the preparations, had loved seeing the sheer delight on Louisa's face when he'd given her a shiny blue bicycle, her first. But business was business. If he was going to make his flight to Tashkent, he had to leave quickly. So he gently kissed mother and daughter on their foreheads, picked up his suitcase, and slipped out the front door as quietly as he could.

He stepped out the main entrance of the apartment building, relieved to see the cab he'd ordered waiting for him as planned. He moved briskly to the car and gave the driver his bag to put in the trunk. The night air was crisp and fresh. The moon was a tiny sliver in the dark sky, and leaves were beginning to fall and swirl in the light breeze coming from the west. Summer was finally over, Feodor thought as he climbed into the backseat, and not a moment too soon. The sweltering heat. The stifling humidity. The gnawing guilt of not being able to afford to provide his family a simple air conditioner, much less a little dacha out in the country, where he and Irina and Louisa and maybe his parents and hers could retreat now and again, somewhere in a forest, with lots of shade and a sparkling lake to go swimming and fishing, far from the traffic and pollution and frenetic pace of the capital.

"Autumn—finally," he half mumbled to himself as the driver slammed the trunk shut and got back behind the wheel.

Growing up, Feodor had always loved the cooler weather. The shorter days. The start of school. Making new friends. Meeting new teachers. Taking new classes. Fall meant change, and change had always been good to him. Autumn was a time of new beginnings, and he wondered what this one might bring. He was not poor, exactly, but he was certainly not successful. Still, he was content, even hopeful, perhaps for the first time in his life. Maybe one day, if he continued to work very hard, he really could save enough money to move his family away from 19 Guryanova Street, away from this noisy, dirty, run-down, depressing hovel on the south side of Moscow, and find some place quaint and quiet. Some place worthy of raising a family. With a bit of grass, maybe even a garden, where he could till the soil with his own hands and grow his own vegetables.

As the cab pulled away from the curb, Feodor leaned back in the seat and folded his hands on his chest. *Autumn.* He smiled. He found himself reminiscing about the autumn day he'd first laid eyes on Irina. It was the first day of middle school, twenty-two years before.

At that moment, Feodor Sherbatov—so caught up in his own world, his own memories—barely noticed the two burly men dressed in black leather jackets and black leather gloves emerging from the basement of his own building. He paid scant attention to the car parked just down the street, the white Lada with its headlights off but its engine running, to which the two men headed. The driver was smoking a cigarette and tapping on the dashboard, but Feodor would never recall the face, shrouded in shadows and a hat of some kind. When the police later asked about the men and the car, this was all Feodor could tell them.

What he did remember—what he would never forget—was the deafening explosion behind him as the taxi gained speed along Guryanova Street, heading to Domodedovo International Airport. He remembered the searing fireball. He remembered his driver losing control and crashing into a lamppost. He remembered his head smashing against the Plexiglas screen dividing the front seat from the back, and the ghastly sensation of heat as he kicked open the back door of the cab. He remembered jumping out into the street, blood streaming down his face, heart pounding furiously, and looking back just in time to see a secondary explosion as his home—the drab nine-story apartment building at 19 Guryanova Street—collapsed in a blinding flash of fire and ash.

2

Oleg Stefanovich Kraskin awoke in a pitch-black room.

Alone and disoriented, he was covered with perspiration. His heart raced. His hands shook. His sheets were soaked through. He could not see or hear a thing nor even remember for several minutes where he was as he tried to shake off the ghoulish images of what was only a nightmare. But what a nightmare it had been.

The great hall in which he stood—once so elegant and grand, even opulent, with its massive archways and precious oil paintings and glittering chandeliers and glorious circular staircase going up, up, up—was ablaze, shrouded in thick, acrid smoke. His eyes stung. His lungs screamed for oxygen. His skin crackled from the blistering heat as the flames raced through the structure, greedily consuming everything in their path. Walls were collapsing. Beams from the ceiling crashed to the floor. Oleg could find no path of escape. He tried calling for help but could make no sound. Yet he could hear the bloodcurdling screams of others. And one voice he recognized imme-diately—it was Marina, his beloved Marina. She was suffocating. She was burning. And there was nothing he could do to save her.

Oleg pushed the covers away and jumped to his feet. Standing, trembling in the utter blackness, he felt around for his glasses. When he found them and put them on, he grabbed his watch and learned that it was not yet six in the morning. Only then did he remember that he was not in his modest downtown flat but at his parents' palatial home in Rublyovka, the tony gated enclave of Moscow's wealthiest and most powerful families.

Stumbling to his left, two meters and then three, he reached the far wall. Then he groped about until he felt the drapes and pulled them away from the bay windows. Fresh, soft morning light flooded the room. No longer was Oleg staring into the fiery abyss of his deepest fears but into the wooded glade in the rear of his parents' estate. With the house so still in the early dawn hours, he could hear the swallows chirping and the buzz of insects flying about.

Oleg finally began to breathe normally again. Wiping the moisture from his face and neck, he fought to regain his equilibrium. This was not a day to dread. To the contrary, it was one for which he had planned and prepared meticulously. He went back to the nightstand, fished out a cigarette from a pack he'd bought the night before, found his lighter, and took several drags until his nerves settled. When he was finished, he took a long, hot shower, shaved, and dressed in his best suit and new leather shoes. Now he could smell breakfast. He could hear his mother padding around in her slippers, and when he emerged into the kitchen, she greeted him with a kiss and a big smile.

"Come, Oleg, sit—make yourself comfortable," she said, handing him a steaming cup of chai. "Your father wanted to join us. But you know his work. The board meets in two days. He left before dawn. But he's proud of you, Oleg—very proud—and he cannot wait to hear how it goes. He wants you to call him the minute you have your answer. I've actually never seen him like this. He's almost giddy."

Giddy? It was not a description Oleg had ever heard applied to his father. But it made him feel good. At the same time, he was far too anxious to eat, for reasons that had nothing to do with his dream. So he apologized to his mother, kissed her on the cheek, grabbed his overcoat and briefcase, and dashed to the garage.

Moments later, he was sitting behind the wheel of his gleaming new silver Mercedes, lighting another cigarette, gunning the engine, and racing down the Rublyovo-Uspenskoye Highway, heading east for the grueling two-hour slog through morning rush-hour traffic. Trying to get his mind off the night terrors and off the day's business, which alone would have made him jittery, Oleg switched on the car radio and tuned in to a news station.

The news anchor said an eight-story flat along the Kashirskoye Highway had been obliterated. Oleg could scarcely believe it. *How was this possible? Three bombings in ten days? By whom? And for what?* The attack had happened just before sunrise, while most of the building's residents were still sleeping. Already the hospitals were filling up with the wounded. The morgues were filling with the dead. Local authorities were telling reporters that more than three dozen bodies had been pulled from the wreckage already. Oleg had no doubt the death toll would climb throughout the day. A spokesman for the Moscow police being interviewed live at the scene said the explosion had apparently been caused by a large bomb that had been placed in the basement, near the furnace, though he cautioned the public not to jump to any conclusions before a full investigation could be completed.

It was too late for that, Oleg thought. His hands gripped the steering wheel until they were white. He was not scared. He was furious. His country was under siege, and the military would soon be striking back. That much was certain. What wasn't clear was who the enemy was and what their motives could be. The Cold War had been over for nearly a decade. This wasn't the Americans. It wasn't the Brits or anyone in NATO. *Then who?*

Oleg's legal training began to kick in. As the youngest partner in one of Moscow's most prestigious law firms, he was used to asking questions, collecting facts, sifting and analyzing dates and times and places and details large and small. What exactly was known for certain? What was speculation and what was really true? What were the connections between each of the attacks, and what could they reveal about potential suspects and motives?

The first attack had occurred on 4 September in the city of Buinaksk, near the border with Chechnya. It had involved a truck bomb, not one placed inside a building. But there, too, an apartment complex had been the target. Oleg had seen pictures of it on the evening news. A five-story flat had been reduced to rubble. The TV had shown flames and smoke and charred human body parts and screaming children, faces bloodied, desperately searching for parents they would never find. Sixty-four people had been killed, and yet Oleg was ashamed to admit that at the time the whole thing had made little emotional impact on him. To Oleg, it had all seemed so far away. It was terrible—unfathomable—to be sure. But it happened in the Caucasus. What could one expect? The province of Dagestan was an unstable, war-ridden hornet's nest. He had two cousins who had fought the Chechens in Dagestan. There was never good news from the Caucasus. So Oleg had winced but moved on.

The second attack had happened just five days later, on 9 September. It had occurred on Guryanova Street, in a poor but quiet neighborhood in the heart of Moscow, only a few kilometers from Oleg's own flat. This wasn't a crime in some far-flung, godforsaken outpost of the Russian Empire. This was a dagger pointed at the heart of the Russian capital.

Vasily Malenchenko, a prominent investigative journalist for *Novaya Gazeta*, one of the city's most influential newspapers, reported that the explosion had been caused by a large bomb in the building's basement. Malenchenko was well-known for having excellent sources inside the police department and other state security services. He reported that the bomb had been attached to the gas furnace. He also reported that there were no solid leads yet as to who was behind the attack, but the working theory among senior officials was that this was the work of Chechen rebels.

For days the government refused to either confirm or deny Malenchenko's coverage. Yet everyone in Moscow and throughout Russia was fixated on his reports. Certainly Oleg's neighbors and his colleagues in his office were all talking of little else. They had all seen the news. They had seen the smoking, gaping crater, the wrecked concrete, the twisted bicycles. They'd seen the severed arm hanging in a tree, an iconic image Oleg feared he would never forget. Ninety-four Muscovites were dead. Hundreds more were wounded. Burned. Disfigured. Shattered.

Oleg had seen the interview, if you could call it that, with a man who had lost his wife and daughter. Apparently the man had just gotten into a cab. He'd been heading to the airport on business when his apartment had exploded right behind him. The reporter had tried to ask the man questions. She'd done it gently, respectfully, but the man could not answer. He had simply wept unashamedly and uncontrollably, convulsing with wrenching, unceasing grief.

Unlike the attack in Dagestan, this one had unnerved Oleg. As he had stared at the incomprehensible images flickering across his television, he'd actually mumbled aloud what everyone in Moscow was thinking at the time: "It could have been me."

Now, just four days later, it had happened again.

3

Panic was spreading across the country.

Oleg briefly thought about turning his car around and heading back to his parents' home. Driving into the heart of Moscow seemed foolish. This morning's attack had occurred less than a kilometer away from his own flat. What was next?

Still, he had business in the city. He'd waited for this day, planned for it more meticulously than for any trial. So he stayed on course, weaving through stop-and-go traffic for the next hour and a half, heading east into the heart of the capital. As he did, Oleg continued listening to the anchors and reporters on the radio providing further updates and analysis, trying like the ten million other residents of Moscow to process what it all meant. Innocent men, women, and children were dying. They were dying at night. In their sleep.

Oleg recoiled at an ugly, unsettling new thought: Could this be what his dream had been about? Could his building be next? Or his parents' house? Were the places he had known and loved and called home all his life about to go up in flames? Was he about to die—alone, unmarried, barely twenty-seven years old?

Oleg had never had premonitions before. The very notion was ludicrous. He was an educated man. He'd graduated from Moscow State University, the finest in the country. He was an up-and-coming lawyer, making an excellent living. His clients included major Russian oil and gas companies. He wasn't religious or even superstitious. He suddenly felt grateful he hadn't sat down for breakfast with his mother. What if he'd told her about his dream? And she'd told others? He would have sounded crazy. Some things were best kept private.

Just then a new and rather odd piece of information came over the radio. During a live interview, Vasily Malenchenko, the journalist with *Novaya Gazeta*, told a Moscow radio station that investigators at the scene of the blast were puzzled by finding not only traces of TNT but also a substance known as hexogen.

"What is hexogen?" asked the radio reporter.

"It's an explosive compound," Malenchenko said.

"Like TNT?"

"Actually, it's far more powerful."

"So why's that odd?" pressed the reporter. "Isn't that what you'd expect at the site of a bombing?"

"No, not really, not in a terrorist attack like this," Malenchenko insisted.

"Why not?"

"Because terrorists shouldn't be able to get their hands on hexogen," he said. "It's only used by the military."

A shudder rippled through Oleg's body as he turned onto Third Ring Road, heading southeast. *Was someone inside the Russian army helping Chechen terrorists? Had it come to this?* He couldn't imagine anyone cruel enough to perpetrate such atrocities. Who were these people?

Marina's father would know, he thought. Maybe not today, but soon, and he would know how to stop them. He would know how to make them truly suffer for this grave injustice. This gave Oleg a small measure of comfort.

He crossed the river and inched along New Arbat Avenue, past the exit to the massive U.S. Embassy compound off to his left and the exit to the British Embassy and the Hard Rock Cafe—a favorite hangout in his youth—to his right. A few blocks up, but still progressing far too slowly, he decided to get off the main thoroughfare and zigzag through a series of side streets until he reached Kremlevskaya Nab. Finally, with only minutes to spare, he parked his Mercedes in a public garage behind the GUM department store, grabbed his briefcase, and headed for Red Square. The morning autumn air was cool and even a bit breezy, and Oleg was grateful he wasn't heading to this meeting in the dead of summer. Walking this far, this fast, he surely would have melted in his designer suit from London and wound up looking like a wreck by the time he got there. What's more, there would normally have been hordes of visitors from all over Russia and around the world slowing him down. But not today.

On this particular Monday morning, there were no tourists on the streets whatsoever. They had all scattered to the wind. In their place, hundreds of police in riot gear were arriving. They were taking up positions around the State Museum, around Lenin's Tomb and St. Basil's Cathedral, and of course, around the Kremlin itself. Armored personnel carriers were being moved into position at various points to cut off all access to the square. Not one but two police helicopters were circling overhead. Moscow was moving to a war footing.

4

Despite the clock, Oleg dared not break into a run to get to the meeting on time.

He feared he'd be arrested, if not shot, for doing so. Rather, he walked as briskly as he could without arousing suspicion. Yet even as he did, he wondered if it was prudent to proceed at all. Surely his meeting had been canceled. No civilians in their right mind were anywhere to be seen. Perhaps it really was best that he head back to his parents' home and reschedule. But still he kept moving forward.

By the time he had skirted the enormous redbrick walls of the Kremlin and made it to the visitors' center at the Kutafiya Tower, it was clear to Oleg he would not have any lines to wait in. Police carrying automatic weapons were buttoning up every entrance to the seat of the Russian government. All tours had been canceled, as had all but the most essential meetings. Oleg showed his ID to one policeman after another and explained why he was there and with whom he was meeting. Each time—to his astonishment—he was permitted to proceed. When he made it to the appointments desk, he slid his papers into the drawer and waited for the guard behind the bulletproof glass to review them.

"Wait over there," said the stone-faced guard. "Someone will collect you."

"The meeting is on?" Oleg asked, still not clear.

"Wait," the guard grunted without emotion. "Over there."

Oleg turned and saw a bench. But he could not sit. Instead he paced, then checked his watch, then reached for his pack of cigarettes and realized he had left them in the car. His appointment was in eight minutes. He had made it on time. The meeting had not been canceled. He could not explain why. But now he regretted his decision to come on an empty stomach. Anger and self-doubt made a toxic cocktail. He desperately needed a smoke. For the moment he would settle for a glass of water. He would get neither. Moments later a colonel in full dress uniform emerged from a side door, gave Oleg a plastic visitor's badge he was to clip on his suit jacket, and ordered him to follow.

Oleg was led to a security post manned by no fewer than four guards armed with machine guns. The colonel ordered Oleg to take any metal items out of his pockets and put them in a wooden bin. These were passed through an X-ray machine, along with his briefcase, which was also checked thoroughly by one of the guards as well as by the colonel. Then Oleg walked through the magnetometer. He cleared it without setting off any alarms, but this was not enough. A guard patted him down, then made Oleg take off his shoes, which were carefully examined. Only when the colonel and all four guards nodded to one another in agreement that Oleg and his few possessions posed no threat, and only after each man had signed a logbook of some kind attesting as much, was a vault-like door unlocked electronically.

Oleg followed the colonel down a long hallway to the magnificent Troitskaya Tower, eighty meters high and built more than five centuries earlier. A guard standing ramrod straight held open a door, through which Oleg and the colonel exited into the open air. Dark clouds were moving in. Russian flags were snapping in the intensifying breeze. Oleg could feel no rain yet, but clearly a storm was coming.

Oleg had never been to the Kremlin before, not even as a tourist. He had little time or interest for museums and tours and until recently couldn't have imagined a circumstance that might bring him there. Now here he was. To his left stood the Arsenal, a pale-yellow, two-story building commissioned by Peter the Great that currently housed the security services responsible for guarding the Russian capital and its senior leaders. To his right was the massive marble-and-glass complex known as the State Kremlin Palace. Neither of these buildings, however, was their destination. Instead, the colonel led him past dozens more heavily armed soldiers to another pale-yellow building, this one shaped like an enormous isosceles triangle. It was known as the Senate.

This was more heavily guarded than any of the other buildings, yet the two men entered without obstruction. Inside, the colonel led Oleg through the cavernous vestibule to a guard station where they checked in, and where both men and their few possessions again passed through metal detectors and X-ray machines. A smartly dressed aide in her early thirties was waiting for them. She did not smile, did not shake their hands, did not salute the colonel as others at the guard station had. She simply led the two men to an elevator, took them up to the third floor, and ushered them through more security checkpoints and a maze of corridors lined with paintings of all the Russian leaders of the past—from Alexander the Great and Peter the Great to Ivan the Terrible and Nicholas II—until they finally reached an anteroom flanked by security men in dark suits and ugly ties and jackets bulging from the weapons they carried underneath.

A rather dour-looking older woman wearing a frumpy gray dress and sporting a hairdo that struck Oleg as a throwback to the days of the Soviet Politburo sat at a desk behind a large computer screen and a bank of telephones. She looked up at Oleg and the colonel but said nothing. She just pushed a button on one of the phones and then nodded at two agents guarding a large oak door.

To the left of the door Oleg noticed a waiting area with nicely upholstered couches and chairs and a mahogany coffee table. But there would be no waiting. No small talk. No greetings of any kind. Not today. For no sooner had Oleg arrived than the security men opened the door and the colonel motioned him to enter. Alone.

Oleg did as he was instructed and to his astonishment found himself standing before the next president of the Russian Federation.

5

Aleksandr Ivanovich Luganov sat behind his desk, impassive and inscrutable.

For the moment, he was still merely Russia's prime minister.

But Luganov was also the chosen—indeed, the openly anointed—successor of the nation's current president, a man whose health had taken a serious turn for the worse in recent weeks. It seemed an unlikely choice. National elections were less than a month away. Luganov was not particularly well-known or well-liked among the Russian people, though with the president's ill health, Luganov was already acting as chief executive in most ways that mattered. The latest polls showed barely 4 percent of the public supported a former FSB chief to be the nation's leader. Yet Oleg hoped he could find a way to win. The people did not yet see what Oleg saw—a man of strength and great courage, a man willing to do whatever was necessary to keep the country safe and to restore the glory of Mother Russia, so battered and tarnished in recent years. No one seemed better suited or more prepared to lead Russia into the challenges of the twenty-first century. To say that Oleg felt intimidated in Luganov's presence was putting it mildly.

Dressed in a dark-blue business suit, a crisp white shirt, and a navy-blue silk tie with small white polka dots, the man sitting behind the desk was relatively young—late forties—in excellent health and physically fit. He had the lean yet muscular physique of a wrestler or a judoka. His sandy-blond hair was thinning with a touch of gray at the temples. He was not tall—perhaps five feet six inches, a good two inches shorter than Oleg himself. But to Oleg, Luganov was a giant among men, and Oleg had no doubt the nation and the world would soon see and come to admire these qualities.

Luganov didn't smile or nod, much less greet Oleg, who stood frozen in the middle of the spacious, dark-paneled corner office, unsure what to do next. Oleg's eyes darted around the room, taking in the arched ceiling and crystal chandelier above them and then the glass-enclosed bookshelves lining the walls to either side. Behind the prime minister to the left was a Russian flag on a gold stand. Behind him to the right was another flag. It too bore the distinctive broad white, blue, and red stripes but also featured the Russian state seal, embossed in gold. On the floor a large potted plant stood next to a credenza, upon which sat a color television, its sound muted, showing live pictures from the site of the latest bombing. On the paneled wall behind the prime minister was mounted a glistening gold carving of the national coat of arms with its double-headed imperial eagle and mounted horseman slaying a dragon.

As Oleg's eyes drifted downward, he intended to rest them on the ornate carpet and wait until he was spoken to, but when he mistakenly caught Luganov's eye, the prime minister glanced at one of two large wooden armchairs in front of his desk. Tentative at first, Oleg finally took the hint and sat down, his eyes now riveted on the bank of phones and sheaves of papers spread across the vast oak desk. Oleg waited, but the man didn't say anything. The silence grew more unbearable by the second. Again Oleg took the hint. He cleared his throat, dried his perspiring hands on the pant legs of his suit, and forced himself to look up, first at the tie, then at the mouth, and finally into the man's piercing blue emotionless eyes.

"Mr. Prime Minister, I just—well, thank you—I just want to say thank you, sir, for agreeing to see me, especially today," Oleg stammered. "I know you have many—I mean, there are a great deal of—well, it's a very sad, very difficult day, a difficult time for our country. I know you have many responsibilities, so you are most kind to make time for me, of all people, on a day like this."

Luganov stared back at him without comment, without encouragement.

Oleg cleared his throat again and forced himself to press on. "The thing is, what I wanted to talk to you about, sir, is your daughter. As you know, as I'm sure she told you, we met in university almost five years ago. I was immediately drawn to her. She is, well, as you know, she's brilliant, absolutely brilliant. Obviously you know that. I'm sorry. And she's clever. And beautiful. And sophisticated and yet so kind and funny and such a great storyteller. So great with people—children, the elderly. She just has a way about her. And I just, I don't know—well, actually, sir, I do know. . . . I—well, the thing is, I fell in love with her. Not right away. But we became acquainted. And then we became friends. And even though I was ahead of her in my studies, we continued to write letters to each other after I graduated, and in time I came to realize that I couldn't imagine spending my life with anyone else. I was terrified to say that to her, because I didn't want to do anything that would jeopardize our friendship. But in the end, after much discussion with my parents, whom you, of course, know very well, I decided—well, I knew I had to come to you and ask you for your permission to marry her. That is why I'm here. And that's my question to you, sir. Would you allow me to present Marina with an engagement ring and a proposal of marriage?"

Oleg was sick to his stomach. It was all he could do not to vomit on the prime minister's desk. But at least he had said what he had come to say. He had gotten it all out. Not the way he had intended or how he had practiced it so often. But he'd done it. The question was on the table, and now he stared at his hands and waited for a reply.

There was none. Not for some time. The room was silent again, though Oleg could hear the muffled sounds of phones ringing and hushed voices talking in the anteroom. He could feel the eyes of two plainclothes officers standing behind him boring into him. He tried in vain to imagine the expression of the man behind the desk. Then, after what felt like an eternity, he heard his name.

"Oleg Stefanovich," Luganov began, "do you love your country?"

Oleg looked up, wondering if his face registered the surprise he felt, hoping it did not. How many times in recent days had he practiced this conversation with his father? They had discussed his answers to dozens of questions. *Did he feel he knew Marina well enough? How did he know he loved her? How many young women had he dated before Marina? Why had those relationships ended? What were his long-term intentions— for his career, for children, for where they would live? How could he support them, and her educational ambitions, if they were going to be living in one of the world's most expensive cities and he was fresh out of law school and barely a year into his first job?* They had carefully rehearsed and revised his answers to these and so many other queries. But Oleg had never imagined one so direct and yet so profound.

"With all my heart, sir," Oleg replied, gaining confidence from the depth of his convictions on the matter and finally able to look his potential father-in-law in the eye without flinching. "Now more than ever."

"And my daughter?" Luganov asked. "How will I be sure you will never betray her?"

"I have never loved another, sir," Oleg replied. "She is the first and only woman I have ever felt this way about. Sir, you have my word, upon my family's honor, that I will cherish and protect her, provide for her and nurture her, with all that I am and ever hope to be. I come from a good, honorable family. Still, I know that I don't deserve to be Marina's husband. I certainly don't deserve to be your son-in-law. But I do promise to be faithful. If you will have me—if *she* will have me—I will never let either of you down."

A phone on his desk rang. Luganov did not answer it.

There were two quick raps on the door. A general entered. "Mr. Prime Minister, your call with the White House is being placed now."

Luganov nodded almost imperceptibly, then leaned forward in his seat.

"I believe you, Oleg Stefanovich," he said. "Now I have one more question."

Oleg swallowed hard.

"I am looking for a bright young lawyer to serve on my personal staff," Luganov said quietly. "Someone hardworking. Discreet. Someone who can be trusted with sensitive information, especially now. And who can be trusted more than family?"

6

Oleg Stefanovich Kraskin arrived at the Kremlin early.

He could still not believe his good fortune. He was not only engaged to the prime minister's only daughter, he was now working as an aide on the prime minister's personal staff. He had undergone no interview. He had submitted no curriculum vitae. He had offered no references. Then again, when a man who used to serve in the Russian intelligence services—indeed, who had once been head of the Federal Security Service, or FSB—hires you on the spot, you can be fairly confident you've been thoroughly vetted already.

As Oleg reflected upon the whirlwind of the past seventy-two hours, it dawned on him that the FSB had no doubt begun a meticulous investigation of him some five years earlier when he had first met Marina. He was embarrassed that the thought had never occurred to him before. But he knew he could rest assured that the background check had been thorough. Luganov was as protective a father as he was a skilled chief executive. He would protect his daughter as intently as he would protect the motherland. But he was also discreet. Not one of Oleg's friends or teachers or colleagues from childhood up to the present had ever mentioned to him that they had been interviewed by the FSB. But surely they had been, because here he was with a provisional pass into the Kremlin dangling from around his neck.

It was just before six in the morning. He wasn't due in before seven, but this was his first day on the job. The previous two days he had wrapped up his work at the law firm, cleaned out his office there, and said good-bye. All of his partners—most of whom were thirty or forty years his senior—were as stunned as they were thrilled. They threw him an elaborate party, for which he was grateful, though he knew full well they were not just being nice to him; they were ingratiating themselves to the future son-in-law of the next president of the Russian Federation.

Having cleared security and completed some essential paperwork, Oleg was directed to the office of Boris Zakharov, the prime minister's chief of staff and most senior counselor. According to Oleg's father, Luganov and Zakharov had been friends since childhood. The two men had served together in Afghanistan in the early 1980s and later had worked for the KGB before transitioning into politics. Many of Luganov's senior staff, Oleg knew, were longtime, highly trusted personal friends of the prime minister. Some of them were probably unqualified to be working in such sensitive positions. But one thing was clear enough: personal relationships and unquestioned loyalty were prized above all.

Zakharov was a large and rather gregarious man who warmly welcomed Oleg into his office and heartily congratulated him on his engagement. He asked Oleg how he and Marina had met and how he'd courted the prime minister's daughter without making headlines. Oleg answered the first question but demurred on the second, saying he had no idea. The truth was he suspected Luganov's people were running interference with the press.

"Now, I expect that Miss Marina has already told you this, but this will, of course, be no ordinary wedding," the chief of staff said after a minute of pleasantries. "Given that it will occur sometime after the elections, we expect the prime minister will, at that point, be the president. Thus your wedding will be a state affair. As such, my office—working closely with our chief of protocol—will be handling all the details. Any specific requests you and Miss Marina have can be routed through me. We will certainly do our best to accommodate them, but do bear in mind that the venue, the guest list, the musicians, and of course all the security arrangements will have been planned well in advance—*well* in advance."

Oleg kept his mouth shut, but no, Marina had never said any such thing. Then again, he had only proposed to her two nights before at their favorite restaurant overlooking the Moskva River. When she saw Oleg on one knee, the exquisite diamond ring in his hand, and learned that Oleg had already asked her father and been given his blessing, Marina had jumped into his arms and kissed him wildly.

"So that's a yes?" he had asked when they came up for air.

"*Da!*" she'd gushed as she began kissing him again.

They had talked about many things. They had called her parents. They had called his parents. But the specifics of the ceremony? That the wedding would be a state affair, run not by them but by political operatives at the Kremlin? No, that had not come up.

"The Russian people won't have experienced a wedding like this since 1894," Zakharov exclaimed as he buzzed his secretary and asked her to bring him "the Wedding File."

"1894?" Oleg asked, drawing a blank.

"The wedding of the czar," Zakharov replied, lighting up a cigarette and sinking into the chair behind his desk. He beckoned Oleg to take the seat across from him.

Oleg's recall of the history of Russian royalty was, perhaps, a tad rusty. But every Russian knew the basics. Czar Nicholas II had married Princess Alix of Hesse, who had gone on to be known as the Grand Duchess Alexandra Feodorovna, the last czarina before the revolution, when she was summarily executed by the Bolsheviks. The wedding had been held at the Grand Church of the Winter Palace in St. Petersburg. The entire Romanov dynasty had attended, as had royalty from all over Europe.

"Your nuptials will be no less grand—maybe even more so," Zakharov explained. "But of course, unlike Nicholas and Alix, we live in the age of television. So this one will be broadcast live—the entire planet will have the chance to see Russia in all her splendor."

Oleg blanched. *Televised? Broadcast to the entire planet?* All he wanted was a simple, private affair. Immediate families. Close friends. A Russian Orthodox priest. And a honeymoon someplace sunny and warm and very, very private.

Zakharov either didn't notice Oleg's less-than-enthusiastic reaction, or he didn't care.

There was a knock at the door, and Zakharov's secretary entered with two three-ring binders. She gave both to Zakharov, who promptly handed one to Oleg and told him to keep it safe and show it only to Marina and his parents. He pointed to the first six pages of critical questions that needed to be answered immediately and asked that Oleg return the completed forms to him by the end of the week. At that point, Oleg would meet with the Protocol Office. But first there were more pressing matters to consider.

Zakharov handed Oleg his permanent hard pass, an elite biometric card that would provide him access to almost every building and room in the Kremlin other than the most secure military facilities. Then he walked Oleg down the hall to the tiny work space that would now be his.

To call it an office would be to somewhat overstate the situation. It appeared, rather, to be a converted custodian's closet into which a small, narrow desk, a creaky office chair, and one dusty file cabinet had somehow been shoehorned. The room had no windows and little ventilation, but it was twenty paces from Luganov's office, and Oleg had no complaints.

Zakharov gave him the combination to the cipher lock on the door, the password for his brand-new desktop computer, and a classified directory of phone numbers for the offices of everyone who was anyone in the Luganov administration. Then he gave Oleg his own personal mobile number and home number and told him to memorize them and share them with no one.

As the chief of staff began to introduce Oleg to key people who worked on the third floor, there was suddenly a commotion by the elevators. A phalanx of security officers got off first, followed by two men Oleg recognized immediately. The first was Mikhail Petrovsky, the defense minister. The second was Dmitri Nimkov, the head of the FSB. Just then Zakharov's beeper began going off, as did those of a half-dozen senior staff up and down the hallway. Phones started ringing in every office.

"Another bombing," Zakharov said, his demeanor changing instantly. "Stay close to me, Oleg Stefanovich. Take detailed notes of everything that is said, and keep your mouth shut."

7

The previous week, Oleg had been reviewing contracts and billing statements.

Now he found himself at the vortex of the most serious national crisis since the collapse of the Soviet Empire itself.

As he followed the chief of staff into a conference room adjoining the prime minister's office, Oleg vividly remembered the day the Soviet flag was lowered for the last time. Every Russian did. December 25, 1991. Oleg was still a teenager at the time. But he remembered being huddled around his parents' television, watching the momentous events unfolding hour by hour. He would never forget his mother's tears or his father's dumbfounded silence. His parents hadn't been elated like some of their neighbors were, as if the nation were somehow going to be free. Rather, they'd feared their country was going to unravel.

For the first time, Oleg understood their emotions.

A door opened. Prime Minister Luganov entered, flanked by body-guards. Once the door was closed, the cabinet took their seats around the conference table. Luganov, of course, sat at the head. The body-guards took up posts at each of the doors, in the four corners of the room, and directly behind him. Several advisors accompanying Defense Minister Petrovsky and FSB Chief Nimkov sat in a row of chairs against the side walls, behind their principals. Oleg joined them, sitting just behind Zakharov, notebook and pen at the ready.

"Mr. Prime Minister, I regret to inform you that there has been another attack," said the defense minister as he handed Luganov a leather dossier.

"Where?" the prime minister asked, opening the file and sifting through its contents.

"In the south, sir—Volgodonsk," Petrovsky replied.

Oleg looked up from his note taking. He knew Volgodonsk. It was near the Black Sea, not far from the border of Ukraine. His maternal grandmother lived there, as did several of his cousins. As a boy, Oleg had gone fishing along the Don River with his grandfather.

"The initial evidence suggests this was a truck bomb," Petrovsky continued. "It went off in front of yet another apartment building—sheared off the entire face of the building, nine stories. If you'll permit, Mr. Prime Minister, the FSB has video taken on the scene."

Luganov nodded, and the video began to roll. Oleg gasped as unedited images flickered onto three large televisions mounted on the far wall. The devastation was beyond anything he had ever wit-nessed. Certainly images this graphic were not going to be broadcast on nationwide TV. What was visible was mostly rubble, but there was also a severed torso that the cameras kept focusing on. Ash-covered mothers clutched their crying children in their arms.

"How many?" asked Luganov, stoic and dark.

The FSB chief took that one. "We know of seventeen dead so far," Nimkov replied. "But it's early."

"Injured?"

"The latest count I have is sixty, but again, Your Excellency, we expect that number to climb."

"Has anyone claimed credit?"

"No, sir," Nimkov said. "Not yet."

"But the MO is the same as the others?"

"Essentially, yes."

"Chechens," Luganov said coolly.

It wasn't a question, Oleg observed, but a statement. He wrote it all down.

"That's our best guess, sir—yes," said Nimkov.

"Zakayev?" the prime minister asked.

Oleg instantly recognized that name. Ramzan Zakayev was a fundamentalist Muslim warlord in the Russian province of Chechnya. He had become a household name during the period of 1994 to 1996, when he led a separatist movement trying to break Chechnya off from the Russian Federation. He was known for his ruthlessness and barbarism. When Russian air strikes began and ground forces first tried to retake the rebel capital of Grozny, Zakayev had declared a jihad, or holy war, against Moscow. More than a thousand Russian soldiers had lost their lives in the Battle of Grozny. Many of them had been slaughtered in a ghastly manner, and in the process Zakayev had become the country's most wanted terrorist. He had been thirty-six years old.

The FSB chief sat back in his leather chair, took his reading glasses off, and set them down on the notepad before him. He looked at Luganov and sighed. "Based on all we know right now, I would put the probability that Zakayev and his forces are behind all these bombings at 90 percent or better."

Scribbling down the conversation as fast as he could, Oleg felt his blood boiling. Like most Russians, Oleg was certain of Zakayev's guilt—so certain, in fact, that it did not even occur to the young lawyer that no actual facts were being presented, no actual evidence was being offered by the head of the Russian Security Service. Only later would he realize that there was no discussion of incriminating fingerprints found at the scene or intercepted communications between the Chechen warlord and the men who had carried out these attacks. Nothing was being said about wiretaps or recorded conversations with Zakayev or even a single Chechen informant implicating him in these crimes.

Luganov turned back to his defense minister. "Are your forces ready to move?"

"At your command, sir," Petrovsky replied.

Oleg again looked up from his notes. He watched as his future father-in-law signaled his consent, then signed the orders as acting president. The second Russian invasion of Chechnya was about to begin.

8

At five minutes before noon, Zakharov summoned Oleg.

Together the two men entered Luganov's office. It had been hastily transformed into a television studio. Bright, hot lights. Two broadcast-quality video cameras. A teleprompter. A boom microphone. And thick black cables, taped down to the carpet, threading everywhere like a pit of snakes. The chief of staff whispered to Oleg to again take notes of everything he saw and heard. This was his sole responsibility for the time being. He was the official notetaker and secretary of the prime minister's private meetings and public appearances. He was supposed to record the name of everyone in a meeting and everything that was said, make careful note of any action items that were decided upon, and then type up all the notes and provide copies to the PM, chief of staff, and a short list of other senior staff within twenty-four hours for their review. Oleg had no idea how long the assignment would last or when his legal training might be tapped. For now, this suited him well.

Oleg wasn't supposed to speak during the proceedings, nor did he want to. He was sworn to secrecy about every meeting, but that was fine, as he had no desire to divulge anything sensitive, even to his fiancée. For her part, Marina was just thrilled Oleg had the job. She had no interest in prying into her father's business. What's more, Oleg told himself, the job was not difficult, yet it put him in direct proximity with Luganov and all of his top advisors. It would allow him to learn about the man, his leadership style, and the nation he served. It was, in short, the opportunity of a lifetime.

The side door leading to the conference room opened. Oleg could see Luganov conferring with Petrovsky and Nimkov. Then Luganov nodded curtly and entered with his chief bodyguard, a man named Pavel, who shut the door behind them. Luganov took a seat behind his executive desk. He made a final review of the papers before him, marking them at times with a fountain pen he drew from his suit pocket. Oleg wondered what it must feel like to have the weight of the nation on one's shoulders. The official occupant of the office—the man who had served as the president of Russia for eight challenge-filled, exhausting years—was not well. Certainly the responsibilities had taken a heavy toll on the man physically and mentally. So had excessive drinking. If everything went as planned, the man would be out of office by the end of the year. In Oleg's judgment, he had already stayed too long.

Zakharov called for silence, and the last-minute whispering of the crew ceased immediately. The director gave a countdown, and suddenly the red light atop the central camera lit up. Luganov looked up from the pages and directly into the camera. It was the first time Oleg could recall Luganov ever addressing the nation.

"Citizens of Russia—our dear leader, as you know, is ill and incapacitated. He is receiving excellent medical care, and I ask you to pray for his quick recovery and for comfort for his family. But I must come to you today in my role both as prime minister and as acting president to inform you that our nation is under attack. Let me assure you, the terrorist forces responsible for these heinous crimes against the Russian people will pay a great price. Under the authority vested in me by the constitution, and the responsibility I have before God and the nation, I have ordered our air and ground forces into battle to defend our honor. Our forces will hunt down the enemy. We will chase them to the ends of the earth. We will eradicate them completely. Our forces will show no mercy, nor will I. On this, you have my word."

The carpet bombing of Grozny began minutes later.

9

Sergeant Major Ilya Daskin drew his pistol and crouched in the shadows.

The fifty-nine-year-old police officer motioned for his partner, a young trainee named Dima, to draw his weapon as well and cover him as he entered the apartment building on Novoselov Street. Dima did as he was told, but even in the darkness, Daskin could see the kid's hands were shaking.

Besides his service in the military, Daskin had been on the force all of his adult life. He'd been born and raised in this city, Ryazan, as had his parents and both sets of grandparents before him. In May of the coming year he was due to retire. Dima, on the other hand, was all of twenty-four. He had been on the force for less than two months, which was probably why he'd been sent from the academy to Ryazan in the first place.

Located 200 kilometers from Moscow, the city was not of insignificant size. More than half a million people resided there. But it was far off the beaten path. Nothing interesting ever happened in Ryazan, certainly nothing dangerous. Crime was low. Drug trafficking was minimal. Tourism was almost nonexistent. It was, apparently, the perfect city to send a rookie to train, at least according to those far up the food chain. Daskin couldn't have disagreed more. In his view, new cops should be sent to the toughest beats in the most crime-ridden cities. That's how they would learn the ropes, not out here in the sticks.

He wiped his brow with his sleeve and moved through the vestibule of the apartment building, sweeping his weapon from side to side. The entrance was poorly lit, but Daskin was confident no one was there. He did, however, notice that the service door to the basement stairwell was ajar. He gripped the pistol tighter and inched toward the door.

The building seemed unnaturally quiet for an autumn evening. Where were all the children? Why weren't they out playing in the courtyard? Where were all the young couples? Usually, in a neighborhood like this, they'd be strolling in the moonlight, as would the retirees walking their dogs and packs of teenagers heading to the mall. Ever since the bombings across the country, the streets had been quieter, to be sure. Many were too scared to sleep at night, terrified their building might be next to be blown to smithereens. But they were simultaneously scared to be out, fearing the terrorists were hatching new plots, especially now that the massive and unrelenting bombing of Chechen strongholds was under way.

Daskin eased the basement door open with his foot. Holding his weapon in his right hand, he quietly drew his flashlight with his left hand and clicked it on. Then he pivoted into the stairwell, pointing both the flashlight and the barrel of his sidearm downward. He saw nothing, heard no one.

This call, like so many others in recent weeks, was almost certainly another false alarm. The public was on edge. People were overreacting, it seemed, to every strange sight, every unfamiliar person, as if Chechens were lurking in every shadow. The public wanted every noise to be checked out by the police, and Daskin knew he and his colleagues had no choice but to respond. People needed not simply to be protected. They needed to be reassured. Even in Ryazan.

Daskin flicked the light switch on the wall to his right and waited a few beats, listening for voices, for breathing, for movement of any kind. Hearing none, he clicked off the flashlight and slipped it back into the loop on his belt. Then, returning his left hand to the pistol, he slowly moved down the stairs, careful to set his feet at the far edge of each step to minimize the chance of the wood creaking from his weight. That was just the force of habit, of course. Anyone who might be hiding down there now knew full well he was coming.

As he descended the stairs, Daskin could feel his heart pounding and sweat collecting on his face and neck and dripping down his back. He wondered if Dima was okay and began to second-guess himself. Had he been right to leave the young man watching the door rather than ordering him to come to the basement as well? Probably. If there was something to this call—which he highly doubted, but if there was, in fact, a shoot-out, which he doubted even more—Dima would be no help in such close quarters. Far better that he hear the gunshots and radio for backup than that he be caught in the cross fire.

It had been less than six minutes since Daskin and his partner had received the radio call to "check out suspicious activity at 14 Novoselov Street." The dispatcher had just received a panicked call from a man calling himself Alexei, who said he lived in the building. Alexei told the dispatcher he had seen two suspicious men entering the basement. He added that a third person—possibly a woman—was waiting across the street in an idling white car. Like Daskin, the dispatcher hadn't been particularly worried—until the man mentioned, almost in passing, that the car was a white Lada, a four-door model. It was those details that had quickened the dispatcher's pulse and now Daskin's. After all, such information had not been released to the public. But every police department in the country was looking for just such a car after a witness had reported a similar vehicle at the site of the Guryanova Street bombing two weeks earlier.

The sergeant major continued sweeping his weapon from side to side, moving slowly, steadily, cautiously past the rows of cardboard boxes and piles of old furniture that cluttered his path. The place smelled of mold and cat urine. But Daskin kept pressing forward, and when he came around the next corner, his heart nearly stopped. For there, set under the massive furnace, was the first bomb he'd seen since his days as a sapper in the army.

Daskin told himself to take a deep breath and make sure he truly understood the situation before radioing for help. He continued to search the basement, but finally, convinced that no one else was there but him, he holstered his pistol, pulled out his flashlight, and got down on his hands and knees to examine the device more carefully. He could see several dozen sticks of what looked like TNT, duct-taped together. Each was connected to the others by a series of black, red, and green wires. What he did not see was a remote detonation trigger, and this gave him a small measure of comfort. Had there been one, and if the terrorists were watching the building and had seen him go inside, they could have detonated the bomb immediately. But this did not appear to be the case. What Daskin did see, however, that he could not explain, were wires running from the sticks of TNT to what looked very much like three sacks of sugar. He had no idea what might be in the sacks, so he maneuvered around to the other side of the furnace and dropped to his stomach, trying to get as close to the odd contraption as he could. Only then did he find the detonator, connected to a timing device, switched on, blinking furiously, and set for 5:30 a.m.

Horrified, Daskin slowly backed away from the bomb. Getting to his feet and trying to steady his breathing, he called his partner and instructed him to start waking up everyone in the building and ordering them to evacuate immediately. Then he radioed headquarters to tell them what he'd found. Within minutes, sirens and flashing lights filled the night. Dozens of squad cars converged on Novoselov Street from all directions, followed by fire trucks and ambulances. Quickly thereafter, reporters and TV news crews arrived.

As the police cleared the building and set up a perimeter to keep bystanders out of danger, the bomb squad arrived. Two specialists suited up and headed into the basement while a half-dozen more officers took bomb-sniffing dogs into the nearby buildings, just in case. The tension throughout the neighborhood was unbearable. The police were not giving out any information, but rumors were spreading like wildfire. As midnight approached, most of the people of Ryazan knew their quiet corner of Russia had been targeted for disaster. Eventually, two perspiration-soaked specialists reemerged from the building. They removed their bombproof suits and toweled off. Then they huddled with their police chief, the fire chief, and Daskin.

"It's done," said the lead bomb squad officer. "All clear."

"Why did it take so long?" the police chief asked.

"This one wasn't like anything we've seen before," the officer replied.

"Why not?"

"Several reasons—one was the detonator."

"What about it?"

"It wasn't your garden-variety type—this thing was heavy-duty, combat quality, the kind of detonator we used to use in the Spetsnaz."

Daskin gave the officer an appraising look. If he had served as an explosives expert in Russian Special Forces, he clearly knew what he was talking about.

"How would terrorists get their hands on something like that?" the chief inquired.

"I have no idea, but there was something else very odd—three sacks."

"Right, what were those?" Daskin asked.

"Well, they sure weren't filled with sugar, I can promise you that."

"Then what?"

"We were stumped, so I told Misha here to bring me a portable gas analyzer."

"And?"

"Hexogen. Military grade. This thing would have leveled this building and maybe several more. Hundreds would have died. A real bloodbath. We're very lucky the sergeant major here found it in time."

The men stood silently, contemplating the gravity of the disaster they had just averted.

Then Daskin turned to his boss. "Sir, with your permission, I think we should alert the FSB."

Had the police chief simply followed Ilya Daskin's advice, he might have lived.

Instead, the chief called Vasily Malenchenko, the reporter for *Novaya Gazeta* who was breaking one story after another about the bombings, for an exclusive over-the-phone interview. The chief told Malenchenko that he and his men had just foiled a major terrorist plot. In exacting detail, he explained how his men had discovered and defused an enormous bomb. He praised his officers, his bomb squad unit, and his detectives while also detailing just how much devastation would have been wrought given that the material was not the kind "normal" terrorists could get their hands on. No, he explained, meticulously describing the bomb itself, the detonator, the timer, the sticks of TNT, and the three mysterious sacks, this weapon was extra dangerous because it contained explosives produced specifically and exclusively for the Russian army.

Malenchenko immediately jumped in a taxi and raced to the news studios of NTV, one of Russia's biggest television networks. Soon he was being interviewed on a live broadcast seen in all eleven of Russia's time zones. He didn't cite his sources, but he did relay everything he'd learned, including the part about the three sacks of explosives that "were produced specifically and exclusively for the Russian army" and effectively "impossible for Chechen terrorists to get."

Malenchenko's interview dominated the news cycle all day as the recording was rebroadcast over and over again. The impact on the nation was immediate and catastrophic. All the fears the average Russian felt about a Chechen attack killing them and their children in their sleep were ratcheted up a thousandfold by the notion that the terrorists had access to the most advanced nonnuclear explosives in the Russian military's arsenal.

Oleg was up much of the night, chain-smoking, glued to the non-stop coverage, asking himself what everyone in Russia was asking: *How in the world could Chechen terrorists have acquired military-grade bomb-making ingredients—not once but at least twice? Who inside the Russian army had given it to them? It couldn't have been enlisted men. It had to be officers. High-ranking officers. But why would high-ranking Russian army officers agree to help kill women and children in such a barbaric manner? How many such traitors were there? How had they not been noticed? Where would they strike next? How soon could they be caught? And in the meantime, who in the military and in law enforcement could really be trusted?*

These questions and hundreds of others quickly dominated the discussion in the media. Everyone had a theory, and each was more bizarre and scarier than the last.

At just after 4:30 in the morning, Oleg's secure phone rang. It was Zakharov's executive assistant. The chief of staff was ordering every member of the staff to get into the office immediately.

When Oleg arrived, the place was in crisis mode. The prime minister was coming by helicopter and would arrive at the Kremlin within the hour. Meanwhile, Zakharov was working the phones to manage the story, if not contain it. He had set himself up in the conference room. Generals, FSB officials, political aides, and public affairs officers were streaming in and out to provide updates and receive new directives, some of which were coming straight from the top. Initially, Oleg's responsibility was to keep a written record of every fact, every instruction, every response and counterresponse. But soon the chief of staff directed Oleg to answer incoming calls from Duma members and mayors and political bosses. People were calling from all over the country, demanding answers, and it was up to Oleg to supply them.

Zakharov gave him the script.

First, Vasily Malenchenko was completely mistaken, Oleg was instructed to say. There had never been a real terror threat in Ryazan. What the local police had stumbled over was a training exercise, organized by the FSB to simulate a possible bomb threat. The whole thing was a giant misunderstanding. The bomb looked real, but it was merely a prop. No one had ever been in real danger.

Second, the three sacks of sugar did not contain military-grade explosives. They didn't contain explosives at all, and certainly not hexogen. The sacks actually did contain sugar. Again, the whole scene was set up to look like a terror plot to test the instincts and reactions of local authorities and interagency cooperation with security officials in Moscow. But signals got crossed and a series of miscommunications had occurred.

Third, Malenchenko was a terrible journalist, a disgrace to the country, and should be fired immediately. If he was a loyal Russian and a good reporter, he would have done his job thoroughly and learned that this was simply a test. He could have cleared up the whole confusion rather quickly with just a few phone calls. Instead, Malenchenko had injected fear into a nation already rattled by the last several weeks of actual terror attacks by Chechen Islamists. He had gotten the story completely wrong, but now the citizens of Russia should carry on with daily life with the confidence that the military would crush the terrorists. The FSB was doing a first-rate job protecting the country.

Furthermore, the simulation had, in fact, been highly successful. No one was killed. No one was injured. The cops on the beat in Ryazan performed well. So did the bomb squad and all the first responders. They all deserved medals. Malenchenko deserved Siberia.

Oleg dutifully delivered his message on dozens of calls as Zakharov and other members of his staff did the same. Oleg was relieved to learn the whole thing had been an FSB exercise, and he was honored and excited to be part of the rapid response team. That evening, he even got to be in the room as Prime Minister Luganov once again addressed the nation on live television. Luganov denounced Malenchenko by name while praising the police and first responders of Ryazan. He encouraged the nation not to worry and provided an update on how many Chechen terrorists had been killed and how proud he was of the resolve of the Russian people in the face of such "savagery and barbarism."

National public opinion polls moved quickly and dramatically. By the end of that fateful week, Luganov's approval rating had shot up from a mere 4 percent to 21 percent. Images of Russian bombers devastating Chechnya filled the evening news. Two weeks later, Chechen rebel leader Ramzan Zakayev was killed by a Russian sniper, and Luganov's approval ratings doubled to 45 percent. By the time the presidential elections were held later that fall, Luganov won in a landslide, capturing more than 63 percent of the vote.

The Russian people were terrified no longer. The terrorists were dying in massive numbers. Not a single new attack had occurred on Russian soil. Luganov was being praised by presidents and prime ministers all over the world for being tough on terror. Oleg Kraskin was ecstatic. He found himself an increasingly trusted member of the inner circle. What's more, he would soon be married and become a member of President Luganov's family.

While driving home from the Kremlin several nights after the election, eager to meet Marina and take her to dinner and the ballet to celebrate, Oleg heard an odd and disturbing story on the radio. The body of Vasily Malenchenko had been found in a Dumpster on the outskirts of Moscow. The reporter had been shot in the back of the head, execution-style.

Four days later, Oleg read a small item buried deep inside *Novaya Gazeta*. The body of the Ryazan chief of police had also been found, in a parking garage in downtown Moscow. No one knew why the officer was in Moscow, the story noted. He had not been scheduled to visit the capital. He was actually scheduled for a minor surgical operation in Ryazan the following morning. There were no suspects at this time, nor was there any known motive. But one thing was clear: the chief had not been mugged or set upon by a gang of youthful hooligans. He had been hog-tied. His throat had been slit. His tongue had been cut out, and his body was riddled with twenty-three bullets. Someone was sending a message. But who? And why?

Yaroslavl
Ярославль

Kostroma
Кострома

Tver
Тверь

Ivanovo
Иваново

Nizhny
Novgorod
Нижний
Новгород

Vladimir
Владимир

Moscow
Москва

Dzerzhinsk
Дзержинск

Tula
Тула

Voronezh
Воронеж

PART
TWO

11

Marcus Ryker tore north on Interstate 25 like a man possessed. Someone was going to die tonight, but it was not going to be him.

Weaving in and out of traffic—racing up the shoulders on either side of the highway when he had no other choice—the twenty-one-year-old rising college senior blew past the posted speed limit of sixty-five miles an hour. He was soon doing eighty, eighty-five, ninety, ninety-five. Yet he kept pushing the accelerator closer and closer to the floor and would not let up.

Colorado Springs rapidly dissolved in the rearview mirror. The exit for Monument, population two thousand, was coming up fast, and the rusted maroon '78 Mustang he'd bought from his uncle was shaking violently.

So was his girlfriend.

Elena Marie Garcia had known Marcus since the sixth grade. They'd started dating in the tenth. No one knew his love of speed and risk-taking better than she. But this was insane.

"Marcus, for heaven's sakes, slow down—you're gonna get someone killed!" Elena screamed as he veered around a sluggish oil tanker, a Greyhound bus, and two minivans clogging his way.

She pleaded with him to calm down and tell her what had just happened, what in the world that phone call could possibly have been about. But she wasn't getting through, and for a moment she wondered if he could even hear her at all.

Elena had never resisted—never even flinched at, much less criticized—any of his crazy adventures. Maybe she'd raised an eyebrow once or twice, but she was almost as much an adrenaline junkie as he was—*almost*, though not quite. Coming from a staid and quiet home where nothing exciting or unexpected ever seemed to happen, she felt energized by Marcus's passion for life and absolutely loved trying to keep up with him.

He had, in fact, once confided to her that this was one of the reasons he had fallen in love with her in the first place. It wasn't just her warm brown eyes, her long jet-black hair, or her soft mocha skin. It was her zest for life. Together they'd hiked more fourteeners than she could remember, both in the blazing heat of summer and in the brutal Colorado winters. They'd skied some of the steepest mountains and the biggest moguls. They'd gone white-water rafting through some of the most intense rapids in any river in any state within two hundred miles of Monument. They'd taken flying lessons, and Marcus had earned his private pilot's license. They'd even taken skydiving lessons the summer after their junior year in high school—without their parents knowing—and laughed until they cried when they finally hit the ground alive and intact.

But as Marcus screeched around corners and blew through red lights and stop signs, Elena burst into tears. She was grasping the door handle for dear life, but she had stopped trying to make sense of what had come over this man she loved.

The evening had started off magically enough. Marcus had arrived at her house at precisely 5:00 to pick her up for a big fund-raising banquet put on by the Air Force Academy to raise money for children of parents killed in action. It was being held at the Broadmoor, the swankiest hotel in the Springs, and they'd been given two free tickets. It was a great treat for the two college students, home and working hard for the summer. Marcus had looked handsome, decked out in a snazzy black rented tux. Given that they'd skipped their high-school prom to go white-water rafting with friends, it was the first time she remembered him wearing anything but jeans, a T-shirt, and Timberland boots. His wavy blond hair was freshly trimmed. His rugged, chiseled face—the heritage of his Dutch roots—was freshly shaved. His blue eyes danced with anticipation of the evening ahead, and he had brought her a bouquet of dazzling red and blue and purple wildflowers that he had picked in the foothills.

She'd loved that he had noticed and complimented not only her dress and shoes but new pearl earrings and necklace, which she'd saved for and bought herself. She'd loved watching him banter with her bow tie–wearing, corporate lawyer father and her every-hair-in-place, every-syllable-just-so, church organist mother. She'd loved how he'd listened to her giggling younger sisters like he had all the time in the world for them.

They'd arrived at the Broadmoor, taken in the glamorous surroundings, and enjoyed the hors d'oeuvres being passed around by stewards. It was all going so well. And then Marcus had taken an unexpected call on his cell phone, and the trajectory of the night took a sudden and devastating turn.

Now the man she planned to marry once they both graduated from the University of Northern Colorado the following year turned the wheel hard to the right and went barreling around one more corner, tires squealing. Then they were on Marcus's street. They tore into his cul-de-sac, and when he slammed on the brakes and came screeching to a stop on the freshly mowed lawn of his childhood home, Elena silently thanked God for the seat belt she was wearing, fully convinced that otherwise she would have been thrown through the windshield.

Marcus immediately shut down the engine and pulled the keys out of the ignition. "Go next door—*now*," he told her. "Call 911. Then call your father, and don't leave the Matthews' house till this thing is over. Do you hear me?" With that, he threw open the door and bolted across the lawn.

"*Till what's over?*" she yelled after him. "*What's wrong?*"

Marcus didn't answer. Yet he didn't seem angry—not at her, at least. His voice had seemed surprisingly calm given the way he'd been driving. But there was a sense of authority and urgency Elena had never seen or heard in him before.

As he disappeared from view around the far side of the house, Elena just sat there for a moment, in shock. But then she heard the sounds coming from inside the house, and it began to dawn on her what was unfolding. She heard something glass smash against a wall. She heard pots and pans striking walls and countertops. The man who was now Marcus's stepfather was throwing things. She heard him shouting obscenities so loudly that fathers and mothers up and down the street were emerging from their doors to see what in the world was going on. Children were standing frozen in their yards, staring at the Ryker house, unable to continue playing.

A flash of fear rippled through Elena. She imagined Marcus's stepfather suddenly rushing out the front door and finding her—alone—in the rusty old Mustang in the middle of his finely manicured lawn. She needed to go, now.

Bursting out the passenger-side door, she raced to the Matthews' house in her ball gown and matching heels and pounded on the front door. Mrs. Matthews was there, trembling and alone with her cats. But she knew Elena and quickly pulled her inside, locking the door behind them both. The police had already been called, the woman assured her, but she handed over the phone so Elena could call her father.

12

Don't die, and don't get arrested.

For years, that's what his mother had told him. She'd said it every time he left the house. She'd been saying it since he'd entered puberty. But now, as he raced to the backyard, adrenaline surging, Marcus knew full well that before the night was finished, it was going to be one or the other.

Stripping off his tuxedo jacket and bow tie, he unbuttoned his collar, ripped the silk lining out of his jacket, then tore the lining into two long strips. As his stepfather's cursing grew all the louder and more vicious, Marcus wrapped the strips of fabric around his hands to protect them, then began scrambling up a wooden trellis covered with his mother's climbing roses, now in full bloom. Reaching the top, his hands scraped and bloodied from the thorns—though not nearly as badly as they could have been—Marcus pulled himself up onto the roof of the screened-in porch and moved toward the window of the master bedroom.

Roger DuHaime, the man who had terrorized their lives for the last eighteen months, was pounding furiously on the bedroom door. He was demanding to be let in and threatening to get an ax and smash the door down if his wife didn't comply immediately. Marcus's mother was cowering in a corner, shaking uncontrollably. Her blouse was ripped and splattered with blood. Her nose appeared broken, and Marcus could see bruises and welts on her face and arms. As he scanned the room, he could see that the lock on the bedroom door was engaged and that his mother had tried to push the heavy oak dresser against the door for extra protection, though she hadn't gotten it very far.

Marcus rapped on the window. Startled, Marjorie Ryker whipped around, fear in her eyes. She didn't move. She didn't say anything. She just gripped a cordless phone in her right hand. She shouldn't have been surprised to see her son on the roof. She had, after all, warned him not twenty minutes earlier not to come through the front door.

"He just snapped," she'd whispered to Marcus over the phone, the sense of urgency in her voice palpable. *"I think he really means to do it this time."*

She had apologized over and over again for interrupting his date, his special night, but Marcus would have none of it. He'd told her to lock herself in her bedroom, call the police, and wait for him to get home and take care of everything. That's when she had begged him not to come into the house, not to get into a confrontation with Roger. *"Don't get in his face, Marcus—he'll kill you,"* she'd warned him in no uncertain terms. *"He's been drinking all day. He'll kill us both."*

But Marcus had dismissed her warnings. He'd told her he was coming. He'd protect her. Everything would be okay. All he asked was that she unlock and open her bedroom window so he could get her out quickly when he arrived.

Yet now that the moment had come, she seemed completely caught off guard. She just stared at him. She hadn't opened the window, nor had she unlocked it, nor was she about to. Instead, she was backing away from him, terror growing in her eyes.

It occurred to Marcus that his mother couldn't see his face. The sun shining over the Rocky Mountains was illuminating him from behind, making just a silhouette.

"Mom, it's me, Marcus. Open the window," he said.

But then came a chilling new sound. It was not that of an enraged man pounding on the bedroom door with his bare fists. It was that of an ax splintering the wood. Marcus couldn't wait any longer. He slipped off his polished black dress shoes, plunged one fist in each, and then, wearing the shoes like boxing gloves, punched his way through the window.

For a moment Roger stopped hacking at the door and demanded to know what was happening. But when his wife didn't respond, he started attacking the door all the more furiously. Marcus scraped the glass away from the window frame, then put his shoes back on, reached in, and unlocked the window. As he climbed inside, he immediately moved to his mother's side. Her eyes registered both the relief of seeing her son and the simultaneous fear that at any moment her husband would smash through that door and hack them both to death.

Marcus knew he was running out of time. His mother would never make it across the roof and down the trellis. She was obviously in great pain after the beating she'd just taken, and he feared she could fall off the roof and break her back or neck. Not hearing any sirens yet, Marcus told her to go into the bathroom and lock the door. At first she hesitated when he said he wasn't going to join her. But when he calmly insisted even as the hole in the door grew, she complied.

Splinters were flying through the room now. Marcus knew he had only seconds to act. He pushed the dresser in front of what was left of the door. Then he raced to his mother's closet and flicked on the overhead light. Stepping onto a small wooden stool, he pushed away a row of shoe boxes, feeling around until his hands brushed the cold metal barrel of a Remington 870 Wingmaster. The dusty 12-gauge pump-action shotgun was more than thirty years old. It had been his father's. His real father's. After his death when Marcus was eleven, his mother had planned to sell it or give it away, just as she'd done with many of his things. Marcus hadn't exactly begged, but he had made an impassioned and rather well-reasoned plea that the gun was a keepsake, a part of their family history, and that she should hold on to it until he was old enough to learn to hunt like his father and his grandfather before him. Impressed and surprised by his logic and articulateness at such a young age, she'd relented and tucked the gun away in her closet for safekeeping. Since then she'd probably forgotten about it.

But Marcus never had. Every few months growing up, he'd secretly snuck into his mother's room and checked to make sure the shotgun was still there, that she hadn't given it away.

As Marcus scrambled to find ammunition, and amid the murderous rage and deafening vulgarities, he could finally hear sirens in the distance. The police were coming, but it was clear they weren't going to arrive in time. He continued working methodically through the cramped closet, shelf by shelf, drawer by drawer, until—in one of the shoe boxes—he finally heard what he needed. He ripped it open. Finding five shells, he quickly loaded two, pumped, then turned and pulled his cell phone from his pocket. He dialed 911. When he heard the call connect and an operator's voice come on the line, he stepped back into the bedroom and tossed the phone onto the bed just as Roger DuHaime smashed through the door and shoved the dresser aside.

Suddenly Marcus was standing just a few feet away from a haggard, unshaven man in his late fifties. He wore a dirty pair of work jeans and a T-shirt stained with oil. His bare feet were tinged with the green of freshly cut grass. His filthy hands were shaking, and as he tightened his grip on the ax, he demanded Marcus put down the gun and tell him where his mother was.

Marcus said nothing. He just stood there and locked eyes with his stepfather, holding the shotgun low, at his hip, aimed at the man's chest. DuHaime was soaked in sweat. His hair, what was left of it, was askew. His eyes were bloodshot and glaring with hatred but also confusion. He scanned the room, looking for his wife and not finding her. For a moment, it seemed he was going to come at Marcus, but Marcus did not move, did not flinch. Nor did he fire. He simply stood his ground and waited.

Then DuHaime heard Marjorie crying in the bathroom. The moment he did, his mouth broke out in a twisted smile. He glanced behind him and began to back up, away from Marcus and toward the bathroom door.

"This isn't between you and me," he growled. "This's about your mother and me, and you'd best stay out of it."

Marcus remained motionless. But calmly and clearly, he told his stepfather to put down the ax, back out of the room, and leave the house, and no one would get hurt. The man just laughed. Marcus repeated the instructions and explained precisely what was going to happen if his stepfather did not put down the ax and leave the room and the house immediately. But his words had no effect. The man did not comply. His stepfather was swaying now, side to side. He was laughing. He raised the ax, mumbled something incomprehensible, and lunged at Marcus.

Marcus didn't hesitate. He pulled the trigger, not once but twice.

13

Two shotgun blasts echoed through the neighborhood.

Then all was quiet.

Elena screamed as she burst out of the Matthews' house, tears streaming down her face, and ran toward Marcus's front door. She was stopped by one of the police officers who had just pulled up. A half-dozen squad cars filled the street, along with a SWAT vehicle and two ambulances. The chief of police was ordering his men to set up a perimeter around the house. Then he ordered all the neighbors back into their homes.

Frantic to see if Marcus was okay, Elena insisted she be allowed into the house. The chief refused. Multiple gunshots had just been fired, and it was not clear by whom. Nor was it clear what might happen next. There was an active shooter in the house. The crime scene needed to be secured, and there was no way he was going to allow anyone into that house, no matter what her relation to the people inside.

Mrs. Matthews came up behind Elena. She gently put her arm around the trembling young woman and coaxed her back into her house. She locked the door again, then put a sweater and a thick blanket around Elena. She made a pot of tea and brought a small tray of things to eat, but Elena had no appetite. Rather, she parked herself in the living room, staring out a bay window, riveted on the drama unfolding before her.

Soon SWAT team members in full battle gear entered the front and the back doors of Marcus's mother's house, guns drawn. Elena tensed, terrified at what might happen next. Minutes later more uniformed officers entered the front door, followed by men in plain clothes. Detectives, Elena thought. Some time later, a team of paramedics entered with a stretcher.

Mrs. Matthews turned on the television and flipped back and forth between the local channels whose news crews were broadcasting live from the scene. One station reported that two hostages had been held inside the house until a police sharpshooter had taken out the alleged perpetrator. A different station cited a source in the police department and claimed someone in the home had committed suicide. A national cable news station said one person had been shot and killed. Another claimed two people had been shot and one was dead while the second was severely wounded. Elena wasn't sure what to believe, but it was surreal to see photos of Marcus's family on the news.

One of the networks eventually showed a photo of Roger DuHaime. Elena knew Marcus's stepfather was an alcoholic. Marcus had begged his mother not to marry him. She'd done it anyway, and it had been a disaster. The man had abused her emotionally and physically, leading to not one but two restraining orders. Both had been lifted. Marcus had pleaded with his mother to leave him, pleaded with his sisters to get her out of the state. The man was dangerous. He needed help. He certainly needed to be kept away from their family. But no one had listened, and now here they were.

Elena had never met Marcus's real father, but she'd heard all about him. Captain Lars Ryker had been shot down by a surface-to-air missile on January 16, 1991, while flying an F-16C Fighting Falcon on a combat mission in southern Iraq during Operation Desert Storm. Marcus had been just eleven years old.

Night fell. The streetlamps came on. The police aimed floodlights at the house. Down the street, Elena could see the lights from all the TV cameras. Suddenly the front door opened and a stretcher emerged—one, not two—and on it was a body covered in a bloody sheet. Elena gasped. As the stretcher was loaded into the back of a waiting ambulance, Elena's hands began to shake. Her lips began to quiver. She was trying not to jump to any conclusions, but she'd had enough of all the speculations. She had to know the truth, however brutal.

She jumped up from the couch and headed for the door. Mrs. Matthews tried to stop her, but Elena kept running. She crossed the freshly cut grass toward Marcus's house just as the front door opened again.

Elena stopped dead in her tracks. Two officers were coming out the door and down the driveway.

Marcus was with them, his hands cuffed behind his back.

14

The steel doors slammed shut.

It was now 2:46 in the morning. Marcus Johannes Ryker had been read his legal rights by local sheriff's deputies. He'd been strip-searched. Interrogated. Booked. Photographed. Fingerprinted. And given an orange jumpsuit to wear. Now he found himself incarcerated in the El Paso County Criminal Justice Center.

Some fifteen hundred inmates were housed in this complex. Some were waiting to be charged with a crime. Most were awaiting their court dates or their sentence and transfer to state or federal prisons for the long haul. Marcus wondered what his cellmate was in for. The guy was over six and a half feet tall and must have weighed more than 250 pounds. Marcus took him for Samoan in origin, though he couldn't be sure. The man said nothing as Marcus entered the cell. He just lay motionless on the bottom bunk as Marcus climbed up to the top bunk.

Marcus wasn't too worried. He was not a small man himself, despite his relative youth. At six foot one, he clocked in at 175 pounds and had been a star left guard on his high school football team all four years. He was in excellent physical shape and had never lost a fight. He hoped there wouldn't be any trouble tonight, but he was prepared to hold his own if it came to that.

The cell block was as quiet as it was dark. Most of the inmates were asleep. Marcus lay on his back and stared at the ceiling just a few inches from his face. Soon enough he could hear the man on the lower bunk snoring.

He looked around. The space was simple enough. The concrete-block walls were painted a light green. The metal-frame bunk bed was bolted to the floor and the left wall. The mattress was thin. The pillow was small. The blanket was scratchy and too small to cover his entire body. Next to the bunk there was a metal toilet bowl. Beside it was a small stainless steel sink. The cell smelled like body odor and disinfectant. He could hear lots of men snoring. He could also hear guards making their rounds on a precise rotation, their boots clomping along the freshly mopped halls, keys jangling at their sides.

"The belly is an ungrateful wretch, it never remembers past favors, it always wants more tomorrow." The line was Solzhenitsyn's, from one of Marcus's favorite novels, *One Day in the Life of Ivan Denisovich*. It was a story of a hapless soul, falsely accused and locked away in a Soviet gulag during the Second World War. Not once since he first read it as a freshman in high school had Marcus ever actually imagined being in prison. And never had the line rung so true as it did right now. Marcus's stomach was grumbling so loudly he wondered if it could be heard up and down the corridor. He'd hardly eaten anything since breakfast.

"You should rejoice that you're in prison. Here you have time to think about your soul." Another line from the novel. Marcus chewed on the words as he pondered all that had happened in the span of just a few short hours. One thing was clear—he'd had no choice but to shoot. His stepfather had been coming at him with an ax. He didn't think he would have any regrets about his actions.

But then he pictured his mother's face when she'd come out of the bathroom and found her second husband lying in a pool of his own blood. Marcus had expected to see relief in her eyes—gratitude, even. He had, after all, saved her life. Instead, she'd collapsed to the floor in unspeakable grief.

A second image that haunted him was that of Elena's face, the moment their eyes had met, just before he'd been transported away from the scene in the backseat of one of the squad cars. He'd expected to see sympathy in those beautiful brown eyes. He'd seen something else instead. What was it? Fear? He couldn't say for sure, but it wasn't good.

With these unsettling thoughts in his mind, he finally drifted off to sleep.

"Ryker, you have a visitor."

It was morning. Marcus felt peaceful and refreshed. He was eager to see Elena. The lock clicked open. Two guards accompanied him down the hall to a semiprivate holding room. There, he was ordered to sit on a chair in a small booth, next to a bulletproof window, and wait. After a few minutes, his visitor appeared. It was not Elena. It was her father.

Marcus had told Elena to call her father the night before because he knew he'd need a lawyer, even if Mr. Garcia had zero experience in criminal law. Still, seeing him now reminded him this wasn't just about getting out of jail and clearing his name with the authorities. It was also about clearing his name with the Garcia family. He'd done nothing wrong, and he needed them to know that.

Wearing a freshly pressed, dark-blue pin-striped suit and a crisp white dress shirt, Mr. Garcia—as stern-faced and dour as Marcus had ever seen him—sat down on the other side of the glass. He set a yellow legal pad on the counter, pulled a Montblanc pen from his breast pocket, and picked up the telephone receiver mounted on the wall.

Marcus took a deep breath and picked up the receiver on his side as well.

"First things first," Mr. Garcia said, "these conversations are monitored. Remember that."

"Okay."

"Next, I just came from seeing your mother," Mr. Garcia continued.

"Good—how is she?" Marcus asked.

"Well, I'm sorry to have to tell you this, but she was hospitalized last night. I'm afraid she had a heart attack. It was a minor one. The doctors say she's going to be all right. But they want to keep her for observation."

Marcus just sat there, stunned.

"She wanted me to tell you she loves you. She doesn't blame you. She knows you were just trying to protect her, and there really wasn't any other option. She wished she'd said it to you last night in person, but she wanted you to know right away."

Marcus took in the news. At first he did not speak. He simply nodded to acknowledge he'd heard the man and appreciated the report. He was grateful for his mother's understanding. But he was worried both for her physical and mental state. He needed to be with her, to take care of her, to protect her.

"Please tell her thank you," he said finally. "I can't wait to see her."

Mr. Garcia nodded and continued. "I also spoke to the DA."

"Good."

"I'm afraid it's not good news."

"What do you mean?"

"He wants to charge you."

"With what?"

"Manslaughter."

15

"But it was textbook self-defense," Marcus said.

"The DA says otherwise. He's going to push for the maximum sentence."

"Twelve years?"

Mr. Garcia looked surprised that Marcus would know such a fact. "I'm afraid so—and a fine."

"How much?"

"Could be a lot. Again, he's saying he'll ask for the maximum."

Marcus was stunned. "That's three quarters of a million dollars."

Once more Elena's father seemed surprised, but he nodded. "That's what he said."

"That's crazy," Marcus said. "He's bluffing."

"That's not the impression I got."

"But Colorado has a 'Make My Day' law."

"The DA says it doesn't apply."

"Of course it does," Marcus shot back. "The statute is clear. 'Any occupant of a dwelling is justified in using any degree of physical force, including deadly physical force, against another person when that other person has made an unlawful entry into the dwelling, and when the occupant has a reasonable belief that such other person has committed a crime in the dwelling . . . or intends to commit a crime . . . and when the occupant reasonably believes that such other person might use any physical force, no matter how slight, against any occupant.'"

"How do you know all that?" Mr. Garcia asked.

"I'm studying criminal justice."

"But how do you know it by heart?"

Marcus shrugged. "I just do."

"Well, the DA says your stepfather didn't make an unlawful entry. It's his home."

"But it's in my mother's name."

"That doesn't matter—they were married."

"What about the restraining orders?"

"Both lifted."

"But they show a pattern of aggression."

"I'm not sure that would be admissible."

"But he was clearly there to commit a crime," Marcus insisted, his voice steady and firm. "He'd already beaten my mother. He'd broken her nose, and he said he was going to kill her."

"Even so, the DA says the statute doesn't apply."

"What about CRS 18-1-704?"

"Which one is that?"

"'Use of Physical Force in Defense of a Person,'" Marcus said, again reciting from memory. "'A person is justified in using physical force upon another person in order to defend himself or a third person from what he reasonably believes to be the use or imminent use of unlawful physical force by that other person, and he may use a degree of force which he reasonably believes to be necessary for that purpose.'"

Mr. Garcia just looked at him.

"Is there a problem, sir?" Marcus asked.

"It's just that . . ."

"What?"

"Well, I'm not sure it's helpful that you know these statutes by heart."

"Why not?" Marcus asked. "I've wanted to be a police officer since I was a kid. You have to memorize these things."

"I understand," said Mr. Garcia. "I'm just saying it could look like . . ."

"Like what? Mr. Garcia, do you really think I would have asked Elena to call you last night if I was preparing to carry out a premeditated murder?"

When Mr. Garcia didn't reply, Marcus added, "If ignorance of the law is no defense, how can knowledge of the law make you guilty?"

"I'm just saying you need to be careful, Marcus. Don't try to be your own lawyer. Let me handle everything."

"I will, but please remind the DA that even though my mother had no legal responsibility to retreat to her bedroom, that's exactly what I told her to do," Marcus said.

"Got it."

"That's the castle doctrine."

"I know," said Mr. Garcia. "My partner brought it up when we met with the DA."

"And?"

"And the DA said the police were already arriving on the scene, that they would have taken care of everything, that you didn't need to fire the gun at all, and you certainly didn't need to shoot twice."

"Has he listened to the 911 recording?"

"What recording?"

"The one I made from my mother's bedroom."

"I don't know. It's been a busy night. Look—"

But Marcus cut him off. "Why do you think I made the call, Mr. Garcia?" he asked. "I knew police had been called. I *told* Elena to call them, even before calling you. I knew they were on the way. But I also knew Roger had lost it. I was pretty sure what was about to happen, and I wanted every second recorded. I wanted the cops, the DA, you, and the rest of the world to hear everything Roger said—the screaming, the cursing, everything. And me warning him—*twice*."

Mr. Garcia stopped taking notes, set down his pen, and leaned back in his seat. "You're not worried, are you?" he asked.

"About what?" asked Marcus.

"Going to prison."

"No, sir, I'm not," Marcus replied. "The law on this is clear. The DA should drop the charges immediately. But even if he doesn't, even if he puts me on trial, no jury would convict, not when they know the facts."

Of this, Marcus was certain. What did worry him—though he didn't say it, certainly not to Elena's father—was that his dream of becoming a police officer might have just been scuttled. Even when the case was dismissed or a jury found him not guilty, was it possible that the stigma of such a high-profile case could stain him forever? Maybe, maybe not, but not even these fears were foremost on his mind. What really bothered him was the prospect that Elena would never look at him the way she used to, if she was even willing to keep dating him at all.

16

"Ryker, you have a visitor."

It was late afternoon. Marcus was playing basketball outside, drenched in sweat, not expecting any visitors. An Asian kid covered in tattoos drove hard toward the basket, began to make a layup, then thought better of it and flipped the ball to Marcus. Coverage was tight. These guys were good. It went without saying they were tough. Marcus faked right, then rolled left and went for the three-pointer.

Swish.

Now they were only down by six, but the guard shouted again.

"Ryker, move it—let's go!"

That was it. The game was over, and so, it turned out, was his time behind bars. Ten minutes later, having toweled off, changed back into civilian clothes, and signed a bunch of forms in triplicate, Marcus found himself sitting in the plush leather seats and cool air-conditioning of Mr. Garcia's gleaming new silver Lexus.

"So . . . ," Mr. Garcia said, sitting in the driver's seat in a brown wool suit, brown leather shoes, and turquoise bow tie. "Turns out you were right. The DA called me this morning. He finally listened to the 911 tape. He read the statement your mother gave the police and reviewed all the forensic evidence. He also went back to the case files that led to both restraining orders, and based on all that, he dropped the charges."

"All of them?" Marcus asked.

"All of them. And not only that—at six o'clock this evening he's going to hold a press conference announcing that he's clearing you of all wrongdoing and stating that given the circumstances, you acted honorably and within the law to defend your own life and that of your mother. He expects all the local stations to cover it live."

"Does Elena know?"

"She was the first person I called."

"What'd she say?"

"She burst into tears."

"And my mom?"

"She was the second person I called."

"She's still in the hospital?"

"Yes, but the doctors say she's making great progress. She should be released tomorrow. She's so happy for you and can't wait to see you face-to-face."

"Thank you, sir," Marcus replied. "For everything."

"Happy to do it, young man."

So much was racing through Marcus's head at that moment.

"I'm really a free man?" he asked, trying to process it all.

"You are," Mr. Garcia replied. "But before I take you home, there are a few things we need to talk about."

"Actually, since my mom isn't there, can we go straight to your house?" Marcus asked. He could hear the relief in his own voice. "I'm dying to see Elena."

"I'm sure you are, son, but that's what I wanted to talk to you about."

He paused, and Marcus immediately tensed.

"Look, Marcus, you've just been through a terrible ordeal," Mr. Garcia said softly. "You shot and killed someone. You spent the night in jail. That's a heavy burden to bear, and it's going to take a toll on you. You were certainly justified in what you did—morally and legally. Don't get me wrong. I'm not criticizing you. But I think you need to take some time to process what just happened."

"Meaning what?"

"It's not uncommon for people in your situation to go through some sort of trauma, to have nightmares, anxiety attacks, and whatnot."

"I'm fine, sir; really, I am."

"You just watched a man die, Marcus, and die at your hands," Mr. Garcia said. "That's got to leave some emotional scars. No one your age—any age—should have to go through that. And I'm so sorry it happened. But now I think you need some time."

"Time for what?" Marcus asked.

"To recover, to heal," Mr. Garcia replied. "Look, I'm not your father. But I think you need to have a serious talk with your mom, and even more with your pastor and maybe a professional counselor. Work this thing through, Marcus. Take it seriously. And then we'll see."

"What does that mean: 'we'll see'?" Marcus pressed. "What are you really saying?"

"Marcus, this isn't easy for me, but I have to do what's right for my daughter."

"Meaning?"

"I'm asking you to take some time off from seeing her, calling her, writing her."

"How much time?"

"I don't know. Let's say a year, then see where we are."

"A *year*? Please, Mr. Garcia, I just bought a ring for Elena. I was about to ask you and your wife for permission to ask her to marry me the moment we graduate. Please, sir, don't do this. I'm fine. And I'm in love. Don't tell me I can't see her."

"Marcus, I know you two are very fond of each other. I know you've discussed marriage. But you don't seem to appreciate the gravity of what has happened."

"I had to do it, Mr. Garcia. I didn't have a choice. Elena knows that, doesn't she?"

"I'm not here to argue with you. I've done everything I could to help you, and I've done it from my heart. But I'm asking you to respect my wishes. Let's talk again a year from now."

Marcus was speechless. He didn't need time to process or heal. Mr. Garcia was the one who needed time, not Marcus or Elena. But he could see it was pointless to argue. He certainly wasn't going to get the man's blessing to marry his daughter now. But waiting an entire year? Why not just say he could never see her again?

They drove back to Monument in silence, but Marcus couldn't actually go home. The house was no longer a crime scene. All the yellow tape had been taken down. But it still needed to be thoroughly cleaned, especially his mother's room, and that would take several days. So Mr. Garcia dropped him off at the Matthews' house. They had left town for the week and offered the house to Marcus if he needed it. Mr. Garcia pulled up out front, handed over the keys, and explained that Mrs. Matthews had left some instructions on the kitchen counter and some food in the fridge. Then he drove away, and Marcus entered the large, empty house feeling more alone than when he was behind bars.

The summer of 2001 was hot, lonely, and cruel for Marcus Ryker.

He did meet for several months with his pastor and separately with a counselor his pastor recommended. Neither of them believed Marcus was suffering from PTSD or any other side effects from the shooting. It had been a brutal and ugly matter, to be sure. But it had been justified, and neither man saw it negatively affecting Marcus's emotions or behavior. Marcus asked them to put their thoughts in writing. They did, and Marcus mailed both letters to Mr. Garcia. A week later, he received a brief, typed reply.

> Dear Marcus—I have received and read both letters. Thank you for your thoughtfulness in sending them to me. I wish you well in your senior year and look forward to discussing this matter with you again upon your graduation. Until then, I would be grateful if you would continue to honor my wishes. Sincerely, Javier Garcia, Attorney-at-Law

In August, Marcus returned to the UNC Greeley campus for his senior year as a criminal justice major, only to find out that Elena had transferred to the University of Denver. Her friends said her father had insisted. Marcus couldn't believe she hadn't even let him know.

At the gym one night, one of the guys he lived with asked what he was planning to do when he graduated. A few months ago, he had been so certain—graduate, marry Elena, become a police officer somewhere in Colorado, hopefully close to home. Now he was all by himself and drifting.

"I want to do something special with my life, something important," Marcus said. "I believe God gave me the ability and willingness to take big risks, but why? It can't just be for me. It has to be for something bigger. But the truth is, I have no idea what."

Less than a month later, Marcus woke up early on a Tuesday morning and went for a run, then came back to the apartment he was sharing with several guys in the same program. He was prepping for his favorite class, History 388—Imperial Russia from 1700 to 1917, and had barely finished showering when one of his roommates pounded on the bathroom door and insisted he come to the living room immediately. Marcus dried off, threw on jeans and a T-shirt, and joined everyone just in time to see a jumbo jet fly into the South Tower of the World Trade Center. Together they stood and watched in shock as both towers collapsed before their eyes. Then they heard that another plane had already crashed into the Pentagon.

Marcus slowly sat down. He wasn't going to class. None of them were. He called Elena's mobile phone. She didn't answer. He texted her, saying he didn't mean to violate her father's instructions but just wanted to make sure she was all right. Then he called his mom. She, too, was watching the coverage on television. They took a moment to pray for the nation and for the president.

That night, Marcus and his roommates remained huddled around the television. They watched the commander in chief address the nation.

"The search is under way for those who are behind these evil acts," the president promised. "I've directed the full resources of our intelligence and law enforcement communities to find those responsible and to bring them to justice."

Marcus found himself moved by how the president closed his address.

"Tonight I ask for your prayers for all those who grieve, for the children whose worlds have been shattered, for all whose sense of safety and security has been threatened. And I pray they will be comforted by a power greater than any of us, spoken through the ages in Psalm 23: 'Even though I walk through the valley of the shadow of death, I fear no evil, for you are with me.' This is a day when all Americans from every walk of life unite in our resolve for justice and peace. America has stood down enemies before, and we will do so this time. None of us will ever forget this day, yet we go forward to defend freedom and all that is good and just in our world. Thank you. Good night, and God bless America."

The following morning, Marcus again woke early. Again he went out for a run, and when he had showered and dressed and eaten some breakfast, he fished out a phone book from the front closet of the apartment, looked up the nearest Marine recruiting station, and dialed. It was busy. Ten minutes later, he tried a second time. It was still busy, and it remained so for the next hour. So Marcus grabbed his keys, jumped in his Mustang, and drove down to the station. It was a mob scene. Young men were lined up around the building and down the block. Marcus parked and got in line. It took him nearly four hours to get inside, fill out a stack of forms, and meet with someone in person.

"I want to enlist," he said without emotion. "How soon can I start?"

The recruiter was impressed with the fact that Marcus was nearly done with college and tried to persuade him to become an officer. Marcus told him he didn't want a career. He just wanted to defend his country, kick some terrorist tail, and get back home to start a family.

The Marine finally relented. On one issue, however, he was adamant.

Marcus needed to graduate. There was no point in throwing away all the time and money he and his mother had invested in his education by dropping out now. Marcus could enlist today, but he would not leave for basic training until May, the day after he graduated.

Marcus looked at his phone. It had been twenty-four hours, and he still hadn't heard back from Elena. If she was done with him, it was time to move on. He picked up a pen and signed on the dotted line, then drove back to campus and went to class.

PART
THREE

18

Be polite, be professional, but have a plan to kill everybody you meet.

The line had been drilled into Marcus Ryker and his buddies in Charlie Company by a Marine general they both feared and loved. Not a day went by when they didn't ask themselves how to live it out, and that was no less true on the fifth of May.

American Special Forces units had been steadily inserting themselves all over Afghanistan since December 2001, and the Taliban and al Qaeda were on the run. Working with a coalition of tribal leaders known as the Northern Alliance, the U.S. military was systematically strengthening local forces fighting against the jihadists—and hunting for Osama bin Laden—throughout Afghanistan, providing them with professional training, arms, communications equipment, and suitcases full of hard cash. It was a high-profile operation and one the American people were watching closely, eager to know their leaders were responding to the shocking and unprecedented attack on America with decisive speed and overwhelming power.

The day began as any other in a godforsaken country crawling with radical Islamist terrorists. Marcus expected monotonous hours in a cramped, deafening, sweltering chopper, traversing to and fro across the Hindu Kush. Visits to countless dust-ridden, poverty-stricken villages whose names most of Marcus's colleagues could hardly pronounce, much less remember. Standing for hours in the blazing sun and blistering heat while a U.S. congressman or senator or deputy assistant secretary of something-or-other met with one warlord and provincial governor after another. Meaningless photo ops. Mind-numbing political speeches. Lousy meals. Not nearly enough coffee. And always the gnawing knowledge that at any time the endless boredom could be shattered by moments of searing terror.

As Marcus awoke in Kabul, flies buzzing about his head, the Afghan capital was experiencing the ninth day of a historic heat wave. The mercury had reached ninety-four degrees Fahrenheit by eight in the morning and was expected to hit a hundred ten by midday. Dressed in full combat gear and carrying his M4 carbine assault rifle, Marcus was already drenched with sweat as he clambered into the back of the Sikorsky CH-53E Super Stallion, took his assigned seat, and buckled up. On most days he was grateful the Marines had done their own investigation of the incident with his stepfather and cleared him just as the local DA had. Still, sometimes he half wished his background check had coughed up something disqualifying, something that would have kept him from coming here of all places.

Climbing in after him as the rotors began to turn were his sergeant and his two closest friends in the theater. William Sanford McDermott was their squad leader. Hailing from Pittsburgh, he got his dark complexion from his Kenyan mother and his toughness and fearlessness from his father, a lapsed Irish Catholic with skin "as white as the wind-driven snow," he loved to say. Everyone in the squad called him Sarge to his face, but behind his back he was known as Big Mac. He was enormous—six foot five and almost two hundred and sixty pounds—and he literally consumed (inhaled, actually) more McDonald's burgers and fries than anyone Marcus and his colleagues had ever met.

Peter Hwang was a Texan, born and raised just outside of Houston, though his parents were from Seoul, South Korea. A hospital corpsman third class, he served as the unit's medic. He was a devout Catholic, and the guys all called him St. Peter.

Marcus was probably closest, though, to Nicholas Francis Vinetti. He hailed from North Jersey and was the youngest of a huge family, with four brothers and three sisters. Vinetti had been trained as a sniper. He was without question the best marksman of the lot. But he talked funny, and Marcus had dubbed him Vinnie Barbarino since he sounded an awful lot like John Travolta's iconic character in the long-defunct TV sitcom *Welcome Back, Kotter*.

Marcus had met Hwang and Vinetti the first day of boot camp in San Diego in May of 2002. They'd been assigned to the Twenty-Second Marine Expeditionary Unit and arrived together at Camp Lejeune, North Carolina, to serve on a battalion landing team known as the One-Six—First Battalion, Sixth Marines—which was where they'd met Sarge. Twenty-six additional weeks of grueling training, along with hours of card playing, debates on every topic under the sun, and of course, far too much McDonald's, had forged some tight bonds, and by the time they were eventually shipped out to Afghanistan to fight al Qaeda and the Taliban in Operation Enduring Freedom, they knew each other better than their own families.

Now, just before the side door of the chopper slammed shut, a dozen or so civilians climbed aboard, joining them for the day's tour. From behind his polarized combat goggles, Marcus quickly sized them up, one by one. All were young, certainly under thirty. Seven were career State Department foreign service officers, assigned to the U.S. Embassy in Kabul. Six were political appointees working for the DoD, having just landed in Kabul less than an hour before. They were paper pushers. Bureaucrats. Functionaries. And they were liabilities in a war zone. They'd read about combat, but they had little experience and certainly no training in how to handle themselves in a fight. They were here to take pictures and make notes and file reports and return to the safety of walled compounds and glass-and-steel offices with air-conditioning and leather executive chairs and flat-panel television screens and gourmet meals and Starbucks coffee. Anyone more senior to this group—whomever these young staff members worked for—was sitting in one of the two choppers spooling up beside them.

The last person to scramble aboard commanded the attention of the entire One-Six. The attractive young blonde with big green eyes and a short shag haircut was Annie Stewart. Marcus remembered her from her bio, distributed during the mission briefing, but she introduced herself to them all just the same. She was a deputy press secretary for Senator Robert Dayton, the Iowa Democrat who was the ranking minority member on the Senate Select Committee on Intelligence. Marcus suspected she was fresh out of graduate school, twenty-four or twenty-five at most. His age, or thereabouts. She was a long way from home.

As the three Super Stallions lifted off and headed southwest toward Kandahar, Marcus cringed as Sergeant McDermott—predictably—began flirting with Annie almost immediately. It might not have looked like flirting. It was a bit more subtle than that. But Marcus, St. Peter, and Vinnie glanced at each other knowingly—they'd seen it all before.

What brought Senator Dayton to Afghanistan? Big Mac began as if the answer wasn't obvious. *How does the senator feel the war is going? What do the American people think about the war so far?*

Then came the pivot.

So how long have you worked for the senator? Just six months, my goodness, that's not long. Do you like it? Where are you from? Charleston? Really. That's crazy. I have a cousin there. Love South Carolina. Ever been to Parris Island? So where did you go to school? Sure, I have lots of friends who went to Georgetown. Did you ever expect to come to Afghanistan? Well, yes, as a matter of fact, that's why I signed up. That's why all of us enlisted—to come here and kill bin Laden.

McDermott occasionally tried to misdirect the young woman by asking similar questions of some of the folks from State and the Pentagon, but he invariably got back to her. If she was bothered by all the attention, she was too polite to let on. She did make one mistake, however. She asked McDermott if he and his unit had seen any real combat. Marcus rolled his eyes and looked out the window as his commander leaned forward with his hands on his knees and began to answer.

Perhaps they'd given their squad leader the wrong nickname, Marcus thought. *Big Mac* didn't really capture the tales he was telling now. *Whopper* would have been far more appropriate.

That said, the man was certainly a world-class storyteller—funny, engaging, even mesmerizing at times, if not completely accurate. Marcus didn't recognize having been part of any of the firefights Sarge was claiming they'd engaged in, but he had to give the man credit. He certainly made the time pass. The cabin roared with laughter. Given how loud the engines were, McDermott had to shout, and everyone had to lean in to hear him. But he had them all eating out of his palm now, Annie Stewart included. Even Vinnie and St. Peter were enjoying the show as one cleaned his weapon and the other one restocked his medical bag with pharmaceuticals.

Marcus's thoughts, however, were half a world away. Elena had written him just one letter since he'd shipped off to boot camp. Her father, she wrote, had been impressed when he learned that Marcus had enlisted, but he still didn't think the two of them should be in contact yet. Not only that, but he had declared that life married to a Marine was no life for his daughter and had suggested it might be time for Elena to move on. Marcus couldn't tell from the letter how Elena felt about it. He was still devoted to her, but now he was less sure than ever what the future might hold for them.

Just then he heard his name.

"Now, the guy you really want to stick close to, Miss Stewart, is Lance Corporal Ryker here," McDermott said.

Marcus turned and was surprised to see nearly every eye on him.

"Really, and why's that?" Annie replied with a curious smile that Marcus couldn't quite decide was bemused or slightly flirtatious.

"Because Vinnie and I are notorious bachelors," McDermott said, grinning. "And St. Pete—well, don't be fooled by his cherubic face. But Ryker here, he's a good Christian and a real family man."

Annie laughed. "You don't say."

"Oh yeah, a real straight arrow," said McDermott. "Fell in love with his high school sweetheart, practically engaged, and planning to get married as soon as he gets out of the corps. When the chips are down, you can count on this guy."

No sooner had the words come out of McDermott's mouth than they all heard and felt the explosion.

19

The lead chopper disintegrated in a ball of fire.

Marcus stared in disbelief as parts of the fuselage fell to the earth. Then antiaircraft fire erupted below them, and the pilots took emergency evasive action. The Super Stallion lurched left, then right. The pilots fought to gain altitude and get out of range of whoever was firing at them. They had been flying at about ten thousand feet. Now they were racing for the ceiling—about eighteen thousand feet, give or take.

Marcus couldn't believe what was happening. Charlie Company had run this route a hundred times before. It had always been secure. But then he saw the second helicopter, the one directly in front of them, take several hits. Black smoke started pouring out of its engine. The chopper careened to the left. Her pilots were rapidly losing control and altitude. It quickly became clear she was going down—with a United States senator on board.

For the moment, Marcus's chopper kept climbing at a rate of about twenty-five hundred feet per minute. But Marcus had no illusions. They were no longer headed for the ceiling. Their mission had radically changed. They were supposed to be protecting Senator Dayton. That meant they had to follow the ailing chopper.

Anticipating a sudden and very rapid descent, Marcus tightened his shoulder harness, then reached over and tightened Annie Stewart's. Everyone else followed suit, holding on for their lives as the Sikorsky began diving for the deck.

They landed hard on a narrow outcropping on the side of a mountain. The civilians screamed as the landing gear collapsed and they skidded toward the edge of the cliff. Fortunately, they ground to a halt with ten or fifteen yards to spare. But they had no time to lose. The helicopter carrying the senator had crashed on a rocky slope about two hundred yards ahead and below them. Marcus could see smoke pouring out of the cabin, along with some of its occupants. He had no idea whether it had been the Taliban or al Qaeda operatives who had fired upon the three choppers. But whoever it was, surely they had seen the results. They had to know the Americans were on the ground, which meant they'd be racing toward them and radioing for reinforcements as they did, the billowing black smoke acting like a beacon and providing precise coordinates.

Sergeant McDermott moved fast. Pushing aside the civilians—most of whom were in shock or nearly so—he heaved open the side door and jumped out. He motioned his men to follow and everyone else, including the pilots, to stay put. He ordered Nick Vinetti—the sniper—to set up an overwatch position. His job was to take out any hostile forces that might approach from any direction. At the same time, McDermott ordered Pete Hwang—the medic—to scramble down the mountainside with Marcus and provide aid, medical or otherwise, for those in the senator's chopper. Meanwhile, he said, he would work the radios and call for assistance.

Marcus and Pete did as ordered. When they reached the crash site, they were horrified at what they found. Both the pilot and copilot had been killed immediately upon impact. Four of the dozen Marines on the chopper had also been killed. Two more were severely wounded. The senator himself was wounded in the leg and bleeding profusely. His chief of staff, the political officer from the U.S. Embassy in Kabul, and a senior public affairs officer were badly shaken up but physically had only minor cuts and contusions. Pete immediately put a tourniquet on the senator's leg, then turned his attention to the two Marines. The others set up a defensive perimeter while Marcus radioed a situation report back to McDermott.

"Sir, permission to move these people up to your location?" Marcus asked, explaining that the fire inside the crumpled fuselage was out of control and risked setting off the fuel tanks in short order.

"Permission granted," came the response. "Bring the senator first."

Marcus ordered the able-bodied civilians to follow him back up the mountain to the working chopper as he slung Senator Dayton over his shoulders in a fireman's carry and led the way. When they reached the others, Marcus set the senator inside the chopper, then scrambled back down the slope to help Pete, only to find that one of the most severely wounded Marines had just died.

That's when the first crackle of gunfire echoed through the canyon. Marcus spun around, M4 at the ready. He spotted two rebels moving across the ridge to their south, both of them firing AK-47s. He took aim but before he could pull the trigger, he heard two sharp cracks in rapid succession. He turned to see Nick Vinetti reloading his M40 bolt-action sniper rifle. Beaten to the punch, Marcus turned back to see two lifeless bodies crashing down the rocky slope. They were dressed like Taliban. From this distance Marcus couldn't positively identify them, but it didn't matter. Whoever they were, there were surely more to follow.

Marcus thanked Nick over the radio, then scanned for more hostiles. But Pete needed help.

"Get this one back to the other chopper," the medic said as he injected one of the badly wounded Marines, now writhing in pain, with another dose of morphine. "Tell Sarge we need to get him to Kandahar immediately along with the senator."

"No can do," Marcus replied. "Sarge says there's a sandstorm over Kandahar. Nothing's taking off or landing right now, and they're not sure how long it'll be till it lifts. They're sending backup from Kabul, but they're at least an hour out."

"Then another hour back to Kabul?" Pete said. "No way—this guy has lost too much blood. He can't wait that long. Tell Sarge they need to head back to Kabul immediately."

"Roger that," Marcus replied, then heaved the Marine over his shoulders and started working his way back up the mountain.

He'd climbed about halfway back to McDermott and the civilians when he heard a high-pitched whistle coming from his right. He turned just in time to see the contrail of an RPG slicing through the air. He followed the arc until he saw the rocket slam into the only working helicopter they still had. The Sikorsky erupted in a huge fireball, raining metal and rock from the sky. Marcus set down the Marine and covered him until the worst of it was over. He turned around and thought about climbing back down when, below them on a winding dirt road, he spotted two pickup trucks filled with cheering jihadists.

Suddenly there was a flash of light and then came another RPG. Stunned, Marcus watched as it hit the chopper below him, killing most of the Marines positioned nearby.

20

Marcus opened fire on the guerrillas down below.

He killed two that were standing in the bed of one of the trucks, reloading their rocket launcher. With another two bursts, he wounded two more crouching near the second pickup. Then he grabbed the wounded Marine and moved right, concealing his position behind the smoke pouring out of the destroyed Sikorsky above him. He ejected his partially spent magazine and loaded another, this one packed with tracer rounds. Then he aimed at the gas tank of the second truck and fired again. In an instant, the gas tank ruptured. Fuel began pouring out like a river, and Marcus had created his opportunity. He continued firing, one burst and then another. The tracer rounds ignited the fumes. The truck exploded, causing the fuel tank of the other truck to detonate as well. The booms could be heard up and down the valley.

Marcus hoisted the wounded Marine back over his shoulder. He knew he had to get to higher ground. He'd seen a cave near the top of the ridge, about seventy-five yards beyond the wreckage of the helicopter he'd been flying on. This was his new objective. Using the chaos of the moment, he proceeded to work his way farther up the mountain. But just then gunfire erupted again from the road below them. Marcus could hear rounds whizzing past his head and ricocheting off the rocks around them. Fortunately, Nick Vinetti reengaged, providing desperately needed covering fire. One by one, the sniper picked off the remaining Taliban fighters. Yet when Marcus finally reached the burning wreckage of the Super Stallion in which they had arrived, he found Nick badly burned, in terrible pain, and nearly out of ammunition. What's more, he was surrounded by charred and smoking bodies.

Sergeant McDermott was not there. Nor was Senator Dayton.

Through gritted teeth, Nick quickly explained that after the first spray of bullets had riddled the chopper, the sergeant and several of the young DoD guys had decided to carry the senator up to the cave to keep him out of the line of fire. They had just come back to get a first aid kit, bottles of water, and other supplies when the RPG had hit. Most of them were killed, Nick said. Sarge was alive but in pretty bad shape. Still, he'd led the survivors back up to the cave. That's where Marcus should take the Marine on his shoulders, Nick said, then wait there for him. He'd get there as soon as he could. Meanwhile he would stay here and provide cover until his dwindling ammo was gone.

Marcus took the advice—part of it, anyway. There was nothing he could do for Nick just now, and he did need to get this wounded Marine to safety. But he would not stay and wait in the caves. Instead, he promised to be back with painkillers and more ammunition. It took longer than he'd figured to make the climb, however. The terrain was far steeper than he'd expected, and when he got there, he was stunned to find so few survivors. The only passengers left alive were McDermott, the senator—who had blacked out—Annie Stewart, and two foreign service officers. All had been injured in the explosion to one degree or another. One of the FSOs had also been shot and was bleeding badly. McDermott had second- and third-degree burns on his hands and face, but despite his own pain he was doing everything he could to stanch the man's wounds.

The other FSO was in shock. He was sitting to one side of the cave, shivering and mumbling incoherently. Miss Stewart, on the other hand, was at McDermott's side. From the looks of it, she actually had some medical training and was presently injecting the FSO with a shot of something. The woman had blood all over her face and hands. Whether it was mostly hers or someone else's wasn't immediately clear. She had obviously been hit by shards of flying glass and burning metal. But she was alive, and now she was valiantly trying to save her colleagues.

"I need something for Vinetti," Marcus said as he caught his breath.

"Painkillers?" McDermott asked.

"Right—something—he's in bad shape."

"We don't have any more," McDermott replied. "We just used the last of it."

Marcus asked for more rounds for Nick's M40 sniper rifle. Again McDermott had to inform him there were none to be had. All their supplies had been on the chopper.

"How soon till reinforcements arrive?" Marcus asked.

"They'll get here when they get here."

"Sir?"

"The radio was destroyed in the blast."

"We're not in communication with Kabul?"

"No, Lance Corporal Ryker, we are not. Now let me do my job."

Marcus looked at the FSO dying in front of him. He'd stopped breathing. He was pale. His blood pressure was visibly dropping. They were losing him. McDermott began giving him mouth-to-mouth. Just then, Pete and the surviving Marines from the second chopper arrived at the mouth of the cave. Pete raced to McDermott's side and took over. His comrades moved to help the others. Marcus said a silent prayer. They needed more than luck to get off this mountain alive. They needed divine intervention.

When he'd whispered an amen, he told Sergeant McDermott he

needed to get back and help Vinetti. Sarge didn't need to be asked twice. He gave his assent, and Marcus raced back down the mountain. As he did, he could see a cloud of dust on the dirt road, approaching from the south. As it neared, he could make out a convoy of a half-dozen white Toyota pickup trucks. Each was filled with Taliban. Their situation, already precarious, was worsening by the minute.

The closest U.S. military presence was at the forward operating base near Kandahar. But that was at least sixty miles away to the south, and it was currently consumed in a sand- and dust storm that could last for hours. Kabul was some two hundred miles away to the north. The closest American aircraft carriers were operating in the Indian Ocean, and that was a good four hundred miles away, maybe more. So who was coming to help them? From what direction? How long was it going to take them to get there? Marcus had no answers, and McDermott no longer had any means of contacting his superiors, much less any friendly forces in the region.

21

Vinetti was lying on his stomach, looking through his scope at the approaching storm.

When Marcus reached him, he didn't waste any time, just told him the bad news. No morphine. No extra sniper rounds. Then he demanded his friend's sidearm.

"What for?" Vinetti asked, looking up for the first time.

Marcus set his fully loaded M4 assault rifle down beside his comrade, along with the rest of his own magazines and those he'd grabbed from McDermott.

"What are you doing?" Vinetti asked.

"Just give me your .45," Marcus replied. "I need to move fast."

Reluctantly, Vinetti unholstered his sidearm and handed it over, along with the last two mags he had. Then he looked back through the scope. "Good luck," he said. "Be fast."

Marcus holstered the .45 and once again began scrambling down the side of the mountain. He could see the Taliban caravan approaching. They were still about a klick and a half away, but they were coming fast. He thought he could beat it, though it was going to be close. Perhaps his only advantage was that he had the element of surprise. Unless they were watching with binoculars, it was very unlikely the guerrillas knew he was careening down the mountain toward them. To be sure, he was kicking up a fair amount of dust. But he was betting that none of it was noticeable given all the smoke from two blazing jet fuel–driven infernos.

At one point, he lost his footing and nearly went down the mountain headfirst. He recovered fairly quickly, but his hands and knees were bleeding and he was covered in dust. What's more, he'd lost one of the extra magazines he'd been carrying. But there was no time to go back for it. The lead pickup in the procession couldn't be more than a half kilometer away now.

When he reached the dirt road, Marcus set off in a dead sprint. He was aiming for the burning vehicles. He estimated they were fifty yards ahead. That was only half a football field. He could do that, he told himself. He'd run far longer as a player in high school. His coach had called them suicide drills. He had no idea.

Marcus expected to hear Vinetti open fire at any moment. But he hadn't started yet, and Marcus suddenly wondered if either or both of his guns had jammed. *Focus*, he told himself. *Focus. Keep moving. Keep running. Don't look up. Don't look back. Focus.* There was nothing he could do about Vinetti. All he could account for was himself. But that was the problem. He thought he'd been in good shape. The best of his life. But his heart was pounding hard enough to explode at any moment. His lungs were sucking in dusty, smoke-filled air. His body was drenched with sweat. His mouth and tongue were bone-dry. Every muscle in his body was in searing pain—straining, pushing. He felt like he was going to vomit. *Thirty yards. Twenty. Ten.* He was almost there, but that convoy was closing in fast.

He reached the first body and grabbed the dead man's AK-47 and every mag he could find. Slinging the machine gun over his back, Marcus kept moving. He found another body. Another Kalashnikov. More ammo. He took it all. Darting through the smoke and around the flames, he found two more machine guns and then spotted the prize he'd come for in the first place—a rocket-propelled grenade launcher lying on the side of the road beside four charred but usable RPGs. There was only one problem. He was never going to have time to get back up the mountain with the loot. The convoy was less than forty yards away, and they had spotted him.

Marcus heard the crackle of gunfire.

Then Vinetti finally engaged. His first shots blew out the windshield of the lead Toyota, instantly killing both the driver and the man riding shotgun. The truck swerved violently and plunged into a large ditch. That gave Marcus just the time he needed to load the first RPG, aim, and fire at the second Toyota. The grenade exploded on contact, killing everyone in and on the truck, while the third pickup smashed directly into the back of it.

Boom, boom . . . crack, crack, crack.

The sounds from the mountainside changed as Vinetti fired the last of his sniper rounds and switched to Marcus's M4, felling one jihadist after another.

Marcus knelt close to one of the burning trucks to give himself some cover.

He feverishly reloaded the RPG launcher, wondering if at any moment the heat would cook off the explosives before he could pull the trigger. It hadn't happened yet, and Marcus begged God that it wouldn't. He took aim once again, settled himself, and fired.

Again the grenade hit its mark. He felt the concussion and thought he'd been nearly deafened by the blast until he heard the pinging of multiple rounds off the pickup beside him. Then he felt the bone-rattling impact of two rounds hitting his bulletproof vest, sending him sprawling and the grenade launcher skittering across the road. The heat was unbearable. He was just a few inches from the flames. All the air had been knocked out of him and he was immersed in thick black smoke. Unable to breathe, unable to see, he jerked away from the roaring truck. He scrambled desperately to his feet, knowing he needed to find cover, and then he felt the searing pain of a round slicing through his left shoulder.

An instant later he landed face-first in the gravel, then slid off into a ditch along the side of the road. For a moment, everything seemed to go into slow motion. But at least he was somewhat shielded by the berm and thus from the worst of the heat. His lungs greedily sucked in as much air as they could. But he could hear the crackle of more automatic gunfire. He could hear bullets whizzing overhead, and he felt his hand moving to his holster.

Then the slow motion came abruptly to an end. Suddenly everything was clear. Everything was sharp. He grabbed his pistol, flicked off the safety, and peered up over the road. A Taliban fighter was coming on fast. He had an AK-47 aimed directly at his face. Marcus pulled his trigger first and the man went down. Right behind him was another fighter. This guy, too, was charging directly at him and unloading his Kalashnikov as he came. Marcus had two options—duck and cover, or fire back. He didn't remember deciding. He just remembered pulling the trigger again and again until the man dropped.

Marcus grabbed one of the AK-47s slung over his back and worked his way through the roadside ditch, toward the convoy. *Shoot, reload, repeat, and keep moving.* That was his mantra as Vinetti rained down death from the mountainside. They made a pretty good team, but they were no match for what was coming next. The last thing Marcus Ryker saw before he took another bullet and blacked out was an American A-10 Thunderbolt swooping down from the sky unannounced and lighting up the road with 30mm shells that destroyed everyone and everything in its path.

The good guys had arrived, and not a moment too soon.

22

Luganov's chief of staff had not been kidding.

The winter wedding of Oleg Stefanovich Kraskin to the only daughter of the president was a spectacle beyond anything the Russian people had witnessed in the modern era. The event, patterned precisely after the marriage of Nicholas II to Alexandra Feodorovna in 1894, down to the smallest detail, had taken years to plan. And all of it was designed to evoke every bit of the pomp and circumstance and glory of the czarist era, before the Russian Revolution, before the Soviet Union, before the collapse of the Soviet Empire and the humiliating decline of Russian power and prestige.

Oleg had barely been included in any of the planning. Indeed, he had been so busy with his work at the Kremlin that he had never even been to the Winter Palace, much less the Grand Church anytime during their long engagement. So when he and his parents arrived from the airport on that snow-covered yet sunny Saturday morning in a heavily guarded motorcade about an hour before the ceremony began, Oleg found himself overwhelmed by the stunning locale.

The Winter Palace, Oleg knew, was once the official residence of the czars. The green-and-white structure on the banks of the River Neva in St. Petersburg was long and low, rectangular and mammoth, with more than one thousand rooms and more than one hundred staircases. The cathedral known as the Grand Church was located on the east side of the palace grounds and was spectacularly ornate with its massive onion dome, gilded and gleaming in the sunshine so rare at this time of year. Inside, the main sanctuary was more beautiful than anything Oleg had ever seen before. The white marble walls and columns were trimmed with gold. The high ceilings were adorned with gold sculptures. The chandeliers and lamps were made of pure gold. Enormous gold statues of angels, each bearing wings, some holding trumpets, were mounted on the walls. Pews accommodating a thousand guests had been set up in the long hall before an altar under a soaring dome. Light streamed down onto the altar through stained-glass windows, and mounted on the wall above was a gold statue of the Christ, hanging on a cross, surrounded by golden angels.

Despite the beauty, Oleg shuddered at all the iconography. Neither he nor Marina was religious. It all seemed so antiquated and banal. If it had been up to him, he would have whisked his fiancée off to Monaco for a quick civil wedding and a honeymoon among the glistening beaches of the Mediterranean and the high-rolling casinos of Monte Carlo. Unfortunately, as had been made clear to him time and time again, it was not up to him. So here he was, ready to participate in a spectacle designed to showcase the glory of Russia to the world.

Oleg excused himself from his parents and stepped into a back room to have a cigarette and change clothes. When he came out, he was not only in full regimental dress; he was wearing the exact uniform in which Nicholas II had been married, as his father-in-law-to-be had insisted. Oleg had initially chafed at the idea, but Aleksandr Luganov was not a man to whom one said no. Oleg's mother dabbed away tears with her handkerchief as her son stood there in the hall wearing the tall, black leather riding boots, black trousers with a single gold stripe running down the outside of each leg, a bright-red tunic adorned with gold, gold epaulets, and a sword in a beautifully designed scabbard attached to a thick leather belt.

"It's time," said the Russian Orthodox archbishop, stepping out of a side chamber.

The cleric, the highest-ranking bishop in the Russian Orthodox Church, was stooped and graying. He wore a bulbous, bejeweled miter adorned with icons of Jesus Christ and two other figures Oleg couldn't identify, a liturgical gown that reached to the floor, and a golden cape festooned with crosses and other Orthodox icons. In his right hand he held an enormous golden staff topped with a cross. He led them down a long, dark corridor and then through a door that opened into the grand hall. An aide to the archbishop directed Oleg's parents to their seats as the organist began to play and Oleg's heart began to race.

Had the ceremony—both the first portion known as the "betrothal" and the second portion known as the "crowning"—not been broadcast live to the world in its entirety and videoed so that the young couple could savor it later, Oleg would have been hard-pressed to remember much of it, so overwhelmed was he by all the guests, the klieg lights, the heavy aroma of incense, and his own dizzying emotions. The bishop's words, the Scriptures that were read, the long passages of the liturgy, and the Communion service after the vows all went by in a blur. Oleg could not remember the names or faces of any of the dozens of heads of state and ambassadors and scores of Russian oligarchs and their trophy wives who attended.

What he would never forget, however, was the sight of the president leading his daughter down the aisle and the look of immense pride mixed with a father's tenderness when he put Marina's hand in Oleg's. Even more, Oleg would always remember how stunningly beautiful his bride looked in the flowing white-and-gold silk dress and diamond-studded crown, the very one worn by Czarina Alexandra in 1894. He would remember the flicker of firelight dancing in her eyes as each of them held a single golden candlestick during the ceremony. And he would remember the moment her soft and supple lips parted and she affirmed her love and loyalty to him until their dying breath.

Afterward, the wedding party and all the guests moved into an exquisitely appointed state room housing the original wooden dining table used by the czars to entertain European guests back in the day. It could—and did—seat exactly one thousand guests and featured original china settings used by the Romanovs. The president and first lady sat at the head of the table. The newlyweds sat to their right, Oleg's parents to their left. Oleg cared little for the gourmet menu or the wide variety of vodka and wine that was served or any of the toasts or the dancing. He hated all the eyes staring at him, all the cameras flashing, and the bright lights of the TV crews. He just wanted it to be over so he could sweep away his bride and enjoy their honeymoon in peace and quiet, alone and far from the hoopla.

His impatient daydreams were interrupted, however, when Luganov leaned over and whispered to him at one point during the reception. Having just lit up a Cuban cigar for himself and offered one to Oleg, the president had pulled his son-in-law close to him and kissed him on both cheeks.

"Oleg Stefanovich, I would not have given my Marina to just any young man. I trust you, my son, and I see great potential in you. I know you will give me many grandchildren and raise them to be princes and princesses, loyal and brave. And I want you to know that if there is anything you need, you have only to ask."

The man looked deep into Oleg's eyes. "We are family now," the president added. "Come what may, we must stick together, for the glory of Russia, for the glory of our dynasty."

23

Marcus Ryker's wedding to his high school sweetheart was hardly a spectacle.

It was a miracle.

And Marcus had the Taliban to thank.

Elena Garcia had seen the story of the helicopter crashes and the shoot-out in Kandahar on the evening news. When the story about Marcus being wounded in combat appeared in the local media a few days later, Elena broke up with her new boyfriend, a medical student at UC Denver, and called Marcus on every number she had for him. When she couldn't reach him, she called his mother. Then she called her father. By the time Marcus was awarded the Purple Heart, he and Elena were a couple again, and after he'd recovered and been given a brief leave for Christmas, they were married.

The ceremony in which Marcus Johannes Ryker pledged his undying love to the eldest daughter of Javier Rodriguez Garcia was so small and understated it didn't even get reported in the local newspapers. The Garcia family had money, but Elena begged her father not to use any of it on a big wedding. She didn't want all the fuss. Nor did she want to do anything that might cause embarrassment to her mother-in-law-to-be. Marjorie Ryker was now a widow twice over. Surviving on Social Security and a modest Air Force pension, she was barely making ends meet, especially given all she'd done to help Marcus through college.

Marcus didn't want anything showy either. The incident in Afghanistan had already brought him far too much attention. Something simple and quiet sounded just right to him. So Marcus's mother hosted the two families for dinner at her home on a snowy Wednesday evening. She made lamb chops, mashed potatoes, green peas, and mint jelly—Marcus's favorite. The next afternoon, the couple were married in the Garcias' living room. The pastor who had discipled Marcus during his senior year of college officiated. Only immediate family and a few close friends attended. The reception was catered by Famous Dave's barbecue. Afterward Marcus and Elena drove to Aspen for a honeymoon of skiing and snowboarding, a wedding gift from her parents.

Friday was New Year's Eve. With a massive snow squall bearing down on everything west of the Continental Divide, Marcus heated up the leftover Chinese food they'd had for lunch. He opened a bottle of champagne that had been chilling in the small refrigerator, compliments of the resort, glad their Baptist friends were, for the moment, nowhere to be found. Then they curled up by the fire in their rented two-level villa, and Elena gave her groom not one gift but two.

Marcus tore the wrapping paper off the first, and what he found took his breath away. It was a single-volume first edition of Solzhenitsyn's *The Gulag Archipelago*, and it was signed by the author himself.

Marcus gasped. "This must have cost you a fortune!"

"You're worth every penny," she replied, her eyes dancing with desire. "I would have paid ten times more."

They kissed with abandon until Marcus realized he had not opened the second gift. They took a pause, caught their breath, and sipped more champagne. Next Marcus unwrapped the somewhat-larger gift.

"What's this?" he asked.

"You'll see," she said playfully.

What he found was a scrapbook Elena had made for him. On the first page was a faded class photo of Marcus in the sixth grade.

He stared at it.

Elena laughed.

Marcus did not.

He looked hideous. His hair was long, his clothes were too dorky to describe, and he was wearing braces and battling acne. He was not smiling. Instead, he looked forlorn, and Marcus knew why. All those memories started rushing back, and he fought to control his emotions. He didn't want to ruin the moment or make Elena feel bad. But the photo was taken not long after he had lost his father.

He thanked her and was about to kiss her, but Elena nodded to the note she had written under the picture.

June 2, 1991—Photo Day—Lewis Palmer Middle School.

This was the day I fell in love with you, Marcus Ryker. This exact day.

My family had just moved to Monument from the Springs. I had cried for weeks. I pleaded with my father not to make me change schools so close to the end of the year. But he didn't listen. He'd found a house he and Mama liked. So we moved, and there I was. My sisters weren't born yet. I was lonely, depressed, angry, furious, and yet suddenly curious about this cute boy in English, social studies, and PE.

The only reason I came to school every day was to see you. You were taller than the rest of the boys. You were quiet but strong— and fast. Fast like the wind. And crazy. Always climbing on things. Jumping off things. Doing backflips. Pulling pranks. You were always getting in trouble, but not real trouble. Not big trouble. The teachers liked you. You always seemed to get off with a warning. You were just having fun, and you were fun to be around.

I had only one friend, Marcy Gallagher. She sat in front of me in homeroom. Her dad was the mayor. She knew you. She liked you. She would talk about you all the time. So I never told her about the crush I had on you.

Then came the day for class pictures. My mother sent me to school that day in the ugliest brown dress I had ever seen. She had just bought it for me the night before. She insisted I wear it. I screamed at her and told her she was ruining my life. I threatened to sue her for child abuse, but she wouldn't relent. She sent me to school in that hideous dress, on photo day, of all days!

Somehow, when I got in line to get my picture taken, lo and behold, I found myself standing right behind you. I was so mortified. I kept praying you wouldn't turn around and look at me. But you did. That was the day you introduced yourself to me. You asked if I was new to the school. I was so scared I couldn't speak. So I just nodded and blushed. And you smiled at me—not a big smile, just a little smile, but it was such a sweet smile—and you told me you liked my dress. When the photographer said it was your turn to have your picture taken, you sat down and your smile faded. All at once you looked sad. I wondered why. I wanted to ask you, but you said good-bye and ran off to class.

The photographer called my name. I just stood there, transported into a dreamworld where Marcus Ryker had actually talked to me—to me! Smiled at me! Complimented me! You were either a big, fat liar or a very kind boy. I decided it was the latter, and I told God right then and there that I wanted to marry you. I told God I didn't know why you were sad, but I wanted to make you the happiest boy in the world. And then I ran off, in that hideous brown dress, without ever having my sixth-grade picture taken. My parents were furious. But they got over it. And I got you.

So just in case you didn't already know it, that's my mission in life, Marcus Johannes Ryker—making you happy for the rest of your life. You can't shake me now. I'm yours forever.

Marcus held his wife tightly. "You can't shake me either," he whispered in the candlelight. "I'm going to stick to you like glue."

FOUR

24

Marcus Ryker tore south on I-25, but this time he was not a man possessed—someone was going to be born tonight, and he'd never been so excited.

With Elena in the backseat of their Ford Expedition, groaning in pain and pleading with him to be careful, Marcus abruptly flashed back to the night his mother had been in such danger, the night he'd driven like a maniac to come to her aid. He was still a risk-taker, but he'd learned a few lessons along the way. He was older now, wiser he hoped, more focused, more experienced, and more careful. He wasn't going to do anything to put his wife and child in danger. Not now. Not ever.

That said, he was going ninety miles an hour as he blew past the exit for the Air Force Academy on his right, then the Focus on the Family campus on his left. Before long, he was getting off on Highway

87, zigzagging through a series of side streets, pulling into the parking lot at Memorial Hospital, and racing toward the emergency room entrance. Elena was just shy of forty-two weeks. She was, therefore, almost two weeks late. She had been experiencing intensifying labor pains for much of the last two weeks yet showed no signs of dilating. She was scheduled to be induced in three more days. But just after 10 p.m., her water had finally broken.

It was now 10:27. Elena's contractions were coming harder and faster. Marcus screeched to a halt, jumped out, and carried his wife inside, abandoning the Expedition and tossing the keys to a security guard inside the door.

Elena's ob-gyn met them in the lobby accompanied by two nurses. They helped Elena into a wheelchair and whisked her off to labor and delivery, Marcus following close behind. Once there, a team of medical professionals immediately surrounded her, but Marcus wasn't about to be boxed out. He moved to her side, took her hand, and watched the blood drain from his own as Elena gasped and cried out and squeezed with all her might.

For the next two hours, Marcus coached her along. He reminded her to breathe deeply. He dabbed the sweat off her face with a cloth. He offered her ice chips and fought not to comment on just how powerful her grip could be with this much adrenaline coursing through her body. All the while, he silently thanked the Lord for his timing. Only weeks before, he'd finished his four-year contract with the Marines and raced back from Baghdad to be at Elena's side.

Eventually, however, it became clear that a serious problem was developing. As Marcus watched a bank of monitors digitally displaying the latest second-to-second data from mother and baby, he could see what the doctor and every nurse in the room could see. With every contraction, the baby's heart rate was beginning to drop precipitously.

Initially, between contractions, the baby's heart rate had settled at between 140 and 150 beats per minute. But now, during the peak of the contractions, it was plunging. The first time Marcus noticed it, the heart rate had dipped to 83. The next time it dropped to 76. Then 72. Then 64. Then just 61. Worse, when each contraction was over, the baby's heart was not returning to normal. Rather it was returning to barely over 100, and now the ob-gyn informed her team that she was concerned the baby was going into fetal distress. She ordered them to prep for an emergency C-section.

"*No!*" Elena cried out when she heard that. Then she dissolved into tears.

Her body was trembling. Her lips were starting to turn blue. Marcus thought he'd seen everything. He'd been in combat. He'd seen friends die. He himself had been shot and nearly burned alive in the wastelands of Kandahar. He thought he'd become impervious to fear. But seeing his wife in such pain and seeing their baby experiencing such trauma was almost more than this Marine could bear.

"Doc, she wants a natural delivery," Marcus said, his voice nearly faltering midsentence.

"I know," said the ob-gyn. "But the baby can't take much more."

The doctor checked the monitors again. The baby's heart rate was just 95.

"Mrs. Ryker, I'm going to ask you to push again," she said. "You're doing great. You're doing everything I'm asking, and I want to give you the chance to try again. But if your baby's heart rate drops too far, I'm going to do what we call a crash C-section. But don't worry. I can have the baby out in thirty seconds. Everything's going to be okay."

Elena said nothing. She couldn't. Tears were streaming down her face, but she was doing everything she could not to make a sound. Marcus knew why. She wanted to be strong. She didn't want him to see her falling apart. But her hands were clammy. Her body was getting weaker. The whole thing was taking a terrible toll on both mother and baby, and Marcus was fighting back his own emotions. His bottom lip quivered. His eyes were moist. He was scared. Not for Elena. She was tough. She'd be fine. He was terrified that the baby—his little daughter or son; they still didn't know which—might not pull through.

"Okay, Mrs. Ryker, take a deep breath and push one more time," the doctor said.

Elena squeezed Marcus's hand and did as she was told. Immediately the baby's heart rate began to drop again: 90. Then 80. Then 70. Then 60. When it dropped under 60, the doctor made the call.

Marcus was pushed away from the table, and the team went to work. He couldn't see everything that was going on, and it was all happening so fast. But he heard a gurgling sound as the scalpel plunged into his wife's belly. He saw blood gushing from her, blood mixed with amniotic fluid. It was spraying everywhere. His hand immediately went to his mouth, covered though it was by the surgical mask. He felt lightheaded. Tears poured from his eyes, though he dared not make a sound. He took several steps back, then felt the reassuring touch of a nurse's hand on his arm. He'd seen more blood than this. On that mountainside in Afghanistan and in that cave. But he'd never seen it flowing out of his wife. He hadn't prepared himself for this. Neither of them had. They'd never seriously considered a cesarean might really be necessary. That was foolish, of course. He'd been trained to not only consider but plan for every eventuality. But he hadn't, and now he regretted it.

Elena had been given general anesthesia, so she was out cold, and for this he was grateful. Because the baby—covered in blood and mucus—was not crying, was not making a sound of any kind. Everything in him braced for the worst. This baby was dead. He was sure of it now. Elena was giving birth to a stillborn child. He was watching it happen with his own eyes, and when Elena awoke, he would have to be the one to tell her. He didn't know if he could.

But suddenly he saw the legs begin to flutter, then heard a cry and then wailing.

No sound had ever seemed so precious.

"It's a boy!" Marcus shouted as he rushed into the waiting room.

Marjorie Ryker burst into tears and flung her arms around him. "I don't believe it," she said as she held him tight. "I'm so proud of you."

"Congratulations, Grandma," he said. "How long have you waited to hear that?"

"Too long!" she cried. "Is he healthy?"

"Healthy and beautiful and I can't wait for you to meet him."

"Me, either," she said, laughing through her tears, then finally let him go after a moment and fished some tissues out of her purse. "You should call your sisters," she said as she dabbed her eyes. "They'll be tickled pink."

"Blue," Marcus corrected.

"What?"

"It's a boy, Mom—they'll be tickled blue."

She laughed again and the elevator dinged. When the doors opened,

Mr. and Mrs. Garcia and Elena's sisters—now teenagers—rushed out, flowers in hand. Mrs. Ryker couldn't contain herself, blurting out the news before Marcus could, and the whole family squealed with delight.

"Congratulations," Marcus said to the girls. "Today you are both aunts."

They oohed and aahed, and he answered their questions and gave them all the details he could think of, only omitting for now any mention of fetal distress and the touch-and-go moments.

Mr. Garcia beamed as he shook Marcus's hand vigorously. "You're going to make an excellent father, Marcus," he said in that elegant and distinctive Spanish accent. "You just need to get a job that's safer than the Marines."

"I'll do my best, sir."

"Sorry, son; if Kandahar was your best, you're going to have to do a lot better."

They laughed together as Elena's ob-gyn approached.

"Mr. Ryker?"

"Yes."

"Your wife is out of surgery now. She did fine. Everything went very well. The C-section was picture-perfect. No complications."

Marcus breathed a sigh of relief.

"She's in recovery. She's awake—a bit groggy still, but awake—and she's asking for you. Can I take you to her?"

"Yes, please," he said. He turned to make sure everyone else was okay. They told him they were, especially with this reassuring news, and urged him to go and give Elena their love. They would see her soon enough.

The doctor led Marcus through a set of secure doors and down several hallways until they reached the recovery room. Marcus poked his head between the curtains. Elena was holding their baby, and when she saw Marcus, her eyes lit up.

"Hey, *madre*," he said with a smile, coming over to her side and giving her a kiss on the forehead.

"Hey, *padre*." She smiled back.

"How are you feeling?"

"Tired, but good."

"Pain?"

"Not yet."

"Keep those drugs comin'!"

"Amen."

"Your folks are outside, and your sisters," he said.

"That's fun. And your mom?"

"Right there with them. I just gave them a briefing. They all send their love and can't wait to see you."

Marcus leaned down and looked into his son's eyes, milk-chocolate brown like Elena's. "Pretty cute, huh?" he said.

"Adorable, just like his father."

"I don't know," Marcus said. "He looks a lot like your side."

"True, I was just trying to be nice," Elena teased, punching him playfully in the arm. "So what are we going to call him?"

"I don't know. You don't like any of the names on my list."

"That's because all of your names are ridiculous," she teased. "Zadok? Really?"

"Zadok is a great name," he protested. "Right out of the Bible. He was a priest, for crying out loud."

"It's never going to happen."

They went through several other names, rejecting each for various reasons.

"What if we name him after your father?" Elena said after a long pause.

"Lars?" he asked.

"Yeah," she said. "He's always been your hero. It's a great name. Strong. Masculine. Dutch. And it certainly goes with Ryker."

He smiled again. He loved this girl and never ceased to be amazed by her.

"What if we give him your father's name, too?" he asked.

"Lars Javier Ryker?" she asked.

"In a country of 300 million people, I seriously doubt there's another one like it."

They kissed to seal the deal. But there was more to discuss.

"So listen," Marcus said, easing into the pool, "I've been giving this a lot of thought, and I've decided not to re-up."

"What?" Elena asked. "I thought you wanted to be an NCO."

"I did, but this changes everything."

"But the Marines love you, and you love being a Marine."

"What about your father?"

"Once you became a hero, he seems to have made his peace with it."

"Still, I don't want to be an absentee dad. I want to get a little house with a white picket fence and a big backyard where Lars can play—here, on the Front Range, if God lets us. I want to teach him to ride a bike and throw a football and go fishing and hiking and white-water rafting, and I can't do that in the Marines, not the way I want."

"So what would you do?" she asked.

"I think I could find a decent job of some kind in law enforcement—and if not here, then somewhere farther out west. How does San Diego sound?"

"Lovely."

"What about Seattle?"

"Rainy, but great coffee."

"Exactly, or Santa Fe or Salt Lake City . . ."

"Any place that starts with an S," she quipped.

"Anywhere we can be together," he replied. "Deal?"

"Deal," she said with a smile and another kiss. "You can't shake me, Ryker."

"And I don't want to, Ryker. I'll stick to you like glue."

26

After two bitter miscarriages, Marina delivered their first child.

It was a healthy baby boy, and Oleg was ecstatic, as were the rest of his and Marina's extended families. Yet no one was more pleased than his father-in-law, who promptly insisted that the archbishop of the Russian Orthodox Church himself—the one who had originally married the young couple—come to the hospital and pray for the baby and his parents.

Luganov further insisted the bishop also perform the dedication. In the tradition of the church, the ceremony would be performed on the eighth day. This was also the day the baby would be named. In the times of the czars, before the Communist Revolution of 1917, it was tradition that the local priest—not the parents—would name the baby. This is precisely what Luganov wanted. Privately, Oleg strenuously protested to Marina. His heart was set on naming his firstborn son after his own father, Stefan Mikhailovich Kraskin, but Marina pleaded with Oleg to let her father have his way.

"I love you more than life itself, Oleg Stefanovich—you know I do," she said as the two headed to their bedroom and undressed for the night. "But my father is not merely the patriarch of my family; he is by all rights the patriarch of Mother Russia, and thus our shepherd, guiding us as a family and as a nation down the path he knows is best. Everyone is watching us because everyone is watching him. Please, my love—do not deny my father the honor of following tradition or the right to uphold the heritage of our people."

"But they are not *our* traditions," Oleg pushed back, rooting through every drawer for a cigarette but finding none. "We are *not* religious people. This is nonsense. We'd be doing it just for show."

"That's not true, darling," Marina argued. "We may not believe in God, but certainly we believe in honoring our parents, do we not? Even more, we believe in upholding the glory of Mother Russia."

"Of course, but—"

"Then I beg of you," Marina interjected, "let us not concern ourselves with these myths and legends. They are not important to us. I don't even think my mother cares. Your parents certainly aren't pious. But my father is."

"Pious?" Oleg asked, his voice tinged with cynicism.

"Well, religious," Marina replied. "The point is: this *matters* to him. So why not give him this gift, this very simple but precious gift?"

"The name of our child? The very name he will bear for eternity?"

"Eternity? Why must you be so melodramatic, Oleg Stefanovich?" Marina said. "In the grand scheme of things, this is so trifling a gift for so great a leader, no?"

"No, that's just it—it's an enormous gift for a man who already has everything," Oleg shot back, increasingly desperate for a smoke. "Marina, my darling, we finally have a son of our own, an heir, someone to carry on our name and our values. This baby is everything to us, especially after losing two others. Should we not be free to name him as we wish?"

Love is a stubborn thing. In the end, Oleg relented to his beloved wife, if not her father. Not only would he allow the bishop to name their son, but he also agreed to ask Marina's parents, not his own, to be the child's godparents.

Thus it was that on the eighth day after his birth, their baby was dedicated by the patriarch at the Church of the Twelve Apostles, on the grounds of the Kremlin. The bishop gave him the name Vasily. Neither Oleg nor Marina could remember a branch in either family tree bearing anyone with this name. But Oleg knew exactly where the name had come from. It was the Slavic version of the name Basil, which came from the Greek name Basileus, meaning "king." There had been at least four or five Russian czars and princes named Vasily. The name hadn't come from the archbishop at all. It had come from the president himself.

On the fortieth day after their baby's birth, Oleg and Marina met again with their two families, not inside the Kremlin's walls but in St. Basil's Cathedral, the iconic onion-domed church planted in the heart of Red Square. The occasion was the baptism of little Vasily Olegovich Kraskin. Once again the president had chosen the venue. He had insisted that the archbishop and several priests be in attendance along with every member of his cabinet and dozens of other VIPs. As with his daughter's marriage, Luganov wanted a national spectacle. The press was there, and the brief ceremony was the lead on the evening news.

This time Oleg did not resist, even in private. This was important to Marina because it was important to her father. He was willing to swallow his pride and go along. But he remained deeply uncomfortable with the religious commitments he was being asked to make in front of the entire country.

As the service began and incense wafted through the darkened sanctuary, Oleg stood beside the altar. He held a single lit candle in his hand. At his side, Marina—wearing a traditional headscarf—held their crying baby in her arms as the bishop, wizened and gray, led them through the liturgy.

"Oleg Stefanovich, do you renounce Satan and all his angels and all his works and all his services and all his pride?"

"I do," Oleg said. "I renounce Satan and all his angels and all his works and all his services and all his pride."

Marina was asked the same, and she responded in kind.

"Oleg Stefanovich, do you unite yourself to Christ?" the bishop asked.

Oleg took a deep breath. "I do," he said through gritted teeth. "I unite myself to Christ."

Marina answered in the same manner. Then came more prayers, more incense, readings from Scripture and from various Orthodox prayer books Oleg had never heard of. Eventually, after nearly an hour, though it seemed much longer, the bishop took their baby, held him over a large silver urn, and poured a silver pot of lukewarm water over his head. Vasily did not cry, but Oleg nearly did.

Oleg was surprised by how emotional he felt as a final prayer was said and Marina wrapped their son in a towel and held him to her breast. Marina was crying. So were Oleg's parents, even as they beamed with pride.

Oddly, Yulia Luganova neither cried nor smiled. Indeed, she showed little emotion at all. The president, however, seemed genuinely and deeply touched, especially when Marina turned and put her son in her father's arms. For only the second time Oleg could recall—the first being at their wedding—the hardness in his father-in-law's fierce and forbidding features visibly softened. His eyes were red and moist. He struck Oleg as uncharacteristically vulnerable, even a bit self-conscious in that vulnerability. In that moment he was not the sovereign ruler of a great people. He was a simple grandfather who now held the grandson he had so long desired.

Oleg stood in the great and shadowy cathedral, the flickering light of candles and the intoxicating aroma of incense enveloping him, and pondered a thought that he had never dared consider before. Was there now, perhaps, a pathway to the kind of relationship with his father-in-law Oleg had always longed for? Were the cold steel barriers between him and this man he both feared and admired finally coming down?

Nine days later, Russian forces invaded the Republic of Georgia.

Oleg never saw it coming. He was not even in Moscow at the time. Rather, he had been sent to Beijing as part of the official Russian delegation to observe the opening ceremonies of the summer Olympic Games. He learned the news the same way every other world leader at the games did, first from the BBC and then via every other news service on the planet. Three hundred fifty Russian tanks, hundreds of armored personnel carriers, and more than nine thousand ground forces—including elite Spetsnaz units—were blasting their way into South Ossetia. Under cover from Russian fighter bombers and heavy artillery fire, they were taking the main roads in South Ossetia and pushing toward Georgia proper. Another thirty thousand Russian troops were massing in Abkhazia, the Russian territory directly adjoining the Georgian Republic, and a sizable Russian armada was steaming across the Black Sea, headed for Georgia's western coast.

Oleg was not simply stunned. He felt betrayed. While he had participated in meetings where snap military exercises in Abkhazia had been discussed at length, he hadn't been in a single meeting or on a single call or seen a single document or email or cable in which an invasion had even been hinted at or alluded to, much less stated outright. Aside from the feeling of utter embarrassment at being so far from home and having to represent and defend his nation and his president among dozens upon dozens of world leaders who were condemning the invasion in no uncertain terms, a flood of painful questions rushed through Oleg's thoughts.

Why *had* the president invaded Georgia? Why would he invade *any* former Soviet republic? Was he really intent on capturing and occupying the entire nation, even Tbilisi, the capital? What in the world for? What was the upside? Wouldn't this seriously damage Russia's reputation, not to mention harm her economy in volatile and uncertain times?

And why hadn't the president trusted Oleg enough to let him in on the secret?

27

KUBINKA AIR BASE, MOSCOW—15 MARCH 2009

President Luganov's motorcade roared up the tarmac at precisely 9 a.m.

Stepping out of his armor-plated limousine, the Russian leader walked briskly past the honor guard standing at attention on both sides of the red carpet, with Special Agent Pavel Kovalev, chief of the president's security detail, close behind him. There was no crowd to cheer, no members of the press or any cameras to smile for. This trip was not on his official schedule. Indeed, only a handful of people on the planet knew it was going to happen. Luganov bounded up the metal stairs and entered the presidential aircraft—a wide-body, specially outfitted, four-engine Ilyushin Il-96 jet—and took his seat in the back.

Defense Minister Mikhail Petrovsky followed the president onto the plane, as did Dmitri Nimkov, the head of the FSB, and Boris Zakharov, the president's chief of staff, along with a phalanx of bodyguards and several military aides. Last, and for the first time since joining the presidential staff, Oleg Kraskin boarded the plane. He worked hard to maintain a professional demeanor, but the truth was Oleg was terribly excited to have been asked to join the delegation, though not nearly as excited as Marina was for her husband to be taking another step deeper into her father's confidence.

Since Luganov's decision to invade Georgia and occupy no less than 20 percent of that former Soviet republic—and since Oleg's decision not to simply defend but to fully and even aggressively support the president in each and every tense conversation with leaders in Beijing—Oleg's relationship with his father-in-law had deepened considerably. Word of his fierce and vocal loyalty had gotten back to Luganov and had been both noted and appreciated.

Though Luganov never said a word to him, Oleg could see that his duties and responsibilities were steadily expanding, and he was certain it could all be traced back to the summer of 2008. Increasingly, he was being asked not merely to take notes of the most confidential of meetings the president had in the Kremlin and elsewhere in Moscow. He was also given recordings of all the president's phone calls with members of the Duma and various world leaders and instructed to produce official transcriptions. In fact, in recent months, the chief of staff had invited him to actually be on most of these calls live, taking notes in real time. He was included in all senior staff meetings. He was given various follow-up assignments of increasing complexity and sensitivity, and he had even begun traveling with the president on most trips within the Russian provinces.

But until now Oleg had never been included on any official state trips. Instead, two colonels from the Defense Ministry typically rotated in the role of private secretary when Luganov traveled abroad or to meet with foreign heads of state. Oleg certainly had been given a tremendous window into the thinking and the actions of Luganov and those in his inner circle, and for this he was grateful. But he secretly yearned for more. While he often reminded himself that 142 million other Russians would give their right arm to have his job, the truth was he wanted to travel abroad with the president. He wanted to counsel and advise him, to be a participant in history, not simply the recorder of it. He privately resented being treated somewhat like a child, being "seen but not heard." Back at his law firm, he had been a partner— the youngest in the firm's history. He'd been an active member of the team, looked to for his opinions and insights in addition to his loyalty and hard work. This had not been the case since coming to work at the Kremlin. But now, without explanation, the president had personally asked Oleg to accompany him on a mysterious trip to meet with an as-yet-unidentified world leader, and neither of the colonels were anywhere in sight.

Oleg marveled at the luxurious interior of the presidential aircraft code-named "Command Point" as he took his assigned seat just behind the president, buckled up, and prepared for takeoff. The dozen oversize seats located in the center of the plane were all upholstered in white leather with the seal of the Russian president embossed in gold on each headrest. There was also a white leather couch that seated four. In the rear of the plane were a conference room and the galley, from which stewards prepared everything from snacks to hors d'oeuvres to gourmet meals and served vodka and wine as well as soft drinks, coffee, and chai. Toward the front of the cabin, adjacent to the cockpit, was a bedroom for the president, a medical bay, and a communications center providing secure voice and data links to anywhere in the world.

Ten minutes later, the Ilyushin was airborne. The moment they reached a cruising altitude of thirty-six thousand feet, the seat belt light went off, and Luganov asked Petrovsky, Nimkov, and Zakharov to join him in the conference room. Oleg, still not briefed on exactly where they were going, gazed out the window at the clouds and the sunshine, just glad to be on board at all.

"Come, Oleg Stefanovich. What are you waiting for? Bring your notebook."

Oleg looked up at his father-in-law and then at the other aides, who appeared nearly as surprised as he was. Oleg was being summoned into the inner sanctum, and he was as thrilled as he was stunned.

Once the door was shut behind them, Luganov took his seat at the head of the conference table, impassive and inscrutable. Oleg went to sit at the far end, but the president told him to sit next to Zakharov instead. Oleg complied. As he opened a fresh notebook and took a pen from his breast pocket, he noticed that Luganov was dressed in a dark-blue business suit, a crisp white shirt, and a navy-blue silk tie with small white polka dots. It was a small detail, but he remembered that this was precisely what his father-in-law had been wearing the day they had first met, the day Oleg had asked for his daughter's hand in marriage.

It quickly became apparent where they were heading—Vladivostok, site of Russia's largest naval base, located on the Sea of Japan at the extreme southeastern corner of the Russian Empire. Defense Minister Petrovsky explained that he had ordered his staff to arrange the trip on the premise that he would be conducting a surprise inspection of the submarine fleet that constituted the bulk of Russia's ability to project power into the Pacific. Petrovsky would, in fact, do just that, accompanied by Zakharov. But the real purpose of the trip was something entirely different. Once in Vladivostok, the president, FSB Chief Nimkov, and Oleg would be driven to a secret military facility where they would have dinner with the reclusive leader of North Korea, who would be arriving by train.

"Why by train?" Luganov asked.

"He is petrified of flying, Your Excellency."

"How far is that journey?"

"Almost five hundred miles."

Oleg stopped writing for a moment and looked at Petrovsky. *Five hundred miles by train?* he wondered, though he said nothing. *This North Korean really is insane.*

That turned out to be an understatement. Nimkov reminded Luganov that the man had several titles he would appreciate being used when they met. He wanted to be referred to as the "Ever-Victorious, Iron-Willed Commander." He also wanted a reference made to the "Glorious General Who Descended from Heaven." While he was partial to "Highest Incarnation of the Revolutionary Comradely Love," he would not be offended if Luganov preferred to simply call him the "Guiding Star of the Twenty-First Century."

Oleg could have written a book about the absolutely bizarre eccentricities of the North Korean dictator he observed during the two-hour meeting between the two leaders, from what he wore to what he ate to how he expressed himself. But what truly disturbed Oleg was how close Luganov seemed to be to this madman. Oleg had never participated in—much less created a transcript of—a single call between the two leaders. Yet the evidence suggested the two men had spoken dozens of times over the past few years. They clearly had a history together, and they were using a personal shorthand to build their framework for an entirely new bilateral relationship.

At first, none of it computed. On the plane, Petrovsky had advised Luganov on ways to persuade the North Koreans to end their nuclear weapons program and enter into a new round of six-party peace talks with South Korea, China, Japan, Russia, and the United States. Luganov had acted as if he fully agreed with his defense minister. But once Petrovsky left the room, it became obvious that defusing the North Korean threat was not Luganov's objective at all.

As Oleg took notes during the meeting between the two heads of state, it was clear that Luganov was trying to clandestinely flip Pyongyang's allegiance from Beijing to Moscow. In so doing, he seemed willing to help Pyongyang become a regional powerhouse ready and able to intimidate and even dominate Seoul, Tokyo, Taipei, and everyone else in the Pacific Rim. To accomplish this, Luganov offered to cancel North Korea's $11 billion debt to Russia and provide some $2 billion in new Russian grain shipments. That's why, Luganov said, he'd persuaded five oligarchs to be prepared to invest upward of $25 billion in developing North Korean natural resources like coal and iron ore over the next decade. That was also why Luganov was offering Moscow's technical assistance with helping Pyongyang build ballistic missiles capable not only of carrying nuclear warheads but of reaching the continental United States.

Luganov's chilling offers were immediately accepted, but there was more to the conspiracy the two leaders were concocting. They agreed that to throw the West—as well as Beijing—off the scent, Russia would publicly and forcefully condemn Pyongyang's ongoing nuclear weapons tests. They even wrote the press release together. What's more, they agreed that Russia's Foreign Ministry would actively support *additional* economic sanctions against North Korea at the U.N. Security Council meeting later that month.

It would all be a show. The "Guiding Star" couldn't have made himself more clear that he eagerly sought to be the Pacific arm of a "rising new Russian Empire." He agreed to fully share the results of North Korea's ICBM testing with scientists from Tehran in order to help the Islamic Republic of Iran become the Middle Eastern arm of the new Russian Empire. Then, in the final minutes of their time together, the two men lowered their voices and somewhat cryptically agreed to be helpful to each other on "additional projects of mutual concern." Oleg wasn't sure what they meant. Nor was he certain he wanted to know. But he dutifully wrote down every word he heard through the official translator and kept his mouth shut.

The flight back to Moscow was surreal.

Luganov lied to the defense minister's face. He spoke of the "sober but successful" talks he'd had with the "Guiding Star." He said he believed new Russian financial assistance to Pyongyang was going to help curb the "lunatic's nuclear ambitions" and bring North Korea back to the six-party peace talks. He insisted Russia should pursue a policy of both carrots and sticks. They would surprise the world by supporting the French draft of the U.N. Security Council resolution condemning Pyongyang's latest nuclear tests, and actively work to ratchet up international pressure on the "rogue regime."

Yet when Petrovsky stepped out of the conference room to take a call from his deputy in Moscow, Luganov sketched out an entirely different strategy with the FSB chief. Then, as if suddenly remembering that Oleg was sitting there, he turned to his son-in-law and ordered him not to transcribe anything he was about to say next. Clearly the president wanted no record of his daring gambit to flip Pyongyang from Beijing's sphere of influence to his own. Oleg obediently put down his pen. He fully expected to be asked to step out of the room. But that order never came. The two men spoke in hushed voices for several minutes. Then Luganov instructed Nimkov to step out of the room and ask for fresh chai and some snacks to be brought in.

After a steward delivered the order, he bowed slightly to the president and backed out of the conference room, shutting the door and leaving Luganov and Oleg sitting alone together. Not even Agent Kovalev was with them.

Oleg had a thousand questions, none of which seemed prudent to ask. The truth was he felt deeply conflicted. He abhorred what the North Koreans were doing and saw them as a grave threat not only to the whole of the Pacific Rim but also to Russia herself. Their megalomaniacal leader would soon be armed with fully operational nuclear warheads and intercontinental ballistic missiles. Wouldn't he be difficult, if not impossible, to manage? How did the president not see he was creating a monster?

At the same time, these were strategic matters far above his pay grade. He had tremendous respect for his father-in-law's ability to defend Mother Russia from all threats, at home and abroad. He'd seen the strong hand Luganov had used in Chechnya, to great effect. The terrorist threat to the Russian people had largely disappeared. He had seen President Luganov show admirable strength and unexpected resolve in invading eastern Georgia, and while Oleg regretted the loss of Georgian lives that had resulted, there was no question that his father-in-law's standing on the world stage had significantly—and counterintuitively—improved. Global leaders, and especially the Americans, now respected and even feared Luganov in a way they hadn't before the invasion. Oleg could see the way the current American president, a weak and pitiful creature, was showing great deference to his father-in-law and granting him surprising concessions in various trade and arms-control negotiations and a host of other matters.

If that weren't enough, Luganov's approval rating among the Russian people had soared following the invasion of Georgia. Before, it had hovered in the low to midsixties. Afterward it shot up to the mideighties. Rather than be frightened or bothered by the move, the people had loved Luganov's show of raw Russian strength. They had loved his utter defiance of the global order and especially his flouting of NATO and the Americans. They had certainly had their attention diverted from systemic economic troubles throughout the motherland and the rampant corruption inside Moscow, and they seemed happy to be so diverted. Their leader looked tough and decisive, especially while the weaklings in the West issued meaningless press releases and wrung their hands and whined about the need for "order and stability" and "respect for international law." Contrary to Oleg's concerns, there had been no negative consequences for Russia at all.

This, in turn, had given the president a robust hand to demand the Duma provide hundreds of billions of additional rubles to rebuild Russia's military might and even modernize Russia's aging strategic nuclear forces. What's more, it gave Luganov tremendous leverage to exploit emerging vacuums in Central Asia, the Middle East, and Eastern and Central Europe.

While he would never dare to say as much, Oleg often sharply disagreed with his father-in-law's specific decisions. Still, he could not deny the man's take-no-prisoners brand of national leadership and global brinkmanship stirred something deep in the Russian soul, even his own. Selfishly, Oleg hungered to be useful and successful and thus respected by this man who dominated the stage. Now, after so many years, he was finally being entrusted with state secrets—indeed, with secrets apparently too sensitive for even the defense minister himself.

Luganov lit a cigar and leaned back in his white leather executive chair.

"Oleg Stefanovich, what would you say was the worst disaster of the twentieth century?" the president asked out of thin air.

"I don't know," Oleg mumbled, caught off guard by the randomness of the question. "World War II? Hitler's betrayal of Stalin? The siege of Leningrad?"

"Ah, my son, you still have so much to learn," Luganov replied, puffing on the aromatic cigar. "These developments hardly compare to the greatest catastrophe."

Oleg's mind raced through the pages of modern Russian history. "The Bolshevik Revolution and the end of the czars?" he offered.

"Tragic, but not the answer I am looking for," said Luganov. "Think, Oleg Stefanovich. Think harder."

Oleg tried. But to his shame, he drew a blank.

"The collapse of the Soviet Union," Luganov said at last. "I am not now, nor was I ever, a true Communist. I cannot say I truly approved of the rise of the Soviet system, its leaders, or its ways. But its utter collapse was without question *the* major geopolitical catastrophe of the century."

Oleg said nothing.

"In that moment, the greatness of the Russian mind, the beauty of the Russian language, the dominance of Russia's military, and the glory of Moscow itself were called into question around the globe," Luganov expounded, smoke curling around his head like a halo. "Tens of millions of our citizens found themselves outside Russian territory. And of course the epidemic of disintegration infected Russia itself."

Oleg wasn't sure whether he should be taking notes. He would have preferred to. It would have given his hands something to do and a place for his eyes to focus. But in the end, he chose not to write, just to listen. He stared for a while at the conference table, then mustered up the courage to look at his father-in-law.

"Every man has a destiny, Oleg Stefanovich," Luganov said. "Yours was to fall in love with my Marina and give me a grandson—a godson— a heritage, a legacy. This is good. It may be small, but it is noble. You are a family man, and you must always cherish and protect your family. You must always be loyal and true to your family."

He puffed away on the cigar.

"My destiny is on a much grander scale," Luganov continued. "The Russian people are my family. They are my children. I am their father, and my loyalties must be to them. They have suffered a cruel and humiliating blow—from the barbarians in Washington, from the Zionists, from the bloodsucking bankers and the corrupt corporate chieftains and sleazy swindlers and the cruel conspirators of the NATO alliance and the eunuchs of the West. My children have had the bread ripped out of their hands, stolen right out of their mouths. Their jobs. Their dignity. Their glorious heritage as Russians."

Oleg had never heard the man speak this way. Not in private. Certainly not in public. And he was not finished.

"What did Dostoyevsky say? 'Pain and suffering are always inevitable for a large intelligence and a deep heart. The really great men must, I think, have great sadness on earth.'" The president stared out the window, and Oleg followed his gaze. The night was dark. The moon was full, but it was on the other side of the plane. The only lights visible were those at the end of the wing, blinking red in the coal-black sky. Luganov set his cigar down and seemed to ponder the words.

"'The really great men must, I think, have great sadness on earth,'" he said again, no longer to Oleg but to himself. "It falls to me to make things right, to cure the sadness of my people. My destiny is to restore the glory of Mother Russia. She must not only *be* great again, she must be *seen* as great—strong, proud, indomitable, invincible. This will take great courage. This will take great cunning. Not every step will make sense to the masses or even to some of my cabinet. I will have to take risks that would cause lesser men to stumble, even if this brings us to war."

It was quiet for several moments. Oleg briefly wondered if the man was expecting a response, though he had nothing to say.

Then Luganov turned to him. "I have a mission, a destiny, Oleg Stefanovich, and in this task I dare not fail. The gods have determined that I am to save this great people from deprivation and deepest shame. For this—and for this alone—my name, and that of my family, shall be recorded in the annals of Russian history, like the great princes of our past."

Luganov abruptly leaned forward in his chair and motioned for

Oleg to come sit beside him. Oleg complied. The scent of the cigar smoke was thick, but Oleg did not mind it. His grandfather had loved cigars, Cubans when he could get them, and the aroma brought back fond memories of sitting in his lap as a child, at his dacha on the Black Sea, listening to him tell stories of the czars and their exploits.

"The people say I am brutal," Luganov said in a voice barely above a whisper. "I know it. I hear the talk. And it is true. I won't deny it. In defense of my nation's honor, I am more than willing to be brutal—vicious, even—but this is no vice."

Once again, Oleg felt deeply conflicted. He had longed to be close to this man, a true associate, an intimate, needed and respected. Yet just at the moment his father-in-law was really drawing him into his confidence, Oleg felt unnerved by the man. He was not a normal leader, and Oleg was uneasy when he considered the amount of power Luganov possessed and his lack of accountability. To whom did he answer? Did he have any constraints at all? This was not what Oleg had anticipated when he'd accepted a position in the government. Yet he understood the price of crossing this man. So Oleg was becoming a master of personal discipline. He could not show the slightest flicker of fear, much less moral disapproval, not unless he first made a careful exit strategy.

Just then Luganov looked in Oleg's eyes and said something that nearly made him shudder, as if the man could read his most personal thoughts.

"A dog can smell fear, Oleg Stefanovich. When someone is afraid, a dog knows it, and he attacks. The same is true with an enemy. If you show the slightest hesitation—fear, doubt, lack of surety—your enemy will think he is stronger, that he has the upper hand. So you have only one option—when the moment is right, you must strike. You must go on the offensive. Hit first, and hit so hard that your enemy will not—cannot—rise to his feet. You must hit him with a crushing blow. And when you take him down, everyone else will be watching. Then they will fear you. Then they will respect you. That's when you have them. That's when you know you are the master, and they are the slaves."

29

JAMES J. ROWLEY TRAINING CENTER,
BELTSVILLE, MARYLAND—3 DECEMBER 2010

Looking back, Elena Ryker wished she had just flat out said yes.

After Marcus left the Marines with numerous medals and commendations—including the Navy Cross to go along with his Purple Heart—and worked in local law enforcement in Colorado Springs for several years, Marcus had asked his wife on numerous occasions if she had any problems with his desire to join the United States Secret Service and eventually protect the president of the United States. There simply weren't enough high-stakes responsibilities to keep Marcus satisfied in the Springs. Climbing fourteeners, cliff diving, rock climbing, and skydiving didn't satiate his need for something bigger and more important. And while Elena had never actually said no to the question—as in, "No, I don't have any problems with you joining the Secret Service"—she could hardly blame Marcus if he thought she had.

The first time he'd asked, Elena had replied that she wasn't a big fan of moving to Washington, D.C. Still, she'd quickly added that she loved him and would support him wherever he wanted to go. The next time he'd asked was during the application and interview process. At that point, she'd said she loved the Front Range and the Rockies and wished they could live in the West for the rest of their lives.

The last time he'd asked her was the day he'd received his acceptance letter in the mail and his start date for training. He'd apparently detected a look of concern in her eyes, which had likely prompted the question. By then, however, Elena concluded it was too late. No, she didn't like the idea one bit. But she really did love him. She knew better than anyone his thirst for adventure and his love of country. She felt selfish for wanting him to take a less dangerous road just to please her and their young son. And how could she say what she really felt now that he actually had the job?

If she could only dial back the hands of time.

Elena slipped her driver's license under the bulletproof glass and waited. She looked down at Lars. Having celebrated his fourth birthday in June, he looked adorable in his new suit, white dress shirt, and clip-on tie, all fresh off the rack from Sears. That morning at the hotel, she'd made him take a bath, trimmed his jet-black hair, and slicked it back with a bit of the gel Marcus used. She'd even bought him a cheap pair of sunglasses from Walgreens so he could look "just like Daddy."

Now their son was beaming, full of anticipation, as he held Elena's hand and kept asking when they could go into the auditorium. A moment later, Elena was handed back her ID and given two visitor passes. She put one lanyard around her neck and the other around Lars's. Then they got in line, put their belongings through the X-ray machine, passed through the magnetometers, and entered with the other nicely dressed and freshly scrubbed families.

Lars picked the seats, in the middle and close to the front, as usual. He was off-the-charts excited about this day, one he'd been anticipating since Marcus had started his training. And Elena remained on her best behavior, keeping her many and growing reservations to herself. Her husband had been selected out of thousands of applicants. He had passed his training with the highest marks. Maybe this really was God's perfect plan for his life, for all their lives. Who was she to say otherwise?

The ceremony began precisely at ten that brisk December morning. A senior agent who looked to be in his midforties walked onstage and stepped up to the microphone. He gave some introductory remarks and then introduced the director of the United States Secret Service.

"Good morning. It is my great honor to welcome all of the spouses and children and families and friends who have traveled, some a great distance, to be with us today," the director, a silver-haired gentleman in his sixties, began. "I remember this day well, both as the son of a special agent, watching my father take the oath of office in 1967, and years later as a graduate myself, taking the oath to join this elite cadre of America's brightest and most brave. I remember the pride I felt becoming part of a team dedicated to defending our most sacred national institutions— our leaders and our currency and financial systems. I remember how difficult it was to explain to family and friends why I would be willing to train so hard and work such long hours and be away from home so often and even lay down my life, if necessary, to safeguard our values and our democratic system of government. But I also remember the pride and sense of accomplishment I felt that day, and every day since, and I see that same sense of pride and devotion in each of your eyes."

The director commended the graduates for passing the exhaustive background checks and rigorous testing and demanding physical preparation required to join the thirty-two hundred special agents and thirteen hundred uniformed officers of the Secret Service. He spoke of the history of the organization: its founding in 1865 and its evolving roles and responsibilities over the years. Elena knew Lars would remember none of the words. She likely wouldn't either. She doubted that even Marcus would. But none of them would ever forget the feeling of being inducted into something special, something honorable and good.

Then came the big moment. The director asked the trainees to stand, raise their right hands, and repeat after him. Elena lifted Lars up so he could see his father. They were just a few rows behind him, so they had a great view. Lars had chosen well.

"I, Marcus Johannes Ryker . . ."

"*I, Marcus Johannes Ryker . . .*" his wife and son repeated to each other in a whisper.

". . . do solemnly swear . . "

"*. . . do solemnly swear . . .*"

". . . that I will support and defend the Constitution of the United States . . ."

"*. . . that I will support and defend the Constitution of the United States . . .*"

". . . against all enemies, foreign and domestic . . ."

"*. . . against all enemies, foreign and domestic . . .*"

". . . that I will bear true faith and allegiance to the same . . ."

"*. . . that I will bear true faith and allegiance to the same . . .*"

". . . that I take this obligation freely, without any mental reservation or purpose of evasion . . ."

"*. . . that I take this obligation freely, without any mental reservation or purpose of evasion . . .*"

". . . and that I will well and faithfully discharge the duties of the office on which I am about to enter."

"*. . . and that I will well and faithfully discharge the duties of the office on which I am about to enter.*"

"So help me God."

"*So help me God.*"

So that was that, Elena thought as the room erupted in applause. She was now the wife of a special agent of the United States Secret Service. She had known since the sixth grade that she'd fallen in love with a boy who loved big risks and great adventure. She could hardly hold it against him now.

Yet truth be told, she did.

30

"I say let the world go to hell, but I should always have my tea."

Dostoyevsky's line in *Notes from the Underground*, his 1864 novella, echoed in Oleg's thoughts as he brewed a pot of chai. Was he becoming the misanthropic civil servant whose notes formed the story? Was he the "sick man, the spiteful man, the unattractive man" of whom the great bard of Russian literature crafted his tale? No, Oleg thought. It was worse. He wasn't merely a despondent man who felt trapped. He was Ivan Denisovich, sentenced to hard labor and unable to escape.

When the president asked Oleg to come with him to a G20 summit, Oleg had, of course, said yes. What else was he to do? Marina was angry with him, though, complaining bitterly that he was never home anymore, that he was neglecting his family, that he was neglecting her. In a rare flash of rage, he slapped her across the face, driving her to the floor. "Why don't you go shopping," he fumed.

This was not like him. But rather than apologize, he packed his suitcase and headed outside to the car waiting to take him to the airport. Despite smoking half a pack on the way, he was still shaken by the fight with his wife as he boarded the plane. He was shaken further when Luganov told him to write him a speech that would dazzle the leaders of the Western powers. The president wanted to make a forceful denunciation of all nuclear and ballistic missile programs of the regime in Pyongyang, including a powerful argument for the denuclearization of the Korean Peninsula. Oleg had never written a speech before. He wasn't sure he could now. He agreed reluctantly. The position Luganov had outlined was one Oleg privately but heartily held, so it would not be difficult for him to make that case. What gnawed at him was the knowledge that he had just been commissioned to draft a speech explicitly designed to camouflage the president's true position. The man was, after all, actively if clandestinely aiding Pyongyang's nuclear and ballistic missile programs, not seeking to bring them to a halt.

Two months later, Luganov asked Oleg to travel with him to Riyadh, Cairo, Amman, Jerusalem, and Ramallah. The president's trust in him was growing. But so were the tensions between Oleg and Marina. They did their best not to fight in front of Vasily, but the bitter realities of life in this pressure cooker were having a demonstrative and corrosive effect on their marriage. Oleg wondered if the only way to rekindle their love would be for him to stop working for the president and go back to life as a private-sector lawyer, far from the daily pressures inside the Kremlin. But he couldn't see a way out. To be sure, his moral revulsion was growing, slowly but steadily. Yet there was also something intoxicating about being so close to the vortex of power.

There were days Oleg resolved to resign and take Marina and Vasily to another city or country to start afresh. Yet he never acted upon such instincts, and then he hated himself for his lack of courage. It was a vicious cycle of revulsion and regret mixed with approbation and advancement, and it was all wreaking havoc on his digestive system. He was having trouble eating certain foods. He was having trouble getting enough rest at night. In time he began battling heartburn and then colitis. Yet it was easier to change his diet and take a growing handful of pharmaceuticals than to confront his wife, much less her father, and take an exit ramp off this road.

Soon Oleg Kraskin was not simply taking notes but drafting Luganov's speeches, statements, and various other official communiqués. He was also getting an inside look at how the Russian leader wielded power. With the Arab leaders, Luganov offered state-of-the-art weaponry, financing to build nuclear power plants, and muscular political support for their pet issues at the United Nations. Without being so explicit, he was wooing the Arabs away from Washington and back into Moscow's camp, where they'd been during the Cold War. Oleg had to admit, if only to himself, it was a supremely seductive performance.

To the Jews in Israel, Luganov portrayed himself as a man of peace, a fair and balanced interlocutor capable of bringing the Arabs to the table to make a sweeping and comprehensive peace treaty. But all this was a smoke screen, Oleg knew. Luganov's actual objectives were twofold. The first was to lull the Zionists into a false sense of security while the president earned billions in payoffs from Russian oligarchs arming Israel's enemies. The second was to entice them to let Russian companies invest in the massive fields of natural gas recently discovered off the Israeli coast, even as he secretly plotted to disrupt or even destroy those projects. The whole performance was both distressing and breathtaking to behold. Oleg was constantly amazed that such rank dissembling could prove so utterly effective.

Six weeks after the Middle East trip, the two men were jetting off to Berlin, Paris, and Rome. Oleg sat spellbound watching the president wine and dine the highest-ranking European political and business leaders, concluding one lucrative joint venture after another, each crafted in such a way that personally—if always covertly—enriched Luganov. As always, Oleg was in charge of drafting letters and memos on behalf of the president to world leaders and to key figures throughout Russia.

By the end of 2012, Oleg was unexpectedly awarded a promotion and a new title: counselor to the president. With it, he received a sizable bonus and a hefty pay raise—far too hefty for Oleg, as it happened. He was convinced it was dirty money. But he asked no questions, and Marina was thrilled because her father insisted the couple take a few weeks of well-deserved vacation. Frankly, Oleg hadn't seen his wife this happy—or happy at all—in quite some time. She asked if they could go to Monte Carlo for old times' sake, just the two of them. Oleg was touched by the request and quickly made the arrangements. His parents agreed to watch Vasily. Marina and Oleg flew first class. They ate at fancy restaurants. They danced in nightclubs. Marina spent far too much money shopping. Oleg lost far too much money at the blackjack tables and roulette wheels. It wasn't quite the same as their honeymoon in Macau, but it was almost as good, and when they got home, they discovered Marina was pregnant again. Oleg hoped this could be the start of a new chapter in both of their lives.

Sadly, however, Marina lost the baby four months later and developed an infection that nearly took her life. Oleg was away on another foreign trip when she was rushed to the hospital. It was all over by the time he returned to Moscow. Though she never said as much, Oleg was convinced she blamed him somehow. Though he never said as much, he blamed her father, for now the president rarely moved without Oleg at his side.

Aside from putting a further strain on an already-troubled marriage, Oleg's rising prominence in the president's inner circle began drawing the growing attention of the Russian media. Oleg discouraged all of it. He never returned reporters' calls. He never issued public statements or responded to requests for interviews or profiles. Yet this hardly dissuaded the press from writing about him. To the contrary, Oleg's caginess only created more mystery around him and his rising influence in his father-in-law's administration, which led, in turn, to more column inches.

At one point, a front-page profile in one of Moscow's most-read daily papers described Oleg as Luganov's *nadezhnyy sovetnik*, or "trusted advisor." Oleg went pale when he first read the story, certain it would infuriate the very man whose trust he most needed and valued. But Luganov loved the story, even with all its factual inaccuracies, and began describing his son-in-law as his *nadezhnyy sovetnik* to everyone he met.

Yet even as Oleg's stature inside the Kremlin was growing, so was his disquietude. While Marina embraced the astonishing wealth her father was amassing, Oleg knew the president's official annual salary was only $137,000. To shepherd a nation was one thing. To fleece the flock was quite another. And Oleg continued to see a steady stream of Luganov's political rivals and potential rivals heading for prison or at least under indictment on charges that seemed unsupported by evidence.

Growing tensions between the first couple bothered Oleg deeply. He and Marina were invited to the official residence less and less often. His mother-in-law, Yulia, rarely traveled with her husband anymore. Indeed, Oleg couldn't help but feel guilty that the surge in his own travels with the president was somehow responsible for the dramatic decline in the first lady's. When Yulia came to visit her grandson, she was more often than not alone with her security detail. She didn't say anything about her marital troubles, of course. Certainly not to Oleg. Perhaps she confided in Marina. But Oleg felt it too sensitive a topic to ask Marina about. So he said nothing, but he was not blind. He could see that the family strains were growing deeper. Remembering Yulia's sourness at Vasily's baptism, he suspected things had been going south for some time.

What unsettled Oleg most of all, however, were the lies he saw the president communicate to his most senior advisors. The man was playing a dangerous double game with most of his cabinet, ordering them to pursue various foreign policies in various regions of the world while he was independently pursuing policies that were in direct contradiction. Wouldn't all this catch up to him one day?

31

MOSCOW—AUGUST 2013

Oleg was already fearful about the president's plans.

But a late-afternoon meeting in the Kremlin when Iran's new president arrived for a state visit turned out to be downright terrifying.

"Welcome, my friend; you have journeyed a long distance," Luganov said upon receiving the Persian leader in his flowing robes and Islamic headdress. "How can I be of service to the people of Iran?"

"Your Excellency, you are too kind," came the reply, "especially to receive me on such short notice."

Luganov nodded.

"The supreme leader has asked me to express that he is most grateful for your growing and deepening alliance with the Islamic Republic of Iran," the Iranian president explained. "You have already done, and continue to do, so much for us—building the reactor in Bushehr, sending us technicians to get the reactor up and running, selling us the newest and most advanced weapons systems, providing political cover for us at the U.N., thwarting all the sinister tricks the Americans and the Zionists are trying to play."

Luganov nodded again but said nothing.

"These are such beneficent and generous gifts," the Iranian leader continued. "They are acts of kindness deeply appreciated at every level of our society and government."

Luganov's icy-blue eyes bored into the bearded Iranian leader, but he did not shift in his seat. He did not stir. He remained impassive, sitting at an angle, leaning back slightly to the right, his legs spread, yet every muscle tensed, like a mountain lion feigning rest but ready to pounce when his prey least expected it.

Oleg had seen this posture in countless meetings over the years. At first it had not bothered him. In the beginning of his service at the Kremlin, Oleg had thought Luganov was simply disinterested with the petty, pathetic problems of the guests who streamed through this ornate office. But in time Oleg realized this was not disinterest. In truth, Luganov was intensely interested in every thought and every comment of every mayor and president and prime minister and king who walked into his domain. He was an expert at lulling friend and foe alike into a false sense of ease, but in so doing he was watching for signs of weakness, probing for insecurities and areas of vulnerability.

As for Oleg himself, his eyes no longer darted around the room as they did the first time he'd entered Luganov's lair. He no longer studied the arched ceiling and crystal chandelier and the glass-enclosed bookshelves and the flags. He knew this room. He knew this man. That's why he could not risk losing his focus. Despite the fact that it was the middle of a warm afternoon in August, despite the fact that the man from Tehran was droning endlessly on, despite the fact that the cup of tea on the end table beside Oleg was empty and that he was beginning to feel drowsy, he reminded himself that he needed to maintain optimum discipline.

The Iranian leader shifted uncomfortably in his chair. "In light of all these acts of brotherhood and unity, the supreme leader has asked me to visit you and express a sense of urgency about two requests we are hesitant to put forward but about which we believe we have no other choice."

"Please, go on," Luganov said, evincing no fatigue whatsoever.

The Persian cleared his throat. "The first matter is the supreme leader's outstanding invitation for you to come to Tehran for a state visit. I want to assure you, Mr. President, this visit would greatly honor our people and send a powerful message to our enemies around the world that our alliance with Moscow is strong and enduring."

Luganov gave no reply.

"Yes, well, Your Excellency, I have . . . rather, I was hoping to discuss . . . well, another matter too."

Luganov waited.

"This concerns . . . well, the S-400."

At this, Oleg looked up from his notes. Even Luganov seemed to stiffen.

"The supreme leader understands, of course, that this is your most advanced surface-to-air missile system," the Iranian hastened to add, appearing almost embarrassed. "But I have come because the supreme leader believes we need it. And we need it quickly."

"Why quickly?" Luganov asked.

"I believe you know why, Your Excellency."

The tactic was a mistake, Oleg knew from experience. But he kept his head down and stayed focused on his shorthand, transcribing every word of the conversation.

"Enlighten me," Luganov said.

"The Zionists, sir," the Persian replied.

"What about them?"

"We believe the Israeli prime minister is actively considering an air strike."

"I was just with him," Luganov said. "You are mistaken."

"Perhaps, Your Excellency. But we have reason to believe the

Zionists are planning to attack the reactor at Bushehr—and ultimately all of our other nuclear research and development sites—before they become fully operational."

During his years of working for his father-in-law, Oleg had seen Luganov interact with dozens of world leaders, including Russia's most important client states. But he had never seen anyone pursue military hardware more brazenly than the Iranians. They were as shameless as they were relentless. Now they wanted to buy a billion-dollar missile system—arguably the most sophisticated system in Moscow's arsenal—with hard, cold cash, because they believed the Israelis were poised to attack their nuclear facilities before they could build the Bomb. They were asking even though they knew the Israeli government had promised Luganov they would not launch a preemptive strike in the next eighteen months unless Iran installed an air-defense system that would make a future air strike nearly impossible. Thus, by asking for the S-400 system, the Iranians were actually accelerating any timetable the Israelis might have for hitting Iran's nuclear facilities.

Oleg did his best not to laugh out loud as he waited for Luganov to dismiss such an audacious and impertinent request. Oleg had seen it happen before. Leaders would come to this office and overreach—sometimes by a little, often by a lot. Either way, Luganov would slap them down. The leaders would apologize profusely and change the subject, and all would be forgotten. Oleg fully expected it to happen again, but to his astonishment it did not. To the contrary, for the better part of the next ninety minutes, he watched as Luganov and the Iranian president negotiated a deal for Moscow to sell Tehran the S-400 system, a simultaneous deal for Iran to purchase North Korean nuclear testing data via Moscow, and a plan for Luganov to make his first state visit to Tehran. Oleg faithfully transcribed every facet of the negotiations, though with each passing minute, his horror grew. They were planning to set the Middle East on fire.

Perhaps the only thing more egregious than seeing the president of Russia agree to sell the S-400 missile system to Iran was seeing the contours of the deal splashed across the front page of one of Russia's most widely read newspapers the next morning.

The moment Oleg picked up the paper at his front door and read the story, a shudder rippled through his body. He had no idea who at the Kremlin had leaked the deal, but he was quite sure heads were going to roll. As he drove to the office, Oleg listened to wall-to-wall radio coverage of the bombshell exclusive that was the talk not only of all Moscow but every capital from Washington to Jerusalem to Beijing.

The article had been written by Galina Polonskaya, far and away the most respected journalist in the country. Now past fifty, the graying, bespectacled Polonskaya had long been one of the best-sourced political columnists in Moscow. Years before, she had been the first to report that Luganov was about to be plucked out of obscurity and appointed head of the FSB. Later, she broke the story that he was going to be named prime minister, and she was the first to profile his remarkable rise to power. She also broke the bribery scandal that felled Luganov's first finance minister, and she exposed the multiple marital affairs and illegal financial payoffs from foreign petroleum companies that brought down the head of Russia's biggest gas company, a scandal that allowed Luganov to install one of his closest friends—a man with no experience in the gas business—as the company's new CEO. For the last two decades, she had painstakingly planted, watered, weeded, and protected her sources. Now all the seeds she had planted seemed to be yielding a bumper crop.

Polonskaya struck Oleg as fiercely independent. She wasn't a wholly owned subsidiary of the Kremlin political machine. She was a courageous if lonely voice against all manner of corruption and shady political goings-on. Six months earlier, she'd written a column alleging that Luganov had amassed twenty palaces and villas, fifteen helicopters, a fifty-three-meter yacht, and nine luxury watches worth more than ten thousand dollars each since becoming president of the Russian Federation. Luganov's press secretary completely overreacted, blasting the story as "malicious lies from the pit of hell." Zakharov had publicly eviscerated Polonskaya as an "enemy of the truth and thus an enemy of the people" and had leaked a bogus story about how Polonskaya had been accused of plagiarizing her thesis while a doctoral candidate at Moscow State University.

The only inaccuracy Oleg could see in the column was that Luganov actually owned *eleven* such watches, not nine. His father-in-law spoke about money all the time. More than politics. More than hockey or hunting or the Olympic Games, all of which he loved. Luganov had not been raised with money. His parents had lived a very modest life. Yet now he seemed obsessed with amassing an unrivaled fortune. Nothing was enough for him. His appetites were insatiable. Initially, Yulia hadn't seemed to mind. At least she hadn't voiced any objections. Neither had Marina. They enjoyed the finer things in life. So, for that matter, did Oleg, though he found himself increasingly embarrassed by, and at times even ashamed of, his father-in-law's ostentatious displays of wealth, especially when most Russians were barely scraping by. It was bad for the image of the presidency. It was bad for Russia's image overall. Yet no one inside or outside the Kremlin had the courage to raise concerns with the president, Oleg among them.

Thirteen days after the article about Luganov's wealth was published, Polonskaya's husband, Mikhail—a renowned oncologist—had died in a private plane crash near the Black Sea. The entire episode was a mystery. The crash had occurred in the middle of the day, in beautiful weather, with an experienced pilot and copilot at the controls. Oleg was sickened when he heard the news, even more so when he saw the pleasure on the president's face after Zakharov mentioned the story during a senior staff meeting. If such a fate had befallen the woman's husband after she had exposed the Russian leader's exorbitant wealth, what fate would now befall her for exposing the arms deal with the tyrants in Tehran? And what would happen to whoever had leaked the story?

Oleg got into the office early. But no sooner had he made himself a cup of chai and begun returning emails than he was summoned to the office of the chief of staff. Zakharov's executive assistant looked pale when Oleg came in. She immediately hit a buzzer on her desk and nodded to a security agent standing in front of the door to the inner office. The agent stepped aside and opened the door. The assistant gestured to Oleg, and Oleg entered. As quickly as he did, the door shut behind him.

"*What do you have to say for yourself, Oleg Stefanovich?*" Zakharov bellowed.

Oleg stood there speechless. He'd known heads were going to roll, but he'd had no idea it would be *his* head on the chopping block.

"*How many people were in that meeting yesterday?*" the chief of staff demanded, shouting so loudly Oleg was sure he could be heard throughout the entire floor. He did not wait for an answer. "*Four. Just four people were in that room—the two presidents, the Iranian notetaker, and you. That's it. Yet this morning Galina Polonskaya is telling the world all about one of our most sensitive alliances and arms deals. How is that possible? We trusted you, Oleg Stefanovich. I trusted you. Now get out. Leave. Go home. Reconsider your life. Reconsider your loyalties. If you were not the president's son-in-law, you would already be in prison."*

Mortified, Oleg did not even return to his office to get his briefcase or his suit jacket. Instead, he immediately took an elevator down into the parking garage and began driving around the city. He did not head home. He did not call Marina. What exactly was he supposed to say?

Minutes ago he had been accused of breaking half a dozen laws, and those were just the ones the former lawyer could think of off the top of his head. He had been accused by the president's chief of staff of leaking highly classified national security secrets. Surely a fair investigation would prove his innocence. But would it be fair? Or was someone out to frame him? But why? What had he done wrong? Hadn't he been a loyal servant of the president?

Oleg chewed on such questions for the better part of an hour as he left Moscow and began heading north. Beads of perspiration broke out on his forehead. His hands felt cold and clammy. Whom could he trust right now? Certainly no one at the Kremlin. That much was clear. Certainly not his parents. They nearly worshiped the president. In their eyes, Luganov could do no wrong. He was the guardian—indeed, the savior—of Russia, especially since the apartment bombings and Luganov's brutal and unrelenting attacks on Chechnya.

What about Marina? If there was one person he wanted to spill everything to—all his fears, his doubts, his myriad and growing suspicions—it was the wife he adored. But how could he? The woman he most loved was the daughter of the man he most feared.

33

Galina Polonskaya stepped into the sunshine.

Throughout the morning and early afternoon, she'd had a string of television interviews via satellite uplinks with the BBC and CNN International and Sky News and even Israel's Channel 2. Having just finished a lengthy sit-down interview about the S-400 deal with the Moscow bureau of the *New York Times*, she now put on her sunglasses and strolled down a crowded boulevard, heading to the garage where she had parked her car.

When she reached the historic Hotel National, within sight of the Kremlin, she stopped for a moment and just stood there, staring at the building's facade. She remembered all too well the bitterly cold December day nearly a decade earlier when the hotel had been the target of a suicide bombing. Polonskaya had been browsing the stores nearby along with thousands of other Christmas shoppers and was one of the first on the scene. She remembered the heavy snow and whipping winds. Much more vividly, she remembered the smell of blood and burnt flesh and the sight of severed body parts. It was another bloody day in a city that had seen too many of them over the years she had been reporting.

Feeling spontaneous, she entered the lobby, looked around, found the café, and asked for a table near a window. She ordered a cup of chai and stared out at the traffic and the shoppers and didn't want to go home.

She couldn't exactly explain why. She wondered if she simply couldn't bear the thought of being alone in her big, drafty, empty house on the east side of the city, missing her husband and feeling sorry for herself. She preferred drinking in the hum and rhythm of this metropolis. She sat there for close to an hour, people-watching, returning a few emails, sipping tea, and avoiding the inevitable.

The gaping chasm in her soul was physically excruciating. She had met her husband at Moscow State. He was in medical school. She was studying political science and journalism. They had fallen madly in love and had remained so for almost thirty years. She couldn't remember a fight and barely a quarrel. Now he was gone. His family wouldn't talk to her. His parents had cut her off, accusing her of costing their only son his life because of what they called her "vain ambitions." That had wounded her the most, not because she felt the stab of injustice but because she feared they were right.

The only solace she seemed to find was not lying down and surrendering in the face of the czar rising in their midst. She had to keep digging, snooping, reporting, exposing. If she stopped now, she thought, her husband's death—his cold, calculated, premeditated, and utterly unnecessary murder—would have been in vain. She had no doubt the Kremlin had killed him. Very likely Luganov had ordered the hit himself. She couldn't say this, of course. She certainly couldn't write it. She had no proof. Not enough to publish. Not yet. So she had to find other ways to punish Luganov. The man was a monster. He had to be stopped.

Polonskaya finished her tea, paid her bill, gathered her handbag, and stepped outside. The sun was beginning to set. A full moon hung in the sky. The air was sweet and fresh with no humidity and a slight breeze from the west. She closed her eyes and drank in the moment. Then she walked two more blocks to the garage, fished her keys out of her bag, got in, and turned the ignition.

The explosion could be heard for miles. Every windshield in the garage was blown out, and more than forty cars were completely demolished. The force of the blast could be felt throughout the city. Many people thought it was an earthquake.

Oleg knew instantly it was not.

He still hadn't gone home after being kicked out of the Kremlin by Zakharov. He was just driving aimlessly. He wasn't listening to the news. Rather, he was trying to drown his sorrows with Tchaikovsky when the violin concerto was abruptly interrupted by an announcer with breaking news.

He couldn't pretend he was surprised. The pattern was becoming obvious, though no one spoke of it. To do so, he suspected, would be to pronounce one's own death sentence, and Oleg didn't want to die. Even so, the moment he heard that Galina Polonskaya had been murdered—blown up in her own car in the heart of Moscow, just blocks from the Kremlin—he pulled his car onto the shoulder, leaped out, and vomited repeatedly.

Traffic continued to rush by. No one stopped. No one seemed to notice or care. Not a fellow driver. Not a policeman. No one.

That's when he made the decision not to go home. It wasn't a terribly well-thought-through plan. He was going on instinct now, and his instincts told him to flee the city. But where?

He remembered that his parents were out of the country—in Hong Kong on business for the next week—so he drove out to their multimillion-dollar home in Rublyovka. It would be quiet there. He'd have time and space to think. To be sure, he'd need to call Marina, and soon. He didn't want her to be worried, alone with Vasily. But he couldn't bear to face them. Not yet. Not until he knew what he was going to say.

34

A patrol car was waiting at the entrance to his parents' gated community.

The first thought that crossed Oleg's mind was that he was about to be arrested. But the two uniformed officers merely asked for his ID, then ordered the gate to be opened and waved him through. When he reached his childhood home, there were several more squad cars parked out front, along with two black Mercedes limousines and four black SUVs. Oleg blanched. Marina was here. Was the president with her?

There was no way he could turn around and leave now. So Oleg found a place to park away from the motorcade, shut down the engine, took a deep breath, and walked up the front steps and into the house. He knew these agents, and they knew him. This was not Luganov's detail. It was the first lady's.

He crossed through the foyer and headed toward the rear of the house. When he got to the kitchen, he noticed agents on the back porch. Through various windows, he saw others patrolling the grounds. Then he entered the den and realized why. Marina and her mother were curled up on the couch in flannel pajamas, holding each other and sobbing.

"What is it?" Oleg asked immediately. "What happened?"

He assumed they had learned of the accusations against him. But then why were they crying? Why weren't they angry? And why were they here? How could they have possibly known he was coming when he himself didn't know until he started driving?

Upon hearing her husband's voice, Marina turned quickly, jumped up, and ran to him. With mascara streaked down her face, she threw her arms around him and sobbed all the more. Oleg held her and noticed the floor was littered with used tissues. A wastebasket near the couch where Yulia was curled up in a fetal position was overflowing. There was an empty bottle of red wine on the coffee table, another half-empty bottle, and two empty but lipstick-smeared goblets nearby. Clearly these two had been here for hours. But why?

For several minutes, neither woman could speak, so Oleg just held his wife and let her cry. Eventually Marina wiped her eyes and her nose and tried to compose herself. It was difficult, but she had something to say and was determined to say it.

"It's Father," she finally said.

"What about him?" Oleg said, bracing himself.

"He . . ." Again Marina became choked with emotion.

Rather than becoming flush with anger or fear or even revulsion, Oleg found himself oddly empathetic. Had Luganov just been diagnosed with some life-threatening and incurable disease? Was he dying? Were both the family and the nation about to endure a wrenching upheaval?

"Father wants a divorce," Marina suddenly blurted out.

The word left Oleg unable to respond. Marina wiped her eyes again. She poured herself another glass of wine and took several large sips.

"He says he does not love Mother anymore," Marina continued, pale and shaken. "He says he has never loved her, that he loves someone else."

"Who?" Oleg asked, immediately wishing he had kept his mouth closed.

Marina answered the question before he could apologize. "That skater, that *whore!*"

Marina did not mention the woman's name. She did not have to. Everyone in Russia knew who Katya Slatsky was. The twenty-eight-year-old figure skater had competed in three Olympic Games, winning a gold medal and two silver medals and becoming a heroine for millions of young Russian girls. She had also become the subject of tabloid rumors in Europe as being the paramour of the Russian president. Oleg's father-in-law had strenuously denounced those who trafficked in such "baseless gossip" as those with "snotty noses and erotic fantasies" who had nothing better to do than "prowl into others' lives."

Oleg had never taken the rumors seriously because Marina hadn't. He'd certainly never asked his mother-in-law. It was not his place. Yes, he had seen signs of discontent in his in-laws' relationship. Yet he had never really considered that the rumors of Luganov's infidelity might be true. Why was that? He had developed and harbored so many profound concerns and suspicions about Luganov the leader. Why had he never taken the time to carefully analyze Luganov the man?

"Where is Vasily?" he asked.

"He's asleep in your parents' room," Marina said. "He's fine. I checked on him just before you arrived." Then she whispered to him. "I'm so grateful you got my message to meet us here. Thank you for dropping everything and coming straight to us. I honestly didn't expect you for hours more."

Oleg said nothing. He realized he had completely neglected to check his voice messages. Upon getting in his car and driving away from the Kremlin, he had turned off the ringer on his mobile phone. He hadn't wanted anyone to be able to find him.

Was this the time? he now wondered. *Was this the place?* With emotions running so high in this home against Aleksandr Ivanovich Luganov, was this the moment Oleg should disclose his immense and growing misgivings about the decisions the president was making and the direction he was leading the nation?

Oleg considered this briefly but thought better of it. Yulia and Marina were already grieving so much. It would be terribly unkind to add to their distress. Instead, he nodded toward his mother-in-law, sobbing into a pillow on the couch. Marina nodded back, and together they went to her side to comfort her as best they could.

Just then there was a sharp knock on the door of the den, startling them all. Oleg turned and saw an agent in the doorway, holding out a mobile phone and beckoning Oleg to take it.

"It's for you," the agent said.

"Who is it?" asked Oleg.

"It's the president, sir."

Oleg swallowed hard. But he could hardly ask the man to take a message, as awkward as the moment was. So he took the phone and went to the bedroom that had been his since childhood. He dreaded what was coming and didn't want Marina or Yulia to have any chance of overhearing the conversation. It was quite clear they had no idea the accusations that had been leveled against him in the last few hours. They were dealing with bombshells of their own, and now was no time to add to their burdens.

"Mr. President," Oleg said quietly, "how can I be of service?"

"Oleg, my son," the president began, "I want to apologize."

Oleg was caught off guard. He'd never heard the man say these words, and certainly not to him.

"For what?" he asked.

"Boris Zakharov has been arrested," Luganov said. "The FSB has determined that he, and he alone, was responsible for the leak of the S-400 deal."

Once again Oleg found himself without words. But Luganov continued.

"The investigators believe Zakharov was trying to frame you for the leak," the president explained. "This was the reason for his outburst this morning. I wanted to personally call you and inform you that he was arrested. He has confessed and has been taken to prison. You have been fully cleared of all wrongdoing."

Oleg let out a breath. "I appreciate you taking the time to inform me, Mr. President," he said, reeling from the contradictory emotions surging within him.

"That is not all, my son," the president said.

"Yes?" Oleg said, eager to get off the phone and back to his wife.

"I need you to go to London for me."

"London?"

"Ten Downing Street, to be precise."

"May I ask why?"

"The prime minister and I just got off the phone. He wants to meet with me next week. Iran and North Korea are on the docket, among other issues. I need someone to lead an advance trip. Negotiate the agenda. Make sure the security arrangements are acceptable. You'll have a team of seasoned professionals with you. But I need someone I can trust to manage the process, someone loyal to me, someone who will report back to me directly, not through the Foreign Ministry. And I need you to leave in two hours. One of my planes is already on the tarmac, fueled and waiting for you. Can I count on you, my son?"

How quickly a man's fortunes could change and change again. No longer was Oleg being fired or investigated for treason, a crime punishable by death under Russian law. Instead, he was being asked to go on—no, lead—a highly sensitive assignment to the British capital, a city he'd never set foot in before, with no warning and no time to prepare. And Luganov had referred to him as "my son" three times in less than a minute.

Oleg was torn. If he said yes, he would be drawn still deeper into his father-in-law's web of deceit and corruption. He would give short shrift to his mother-in-law's betrayal and unremitting grief and add to his wife's already-bitter pain. He would be ignoring every flashing light on the dashboard that told him to take these two women and Vasily and flee to the West without looking back.

A line from one of Solzhenitsyn's books came to mind: *"You can resolve to live your life with integrity,"* the great conscience of the Russian soul had written. *"Let your credo be this: Let the lie come into the world, let it even triumph. But not through me."*

And yet, as if detached from his own body, as if disconnected from all his fears and doubts and resentments and revulsion, Oleg Kraskin heard himself say, "Of course, Mr. President. I am, as ever, your loyal servant."

FIVE

35

Special Agent Marcus Ryker was getting noticed by his superiors.

A quick study and always ready to tackle a new assignment with vigor, he'd just been promoted again, and this was the big time: the nation's capital.

Atlanta had been his first assignment, and there he had helped solve dozens of counterfeit cases—including several significant ones—while learning the ropes of protection work when POTUS or VPOTUS would come to town and during the presidential primaries. From there he was transferred to the Manhattan field office, where he helped guard foreign dignitaries each September as the U.N. General Assembly kicked off its fall session. He did occasional protection work for visits by the president and VP. Most of his time, though, was spent on a task force locating and seizing illegal assets from Russian crime bosses.

Elena had never enjoyed Atlanta, and she'd been claustrophobic in

New York. Marcus loved the city's energy and intensity, not to mention all that he was learning and doing and the respect he was gaining among his peers. But Elena wasn't a big-city girl, and she refused to become one. She resented the fact that everything was so expensive. The traffic was horrific. The subway tunnels smelled of urine. The schools were an abomination. The only thing she hated more than sending Lars to the public school they'd found in Atlanta was putting him in the one they'd found in Queens.

Lars had just turned seven, and now they'd moved again. No longer was Marcus learning enough Russian to bust mafia goons from "the old country"; now he was on the vice president's protective detail. They were living in the Eastern Market section of D.C., in a two-bedroom apartment a few blocks southeast of the Capitol. Lars had to go to yet another lousy public school. They simply couldn't afford a private one.

Marcus was working constantly. They rarely had time to eat dinner as a family at home, much less go out as a family, and Marcus and Elena struggled to find time for dates. The problem wasn't simply that Marcus loved his job. It was that he was good at it. He wasn't trying to catch his bosses' attention, but he was doing it just the same. With every passing year, he was being given more important assignments, each of which kept him busier than the last. *No wonder the divorce rate for agents was so high,* Elena mused.

Not that she would ever consider such a thing. "Divorce? Never. Murder? Maybe," she'd recently quipped to Maya Emerson, the wife of their pastor at Lincoln Park Baptist, where Elena and Lars attended church. Marcus did too when he wasn't on duty.

On Thursday Marcus woke up well before the sun rose and certainly well before Elena. He ran his usual five miles, showered, dressed in a dark-blue suit and red-striped tie, kissed his wife and son on their foreheads, and left their apartment for the White House while it was still dark. When the sun finally peeked over the horizon and the alarm beside their bed went off, Elena padded to the kitchen in her bathrobe and poured herself a cup of the coffee Marcus had brewed for her before he'd left. Then she read the Scriptures for a bit in her favorite chair by the bay windows in the living room while their cat, Miles, curled up on her lap. When the alarm on her phone buzzed, she got Lars up, made him breakfast, and walked him to school.

Lars was struggling to make friends, struggling to fit in. He constantly told them he wanted to move back to Monument, back to his grandparents and all the good memories he'd ever had in his life. Elena didn't just sympathize. She fully agreed with him. Yet whenever she brought up with Marcus even the possibility of moving back, he bristled and changed the subject.

By noon the vibrant autumn sun blazed across a bright-blue canvas. There was no humidity, and the temperature hovered in the low seventies. Plenty of tourists were in town, but not nearly as many as during the summer when school was out or even in the spring when the cherry blossoms were in full bloom, vivid pink and delicately aromatic, making the trees look like billows of cotton candy. At this time of year, with American children back in class, most visitors to the national landmarks—from the Capitol Building and the National Archives to the varied Smithsonian museums, from memorials of presidents and veterans and Dr. Martin Luther King Jr. to the White House itself—were from abroad.

With hundreds of people strolling along E Street and down Pennsylvania Avenue, taking selfies and shooting home videos of themselves near "the people's house," the young Asian man in his early twenties hardly drew special attention. He wore a New York Yankees baseball cap he'd bought from a street vendor, tan khakis, and a black polo shirt. He had on a light-blue windbreaker and new Nikes and sported a backpack. A DSLR camera dangled around his neck as he meandered through Lafayette Square, drifting slowly toward the north side of the White House, snapping pictures every few steps. He and his six friends—all with Asian features, though some darker than others—could easily have been graduate students or members of a college sports team. But they were neither athletes nor students. Nor were they alone.

At precisely 12:05, the leader—the one in the Yankees cap—glanced at his watch. Then he shouted something in a foreign language and broke into a sprint. He was heading directly for the black wrought-iron fence protecting the North Lawn of the president's home. The six others were running too, just a few paces behind him. Simultaneously, two other groups of college-age young men—one about forty yards to the right, the other about thirty yards to the left—all began sprinting toward the White House as well.

Uniformed Secret Service officers yelled at them to stop but were immediately shot dead as the young men pulled handguns and fired with deadly accuracy. Others ripped the cameras off their necks and hurled them onto the White House grounds and into the guard stations, where they exploded with horrific force. The grenades hidden inside the cameras were powerful ones. As they detonated and the crackle of gunfire broke the early-afternoon calm, chaos erupted. Secret Service officers were being blown to pieces. Tourists were screaming and running for cover.

In the midst of it all, twenty attackers scaled the fence, jumped onto the grass, and bolted for the North Portico, the closest White House entrance. Snipers on the roof opened fire. They took out five of the men in quick order. Uniformed officers and Marines at the doors opened fire as well. They killed four and severely wounded four more before being killed themselves. But this still left seven able-bodied attackers taking up positions under the North Portico, firing at agents and members of the emergency response team and K-9 units emerging from the West Wing and the Treasury Building. One of the men affixed plastic explosives to the electronically locked north entry door and blew it to smithereens.

Marcus had just finished his shift, standing post outside the VP's office in the West Wing, and was on his way to Room W-16—the Service's White House basement command post, code-named Horsepower—when he heard the gunfire and explosions. Immediately he drew his Sig Sauer P229 automatic pistol. As he did, he received the call on his radio from the watch officer. He was instructed to race back upstairs and assist agents defending the North Portico. He responded at once, bounding up the steps two at a time, and heard a blizzard of situation reports coming in from all sectors.

A car bomb had gone off near the corner of E Street and Seventeenth.

Other agents were reporting machine-gun fire erupting near the fence line along the South Lawn, close to the Treasury Building.

A plane had just entered restricted airspace. It was approaching the White House from the southwest and was not responding to air traffic control commands to divert. Fighter jets were being scrambled out of Andrews, but they were three minutes out.

Marcus headed toward the Entrance Hall, the large vestibule leading to the North Portico. To get there, he had to cross through the State Dining Room, which was being arranged for an event that evening with the Ukrainian prime minister. As he came upon ushers and protocol personnel paralyzed with fear—unsure what to do or where to go—another massive explosion rocked the building. Marcus found himself thrown off his feet by the force of the blast, as was everyone around him. Priceless china, crystal wineglasses, and water goblets smashed to the floor. One of the enormous glass chandeliers came crashing down, shattering into a million pieces.

Marcus checked to make sure everyone was okay. Most were cut and bleeding across the face, neck, and hands. So was he. But they were alive, and to keep them that way, he had to get them moving. He scrambled back to his feet and went to the door as he ordered the staff to run to the southwest stairwell, head to the basement, and take cover in the bowling alley, where they'd be safe.

Once they were in motion, Marcus turned back to the threat at hand. He could feel the adrenaline surging through his system, but it didn't blur his thinking. He'd been trained to channel it, manage it, control it, and let it create heightened focus in the midst of chaos. He began counting to fifty, a trick he'd learned to slow his breathing and steady his nerves. *All stress is self-induced,* he reminded himself. *It's in your mind. You don't need it. Lay it down. Panic is contagious. But so is calm. Stay calm. Do your work. Slow is smooth. Smooth is smart. Smart is straight. Straight is deadly.*

Glancing out from behind a pillar, he spotted several young men pouring through the remains of the breached door. All were pulling submachine guns from their backpacks. He had to move now. Pivoting through the doorway, he fired two shots, shifted aim, fired twice more, then shifted again and fired another three shots. In just seconds, he had taken down three assailants. But as he pulled back for cover, the dining room erupted with machine-gun fire. Bullets were flying everywhere, ripping up everything that hadn't been destroyed by the blast.

Marcus broke right, out of the dining room and into the Red Room. He stopped and fired three times through the open door to the Entrance Hall. He wasn't sure if he'd hit anyone, but there wasn't time to check. He ducked behind another pillar to take cover, then radioed the command post with an update on his location and what he was seeing. Then he sprinted through the Blue Room and the Green Room. When he reached the East Room, he paused just before entering and popped out a spent magazine and reloaded. He whispered a quick prayer and burst into the East Room, hoping to outflank the terrorists by coming in behind them. Sure enough, he found two of the terrorists. He also found a group of White House staffers, facedown on the floor, being executed one by one.

36

Marcus was alone, but he had the element of surprise.

Both terrorists had their backs to him. One held a machine gun and was firing at agents trying to retake the Entrance Hall. The other was wearing a Yankees cap. He held a 9mm pistol and was shooting staff members in the back of the head.

Marcus took aim and fired four rounds in rapid succession. He hit the one in the ball cap in the spine, felling him instantly. He missed the one with the machine gun, though, who now swung around and returned fire. Several of the shots went wild. But two hit Marcus directly in the chest. He was wearing a Kevlar vest, but the impact knocked him off his feet and drove the wind out of him. The terrorist raced toward him, changing out magazines as he approached. Just as he reached Marcus and aimed at his head, the young man's body was riddled with bullets.

Marcus instinctively covered his hands and face as blood sprayed everywhere. When he finally looked up, a member of CAT—the counterassault team—stood over him. He grabbed Marcus by the hand, pulled him to his feet, and handed him a Heckler & Koch MP5. Marcus nodded his thanks, and the two went hunting.

The firefight that ensued lasted all of nine minutes. That's what the surveillance video showed, and Marcus would eventually watch it more than a dozen times. In the moment, however, he would have sworn the battle lasted at least forty-five minutes or an hour. Everything seemed to slow. He and the CAT member fired and reloaded, shifted locations, then fired and reloaded again. They kicked away grenades and even lobbed one back. Eventually reinforcements arrived. That's when the battle turned and finally shut down for good.

By the time the entire episode was complete and the complex had been locked down and fully secured, twenty-two plainclothes agents and uniformed officers of the U.S. Secret Service—plus one CAT member—lay dead. Seventeen more were wounded, twelve seriously. Eleven White House staffers had been murdered, along with six tourists: a Japanese family of four and a retired Jewish couple from Minneapolis.

Nineteen of the twenty terrorists—all from a previously unknown jihadist group from the Philippines—were dead. The twentieth lay in a coma, and doctors at George Washington Memorial Hospital gave him little chance of recovery.

By the grace of God, the president was unhurt. The moment gunshots and explosions began, alarms had sounded throughout the White House complex and his protection detail had immediately moved him down to the bunker known as the PEOC, or Presidential Emergency Operations Center. Simultaneously, the VP had been rushed by his detail through a maze of tunnels underneath the Eisenhower Executive Office Building, then whisked away to a secure, undisclosed location miles away to ensure continuity of government should events at the White House spin even more tragically out of control. The first family had been out of town at the time and were never in danger.

In the days that followed, however, heads rolled throughout the executive branch. The director of the Secret Service was fired. So were his deputy and the shift commander on duty at the White House at the time of the attack. The secretary of Homeland Security was forced to resign, and two inquiries—one by the House Government Oversight Committee, the other by the DHS inspector general—ended up recommending a sweeping reorganization of the Secret Service leadership and its policies and procedures for guarding the White House complex.

Things turned out better for Special Agent Marcus Ryker. After recovering quickly from what turned out to be minor injuries, he and a number of colleagues received both the Medal of Valor and the Distinguished Service Award. These were personally bestowed upon them by the president in a nationally televised ceremony held in, of all places, the East Room of the White House, one week to the day after the attack had unfolded.

Elena and Lars were there, sitting in the center, near the front, in seats chosen by Lars. Sitting with them were Marcus's mother and two sisters, the entire Garcia family, and Pastor Carter Emerson and his wife, Maya, from Lincoln Park Baptist Church. No one in Washington had been kinder or more helpful to Marcus and Elena in their struggles—and especially to Elena as she battled loneliness and the challenges of raising Lars nearly on her own—than this seventy-something African American couple who had known their own share of hardships in life.

Bill "Sarge" McDermott and his wife also flew in for the ceremony. Pete Hwang and Nick Vinetti and their wives came as well. Bill had retired from the Marines as a full colonel and was now making a mint as an investment banker on Wall Street. Pete was still in the Marines. He'd gone to medical school at the government's expense and was serving as a staff doctor at the Marine training facility in San Diego. Nick, meanwhile, had retired from the military with full honors, gone to graduate school to study international relations, and then opted to join the Foreign Service. After working a stretch at the State Department, he'd served in various roles at U.S. Embassies throughout the Middle

East and Asia. At the moment he was serving as a political officer at the U.S. Embassy in Tallinn, Estonia.

Having forged their bonds in battle, the four men had made it a point to stay in touch after going their separate ways. They called and emailed fairly often. They got together every Memorial Day weekend to ride Harleys and raise money for the Wounded Warrior Project. It meant the world to Marcus that they'd all drop everything and fly to Washington at their own expense to be there for him. And it hadn't even been his idea or theirs. It had been Elena's.

MOSCOW—17 OCTOBER

From his corner suite, Oleg Kraskin watched the ceremony live on RTV.

All week he had been transfixed by the coverage of the attacks in Washington, the ensuing congressional hearings, the firings at the highest levels of the Secret Service, and the DHS investigation. Privately, he wondered how he would handle a similar terrorist attack, should it ever happen in the Kremlin. He'd done his required service in the army, like every other able-bodied male in the country, and he'd been trained in basic emergency procedures, as all his colleagues had been. But he was not a military man. He had never worked for the security services. He had no idea how he would respond in a real crisis.

Snuffing out one cigarette and lighting up another, Oleg tried to assess how the attacks might affect Luganov's already-chilly relationship with the American president. Oleg, for all his jet-setting in recent years, had never been to Washington. He had never even set foot in the United States. Since he'd come to work for Luganov, others had handled the American portfolio. That had been fine with Oleg. He had far too much on his plate already, and relations with the Americans had always been considered something of a "holy grail" among Luganov's team— alluring and intriguing, yet forbidding. The stakes were too high, and the margin for error was too thin.

What intrigued Oleg most as he watched the East Room ceremony was the figure of Special Agent Marcus Ryker. His injuries notwithstanding, he was strikingly good-looking, and at first Oleg wondered if he had Russian roots. He had intense, alert blue eyes, a firm jaw, and short blond hair. He wore a trim navy-blue suit, a white oxford shirt, and a solid burgundy tie. There was something rare in Ryker's face, in his eyes—something honest, something earnest and trustworthy that appealed to Oleg.

The American president read a prepared statement explaining not only each agent's bravery under fire but his background. Oleg was struck by the fact that he and Ryker had roughly similar stories. They had gotten married within a month of each other. They each had a son. They had each dedicated themselves to government service when they could have been successful in the private sector. They both worked quietly, in the background, out of the glare of the cameras, serving their national leaders with distinction and honor.

Then the phone rang. It was Luganov, and he needed Oleg immediately.

37

"Agent Ryker, the president would like you to join him in the Oval Office."

The young aide was so earnest and so pleasant, that Marcus—usually a stickler for protocol—asked if Elena and Lars could join him.

"Of course," the aide said.

"Could our family and friends come too?"

At this, there was a brief hesitation, followed quickly by a warm smile and a nod. "The president wants to personally express his gratitude to you, away from the TV lights. I'm sure he would enjoy meeting the people closest to you as well."

Soon they were all in the Oval, including Pastor Emerson and Maya, chatting and laughing with the president of the United States and getting their pictures taken with him. That's when the president decided to make an announcement. As commander in chief, he was taking the liberty of the office to give Marcus a promotion. No longer would Marcus be assigned to the VP. Starting the following morning, he would be assigned to the PPD itself—the Presidential Protective Detail.

The small group burst out in cheers and applause. Marcus beamed. Lars was beside himself with excitement. Marcus's Marine buddies were elated. They slapped him on the back and offered him hearty congratulations, and they personally thanked the president. Marcus's mother hugged him. The Garcias seemed less excited. Elena was crestfallen, though she did her best not to show it. Later she would learn that Marcus had known about the promotion for several days but hadn't said anything. He'd wanted it to be a surprise.

It certainly had been, but not a good one.

Elena had wanted her husband to use this moment to step down from the Secret Service. It was enough, already. Between this and his service in Afghanistan and Iraq, Marcus had cheated death one too many times. As a family, they desperately needed a break—not just a vacation but the opportunity to leave Washington altogether, the chance to move back west and restart their lives together. Elena wanted Marcus to talk to a headhunter, take a six-figure salary doing executive security for a big company, ideally in Colorado. She'd broached the idea a few times, but Marcus either hadn't understood how important this was to her or didn't care. This was what made his unwillingness—or outright refusal—to tell her about the promotion in advance such a bitter pill to swallow. Had he really been too busy to share such a huge development? Or was he just trying to avoid the blowback that was sure to follow if the conversation had happened in the bedroom of their apartment rather than the Oval Office?

That night Marcus took the whole group out to dinner at the Willard InterContinental.

It was a four-diamond hotel just around the corner from the White

House, and it was a pricey evening. Mr. Garcia pulled Marcus aside at one point and insisted that he pick up the tab. Separately, Bill McDermott did the same. Marcus wouldn't hear of it. They weren't together often, he told them. He'd socked away a little money for a rainy day, and this was it. He wanted to treat them. And he had an announcement of his own.

As the dishes were being cleared ahead of dessert, Marcus stood, refilled his glass of champagne, and cleared his throat to get the group's attention. It wasn't easy to do. Everyone was chattering about the extraordinary day they'd had. Bill had been regaling them with stories from Marcus's past that kept them all laughing. Pastor Emerson, a Vietnam vet, had shared about the first time he'd met a president, when Lyndon Johnson visited troops in Cam Ranh Bay. Lars, meanwhile, had been cracking everybody up doing impressions of the president that were frighteningly dead-on. Eventually everyone settled down.

"I'm not the public speaker of this group," Marcus began to knowing smiles all around, "but I just want to say how grateful I am to each of you. Over the years, you've supported me—and heckled and embarrassed me, but mostly supported me. Some of you, especially my mom and Elena and the Emersons here, have prayed for me. For Lars, too. And each of you has been a tremendous encouragement to us over the years. God has been very kind to our little tribe. But for his grace, things could have turned out differently, many times. Yet for reasons only he knows, our Savior has brought me safely here tonight, here with each of you, and this dinner is my way of saying thank you."

The group applauded warmly, but Marcus was not finished.

"I know words like 'thank you' and 'I'm so grateful' don't really suffice," he continued. "Nor does a fancy meal, even in a hotel as nice as this. Nor will what I'm about to propose, but I'm going to do it anyway. Because you all deserve it, and goodness knows we all need it."

Everyone looked at each other, wondering if the others knew what in the world he was talking about. Only one of them did.

"I think it's time for an extended reunion," he said when the suspense had built to a crescendo. "This group of ours has been through a lot over the years. We've been running hard, and I say it's high time we take a break and savor the many blessings the Lord has given us."

The group was buzzing now. They all liked the sound of that. Marcus even noticed that Elena, who had not seemed herself all day, had suddenly brightened, at least with curiosity.

"What are you saying, Mr. Hero?" McDermott asked.

"Yeah," Vinetti chimed in. "What exactly are you getting at?"

"Okay, here's the thing—I'd like to take you all on a cruise," Marcus said at last. "I'm talking about an all-expenses-paid bon voyage to the Caribbean or Alaska or the Mediterranean. I honestly don't care where. You vote and pick a week that suits everyone best, and we'll take care of the rest."

"We?" Elena asked, as amazed as she was excited yet quickly trying to do the math in her head.

"Your father and I." He smiled. "We've been cooking this up for the last few days. The two awards I received today come with generous bonuses, and what I can't cover, Dad has offered to cover himself."

"Really, Daddy?" Elena asked, her eyes welling with tears. "Is it true?"

"Absolutely, sweetheart," Mr. Garcia said. "Marcus is right; you guys need a break. We all do. Am I right?"

He looked at his daughter, then at Marcus and the rest of the group. The entire party erupted in cheers and laughter and tears and hugs. Bill McDermott, moved by the moment, stood up and offered to cover everyone's airfare. This triggered another round of whoops and cheers. Elena jumped out of her seat and threw her arms around Marcus and kissed him and cried while Lars did a hilarious happy dance as the rest of the restaurant's patrons stared on in a mixture of amusement and disdain.

There was just one problem: Marcus Ryker would never make it to the cruise.

38

Russia invaded Ukraine on February 27, 2014.

That was a Thursday. The Caribbean cruise the Rykers had been planning for months was set to sail from Port Canaveral two days later.

Elena had surveyed everyone's schedules and desires. She had meticulously researched the best cruise lines, hunted for the best prices, and kept each family briefed on every detail. Now everything was set. Eight deluxe rooms had been reserved and paid for. Sixteen round-trip first-class tickets had been bought—funded, as promised, by Bill McDermott. Elena had even designed and ordered matching T-shirts for everyone declaring them part of "The Ryker Reunion Cruise" and created a special Facebook page where they could upload and share photos and journal their memories.

Upon hearing the news that Marcus's vacation leave had been canceled and that he was being ordered back to the White House immediately, Elena burst into tears. She didn't want to hear about the president's plans to head to Camp David for a crisis meeting with his national security team in less than an hour. She didn't want to know that one of the agents on the PPD had been incapacitated with stomach flu and another had broken his ankle that afternoon in a training exercise. She wasn't an insensitive person. She was as much a team player as any of the wives of any of the men on the detail. But there was a breaking point.

"I don't care that they need you," Elena said through her tears. "I need you. *Lars* needs you. Call your supervisor back and tell him you can't go."

"You know I can't do that," Marcus said calmly as he began changing into a suit and tie. "The president asked for me by name. I have to go."

"No, you don't, Marcus. You asked for time off. They approved it. That's it, end of story."

"Look, I know this is hard. And I'm sorry. But I took an oath."

At that, Elena lost it. *"You made an oath to me first, Marcus Ryker."*

She unleashed a torrent of pent-up resentment. She didn't want to hear any more excuses or broken promises. If he loved her, he would pick up the phone, call the watch commander, insist he was taking his family on a long-planned and much-deserved vacation. If he really loved her, he would resign from the Secret Service altogether. Enough was enough. This wasn't about the president. It was about their family. It was about their marriage, and it was time for him to choose.

Marcus tried to hold her, but she would have none of it. When he said he'd call her in a few hours when she'd cooled down, she picked up an empty vase and heaved it at his head. It missed and smashed against the wall.

Lars suddenly appeared in their bedroom doorway, ashen. Elena raced to his side and held him. "Lars and I are getting on that plane tomorrow," she told Marcus, wiping her tears and trying her best to compose herself. "You'll either be on the plane, or you won't. It's clearly too much to expect you to do anything to protect my feelings. But God help you, Marcus Ryker, if you won't take your only son on a vacation you yourself promised in the first place."

The anger in Elena's eyes was unlike anything he'd ever seen before. She did not wait for his reply. She scooped up Lars, took him back to his room, and slammed the door behind her. Marcus heard her turn the lock. He asked her to come back out and talk, but she refused. He waited for several minutes, but she continued to sob. Marcus couldn't bear the thought of leaving like this. But glancing at his watch, he finally concluded he had to go. He returned to the master bedroom, opened the safe in their closet, and retrieved his badge and service weapon. Then he grabbed the suitcase he always kept packed and headed for the kitchen. There he quickly scribbled a note of apology to Elena and a separate note for Lars.

Take care of your mom this week and have a great time, he wrote. *Tell Grammie and Paw Paw and everyone else I love them, and I'm very sorry. I'll see you soon, little man. I promise. Love, Daddy.*

39

Marine One lifted off from the South Lawn and headed north.

Sitting behind the president was the SAIC—the special agent in charge—and three additional agents, including Marcus. Directly beside and across from the president sat the national security advisor and the White House chief of staff. Only then did Marcus learn just how much the crisis in Ukraine had worsened in recent hours.

Like his fellow agents and anyone else who was watching the news, Marcus knew that in December, some eight hundred thousand Ukrainians had taken to the streets of Kiev. The protesters had surrounded key government buildings and demanded the ouster of their president as a pro-Moscow puppet. He was bankrupting the economy, selling out Ukrainian sovereignty, and increasingly putting control of the country under the thumb of the Russians. As the bitter winds and heavy snows of January arrived, the crowds were no longer content to camp outside the government buildings. They surged forward, storming barricades erected by riot police and occupying city hall, parliament, the finance ministry, and more. Initially paralyzed by indecision, the government finally launched a counteroffensive in late February. They ordered the police to fire on the protesters using live ammunition and retake all public buildings. Within hours, seventy-seven people lay dead. Hundreds were wounded. Hundreds more had been arrested. But the images of the violence electrified an already-enraged populace. As rumors spread that President Luganov of Russia had ordered the killings of the protesters, and had allegedly done so from his luxury dacha on the Black Sea, hundreds of thousands of Ukrainians poured into the streets, and the country seemed to be teetering on the brink of a full-blown civil war.

For at least two months now, Marcus had heard the American president and the secretary of state issue a series of weak statements. They had called for a restoration of calm and requested that "international law and the rights of the Ukrainian people be respected." The president warned the Russians not to inflame the situation and called for the U.N. Security Council to pass a firm resolution. Not once, however, had they offered the Ukrainian people one bit of practical help or threatened any specific repercussions if Moscow did intervene directly.

Now Marcus was stunned to overhear the national security advisor say the Ukrainian president was missing. Unconfirmed reports suggested he had actually fled the capital with a small group of loyalists and was racing for the Russian border, hoping for asylum in Moscow. Yet what truly chilled Special Agent Ryker was hearing that just at the moment the Ukrainians might have driven the pro-Luganov puppet from office, Luganov appeared to have ordered the Russian military to invade the sovereign territory of yet another Russian neighbor. If this were true, how far would Luganov go? Was he just sending a message, or was he planning to go all the way to Kiev? To Marcus, the situation had the feel of the Russian invasion of Georgia all over again.

The presidential retreat center deep in the heart of Maryland's Catoctin Mountain, some sixty miles north of Washington, was on full lockdown.

With the commander in chief and most of his war cabinet on hand, the Secret Service was taking no chances. No one was getting in or out of Camp David without the highest possible clearance. Every ID of every person trying to enter the outer perimeter of the camp was carefully scrutinized. Every license plate of every vehicle was double-checked to make sure it was authorized to be on the grounds. Everyone aside from the president and members of his family passed through magnetometers. Every possession of every cabinet secretary, advisor, and staff member passed through X-ray machines and through sophisticated sniffers capable of detecting nuclear, chemical, and biological agents.

Surveillance helicopters crisscrossed the skies along with drones equipped with state-of-the-art cameras and thermal imagery equipment, keeping a close watch on the 180-acre camp for possible intruders. Sharpshooters and their spotters took up positions on the rooftops. Agents operating shoulder-mounted missile launchers capable of shooting down any unauthorized aircraft were in place, and K-9 units constantly roamed the grounds.

At exactly 3 p.m., the president gathered his entire national security team—most in person, though some by secure video feed—in a Laurel Lodge conference room to assess the latest developments and formulate an official response and action plan. The SAIC stood post in the corner of the room, directly to the president's right. Another agent guarded the door to the president's left. Marcus was assigned to the only other door in the room.

The director of national intelligence, fresh back from NATO headquarters in Brussels, was the first to brief the president. He reported that thousands of Russian soldiers and commandos were moving throughout southern Ukraine and the Crimean peninsula. They were crushing any and all armed resistance they encountered and had seized government buildings, banks, TV and radio stations, and the airports. What was odd, however, was that none of the olive-drab uniforms of the offensive forces bore the Russian flag or Russian military insignias.

They actually bore no flags or military insignias at all. The DNI asserted unequivocally that there was no question the "little green men" were operating at the behest of President Luganov. But he conceded that by wearing different uniforms, these enemy forces were able to do their dirty work without definitively implicating Moscow.

"Luganov is doing his best to deceive foreign governments and the international media, but the evidence supports only one conclusion, Mr. President," the SecDef added. "The Russians have launched an invasion of Ukraine, and they will likely have full control of Crimea within the next few days."

"Are the Ukrainians fighting back?" the president asked.

The national security advisor took that one. "Initially, and bravely," he said. "But now we're seeing signs they are pulling back and regrouping."

"Why?"

"Keep in mind that the population of Crimea is largely ethnic Russians. Many—most, perhaps—would actually like to be back under the control of Moscow, not Kiev. That means they are far more loyal to Russia than to Ukraine. So we're not seeing significant resistance inside the major cities in Crimea. And with Kiev engulfed in chaos—the Ukrainian president missing and nearly a million Ukrainians in the streets—it's not clear exactly who's calling the shots."

"What's going on with Russian regular forces?" the president asked.

This time it was the chairman of the joint chiefs who responded, speaking via a secure feed from the National Military Command Center at the Pentagon. "Sir, President Luganov has ordered some thirty thousand combat troops to the Ukrainian border. We're seeing upwards of a thousand tanks, thousands of artillery batteries, and SAM batteries."

"And in the air?"

"Russian fighter jets have been penetrating Ukrainian airspace for weeks," the SecDef reported. "Today, however, oddly enough the skies are quiet."

"What do you make of that?"

"It seems consistent with President Luganov's deception campaign, sir. He's going to say Ukrainians loyal to Mother Russia are fighting, not regular Russian forces. He's going to say he had nothing to do with any of this. I wouldn't be surprised if he calls for a cease-fire and a snap referendum asking Crimeans if they want to be under Russian sovereignty or that of Ukraine. If that happens, believe me, anyone who voted against Moscow and for Kiev won't be long for this world."

"What are our military options?" the president asked.

"We really don't have any, Mr. President," said the chairman of the joint chiefs. "As you know, sir, Ukraine is not a NATO ally. We don't have a formal treaty with Kiev. Even if we were inclined to get involved, it would take us several weeks to spool up enough forces to get into the theater and retake Crimea. But that would effectively put us into a head-to-head war with Russia. That could get very ugly, very fast, sir. As was just stated, Luganov has positioned some thirty thousand combat troops backed up by a whole lot of airpower and heavy mechanized divisions just a few miles across the border. We'd be lucky to get twenty-five hundred U.S. forces there within two weeks. It would take quite a bit longer to get any significant number of tanks and APCs on the ground. We'd be outgunned from the first shot. And keep in mind, sir, that even if we did begin to establish air dominance, and even if we were to link up with Ukrainian ground forces and actually started to take back significant swaths of territory—and those are mighty big ifs at the moment—who is to say the Russians wouldn't escalate the situation?"

"How so?"

"It's possible Luganov could order the use of tactical battlefield nukes."

"You can't be serious," said an incredulous president.

"I'm afraid I am, sir. Tactical nukes are a key part of Russian military doctrine, and I don't believe we can rule out their use."

"You really think Luganov wants to start a nuclear war with the United States of America?" asked the president, quickly growing angrier than Marcus had ever seen him.

The chairman didn't respond. No one did. It was quiet for several moments. Marcus looked at the president, then around the room at his aides and military and foreign policy advisors at the table and on the screens. No one seemed to have a good answer to the question, and that fact was as unnerving as anything Marcus had ever heard since joining the Secret Service.

40

The president issued a milquetoast statement.

He denounced the Russian aggression and urged an immediate cease-fire and withdrawal to recognized international borders. Luganov couldn't have cared less. While not admitting that any of the "little green men" were active Russian forces, Luganov went on national television from the Kremlin and announced that he was fully prepared to use military force to protect all the Russian-speaking people of Ukraine, and particularly Crimea, against "crimes of any kind." Within hours, the Duma—the Russian parliament—passed a resolution affirming Luganov's "right and responsibility" to use such force in Ukraine, as he deemed necessary.

Over the course of the next forty-eight hours, the American president took three separate calls from the leader of the Ukrainian opposition, who was clearly terrified that Luganov was poised to drive all the way to Kiev. She pleaded for U.S. military assistance—arms, ammunition, communications equipment, and targeting information, as well as medical supplies and tactical air support. She expressed more distress with each successive conversation, yet no one at Camp David or in the White House thought it wise to intervene to help the Ukrainians, lest it put Washington in a worst-case-scenario showdown.

"We have to be honest, Mr. President. Ukraine is squarely in the Russian sphere," the secretary of state insisted.

"They're not a member of NATO," noted the national security advisor.

"They wanted to be," the SecDef said.

"But they're not," SecState pushed back. "Look, I'm as sympathetic to their plight as anyone, but, Mr. President, we can't get into a shooting war with the Russians over Ukraine—we just can't."

She didn't need to finish the thought. Everyone knew what she meant, and everyone in the room agreed. A war with Russia, a nuclear power, could quickly get out of hand. The U.S. had already fought two major wars in Afghanistan and Iraq over the previous decade and a half, neither of which had been fully resolved, and both of which had drained trillions of dollars from the federal treasury and soured the American people on any further foreign interventions. The last thing the average American could imagine was sending soldiers or Marines to fight and die in another country to which the U.S. had no treaty obligations.

In the end, the president decided to meet with Luganov face-to-face. Most of his advisors were dead set against the idea and said so. But the president refused to be dissuaded. He ordered preparations to be made for an emergency summit, then called the chancellor of Germany and asked if she would host it. She immediately agreed.

Three days later, Marcus touched down in Berlin just after 6 a.m. local time.

The advance team's first stop was the U.S. Embassy. They briefed the ambassador and the deputy chief of mission on the president's itinerary, secured assistance from all the relevant department heads, and met privately with the CIA station chief and legal attaché, a special agent on loan from the FBI. Next they headed to the Hotel Adlon Kempinski, located within sight of Berlin's Brandenburg Gate, where they checked in and began working through a detailed checklist of preparations. They did a walk-through with the hotel manager and head of security, reviewing the presidential suite and every room on three full floors that would be needed for the entire U.S. delegation. They walked through the kitchen and explained that they'd be bringing their own food, their own beverages, and their own chefs. They examined arrival points and the garage, where dozens of U.S. government vehicles would need to be parked and secured. They went up to the roof to see where the White House Communications Agency equipment would be set up and where sharpshooters and spotters would be positioned.

The following day they met with German intelligence officials and senior representatives of the local police force to gather everything they could on current security threats and an updated list of persons of interest. They drove dozens of possible routes from the airport to the hotel, from the hotel to the U.S. Embassy, and from the hotel to the German Chancellery, where the summit would be held. They also drove routes from the hotel to three different local hospitals and made sure each hospital was stocked with plenty of the president's blood type. Then they used a U.S. Army helicopter to examine the motorcade routes by air, identifying possible choke points or other areas of vulnerability and discussing ways to counter such threats.

On the morning of the third day, the White House deputy chief of staff, the deputy secretary of state, and the rest of the political advance team landed in Berlin. They were greeted at the airport by the U.S. ambassador and the DCM. Marcus and his colleagues drove them to the German Chancellery, where they met with their political and diplomatic counterparts in the German government. Finally, after a working lunch to discuss additional logistical issues, it was time for a high-stakes meeting with their counterparts from Moscow.

It was precisely 5 p.m. local time when they all entered the grand conference room where the summit would be held—if it was held. The Germans and Americans entered from the left. The Russian delegation entered from the right. They convened around an enormous circular conference table.

The CIA had prepared dossiers on the Russian participants, and Marcus had reviewed each one carefully prior to their departure from Washington. He knew, therefore, that the Russian advance team was headed by Oleg Kraskin, President Luganov's most trusted political advisor. Oleg would be negotiating the summit's itinerary, agenda, guest list, seating chart, and every other detail on behalf of the Kremlin and would even be in charge of trying to hammer out a public statement that could be agreed upon in advance by the three world leaders and released when the summit had concluded.

In this context, there was no reason for the Russian negotiator to notice, much less speak to, any member of the American security detail. But about twenty minutes into the rather heated meeting, Oleg suddenly stopped himself midsentence and stared at Marcus so intently that everyone turned to see why.

Marcus instinctively tensed. He was not used to being the center of attention. He actually had no specific protective duties in this room and certainly no diplomatic responsibilities. He was simply there to listen to everything that was discussed and process it from the perspective of securing the American principals when they arrived. He had no idea what to make of the fact that the head of the Russian delegation was fixated on him.

"Mr. Kraskin, is there something I can help you with?" the American ambassador finally asked as the awkwardness of the moment threatened to derail their business.

"You," Oleg said to Marcus, ignoring the ambassador. "You're . . ."

Oleg's voice trailed off. Then Oleg stood, startling everyone, and began walking toward Marcus, who stood as well as the man drew closer.

Marcus tried to evaluate the possible reasons for the Russian's unexpected behavior. He had no idea how he was supposed to respond.

What were the rules? What was the protocol? It was unheard of for such a high-ranking Russian political official to address a member of the Secret Service, much less approach him, in a meeting like this or at any other time. Was he about to strike him? Marcus had every right to defend himself if attacked. But he knew that any physical altercation between the two men would pour gasoline on a geopolitical fire already raging and threatening to burn out of control.

Oleg Kraskin stopped dead in his tracks, mere inches away from Marcus's face. For a moment he said nothing. He just stood there, staring. There was an odd, almost quizzical look on his face.

Marcus steadied his breathing, fully prepared to react but determined not to overreact to whatever was coming. In his peripheral vision, he could see that several other officials were also now rising to their feet. The U.S. ambassador was about to speak when Oleg Kraskin beat him to it.

"You're Marcus Ryker, are you not?" Oleg said, pointing at Marcus's chest.

"Yes, sir, I am," Marcus said as politely and diplomatically as he could.

"You're the agent who saved your president's life. I saw you on television. You're a hero."

Marcus said nothing, completely baffled at this point.

"That's you; am I right?" Oleg pressed. "You're the one the president honored in the White House?"

"Yes, sir, I guess so," Marcus replied, not sure what else to add.

"Well, Agent Ryker, I must say, it is a pleasure to meet you," Oleg said.

The Russian extended his hand. Marcus stared at it. He was tempted to look to his superiors for guidance but felt certain this would offend the very man who could alone determine whether this summit happened or not. So he gave Oleg Kraskin a firm handshake, and then, as quickly as it had begun, the moment was over. The Russian returned to his seat, and the meeting proceeded as if nothing had happened.

41

Marcus didn't mind standing post all night in front of the presidential suite.

He was just glad to be back on the Front Range.

Andrew Clarke, the newly elected president, had come to the Springs and was staying overnight at the Broadmoor Hotel and Resort, with several items on his agenda. First and foremost was visiting the headquarters of NORAD, the North American Aerospace Defense Command, once located deep inside Cheyenne Mountain but since 2006 situated at Peterson Air Force Base. Though he'd never served in the military himself, Clarke had entered office insisting he would both restore the honor of the men and women who served in the military and rebuild America's armed forces, which he said had been "gutted" by his "loser" of a predecessor.

The second priority on the president's list was serving as the keynote speaker for a high-dollar fund-raising dinner for Republican senatorial candidates. It was early yet. The all-important midterm elections wouldn't be held until the following year, but the president was determined to create, if at all possible, a veto-proof majority in the Senate that would enable him to pass the sweeping health care and tax reform bills he had so far been unable to get through Congress and signed into law.

Both items had been checked off the list the previous day. This morning the president was focused on the third item on his agenda: having breakfast with a dozen evangelical leaders whom he counted both key to his stunning upset victory and just as key to his reelection campaign.

Marcus hadn't given any of the three a single thought. His sole interest in this trip—aside from keeping POTUS safe—was the chance to catch up with family. With the permission of the special agent in charge, Marcus had taken some personal leave and flown out to the Springs a day before the president arrived. He'd taken his mom up Pike's Peak for the day, then out for dinner at her favorite hole-in-the-wall Mexican restaurant in Monument. He'd shown her the latest pictures of Lars, who the week before had celebrated his eleventh birthday, on his mobile phone and caught her up on her grandson's latest exploits.

Right on time, about halfway through dinner, Mrs. Ryker made her semiannual plea for Marcus to retire from the Secret Service, move back to Monument, and give Lars "a real childhood." Marcus listened patiently and asked his mother—for the umpteenth time—if Elena was actually paying her cash to make this case every six months. When she denied it like every other time, he gave her his standard reply: "Thanks, Mom, but really, we're doing fine."

The cruise disaster had long ago blown over. Marcus had apologized profusely. Elena had forgiven him. They'd met with Pastor Emerson for several months of counseling, and Marcus was finding ways to cut back on his hours and make a little more time for his wife and son.

When he got back to Washington on Friday night, he told his mother, he was going to meet Elena and Lars for a big night he had planned for them at the Kennedy Center. And yes, he assured her, when he finally felt the time was right to retire, they would definitely come back to Colorado.

The morning the president was to arrive in the Springs, Marcus had breakfast with his in-laws. He asked them to come over to the Broadmoor so he'd be ready to meet the motorcade when it arrived just before noon, and they were more than happy to do so. They loved their son-in-law and were as eager as ever to see the latest pictures and to hear the latest news. They just wished their daughter and only grandchild could have come too.

"The Kennedy Center sounds exciting," Javier Garcia said, his eyes brightening when Marcus explained what he was planning. "What are you going to see?"

"Actually, it's all Lars's idea," Marcus explained. "He's been studying *Moby-Dick*. You know, 'Call me Ishmael,' and the like. Anyway, he's gotten kind of into the whole thing, and his teacher heard that there was going to be a performance of an opera based on the novel at the Kennedy Center. Can't say I'm a big fan of opera, but it's gotten great reviews, and you know how your daughter is determined that our son learn about more than just fly-fishing and hiking fourteeners."

"That's our girl," Mrs. Garcia said with a laugh.

"But in this case it's really all Lars," Marcus said.

"What time is the show?" Mrs. Garcia asked. "You're sure you'll get back on time?"

"Oh, it won't be a problem," Marcus assured them. "The opera starts at 1900. Air Force One is wheels down at Andrews at precisely 1736. We'll chopper back to the White House. The moment we touch down, my shift will be over. My tux is hanging in my locker. I'll grab a cab and meet them there. *Chick-chock*. No problem."

But there was a problem. The president's meeting with the evangelical leaders went long—very long—and by the time they got to the airport, Marcus knew he wasn't going to make it back to Washington on time.

42

Marcus called Elena from the tarmac.

"Don't worry; I may be a little late, but I'll make it," he insisted after explaining the situation. "I promise."

"It's okay—don't worry about it," Elena said gently. "How 'bout if we meet you there? I'll leave your ticket at will call."

"Thanks," Marcus said. "And, honey?"

"Yes?"

"I'm sorry."

"I know," she said. "Stay safe, and we'll see you soon."

Just then she started a sneezing fit.

"You okay?" he asked.

"I'm fine. Probably just allergies."

"You sure?"

"Yeah, yeah, I'm good. I love you, sweetheart."

"Love you, too," he whispered. "Gotta go."

They had come a long way. Elena had made her peace with his job and its challenges, and he was making far more of an effort to be a loving and attentive husband and father. It wasn't perfect. But it was working, and he was grateful.

He hung up the phone, checked in with the SAIC, received orders to board, and bounded up the stairs and took his seat. Ten minutes later, Air Force One surged down the runway. When he heard the landing gear retract, Marcus checked his watch again. They were forty-seven minutes behind schedule. He knew the pilots could make up some of that time in the air. They were going east, with the jet stream at their backs. Still, POTUS had nothing on his formal schedule that evening, which meant there was no particular reason the pilots needed to push. But worrying wouldn't get them there any faster. *Stress is a choice,* Marcus told himself. *Lay it down.*

He tilted his seat back, closed his eyes, and uttered another prayer that the pilots would make up lost time. He didn't exactly look forward to a night of opera, but he couldn't bear the thought of missing a single moment of such a special evening with Elena and Lars. He'd missed far too many already.

Lars took the news well.

Better than Elena had feared. After nearly a year of marriage counseling with Pastor Emerson and Maya, it was true that she had made her peace with Marcus's crazy job and crazier schedule. But Lars had not. He was struggling in school, drifting in class, underperforming on tests, and occasionally even getting into fights. The school psychologist said it was only preadolescence. Elena knew it was more. A boy needed the love and discipline and strong presence of his father in his life. It was no more complicated than that. But she was done being angry and worked hard to let go of her bitterness. These were the cards God had dealt them. She'd done herself and her marriage and her son no good complaining about her hand. She needed to be grateful and play them as best she could.

"Wow, you look amazing," she said as she adjusted Lars's bow tie. "Dad's going to be impressed."

"If he even shows up," the boy muttered.

Elena suppressed a sigh. At least Lars wanted to spend time with his dad, she told herself. Not all eleven-year-old boys did.

As Lars went to grab the car keys from a dish in the kitchen, Elena gave herself one last look in the mirror. Aside from a few wrinkles around her eyes, a few extra pounds, and a single gray hair she'd found just that morning—the occupational hazards of being a mom, she'd concluded—she didn't look half bad.

Her eyes were a bit red. She felt achy and a bit warm. She was afraid she was coming down with something, though she refused to let it slow her down, especially tonight. She loved the black cocktail dress and black pumps she was wearing. She loved her classic pearl necklace and earrings, the very ones she had bought herself in high school for special occasions. She was pleased that Marcus had cared enough to call her from the airport to give her an update. He hadn't always done that. But he was thinking about her, about them, and she was grateful.

"It'll only take a second, Lars," she assured him. "Don't worry. We won't be late."

After yet another sneezing fit, Elena pulled into a 7-Eleven a few blocks from their apartment to pick up some cold medicine. Lars wanted to stay in the car, but Elena insisted he come with her. It was still light out, but the corner of Eighth and E Streets in the southeast section of D.C. was no place for an eleven-year-old boy to be by himself on a Friday evening.

Lars complained all the way into the convenience store and then all the way up one aisle and down the other. He reminded her how heavy traffic would be, as if she hadn't ever driven in the city before. He reminded her of how hard it would be to find parking if they got to the Kennedy Center late. He couldn't argue they'd have a hard time getting decent seats, because Elena had already bought the tickets and Lars had chosen exactly where he wanted to sit—in the center, toward the front, of course. But he found other lines of attack and pressed them relentlessly.

Elena did her best to stay calm, if not exactly cheerful. She was feeling worse by the minute. Her eyes were watering. Her head was pounding. Lars's constant grumbling about almost everything concerning life in Washington was already driving her crazy. Tonight's riff was not helping. She didn't want to lose her patience, though. The last thing she wanted was to ruin this special evening. She knew Marcus's sayings about how stress was "all in her head" and she could "lay it down" at any moment. *Blah, blah, blah.* Maybe that worked in the Secret Service. She hadn't exactly found it such great advice when dealing with a preadolescent boy, especially when Dad was on the road. Instead, she said a quick prayer, finished filling her basket, and headed toward the cashier to pay and be gone.

Her heart sank when she saw five other people in line ahead of her, and it sank even further when Lars started saying she should have gone to Walgreens or CVS, which he insisted were "always faster." Elena started counting silently to fifty. She wasn't going to lose it. Marcus was constantly telling her to count to slow down her thoughts and steady her nerves. It was advice she never followed, but there was a first time for everything.

Just then, two young men—both in their late teens—entered the store. Both were dressed in dark-blue hoodies and sunglasses that obscured their faces, but to Elena they looked Hispanic. She immediately sensed something was wrong. Before she could figure out what to do, the two drew handguns and demanded that everyone stay where they were and not make any sudden moves.

43

"*Fork over all the cash in the drawer, Pops,*" one of them shouted at the African American man behind the register, tossing a small duffel bag on the counter.

Elena's heart was racing. She slowly reached for Lars, who just as slowly took her hand and squeezed it tightly.

"*Let's go, let's go; we don't got all night!*" the leader demanded, waving a pistol in the face of the terrified clerk.

The man's hands were trembling. He was trying to open the register, but it was taking too long.

"*Look at me, Pops. Look at me!*"

The gray-haired gentleman looked up. Elena could see the fear in his eyes and knew she had the same look in her own.

"*Now, I'm gonna count to three, and when I get to three, that register better be open, or I'm gonna shoot you in your brain. You got that?*"

The man nodded and immediately went back to work. The register finally popped open, and he began stuffing the duffel bag with cash.

"Move, move; come on, let's go," barked the leader, who then glanced back at his partner to make sure everything behind him was okay.

Elena glanced at him too. The kid was standing a few feet to her left, near the door. He was aiming his pistol at the line of customers, making sure none of them did anything stupid. At the same time he was constantly looking outside at a rusty green Plymouth Duster idling out front. Elena didn't have a good view of the driver, but she could tell he, too, was nervous by the way he kept revving the engine every few moments, like he was trying to signal his partners that they'd already been in there way too long.

She glanced at the door. It was less than ten feet away from them, and it was unlocked. Yes, it was being guarded by the kid to her left. But would he really shoot them if they suddenly bolted out of the store to safety? These punks were thieves, but were they cold-blooded murderers? Elena doubted it.

Elena knew exactly what Marcus would be doing if he were there. He'd have been armed, and she had no doubt he would have drawn down on these two and given them a single and clear ultimatum: drop their weapons or die. She also knew what he'd tell her: do whatever these hoodlums told them, stand still, stay calm, and don't try to be a hero. He was right, of course. It would be foolish to bolt. This would all be over in a moment.

What neither Elena nor the hoodlums had accounted for was the off-duty D.C. cop in the restroom. Hearing all the commotion, he slowly came out of the men's room and down the aisle behind them with his service weapon drawn.

"Police—hands up and no one dies!" he shouted.

The kid to Elena's left turned quickly to see who was behind him.

The moment his gun came around, the policeman fired three shots in a row. One went wide and blew out the glass door. Another struck the boy in the chest. The third hit him in the throat. The boy flew backward through the shattered glass and landed on the pavement.

The store erupted in gunfire as the leader wheeled around and began firing everything he had and the cop returned fire. When it was all over and the smoke cleared, the driver and the second gunman were gone, and four people lay dead—the kid in the hoodie, sprawled out on the pavement, the off-duty policeman, Lars, and Elena.

Air Force One landed early.

With the jet stream working for them, the pilots had made up the forty-seven minutes and more. Marcus couldn't believe his good fortune. But as the plane taxied to a stop, the special agent in charge came over to his seat and asked him if they could talk in private.

"Is there a problem, sir?" Marcus asked, anxious to get moving.

"I'm afraid there is," the SAIC said as the rest of the detail grabbed their carry-on bags and headed off the plane.

At first Marcus thought he was being relieved of duty. He'd never seen his supervisor look so somber or hesitate to say whatever was on his mind.

"Look, Marcus, there's no easy way to say this, so I'll just say it."

Marcus steeled himself for whatever was coming.

"There's been an incident."

"What do you mean?"

"A shooting, at a 7-Eleven in Southeast."

"And?"

"Elena was there, as was Lars."

Marcus froze. "But they're okay, right? Tell me they're all right."

The SAIC shook his head. "I'm sorry," he said. "I'm afraid they're not."

"What do you mean? What happened?"

"There was an off-duty cop in the store at the time. He drew his weapon. There was a gun battle. Elena and Lars were caught in the cross fire."

Marcus heard the words, but he didn't believe them. There was no way his wife and son were at a 7-Eleven in Southeast, he explained. They were meeting him at the Kennedy Center. He needed to get there himself. He couldn't be late.

"Marcus, they're dead," the SAIC said. "Both of them. I'm so sorry."

The SAIC drove.

They raced from Andrews into the city in a government sedan, lights flashing, siren blaring. Marcus couldn't hear it. All his training was failing him. He couldn't think clearly, couldn't count, couldn't focus, much less speak. This couldn't be real. It had to be a mistake. It had to be.

Finally the two men pulled up to the crime scene. A dozen police cars and several ambulances clogged the streets. A half-dozen TV news crews were covering the story live, their satellite trucks taking up nearly a city block. A D.C. detective met them and walked them over a sea of shattered glass to the blown-out front door of the convenience store. The body of the young gunman had already been removed, but his outline remained in the coagulating pool of blood.

"You sure you want to do this?" the detective asked before opening the door.

Marcus said nothing. The detective looked to the SAIC and back at Marcus, then led the two men inside.

What Marcus saw was worse than anything he had let himself imagine. Three bodies, each covered in blood-drenched sheets, lay where they had fallen. Bullet casings were everywhere. An empty handbasket, resting on its side, immediately caught his eye. Strewn about the filthy tile smudged with blood and dirt were unopened packages of DayQuil and Extra Strength Tylenol, a bag of Ricola, a three-pack of tissues, a Snickers—Lars's favorite—and a Dasani water bottle.

Crime scene investigators were still taking photographs, still taking measurements and detailed notes. All the initial interviews with witnesses had already been conducted by the detectives, and the wounded had been taken to the hospital to be treated for shock and various minor injuries. No one was left who had actually been present when the shooting began, no one Marcus could ask for details.

It didn't matter. Marcus hadn't come to solve a crime or even observe the aftermath of one. He had come for one simple, if unimaginable, purpose—to identify the bodies of the two people most precious to him in the world. So that's what he did.

Just a few inches away a woman's hand, cold and stiff, poked out from beneath a sheet. Marcus instantly recognized the rings. They were Elena's. He forced himself to kneel beside her body. His hands were shaking. Taking a deep breath, he slowly pulled back the sheet. There was Elena's face. Her eyes were closed. She looked like she was sleeping. She looked peaceful, so beautiful in her pearl earrings and necklace. Marcus saw blood. Then he pulled the sheet back farther and saw the damage. She'd been hit once in the chest and again in the stomach. His bottom lip quivered. He wanted to look away, but he couldn't. Marcus felt the SAIC's hand on his back, steadying him. Neither man said anything. What was there to say?

Marcus leaned down and kissed Elena on her forehead, then pulled the sheet up over her face and turned to the body next to her. Again, he slowly pulled back the sheet. Lars was lying facedown. Marcus could see the holes in the back of his tux. Blood was everywhere.

Slowly, carefully, he turned the boy over. His eyes were still open, and they looked so scared—haunted and alone. At this, Marcus lost it. He immediately shut Lars's eyes and cradled him in his arms and wept and wept.

The memorial service took place on a Thursday.

It really ought to have been cold and drizzling. Yet it was late June in the nation's capital, and the morning was dazzling, sunny and fresh. The skies were blue and laced with white, wispy clouds. The trees were lush and green, and every garden was in full and vibrant bloom. The humidity was surprisingly, refreshingly low, and there was a light breeze coming from the east as people entered Lincoln Park Baptist Church, just six blocks from the Rykers' apartment.

A rather large African American woman in her sixties knocked twice and popped her head into Carter Emerson's office.

"Whenever you're ready, Pastor," she said, her eyes somber behind her glasses. "Everyone's in place." She caught Carter's eye and nodded respectfully at Marcus, then backed out of the office and closed the door.

Marcus couldn't remember the woman's name. That bothered him.

They had met numerous times. She was in Elena's Bible study. She'd already brought a meal to his home this week. She and her family were pillars of the congregation. Marcus's ability to observe and recall the minutest of details was something he had always prided himself on, a skill that had served him well as a criminal investigator and federal agent. Yet now even simple things were slipping from his grasp. This morning he had forgotten the PIN for his ATM card. The previous night he'd forgotten the combination to the safe in his closet, not that it mattered. In putting him on indefinite paid leave, his SAIC had taken away both his service weapon and his personal weapon when he'd driven him home from the 7-Eleven that terrible night.

Perhaps Nick Vinetti had been right to insist on driving him to the church that morning. Nick, now deputy chief of mission in Moscow, had flown immediately to Washington when Pete Hwang had called him with the news. Both men had been staying with Marcus for the past few days, making sure he was eating and that he didn't do himself any harm. Marcus kept telling them he was fine. They didn't believe him. No one did.

"Let's pray a moment before we go out," Carter said.

Nick and Pete nodded and, following the pastor's lead, bowed their heads. Marcus did not. He just stared at his hands while Emerson talked to God. Right now Marcus was in no mood to pray.

When he heard the *amen*, Marcus rose and followed Carter out of the office and down the hall, with Nick and Pete tailing them. When they reached the sanctuary, Marcus was stunned. The pastor could and did draw quite an audience week after week, but Marcus had never seen the place packed to the rafters. There had to be more than five hundred people crammed into the pews and portable chairs and standing along the side and back walls, and every seat in the balcony sections was taken. It was a mixed group racially and professionally. Most were members of the church and the community in and around Eastern Market. Still, more than a hundred members of the United States Secret Service, including the director and assistant director, had come to pay their respects as well. Marcus even noticed that Senator Robert Dayton and his wife had come. Next to the senator's wife was Annie Stewart, the aide who had survived the attack in Kandahar.

The president and First Lady had, fortunately, chosen not to come, as had the vice president and his wife. Marcus had deeply appreciated receiving handwritten notes from each of them offering their condolences. The president's note had included a PS, explaining that he didn't want to create a security and logistical nightmare that might shift attention off of Elena and Lars and prove distracting for Marcus's family and friends. At this, Marcus had been immensely relieved. He hadn't wanted them to come for precisely the reasons the president had mentioned. But he wouldn't have dared insult them by asking them to stay away.

Marcus went to his assigned seat in the front row and hugged his mother, seated to his right. In the row behind them sat Marcus's two sisters, their husbands, and their children.

To his left were the Garcias. Javier looked numb. Elena's mother and her sisters—now in their twenties—were a mess. They kept dabbing their eyes with tissues and trying to keep their mascara from streaking, but to no avail. After greeting his own family, Marcus embraced them all, holding his mother-in-law as she sobbed. When the organist played the first notes of the opening hymn, Javier finally helped her into her seat, and the service began.

45

The funeral was mercifully short, and for Marcus most of it passed in a blur.

There were hymns and Scripture passages, and Carter gave a moving eulogy. Mr. Garcia spoke, choking back tears, as did one of Elena's sisters.

When the choir rose to sing the final hymn, everyone in the church stood—everyone, that was, except Marcus. He just stared at the two caskets and listened to the music without hearing it. He was furious with God. *How could he have allowed this to happen?* He was in no mood to be spiritual. But at last, when the choir reached the final stanza, he stood, joining the rest of the congregation. He loved his wife and son and didn't want to do anything that might dishonor their memory.

When the choir was finished, the pallbearers came forward, Nick and Pete among them. Bill McDermott stepped forward as well. He'd recently been appointed by the president to serve on the National

Security Council. Joining them were Marcus's SAIC and two special agents from the PPD. Together the six men walked each casket down the center aisle, one after the other, to a black hearse waiting out front.

The police escort to the cemetery was long. The burial service itself was short, for family and close friends only, as Marcus had requested. When the caskets were lowered into the ground, the group returned to the church for a reception of light snacks and soft drinks in the fellowship hall. Marcus and the families greeted all who came, chatting and reminiscing with each of them until Pastor Emerson eventually came up, apologized for the interruption, and asked Marcus to step into his office.

"Thought you might need a break," Carter said when they were behind closed doors. He suggested they sit a spell, then made them both some coffee from a Keurig machine behind his desk. Marcus took the mug, nodding his thanks, but didn't take a sip. He just stared into the steam.

"How you holding up?" Carter asked.

Marcus shrugged.

"Looks like you've got something on your mind, son."

That was true, but Marcus wasn't sure he wanted to say it aloud. Maybe it was better to get back to the reception. Most people had gone, but there were still some lingering. He needed to show his gratitude to everyone who had come, needed to listen to every memory about Elena and Lars they wanted to share. It wasn't perfunctory. He didn't simply feel duty bound to be polite. Rather, he found himself deeply moved by listening to each person share memories. He wanted to reflect and remember. And it was better than him having to talk.

"They all get it," Carter said as if reading his mind. "They'll wait. Believe me. Nobody's going nowhere."

This man was old enough to be his grandfather, Marcus thought. He needed a grandfather just then, someone older and wiser who could show him how to function, how to put one foot in front of the other when all he really wanted to do was hide away in his apartment and shut the whole world out. Someone who knew what he was going through. Carter Emerson had never lost a wife. He and Maya had been married almost fifty-five years. But their daughter, Alicia, had been murdered when she was just seventeen. It came up from time to time in his sermons. Carter was open about how the loss had almost caused him to walk away from Maya and the ministry. He was also a Vietnam vet and had lost some of his closest friends in the war. Those wounds were not fresh, but they were deep. This was a man of sorrows, Marcus knew. He'd been through the valley and come out okay.

"Maybe so, Pastor," Marcus said at last. "But I guarantee you there's not a soul out there who ever imagined I would outlive Elena and Lars. Not a one."

Carter sipped his coffee without comment. After a while, Marcus got up and walked over to the bookshelves. The office was lined with them, wall to wall, top to bottom. Marcus scanned the titles—the tomes of theology and eschatology, the biographies of great pastors and preachers and missionaries, the writings of the church fathers, the works on counseling and rearing children and handling finances and choosing elders and shepherding a congregation.

Finally Marcus turned and went to the window. He drew aside one of the white cotton curtains and looked out on the parking lot. Only a handful of cars remained. He thought again what he had thought during the service. *How could God have let this happen?* He was still angry, still hurting. But a new thought began to work its way around the edges of Marcus's rage, and with it came a new target for his wrath.

"I've spent my whole life protecting people," Marcus said as he stared out at a large oak tree outside the window, flush with green leaves. "I've guarded generals and senators, presidents and prime ministers. I've risked my life to protect my country and our allies. But in the end I couldn't protect the two people I love the most. What does that say about me?"

PART
SIX

Some time later

NOVO-OGARYOVO, RUSSIA—15 JUNE

"It's time, Oleg Stefanovich—we are going to war."

The president pushed back from the dining table, wiped his mouth with a white cloth napkin, tossed an unfinished piece of sausage to his black Lab, Nikita, and strode straight out the French doors and across the lawn to the chopper spooling up on the helipad. Luganov had finished his morning routine—an hour in the gym, an hour in the pool, and a hearty breakfast of fresh black coffee, freshly squeezed orange juice, an omelet made of quail eggs, and a side of cottage cheese. Now Aleksandr Luganov had called for a meeting of his inner circle back in Moscow at precisely noon, and he was not a man willing to be late.

Oleg did not get up from the table immediately. He was still reeling from the astonishing plan his father-in-law had just laid out for him. Over the years, Oleg had tried hard to close his eyes to the man's history of saying and doing the morally dubious. But what Luganov was describing now was downright insane. He was actually talking about invading not one but three NATO countries, doing so simultaneously, and launching this brazen and unprovoked attack soon—within a matter of months—before Brussels, much less Washington, had a chance to know what was coming. Luganov had hinted at and alluded to such ideas before. Oleg had heard him ask questions of his generals and intelligence officials that suggested he was giving some thought to such madness. But Oleg had never taken any of it seriously. Until now.

Oleg turned and stared out the window as the president was saluted by an honor guard and boarded the helicopter. Oleg berated himself for remaining silent throughout the one-sided discussion. He had not raised any objection nor even asked a question. Yet how was he supposed to respond to such a plan? He was counselor to a man who neither sought nor brooked any counsel other than his own. Surely Petrovsky and Nimkov would see it as madness, he tried to assure himself. If anyone could wave the president off such a scheme, it would be one or both of them.

Oleg badly needed a cigarette, but clearly there wasn't going to be time for that. The whine of the rotors pierced the vast rooms of the mansion, and Oleg knew he needed to get moving. The clearest sign that this plan was not a whim but something Luganov was actively weighing was the fact that he was heading back to the Kremlin to meet with his war cabinet. These days his father-in-law seemed increasingly annoyed by any time he had to spend with his cabinet or senior staff. In recent months he had routinely canceled meetings and asked for senior officials to route written questions through his chief of staff or through Oleg himself. Oleg often found himself drafting replies to this neverending flood of queries on every manner of subject. Professionally, this made Oleg a more valuable advisor than ever. He had more access to the president than almost any other human being. Strategically, however, he was worried. The president was slowly yet steadily narrowing his inner circle. He was getting input from fewer and fewer people. The minister of defense, army chief of staff, and the head of the FSB still had a great deal of access and were summoned—or at least tele-phoned—more than most. Those officials who handled such mundane matters as the budget or infrastructure or education got almost no time from the president at all.

As Luganov increasingly withdrew from the petty nuisance of meeting with subordinates, he spent less and less time in his office. Occasionally it was unavoidable, such as when various world lead-ers came to see him. Then the police would block off highways and side streets so his motorcade could whisk him to the Kremlin. Other times, like today, he would chopper in, an arrangement that allowed him to spend more and more time working out of Novo-Ogaryovo, his immense palace west of the city, valued at over $200 million.

Often his mistress stayed there as well. This made it exceedingly awkward when Luganov insisted that Oleg sleep there so they could work late. Katya Slatsky was at least thirty-five years the president's junior. The girl was stunningly beautiful, to be sure. But she was young enough to be the man's daughter. Indeed, she was actually younger than Marina, who hated the whore who had replaced her mother with an intensity that only Oleg saw. Marina had never expressed or even hinted at such feelings to her father. Whether this was out of love or fear, Oleg could not say. Fortunately, Katya had not been there last night, and Luganov had been all business.

The fact that the president was not only willing but eager to go back to the Kremlin meant this war plan—as dangerous as it was—had become a top priority. So Oleg forced himself to his feet and headed to the chopper, and soon they were off the ground and banking eastward for the capital.

When they landed inside the walls of the Kremlin, they headed straight for the conference room adjacent to Luganov's office. The war cabinet was already assembled and waiting. They all stood when the president entered the room and sat only when he took his seat at the head of the table. In the past, Oleg had sat in a chair behind the presi-dent and to the left of the chief of staff. But ever since his promotion to chief counselor, he sat at the main table with the principals, at the end directly opposite his father-in-law.

"Gentlemen, the time has come to restore the true glory of Mother Russia," Luganov began. "This means bringing ethnic Russians outside our fold back under our care, retaking lands that are rightfully ours, humiliating the West, and proving that the U.S. and NATO are paper tigers and that Russia is the sole and dominant power on the earth."

47

Luganov had their attention now.

Everyone grunted approval. Yet as Luganov explained his plan, Oleg saw many of the expressions change ever so discreetly.

What the president was proposing was a full invasion and occupation of Estonia, Latvia, and Lithuania, followed by formal annexation of each. Immediately afterward, snap elections would be held whereby the populations of the Baltic states would vote to rejoin the Russian Federation—voluntarily, Luganov insisted—so they could "enjoy all the rights and privileges of being full Russian citizens."

Luganov said he wanted to launch his blitzkrieg using twenty-seven battalions—roughly twenty-one thousand soldiers—to seize Estonia and Latvia. Based on his calculations, he believed they could reach and capture the capitals of Tallinn and Riga in just sixty hours. He said another fifteen battalions—nearly twelve thousand troops—would be needed to wrest control of Lithuania. He proposed attacking through

Belarus and from the Russian territory of Kaliningrad, west of Lithuania and north of Poland. He believed they'd need another two days to capture and adequately control the Lithuanian capital of Vilnius.

At this point the president opened a leather binder and handed out copies of a ten-page war plan he had drafted himself. He walked his team through the document. The first few pages laid out specific tactical objectives such as roads, power plants, and cities that needed to be taken, by which battalions, and by what specific dates and times. It also laid out a time frame that nearly made Oleg's jaw drop. The president wanted to launch the attack no later than the end of October. That was just four months away.

The next few pages included maps and suggested routes of attack. The last two pages raised specific questions to which the president said he expected detailed answers by their next meeting, set for the following day. Luganov wanted to know from his foreign minister whether he believed the president of Belarus would agree to a snap joint military exercise inside his territory and what kind of sweeteners might be needed to get Minsk on board. He wanted to know how quickly the defense minister could put together exercises for a hundred thousand or more troops on the border of Ukraine in order to divert attention and make it seem like he might actually go for a full invasion not of the Baltics but rather Ukraine in the hopes of seizing Kiev, which he had recently and very publicly called "the mother of all Russian cities."

From the chief of the air force he wanted to know how many squadrons of bombers and fighter jets he could safely move from the Eastern Military District near China to the Western MD without creating a significant vulnerability on the eastern front, how quickly this could be accomplished, and whether it could be done discreetly enough not to immediately draw the attention of the Pentagon. From his FSB chief he wanted to know what kind of progress had been made in surreptitiously providing automatic weapons, ammunition, and explosives to Russian loyalists in each of the Baltic republics and whether they had the proper communications equipment to be mobilized when the time was right.

For several minutes the room was silent, and from Oleg's vantage point quite tense, while the men absorbed the plan and considered the implications for the nation and for themselves. The chief of the army was the first to raise his hand, and the president actually looked pleased to take the general's question.

"Mr. President, just to be certain I understand: you are asking us to seize Tallinn and Riga in sixty hours?" he asked.

The question made it clear to Oleg that this was the first time the army's most senior and experienced commander was hearing of the plan.

"Yes," Luganov confirmed. "And Vilnius within another forty-eight hours."

"You are asking us to capture and occupy three NATO capitals?"

"And secure their annexation so that they might be rightfully reintegrated into Mother Russia," the president said.

"But not Kiev."

"Not right now."

"Would it not be in our interest to seize all of Ukraine instead?" asked the general. "The Ukrainians are very patriotic, and they're able fighters, but they are not members of NATO. Washington and Brussels will huff and puff, but in the end they will do nothing if we take Ukraine. I have war-gamed this with my staff. I'm convinced we could get it done in a month to six weeks."

"But we can have the Baltics in four days," Luganov replied with a rare but telling smile.

Again the room was quiet. Then the army chief of staff pressed forward. "How is it in Russia's interest, if I may ask, to provoke such a confrontation with NATO when Ukraine is ours for the taking with no risk of triggering Article 5?"

Oleg saw the smile disappear instantly from the president's face.

The general was speaking of the mutual-defense pact that lay at the heart of the North Atlantic Treaty Organization's charter. Article 5 stated that each member of NATO would consider an attack against one member state to be an attack against all. Any hostile action against any NATO member would, therefore, obligate the entire alliance to bring its combined political, economic, and military power to bear to repulse such an attack. No state was alone to fend off the Bear by itself. It was all for one and one for all. During the Soviet era, Oleg knew, it was this very alliance that had stopped Russian leaders from invading any part of Europe, lest they trigger war with the West that could all too easily go nuclear. Now Luganov was proposing to invade three NATO countries simultaneously.

"General, are you afraid of NATO?" Luganov fumed, his face growing red as he leaned forward in his chair. "I am not. Just the opposite. I believe they are afraid of me, and rightly so. They are fat and lazy. They are weak and divided. Their day is over. Our day has come. We are strong and getting stronger. We have modernized our strategic forces. We have rebuilt our conventional forces, all while they have downsized their own. So we will storm into the Baltics with such speed and force that the leaders in the White House and at SHAPE headquarters and around the globe will shake in fear. They will not know what has just hit them. They won't dare threaten us with nuclear war, for they know I am willing to unleash our nuclear power upon them. And when this simple truth dawns on them—that I am a man of action and they are cowards—they will surrender the Baltics without a fight, and that, gentlemen, will be the end of NATO. If they do not trigger Article 5— and I guarantee you they will not—then I will have won a great victory for our people. We will be the world's only superpower, the only nation on the planet that has a great military *and* the courage to use it. I alone will have the power to dictate economic and political terms to the West, and we will see riches and glory unparalleled since the days of the czars."

The day started just like any other.

Marcus Ryker woke before dawn and ran his usual five miles. Returning to his apartment in Eastern Market, he showered, threw on a pair of ripped jeans, a denim work shirt, and steel-toed boots, and walked to a diner a few blocks from Capitol Hill. There he sat alone in a booth in the back and ordered scrambled eggs, dry toast, and black coffee. He read the *Post* from cover to cover, then, unable to take any more bad news, trudged over to Lincoln Park Baptist Church.

For the last few weeks, he'd been helping put a much-needed new roof on the 137-year-old building. By noon the sun was beating down from a cloudless sky, and Marcus was drenched with sweat. He took a swig from his water bottle, checked his watch, and decided he could still get another twenty to thirty minutes of work in before stopping to wash up for his weekly lunch with Carter Emerson and some vets who attended the church. They didn't talk about war. They didn't talk about loss. They certainly didn't talk about politics or women. Most of the conversations were about whether the Nats were still in contention for the play-offs and whether the Redskins—or in Marcus's case, the Broncos—had any shot at all at a winning season, to say nothing of going to the Super Bowl.

Marcus was bending over to retrieve his hammer when Nan Warren shouted to him and asked if he could come down a few minutes early. Nan was Carter Emerson's secretary. She was the one whose name Marcus had blanked on the day of the memorial service. Yet for at least three months after Elena and Lars's deaths, she had faithfully brought him a home-cooked meal, usually meat loaf, always on Mondays. Her husband, Jim, was one of the vets Marcus had lunch with on Wednesdays. They had all become friends.

"Be right there," Marcus called back. He assumed Carter wanted to see him before the lunch meeting.

Though he'd never let on, he felt a pang of annoyance at being summoned early. There were already forecasts of big thunderstorms rolling in over the next few days. If he was ever going to get this roof done, he needed fewer breaks and more focus. Yet that wasn't the way Carter and his team rolled. "Jesus wasn't about projects; he was about people," Carter would say with a hearty laugh whenever Marcus mentioned his concern about the roof's progress. "Love your neighbor, not your work."

Marcus didn't care much for such platitudes. A big part of the reason he was working on the roof was to avoid people. Then again, he was pretty sure Carter was onto him and was intentionally trying to get him engaged with as many people as possible. That had to be why he'd asked Marcus to do odd jobs around the church in the first place, starting on the very day Marcus had turned in his letter of resignation to the Secret Service. It also had to be why Carter was always calling him down from the roof to "have some lemonade together" or "meet a brother" or fix a clogged toilet or listen to and critique the latest draft of his next sermon or have a slice of Maya's "crazy-good key lime pie." As annoying as it was sometimes, Marcus was also grateful. This man and his dear wife loved him and were doing their best to keep him from hitting rock bottom.

After descending the ladder and taking a few minutes to wash his hands and face, Marcus exited the lavatory in the church basement and went to the third floor, where Nan was sitting at her desk.

"Go right on in, young man," she said with a warm smile. "He's waiting for you."

When Marcus rapped on the door, heard a hearty "Come in," and stepped into Carter's cluttered office, he was caught off guard to find they were not alone. Sitting on the couch along the back wall near the windows was Robert Dayton, the senior senator from Iowa, wearing a seersucker suit and a pale-blue bow tie that made Marcus think of his father-in-law. Sitting in a wooden chair to his right was Annie Stewart, wearing a black-and-white-striped sweater jacket over a white blouse, black slacks, and black flats. The last time he'd seen them was at the memorial service.

"Marcus," said the senator, standing and putting out his hand.

"Senator," Marcus replied, shaking it and then the woman's. "Miss Stewart."

"Please call me Annie," she said.

Marcus nodded and they stood for a moment in an awkward silence. Everyone was looking at Marcus, but he had no intention of saying more. He was being ambushed. Everyone in the room knew it, and he wasn't exactly happy about it. Then Carter piped up and encouraged them all to sit.

"Annie called me this morning," the pastor began. "Said she'd been trying to reach you but to no avail. Everything okay, Marcus? Phone working properly?"

It was true. She'd left three voice messages and sent two emails and a text. Marcus had responded to none of them.

"Everything's fine, sir," Marcus replied. "And, Miss Stewart— Annie—please forgive me. I wasn't trying to be rude. I simply wasn't interested in meeting with the senator. But clearly we've now passed that point."

Annie leaned forward to say something, but the senator took the lead. "Marcus, I know you've been out of the game for some time, and I respect your reasons," he explained. "But I'm heading for Europe in a few days, and I'd like you to come with me."

"That's very kind, but I need to pass."

"Come on, son," Carter said. "Don't be so quick to say no. We're all friends here. You've known the senator for years. Hear the man out."

49

Marcus looked at his pastor, then back at the senator.

"You're running for president," he said. It wasn't a question but a statement.

"Perhaps," Dayton replied.

"You are. You've formed a PAC and socked away over eight million dollars."

Dayton raised an eyebrow, clearly surprised he knew such things or cared. "Seven and change, but yes, we'll be at eight by the end of the month."

"Not hard to do when you're a member of the Senate Finance Committee and the ranking member on the Intelligence Committee," Marcus noted. "You just happen to hail from the state that holds the nation's first caucuses, and you're rising in the early polls, though they hardly mean much. It's all about name recognition at this stage."

Dayton was too smooth to take the bait. "Look, Marcus, I'm heading to Europe because I'm worried about Aleksandr Luganov," he countered. "More people in this town ought to be, President Clarke among them."

Marcus said nothing.

"America's next president needs to understand that as troubled as the Middle East is and as volatile as North Korea remains, the most serious threat facing the United States—the truly existential threat—comes from Russia," Dayton continued. "It's the Russians who actually have enough nuclear warheads to annihilate 330 million Americans. It's the Russians who actually have the ICBMs to deliver those warheads to our cities. And it's the Russians who are being led by a man who will stop at nothing to rebuild the glory of Mother Russia—hack computers, buy politicians, engage in elaborate disinformation campaigns, arm our worst enemies, even invade small nations in order to intimidate great ones."

"And?" Marcus asked, wondering why any of this should matter to him.

"And the man who is sitting in the White House right now either doesn't get it or—how shall I put this delicately?—demonstrates insufficient concern."

"And?"

"And I think it's time to go over and meet some of our friends in London, Brussels, and Berlin and take a firsthand look at how ready NATO would be to confront Luganov if there were a new leader in the White House, someone who took the Russian threat a tad more seriously," Dayton said. "I'm leaving Friday afternoon with some of my senior staff, and I'd very much like you to come with me."

"Why?"

"You've worked on plenty of high-level delegations abroad. You know the protocol, and you know the security needs and the logistics."

"With all due respect, sir, plenty of people in this town have done that and more. As you say, I'm out of the game, and honestly I have no interest in getting back in."

The senator looked to Annie.

"Peter Hwang recommended you," she said.

The mention of his old Marine buddy blindsided him. "Pete? What does he have to do with anything?"

Annie looked back at the senator.

"Dr. Hwang has joined my staff as a senior policy advisor."

"On foreign policy?"

"No, that's Annie's portfolio," Dayton said. "Dr. Hwang is helping me develop a health care plan and a strategy for reforming the VA, along with several other matters. He started with me a couple of months ago. When I told him about this trip, he urged me to take you along."

"Senator, I'm flattered, but you can find someone younger to carry your bags."

"I don't need someone to carry my bags; I need someone to watch my back," the senator said.

"No one in Washington has been more outspoken against Luganov than the senator," Annie interjected. "He's called him out on the invasion of Georgia and Crimea, plus everything the Russians have been doing in Syria and with Iran, not to mention hacking our elections, throwing dissidents in jail, making reporters disappear . . ."

Still Marcus didn't bite.

"Look, Marcus, everyone knows I'm seriously looking at running for president," Dayton said. "Everyone knows foreign policy will be a major component of my campaign, and when I run—*if* I run—I'll be running directly against Luganov. The man is not just a menace. He poses a clear and present danger to the security of the United States, NATO, and the free world, and that danger is growing. Now, at present I don't have a security team. Pete is insisting that I start to build one. He wants me to start with you, and I agree. I'd very much like you to come on this trip. Keep us all safe, and give me your take on the security situation in Europe while you're at it. That's it. I'm not asking you to join my team full-time. No long-term commitment. Just a robust retainer along with first-class airfare and first-class accommodations.

As you rightly note, we have some money in the PAC. Let me use some of it on you, and then you can be back fixing roofs in no time. What do you say?"

Marcus had no interest. He didn't agree with Dayton on almost any issue of domestic policy. He could only imagine what nonsense Pete was going to cook up for him. That said, he did share the man's concerns about Luganov and found him a credible voice on matters of national security—one of the few in the Democratic Party. He also appreciated that neither the senator nor Miss Stewart had brought up the deaths of Elena and Lars in the conversation. They were treating him as a professional, not out of pity. That was classy and, in his experience, all too rare.

Standing, he thanked them both for the offer but politely declined. Then he shook their hands and took his leave, heading back up to the roof. He would skip lunch with the vets. He'd already had far more human contact than he'd wanted for the day. To his relief, Carter did not come find him after the senator left to prod him to reconsider or even to invite him to lunch. That gave Marcus a good six more hours on the roof, alone with his iTunes and his earbuds.

It was well past seven o'clock when he finally headed back to his apartment alone.

And someone was waiting for him.

50

"You look terrible," Pete Hwang said with a smile.

"You look worse, believe me," Marcus replied as he approached the front steps of his building. "I should have expected you'd be here."

"You're losing your edge, old man."

"I probably am," Marcus conceded as he led Pete upstairs, unlocked his front door, and let them both in. "But Dayton? Really? I didn't take you as that desperate."

Pete shrugged. "What can I say? The man made me an offer I couldn't refuse."

"But he's an arrogant gasbag."

"He's a politician."

"My point exactly."

"Fair enough, but at least he's a principled gasbag."

"At least," Marcus said as he tossed his keys on the counter and urged Pete to make himself at home. "But come on, you can't really want Bob Dayton to be the next president of the United States, can you?"

"Point me to someone better and I'll sign on tomorrow." Pete loosened his tie, set his briefcase on a chair, and plopped onto the couch and put his feet up on the coffee table.

Marcus grabbed two bottles of beer from the fridge, handed one to Pete, and put the other by his La-Z-Boy. Then he went back to the kitchen, found a can of mixed nuts in the pantry, opened it, and set it on the coffee table. He slumped in his recliner and reached for the remote. "For crying out loud, Pete, the man's a socialist."

"He's not a socialist."

"Oh yeah, then what is he?"

"A progressive."

"You mean a liberal."

"But an honest liberal."

"I grant you that—he's honest and a good family man—but seriously, does he even have a real shot?"

"To shape the debate? Absolutely. To win? I don't know. But hey, he's rising in the polls. It's just name ID right now, but if he wins Iowa and picks up a head of steam going into New Hampshire, who knows? Ask me again in a few months."

"Well, tell him to drop the bow ties. He looks ridiculous."

"What are you talking about? Your father-in-law wears bow ties. I thought you liked them."

"Javier Garcia is a highly sought-after corporate trial lawyer, Pete. Nobody cares what he wears, so long as he wins. Your man wants to be the next commander in chief. I'm telling you, drop the bow ties."

"Fair enough. I'll see what I can do."

"Good. Now, tell me you didn't really sign on to do domestic policy for him," Marcus said, turning on the TV and flipping through the channels.

"Of course I did," said Pete, taking his first sip of his beer.

"Full-time?"

"You betcha."

"And you're really leaving your practice?"

"Done."

"But why? I mean, after you left the Marines, you became one of the best cardiologists in the country. Why give all that up?"

"Boredom."

"But you're finally making real money for the first time in your life."

"I'm bored out of my mind, Marcus. And with the divorce final, most of what I make is just going to alimony, after Uncle Sam gets his bite, so really, what's the point?"

"I'm sorry about Jane."

"Hey, what can you do? I should have seen it coming."

"You were a good husband and a great dad."

"Some things aren't meant to be."

Marcus was silent for a moment. Then he switched the channel to the Nats game. The two men watched the entire second inning without saying anything. The Nats were playing the Texas Rangers, and there was no score yet.

"So you're moving to Des Moines?" Marcus asked when a truck ad came on.

"Actually, I just got an apartment here. Moved in a few days ago."

"Here in D.C.?"

"Georgetown."

"That's cool."

"So we're finally neighbors."

"The campaign's going to be run from here, not Iowa?"

"The PAC is run from here, and technically that's who pays me. We'll see what happens if he pulls the trigger. Right now he's just in an exploratory phase."

"Did you let your apartment in San Diego go? I love that place."

"Me, too—no, I'll hold on to it," Pete replied.

"That's the first sensible thing you've said so far."

"For now, I'm subletting it to one of my nephews. He's a sophomore at San Diego State."

Marcus took another pull on his beer.

"Look, buddy, you want the truth?" Pete asked.

His tone had suddenly changed. Marcus had heard it before. He muted the television and turned to look at his friend. "Sure, what's the matter?"

"Nothing's the matter; it's just . . ."

"What?"

"I don't know, man. It's just that when Jane moved out, she went back to Westport. She's got custody of the kids. She took the furniture. I tried to keep living in the apartment, but I couldn't stay. Too many memories. Too many ghosts."

"I'm so sorry."

"What can you do?" Pete said again, returning to his beer.

"Anything but politics," Marcus quipped.

"Yeah, right—you spent the best years of your life in the White House."

"Not doing politics."

"Same difference."

"It *is* different—the Service is scrupulously apolitical."

"Okay, but I've been *scrupulously apolitical* my whole life, and where has it gotten me? The country's in trouble, Marcus, serious trouble. Someone needs to get us back on the right track—or try, anyway. The senator's offered me a shot on developing serious reforms, especially on health care and the VA. I decided it was now or never."

"Go with never."

Pete ignored him and changed the subject. "So, I understand you saw Annie today."

"Yeah. Why?"

"What do you mean, *why*?" Pete asked. "You don't find her attractive?"

"Pete, you just got divorced."

"Which means I'm back on the market, my friend."

Marcus snorted, shook his head, and turned back to his beer and the game.

"Anyway, none of this is the point," Pete said, munching on some cashews.

"So what is?" It was top of the third. The Nats were rallying. They had runners on first and third with only one out.

"You should come with us. Say yes to Dayton."

"Why?" Marcus asked as the Nats' lead-off hitter came to the plate.

"To get out of the house."

"I get out of the house."

"No, Marcus, really out. You need a break, a change of pace, of scenery."

"Like you?"

"Believe me, buddy, you need it even more than I do."

"I'm fine, Pete. But thanks for the concern."

"No, Marcus, you're not fine. You're depressed and stuck in the mud."

Marcus looked at his friend. "No, I'm not—not anymore."

"Yeah, you are, and I'm worried about you. You're not getting past this thing, and you need to."

"Getting past it?" Marcus asked, suddenly angry. "My wife and kid are dead. I'm not getting past anything."

"I know, and I'm sorry—it's unspeakable what happened to you," Pete said. "But it's not going to get any better by quitting your job, avoiding your friends, dodging your family, and not answering your phone or emails. I mean, seriously, when was the last time you went back to Colorado?"

Marcus shrugged.

"When's the last time you talked to the Garcias? Or your mom?"

Marcus said nothing at first, just finished off his beer. "It's been a few months, but—"

"I get it, okay? I do. I'm a doctor, and I'm your friend. And I'm telling you—you can't just shut down and hide from the world. When Jane left, I felt like someone had kicked me in the stomach. And yes, I was devastated and furious. I stopped eating. Lost twenty pounds. But I finally realized I needed a change—a change of scenery, a change of pace, people, everything. And, Marcus, I'm telling you, you need one too."

51

Marcus said nothing.

He just stared at the TV as batter after batter struck out, stranding two runners on base.

"The senator called me a few hours ago—he said you told him no," Pete continued. "I said I'd take another run at you. So here I am. Come on, Marcus. You know Brussels and Berlin better than anyone. You've certainly been there with the president and VP enough times over the years."

It was true. Marcus thought about the last time he'd done an advance for a G7 summit in London but then stopped as abruptly as he'd started. He looked at Pete. "*Us?*"

"Sorry?" Pete asked.

"You said come with *us*," Marcus repeated. "The senator didn't say anything about you going."

"He only asked me after you said no," Pete admitted, setting down his beer and sitting forward on the couch. "Come on, man, what do you say?"

Marcus looked back at the television. Now the Rangers were rallying. The first batter up hit a double. The second hit a triple on a high fastball.

"All right, I'll go," he said finally, turning the television completely off and facing Pete directly. "On three conditions."

"Who are you? Aladdin?"

"You gonna hear me out or not?"

"Fine—name your price."

"First, skip London, Brussels, and Berlin—been there, done that. It doesn't get you anything. Go to Kiev, Tallinn, Riga, and Vilnius instead."

"Why?" asked a bewildered Pete. "Most Americans can't even locate those cities on a map."

"That's precisely why," Marcus said. "If the senator's real concern is the threat posed by Russia, then go talk to people who actually feel threatened by Russia. The British don't. Neither do the Belgians or the Germans. They ought to, but they don't."

"Go on. I'm listening."

"Every politician with national ambitions goes to 10 Downing Street, especially if you're on the Intelligence Committee. But who ever talks to our most exposed and vulnerable allies? I worked on the PPD for years. We never once went to the Baltics. Yet I hear Luganov just ordered exercises in the Western Military District. And the Ukrainians? After the whole thing in Crimea, everyone's forgotten about them. But the Russians have massed something like fifty thousand troops on the Ukrainian border, maybe more. They're saying it's only an exercise, but what if it really is the prelude to an invasion? So get ahead of the story. Meet with the leaders in Kiev. Go see the Ukrainian troops on the front. Take your buddies from CNN and the rest and go make some news."

"Interesting," Pete conceded. "Keep going."

"Second, go to Moscow."

"I beg your pardon?"

"You heard me. Ask for a meeting with Luganov, in the Kremlin, one-on-one."

"Marcus, have you lost your mind? Luganov and Dayton hate each other. Everyone knows that."

"All the more reason to meet with him, mano a mano."

"Are you going to be the food taster?"

"If I need to be."

"Marcus, this guy once ordered his people to slip radioactive poison in the tea of one of his political enemies."

Unfortunately, Marcus knew, that was true. "You want your man to make headlines, right, to show himself a leader?"

"Right."

"Then lead," Marcus insisted. "No one else has the guts to confront Luganov. So Dayton should get in his face and tell him he's leading his country down the path of ruin unless he changes course. *Then* fly to Brussels and meet with the leaders of NATO and tell them that unless they get serious about increasing their defense budgets, they're inviting more Russian aggression in Europe. *Then* come back to Washington and introduce a bill that imposes sweeping new economic sanctions on Moscow and that adds another $100 billion to the Pentagon's budget."

"Uh, Marcus, you seem to forget one thing."

"What's that?"

"My guy is a Democrat."

"All the more reason for him to set himself apart from the appeasement wing of his party. You want to make news, my friend? That'll make news."

Pete sat back, trying to process it all. "Why would Luganov ever say yes to such a meeting?" he asked after a moment.

"To look tough."

"What do you mean?"

"To squash your guy like a bug."

"Thanks a lot."

"I'm serious," Marcus said. "Who is a bigger Russia hawk in the

United States Senate than Bob Dayton? The man constantly sounds like he's ready to start a war with Luganov. Never misses a chance to denounce the Kremlin when they deserve it and arguably even when they don't. No one would expect him to ask for a meeting with Luganov, and no one would ever expect Luganov to say yes, which is probably why he will—either to woo him and charm him or to intimidate him and make him look like a deer in the headlights or to try to make your guy look like a hotheaded blowhard prone to hyperbole and overreaction."

"Then again, if Dayton walks away looking like a serious statesman . . ."

"Now you're getting the picture," Marcus said.

Pete finished his beer and looked at his friend. "So that's what you've been doing, all holed up in this apartment."

"What?"

"Everyone's worried about you, myself included. But maybe you're not in here grieving. Maybe you're plotting political strategy."

"I have been grieving, Pete," Marcus said quietly. "Doesn't mean I'm depressed."

"I'm not so sure," Pete replied. "But whatever you've been up to, you've given me better ideas in the last five minutes—and for free, mind you—than I've given him over the last two months for . . . well, let's just say not for free. So what's your third condition? I'm pretty sure the senator's going to jump at the first two."

Marcus smiled for the first time.

"Promise me that when we get to Moscow, you and I go see Nick and grab a beer."

The group took off from Washington Dulles on Friday afternoon.

They did not fly commercial but rather on a Learjet leased through the political action committee. Joining the senator were his chief of staff, his press secretary, Annie Stewart, Pete Hwang, Marcus, and four former Secret Service members whom Marcus had personally recruited and retained on behalf of the PAC to provide security. Two additional former agents were already on the ground in Kiev, arranging hotel rooms and transportation.

Marcus knew full well that he and the other former agents would hardly be able to guarantee the thorough and airtight protection package they all used to provide heads of state. But no American leader as outspoken as the senator on the grave threat posed by Russia could afford not to take at least basic precautions.

Pete had also convinced Dayton to switch out his bow ties for a good old-fashioned Windsor knot, another small but noteworthy sign to Marcus that Dayton wasn't simply "exploring" a run for president. He was already flat-out running.

They arrived in Kiev just after 9 a.m. Saturday, local time.

The senator and his team were picked up in two armored Chevy Suburbans, driven by the former agents Marcus had sent on ahead, and taken to the Hilton on Tarasa Shevchenka Boulevard. After checking in, showering, and changing, the team drove past several lovely parks along the Dnieper River before passing through security gates, continuing up a hill, and arriving at the enormous and historic Mariyinsky Palace. There, they were taken immediately to the green reception room, as elegant as it was ornate, where they were received by Ukrainian president Dmitri Dovzhenko under a large crystal chandelier.

"Senator Dayton, thank you for coming to Kiev—you are most welcome," Dovzhenko began as a small group of Ukrainian and American reporters and photographers recorded the moment.

"It's an honor to be here, Mr. President, especially now," Dayton said as the cameras clicked away.

"Your support for us in the U.S. Senate means a great deal to us, as does your willingness to come all this way to meet with me. The situation on our eastern border is growing critical, and we need faithful friends like yourself."

"In such times as these, we need good leaders with great courage, do we not?" asked the senator.

"We do indeed."

"The words of Sir Winston Churchill come to mind," Dayton said, playing for the cameras. "'The belief that security can be obtained by throwing a small state to the wolves is a fatal delusion.'"

"Hear, hear."

"Mr. President," Dayton continued, "I cannot account for why the

White House isn't doing more to stand with you, but I vow to do my best to push our president and my colleagues in the Senate to do as much as possible. This is why I've come."

Dovzhenko bade the members of the press corps farewell, then led the senator and his aides through a side door to a book-lined study, where they were served tea. After some pleasantries, they quickly got to the heart of the matter.

"I'm hearing reports that some fifty thousand Russian troops are currently conducting exercises close to your territory," Dayton said. "Is this accurate?"

"Unfortunately, no—the number is considerably higher," Dovzhenko replied. "As of this morning, Luganov has amassed more than a hundred thousand men and more than a thousand battle tanks on our borders. Squadrons of bombers and fighter jets have been redeployed from the Asian theater to the military district immediately adjacent to us. And the number of Russian intrusions into our sovereign airspace has quadrupled in the past two weeks."

"Have you talked directly to President Clarke about all this?"

"We spoke briefly when I congratulated him on his election," Dovzhenko replied uncomfortably. "We spoke again last week for a bit longer. The president assured me he considers Ukrainian freedom a 'major priority.'"

"Has he invited you to the White House?"

"Not yet."

"But he's promised to send more aid?"

"Yes, well, a bit—but 'nonlethal assistance' only, I'm afraid."

"What about the heavy arms and ammunition you've been asking for?"

"Let's just say the president was noncommittal," said the Ukrainian leader. "I will tell you what I told him. We are not asking for American or NATO troops to shed a single drop of blood for us. We are ready to fight the Russians alone. But give us the means to defend ourselves with honor." Dovzhenko leaned forward in his seat and lowered his voice.

"Senator, I know you are familiar with the Budapest Memorandum, but how many other Americans are?"

"Very few, I'm afraid."

"Then I ask you to educate them," Dovzhenko said. "They need to understand that when the Soviet Union collapsed in December of 1991, we in Ukraine possessed almost two thousand nuclear warheads. At that time your president, along with the British prime minister, insisted that we turn these warheads over to Russia to be dismantled and destroyed. As you can understand, we were highly reluctant. Those weapons provided us a guarantee—perhaps our only guarantee—that we would never be reinvaded and reoccupied by the Russians. But Washington and London pushed us hard to give them up in return for so-called 'security assurances'—including assurances that Moscow would respect our sovereignty and borders. On December 5, 1994, my predecessor signed the agreement in Budapest."

Dovzhenko paused for effect.

"Senator, Ukraine kept its part of the deal. We gave up our nuclear weapons. All of them. But Moscow has broken its word. They have annexed Crimea. They have seized parts of our eastern territory. And they are preparing to come for the rest of us. They would never have done so if we were a nuclear-armed power. We are not, because your country and the British persuaded us to give up those weapons with the promise that you would never let us be threatened, much less invaded, by the Russians. Yet here we sit. Forgive my bluntness, but your president does nothing."

"President Dovzhenko, this is a significant reason I am actively considering running for president myself," said the senator. "I see what Luganov is up to. I want to strengthen NATO, and I want to help you—with arms, with intelligence, with whatever you need so you can defend yourselves, by yourselves."

"This is all very well and good, Senator, and believe me, I and my people are grateful for your wisdom and your courage. But let us be frank. I will not get involved in your presidential campaign. I cannot afford to play partisan politics. Time is of the essence. I agreed to meet with you in hopes that you will take a personal message back to the president, back to Congress, and back to the American people. The Russian bear is awake, and he is hungry. He is on the prowl. Our very lives and freedoms are at risk. You made us promises. You must keep them. I implore you, sir—keep them now."

"Dovzhenko is right," Dayton said after they lifted off from Kiev. "We need to figure out how to help him."

"No, sir, he's not right—not entirely," Annie replied.

Marcus looked up from a text he was writing to Nick Vinetti in Moscow.

"What do you mean?" the senator asked. "The Ukrainians did give up their nukes in return for American and British security guarantees. Now they're about to be overrun by the Russians, and the White House is AWOL."

"It's not that simple, sir."

"Sure it is," Pete interjected. "Look, this isn't just a strategic issue. It's a moral one. America doesn't cut our allies loose. Yet that's exactly what Clarke has done. And if you position yourself right, Senator, you can use this to show that Clarke has no idea what he's doing when it comes to foreign policy."

"Annie, Pete's right," Dayton said.

"No, sir, he's not," Annie pushed back firmly but respectfully.

"Why not?"

"For starters, Ukraine is *not* an ally," she replied. "A friend? Yes. But an ally? No. Second, reread the Budapest Memorandum. There's no question the Russians pledged to respect the territorial integrity of Ukraine, and there's also no question that they have clearly and repeatedly broken that pledge. But nowhere in that document does the U.S. explicitly promise to go to war with Russia to defend Ukraine. Nor does it explicitly commit an American president to provide weapons and other war matériel to Ukraine if the agreement is violated. It's not a treaty, and if it were, it never would have been ratified by the Senate—not in 1994 and certainly not now."

"What are you saying?" Pete asked, becoming far more animated about this than Marcus would have imagined. "Are you suggesting Clarke is right to cut the Ukrainians loose to the likes of Aleksandr Luganov?"

"No, of course not."

"Then what?"

"I'm suggesting the senator would be wise to tread with extreme caution and not publicly commit himself to war with Russia in order to protect Ukraine," she replied. "Don't get me wrong. I feel for Dovzhenko and his people. Believe me, I do."

"But . . . ?" Pete pressed.

"But the truth is we simply do not have a treaty obligation to Kiev. We do have one with the Baltics, though. In a few hours, Senator, you'll be sitting with the Estonian prime minister. Estonia is a member of NATO. If the Russians were to move against Estonia or Latvia or Lithuania, then the U.S. would have a legal obligation to defend them. Yet even this raises a critical question, sir, especially for a progressive Democrat like yourself."

"Which is?"

"Are you sure you are willing to risk a nuclear war with Russia to defend three countries that few Americans have ever heard of? On top of that, are you really ready to go to war to defend a country with whom we don't even have a treaty? And either way, how exactly are you going to sell that to the Democratic Party and win your party's nomination?"

They arrived at Toompea Castle just in time for their noon meeting.

The castle, built around the thirteenth century, was a mammoth structure surrounded by a high stone wall. After a brief photo op similar to the one in Kiev, Prime Minister Voldemar Jannsen invited Dayton and the team to join him for lunch along with the ministers of defense and foreign affairs.

As soon as lunch was served, Jannsen got down to business. "My intelligence chiefs tell me Luganov has positioned more than fifty thousand Russian combat soldiers on our border in addition to the hundred thousand troops he's positioned in Belarus and on the borders of Ukraine. In addition, he's moved four hundred battle tanks and fifteen squadrons of bombers and fighters within striking distance of us and our Baltic neighbors. The Kremlin says it's an exercise. But my advisors say it's the prelude to war."

"We heard similar concerns in Kiev," the senator replied.

"I'm sure you did, but you don't have a treaty with Kiev. You do have one with us."

"And we will honor it," Dayton said without hesitation.

Marcus glanced at Annie, who kept a poker face.

"Will you, Senator?" the prime minister asked. "I don't mean to be undiplomatic, but your president seems awfully vague about Article 5."

"Unfortunately, that's true—and that's one of the reasons I'm considering running."

The prime minister shifted in his seat. "Senator, I hope you will not be offended when I say this."

"No, of course not."

"Whether you run for the presidency of your country or not is of little concern to me and my colleagues. We cannot wait for a new American president. Tallinn is less than two hundred miles from the Russian border. I need the man who sits in the White House right now to step up and give us a decisive and demonstrative show of support before it's too late."

"I hear you," Dayton said. "And I'm heading to Brussels in a few days. I'm going to deliver a major speech calling for all NATO countries to step up and fulfill their obligations to invest at least 2 percent of their GDP on annual defense expenditures, as stated in the NATO accord."

"I appreciate that, Senator—I do. We absolutely need every NATO country to do their fair share. We certainly are, and more. Our defense spending has hit 2 percent and usually more nearly every year since Estonia gained membership in NATO in 2004. But again, as important as shining a spotlight on this investment issue is, it's not going to help much if the Russians invade next week or next month."

"I take your point," Dayton said. "What specifically do you need, Mr. Prime Minister?"

"What do I need?" Jannsen asked. "For starters, why isn't NATO flowing in combat brigades, tanks, fighter jets, and antiaircraft missiles, not just here but throughout the Baltics? The Russians have put together an overwhelming force. By all evidence, they are training for an invasion right now. Tomorrow I will take you to the border. I will introduce you to my top generals. I will show you the current disposition of forces. But what have Washington or London or Brussels or Berlin done in response? They've issued meaningless condemnations of Luganov and vague statements of support for the Baltics. What I need is troops and heavy weapons, not more words."

"Again, that is precisely why I have come, Mr. Prime Minister—to see the situation for myself and be able to sound the alarm throughout Europe and back in Washington."

"Good," Jannsen said. "We're not getting many representatives from Washington coming through the Baltics these days, and we're grateful for every friend we can find over there. But may I be even more candid with you, Senator?"

"Of course."

At this, the prime minister leaned close to Dayton and lowered his voice, such that Marcus had to strain to hear every word, even though he was sitting with Annie and Pete just a few feet away.

"Please take this message back directly to President Clarke. At this moment the very existence of my country hangs in the balance. And I must tell you the existence of NATO itself is very much in jeopardy."

"Go on."

"If the Russians invade Ukraine, that's horrible, but it doesn't obligate Washington to take action," Jannsen said almost in a whisper. "But if Luganov invades the Baltics, Article 5 kicks in. If you honor your treaty obligations, then you and the rest of NATO have to come to war to drive out the Russians and reestablish our independence. But let's be brutally honest. If Russians and Americans start killing each other, Luganov is going to use tactical battlefield nuclear weapons. When that happens, many Estonians, Latvians, and Lithuanians will die in a millisecond. Millions more will die horrifying deaths in the days and weeks that follow. And it won't just be us. NATO forces will die as well, including Americans. Then your president will be faced with the ultimate worst-case scenario—will he retaliate against Moscow and other Russian cities with ICBMs and nuclear weapons? If he does, he knows he runs the risk of setting into motion a global thermonuclear war, which will lead to the deaths of hundreds of millions. But if he backs down and chooses *not* to honor the NATO treaty, then he is signing the death sentence not just for us but for *all* of NATO. What's more, he'll be creating a monster—Aleksandr Luganov will have not only seized the Baltics, he will have personally crushed NATO. He will have effectively paralyzed the United States. And in so doing he will have won the right to dictate terms on any matter, anywhere on the globe, financial, political, military, and otherwise."

The prime minister paused to let his words sink in. "You must not kid yourself, Senator," he added after a moment. "These are the stakes, and they are very high—unimaginably high."

"Do you see any hope?" Dayton asked.

"Perhaps," Jannsen replied. "But it's a narrow path, and rapidly becoming narrower still. Go back and implore the president to send us the Eighty-Second Airborne. Send us mechanized units. Order American battle tanks that are in storage to be taken out of mothballs and readied for service. Send fighter squadrons. Send bombers. The only hope to prevent the very real scenario I just laid out is for the U.S. and the rest of NATO to make a clear stand with us and do so immediately. Build up a force here big enough to make Luganov think twice. You don't have to match him man for man, tank for tank, plane for plane. You just have to show that NATO is ready to go toe-to-toe with him using conventional forces. That's how you stop him. And that's how you make sure that all-out nuclear war isn't the only option to protect freedom on the earth."

54

EASTERN ESTONIA, NEAR THE GULF OF FINLAND—22 SEPTEMBER

What stunned Marcus was that the first missile came slicing across the cloudy morning sky—low and sizzling hot—from *behind* them.

The moment it hit its target and created a deafening explosion, Annie grabbed his arm. Seeing that, Pete shot Marcus a look deadlier than the missile. But more were coming. Almost instantly six additional air-to-ground rockets came streaking overhead, all from behind them. The roar of the explosions and the magnitude of the resulting fireballs startled the senator and his staff. For Marcus and Pete, it brought back their years in the corps, both their training and their tours in Iraq and Afghanistan.

As Prime Minister Jannsen, standing beside them, explained why his forces conducted live-fire exercises when most militaries in the world did not, helicopter gunships and attack choppers came swooping in. Each were firing .50-caliber rounds at faux Russian battle tanks constructed out of cinder blocks and wood in a long and heavily for-ested valley stretching out before them for several kilometers. Soon Estonian tanks and armored personnel carriers emerged from a glade to their left. They, too, opened fire, and when they did, the prime min-ister's words were immediately drowned out. Moments later, Black Hawk helicopters came into view from their right. Commandos began fast-roping to the deck and sprinting for cover, firing American-made antitank missiles and tossing grenades as they did.

The entire exercise lasted about an hour. Marcus found himself impressed by the professionalism of the ground troops and their air support as well as by the intelligence briefing Jannsen and his generals provided afterward. These men were deadly serious about defending their nation from the Russians, whether NATO came to help them or not. But the message they were trying to convey was painfully clear: while they would all fight to the bitter end, that end would come bru-tally fast unless NATO—and especially the Americans—kept their Article 5 commitment and came to their rescue.

Over a working lunch in their command bunker, Senator Dayton asked one insightful and penetrating question after another. Marcus could see he was not here to grandstand. He genuinely wanted to understand the latest intelligence that was causing the Estonians and their Baltic neighbors such angst. He also wanted to grasp as much of their game plan for resisting the Russians as they felt comfortable sharing, given that of all the senator's staff members, only Annie had a top secret security clearance.

That evening Dayton and the team dined back in Tallinn with the U.S. ambassador to Estonia inside the embassy compound. Over dwarf herring, smoked eel, plenty of black bread, and red wine, they compared notes with the ambassador—a career Foreign Service officer in her fif-ties who had served in a half-dozen other East European posts and was fluent in Russian, Polish, and German and conversant in Estonian—on the readiness of the local forces as well as the reluctance of NATO commanders to send more manpower and machinery. The senator also pressed the ambassador on what she made of the Russians' snap exercises. She insisted this was "business as usual" and "one of dozens of such exercises I've seen since being posted here." She intimated that the prime minister's growing concern of a Russian move was "slightly overheated, between you and me." That said, she conceded she was genuinely worried Luganov might make a move—and soon—deeper into Ukraine. Whether he was crazy enough to go all the way for Kiev, she couldn't say, but she indicated that she had conveyed her concerns to the State Department as recently as that morning.

Just before dessert came, Marcus received a phone call from Washington. He apologized for the intrusion, excused himself from the table, and stepped out of the ornate dining room into a hallway. The number was from the White House. On the other end of the line was Bill McDermott, who had recently been promoted to deputy national security advisor by President Clarke.

"Bill, good to hear from you," Marcus said when he'd found a bit of privacy. "Congrats on the new gig."

McDermott let loose with a tirade of profanity. "Estonia? With the likes of Bob Dayton? Are you insane?"

"Whoa, whoa, take it easy, Bill. What's gotten into you?"

"The president is preparing for a major reelection campaign, and suddenly I hear you and Pete are cavorting with the enemy?"

"We're hardly *cavorting*, Bill, for crying out loud. But we are taking a hard look at a real enemy. You might want to try it."

"And just what's that supposed to mean?"

"You know very well what it means," Marcus said, fighting hard to keep his voice down to avoid attracting attention from either the Estonian bodyguards or his own team members stationed up and down the hallway. "Luganov is massing forces on the border of the Baltics, but the president isn't sending more troops to create a trip wire. Nor has he made a full-throated defense of our allies here. He's hedging on Article 5. People over here are getting worried, and for good reason."

"So Dayton's going to hit the president—again—for not being

tough enough on the Russians? Give me a break. Dayton's a political dead man."

"I have to say, Bill, you sound awfully defensive for a man in a position to advise the commander in chief to actually get tough with the Russians."

"Just to be clear, Ryker, have you formally signed on to advise a raging left-wing Democrat, one who very well could end up being the president's chief rival?"

Marcus was surprised by how personal McDermott was being, and how political as well, especially given the apolitical nature of his job. Marcus decided to deescalate the conversation. There was no point burning an old friend, much less a man in a position so close to the president. Prime Minister Jannsen had been clear that the only reason he'd agreed to meet with Dayton was to enlist him as a leading voice in the Democratic Party to go back and talk to Clarke in private and try to persuade him to do more on a bipartisan basis to bolster NATO forces in the Baltics.

"No, I haven't," Marcus said, his voice calmer and his tone more circumspect. "Pete has, but I'm just along for the ride. The senator asked me to put together a security detail for him. Pete wanted to get me out of the house. He's worried about me, thought a trip like this might be good for me."

Bill's tone softened. "Maybe he's right."

"Maybe."

"Fine. Come see me when you get back. Maybe I'll hire you instead."

"Hire me?" Marcus asked. "What on earth for?"

"To keep you away from Pete Hwang, for starters," he laughed. "Take care."

"You, too."

And with that, the line went dead.

55

"The war begins in precisely two weeks."

Luganov said it so matter-of-factly, almost casually, as they boarded the presidential jet for the flight back to Moscow that at first Oleg wasn't sure he had heard the man correctly.

"October 7?" Oleg asked, aghast but desperate not to show it. "But that's earlier than we'd discussed."

"It's going to be delicious, my son," Luganov continued as he headed for the back of the plane. "NATO won't know what's hit them."

When they reached the conference room, Luganov asked Oleg to shut and lock the door behind them. Oleg did as he was told as Luganov tore off his jacket and tie, loosened the top buttons of his freshly starched white shirt, and poured himself and Oleg glasses of vodka from the bar behind his white leather executive chair. The president took a swig. Oleg did not. It wasn't even ten o'clock in the morning. He was growing increasingly concerned about how much his father-in-law was drinking, though this was hardly the time to say anything. There were far more urgent issues on the table.

"So it's true, Father—you've decided there is no way forward other than war?" Oleg asked, hoping to appeal to the man as a member of his family, not his staff.

"I have," Luganov replied, opening the folder in front of him marked *CLASSIFIED*, scanning the cover page quickly, and then sliding the entire folder to Oleg. "This is the latest draft of the war plan. I've made several important changes since last week. But this is it. When I sign it, it will become final. But first I want you to take a look at it. Tell me what I'm missing. I want to leave nothing to chance."

Oleg took a deep breath, then picked up the folder with cold hands and began to read it carefully. Soon the jumbo jet was rumbling down the runway and lifting into the air. Oleg kept reading. From time to time he looked up at his father-in-law, worried that he was expecting a response faster than Oleg was prepared to give it. Instead, the man seemed oddly and uncharacteristically detached. He was swirling his drink in his right hand while staring out the window at the massive city of St. Petersburg—home to more than five million souls—shrinking in the distance.

Oleg wasn't trained in the strategies or tactics of the armed services. But he had spent enough time in the company of the president and his generals to perceive that the plan in front of him was flawless. It was built around speed and the element of surprise. To the extent that the West was expecting an invasion of Ukraine, Luganov's calculus was likely spot-on—an invasion of the Baltic states would utterly blindside NATO leaders. Unless they began airlifting men and matériel around the clock, beginning that very night, it was highly unlikely they could prevent the Russian onslaught that was coming—certainly not with conventional weapons.

There was just one critical issue, but Oleg was terrified to raise it. He had seen the army chief of staff ask the same question, and the man had been immediately dismissed from the position he'd held with honor for five straight years—and not simply dismissed. Luganov had ordered the general arrested and sent into exile to who-knew-where on charges of treason. Did Oleg run the same risk now? He had been asked for his opinion. And he was family. Then again, Luganov had dismissed Yulia, his wife of thirty-four years, without any hint of emotion or regret. To this man, even those closest to him were evidently expendable. Still, Oleg mused, wasn't it traitorous to his country, to his people, *not* to ask the question?

Oleg cleared his throat, both to get the president's attention and buy just a moment more to figure out how best to frame the most crucial conversation of his life.

"From a military perspective, the plan is very impressive in every respect, Father," he began, treading carefully. "Yet, in all honesty, I cannot shake my concerns about the intelligence informing the strategic concept."

"How is that, my son?" Luganov said, turning from the window and finishing what was left in his glass.

The president did not seem defensive, so Oleg took another step. "You know I have always had the highest regard for Dmitri Dmitrovich," Oleg continued, referring to FSB chief Nimkov. "But I have to ask, is he really giving us—is he really giving *you*—all the facts?"

"To what facts are you referring?"

"I'm just wondering how carefully Dmitri and his team of analysts have truly studied the American president."

"Andrew Clarke?" sniffed Luganov. "Please—the man is a neophyte, a boorish fool. What more is there to know? He can't get serious legislation through the congress. He knows nothing of NATO, nor does he care. If he did, he wouldn't be so cagey about Article 5. He'd be moving troops and tanks into the Baltics. I've discussed this at length with Dmitri Dmitrovich. Believe me, there is nothing to worry about."

"But, Father, there is something here that worries me," Oleg said, leaning forward in his seat now. "I'm not disputing a single word you have just said, but I do question the psychological profile of Clarke that the FSB has provided. Indeed, I worry that the profile is deeply flawed and thus could be leading us down a very dangerous path."

"Go on," Luganov said.

"Clarke is clearly a neophyte; that is certainly true. And he's obviously made many mistakes, some of which seem astonishing— ridiculous even. But by locking in on Clarke's numerous weaknesses, his self-inflicted mistakes, and his political weakness, the FSB may be missing the man's singular strength."

"Which is what?"

"His capacity to learn from his mistakes."

"Nonsense," Luganov said. "He's the most uninformed and inexperienced leader the Americans have ever elected. This opens up a door to us never unlocked at any other time since our humiliation at the collapse of the Soviet Empire."

"But what the FSB is not properly weighing is that Clarke *was* elected," Oleg calmly but firmly protested, careful to use Dmitri Nimkov as his foil, not targeting Luganov's own analysis. "The man ran arguably the most disastrous campaign in the history of any country. He foolishly steered into not one political storm but many, yet he found a way to navigate to a safe harbor. He vanquished one opponent after another when no one thought he could. Admittedly, his transition was full of blunders, but in time he corrected those as well. He hired staff that did not serve him well, to put it mildly. Yet, one by one, he has fired them and replaced them. Moreover, he chose an experienced VP and a deeply experienced and rather accomplished cabinet. And for all the rancor, even chaos, in the American political system, certainly in the media, Clarke is getting things done. America hasn't imploded. The economy is growing. Millions of jobs have been created. And they're plowing tens of billions into more-robust defenses."

Oleg could see frustration growing in his father-in-law's eyes. He had only a few moments more to make his case without losing his job and perhaps his freedom. He had never spoken to the president like this. He could barely believe what he was hearing himself say, and yet he found himself pressing on just a bit further.

"My point is simply this—Dmitri Dmitrovich is asking you to base the entire premise of your invasion of not one but three NATO countries on the absolute certainty that the current president of the United States is a total beginner and has no idea what he's doing and thus would never launch a counterattack against us using conventional forces and therefore would *certainly* never order a counterattack using tactical nuclear weapons, much less strategic nuclear weapons, even if you went nuclear first. Perhaps the FSB is right. But what if they are wrong? What if Andrew Clarke is more unpredictable than Dmitri Dmitrovich is giving him credit for? What if Clarke's ability to course-correct makes him a far cannier opponent than the FSB has adequately considered? What if the FSB's read on the American president is just wrong enough that this invasion of the Baltics leads us not to glory, but to . . . ?"

"To what?" Luganov asked.

"To ruin."

At first, Luganov glared at him. But suddenly his entire countenance changed. He burst into laughter and poured himself another drink.

"Oleg Stefanovich, what a vivid imagination you have!" he roared. "My son, you are not a military man. You are certainly no intelligence man. But you are a good and loyal boy, and I truly cherish your capacity to amuse me as well as advise me. Now come—drink up! Drink with me to the coming victory that will electrify the masses and firmly and finally reestablish Russia's place as the supreme global power."

Oleg was furious, though he fought not to show it. Luganov was not only ignoring him, he was mocking him. And there was nothing Oleg could do about it. He had to demonstrate his loyalty. So he grabbed the glass of vodka and forced it down with a grimace. As he did, the president signed the war plan, then picked up the secure phone back to the Defense Ministry.

56

THE GRAND PALACE HOTEL, RIGA, LATVIA—23 SEPTEMBER

"You're not going to believe this."

Annie Stewart could barely contain her smile as she found the senator and the team huddled in the back corner of the Pils Bar, its walls covered with the mounted heads of elk and deer and other hunting trophies, in one of Riga's oldest and most elegant hotels. It was nearly midnight. Most of the patrons had turned in for the night. Even the print and cable reporters covering their trip had paid their tabs and gone to bed. But Dayton and his chief of staff were poring over the latest draft of the senator's new Russia sanctions bill they'd been working on for the last few days. Pete was returning emails. Marcus was listening to a Nats game on his iPhone. The security detail was standing post by the front and side doors. But Annie had news.

"What've you got?" asked the senator.

"I just got off the phone with the Kremlin," Annie said, instinctively lowering her voice even though the only one within earshot was the bartender, who, as they'd already found out, barely spoke English. "It's a done deal."

"What is?" Pete asked, struggling to appear more interested in what she had to say than how attractive she looked in her black cashmere sweater, faded blue jeans, brown boots, and Cartier watch.

"Luganov," she said. "He's agreed to a meeting."

"You're kidding," Dayton said.

"No, sir. I've been working on it all evening. That's why I missed dinner with the foreign minister."

"This is tremendous—great work."

"So when is it?" Marcus asked.

"Well, that's the thing—the only time he has to meet is tomorrow at four thirty."

"Where?"

"In his office at the Kremlin."

Pete slapped Marcus on the back. "Wow—this is huge!"

"But we're supposed to be in Vilnius tomorrow," the senator protested.

"I know," Annie said.

"I'm supposed to have dinner with the prime minister."

"It's your call, sir, but if we decline, I don't know that we'll have another opportunity."

"What do you all think? Pete?"

"I say we do it, sir. Definitely. We can always reschedule with the Lithuanians."

Everyone else agreed with Pete. Everyone except Marcus.

"What's the matter, Marcus?" the senator asked. "This was your idea, after all."

"I realize that, sir—and I still support a meeting with Luganov. But I would recommend against looking too eager."

"What's that supposed to mean?"

"Decline the invitation for tomorrow," Marcus continued. "Have

Annie call back and explain that you have meetings in Vilnius that cannot be changed, but you could be in Moscow the following day or the day after that."

"But Annie just said Luganov isn't available for the rest of the week."

"Sir, do you think it's wise to blow off a NATO ally to meet with the enemy? Is that really the message you want to send on this trip? And what if you do and Luganov stands you up when you get there?"

The senator turned back to Annie. "The man does have a point."

"May I make a suggestion?" she asked.

"By all means."

"Let me make a quick call to my contact in the PM's office in Vilnius and explain the situation. If they have a problem with it, then we accept Marcus's advice. But if they're okay with rescheduling the meeting, then we proceed to Moscow in the morning. The following day we can fly directly to Vilnius, and you can brief the PM on your meeting with Luganov. How's that sound?"

Marcus hesitated. He still wasn't crazy about the idea. But it was the senator's trip, not his. "Works for me," he said.

Dayton grinned. "Me, too. Good thinking. Get it done, Annie. This might be the break we've been hoping for."

The Lithuanian prime minister agreed.

They were heading to Moscow.

Dayton and his team landed at Domodedovo International Airport just after 11 a.m. on Wednesday. They checked into the Hotel National a little after one that afternoon. Marcus insisted that they enter from the back and not let the media know where they were staying. He remembered every grisly detail of the suicide bombing that had occurred there, which he'd been briefed about when he'd done an advance trip for the VP a while back. He and his men took the senator up a service elevator to a set of suites on the fourth floor. After making sure the rooms were secure, Marcus posted one man at the main elevators and another by the service elevator. One he put downstairs in the café to keep an eye on the lobby. The rest he posted inside the doors of the senator's personal suite.

None of them had been permitted to bring their weapons off the jet. But a discreet request to Nick Vinetti at the U.S. Embassy had gotten around that. Nick made sure each man on Marcus's team was given a Sig Sauer automatic pistol from the Marine armory. Nick also loaned them several MP5 machine guns and plenty of rounds of ammunition, plus several Uzis rarely used anymore. What's more, the embassy was providing three armor-plated black Chevy Suburbans, drivers from the embassy motor pool, and whatever logistics the senator needed. As a prospective presidential candidate, Robert Dayton had no access to the embassy's official diplomatic resources. But since he was the ranking Democrat on the Senate Intelligence Committee, his trip qualified as a "codel," State Department parlance for a congressional delegation. And for a codel, it was Nick's responsibility as deputy chief of mission to make sure everything went smoothly and safely for Dayton and his team.

The time for the Luganov meeting kept changing. When they landed, Annie was told the meeting had been moved back to 7 p.m. Upon arriving at the hotel, she was told it had been moved up to 3 p.m. Yet as Marcus took a quick shower and changed into a suit, he received an urgent text from Annie to the team that the meeting had been postponed indefinitely.

"They're playing with you, Senator," Marcus said when he arrived at Dayton's suite. "Plan for the original four thirty time slot. If the meeting is going to happen at all, I can almost guarantee it will be then. Let's roll at three thirty as originally planned so we have enough time to clear Kremlin security."

Dayton was skeptical and visibly agitated. As it happened, however, Marcus had called it exactly right. During the brief ride to the Kremlin, Pete leaned over and whispered to his friend that his stock was definitely on the rise with the senator. Marcus nodded to confirm he'd heard, but privately his doubts were growing about whether any of this was a good idea. They were now deep in enemy territory, and as honest and principled as Dayton might be, Marcus knew the senator was no match for Luganov, the reigning grand master of geopolitical chess.

The three-vehicle American motorcade was escorted by the Moscow police's VIP unit. This thrilled Dayton's press secretary and chief of staff. After all, the images of their man entering Red Square and passing St. Basil's Cathedral and then passing through the gates into the Kremlin itself would look great on CNN and MSNBC that night. But Marcus's anxiety began to spike when only the lead Suburban—the one carrying Dayton, Annie, Pete, and himself—was cleared to enter and the other two were not. Even without their security detail, Marcus had few concerns for their physical safety. Besides the White House itself, there was no government compound in the world as secure as this one. There was certainly no way President Luganov was going to allow a prominent American senator—especially such a harsh critic—to be assassinated in the heart of the Russian capital. No, Marcus's real worries were for the senator's reputation and political viability. The man was entering the lair of a wolf. He would likely reemerge, but the question was, how damaged?

They were taken first to the visitors' center at the Kutafiya Tower.

There they were met by a junior protocol officer who escorted them to the appointments desk, where they received visitor IDs and passed through metal detectors. Their possessions went through X-ray machines and WMD sniffers. Only then were they guided through Troitskaya Tower, past the Arsenal and the State Kremlin Palace, and into the pale-yellow building known as the Senate.

Next they were handed off to a more senior protocol officer who was waiting for them. She did not smile. She did not shake their hands. She simply greeted the senator with emotionless indifference, effectively ignored his colleagues, and took them up an elevator to the third floor. They had to stop at another security checkpoint, where they once again submitted to the protocol.

"In such times, one can never be too careful," said one of the security agents, discerning the annoyance in Dayton's eyes.

It struck Marcus as an undiplomatic thing to say to a visiting U.S. senator, but he nevertheless respected the security protocols the Russians had in place, especially given the apartment bombings in Moscow years before, other more recent terrorist attacks in Moscow and various capitals throughout Europe, and of course the attack on the White House that he had personally experienced.

When they were cleared, the Americans were led to an anteroom flanked by armed security men in dark suits with ugly ties. One of the men directed them to a waiting area with nicely upholstered couches and chairs and a mahogany coffee table, where they were served tea and some light snacks.

Marcus took in and memorized every detail—how many men were in the lobby and down the hall, how many CCTV cameras there were and where they were positioned, the sound that the doors made when they electronically locked and unlocked, the number of nonsecurity staff in the vicinity, and so forth. He had been all over the world with the president and the VP. In the process, he had become acquainted with security personnel and procedures in palaces and government office buildings of every conceivable kind. But he had never been here, to the epicenter of the Russian government, and he found himself immensely curious.

The senior protocol officer informed them that the four thirty meeting had been delayed until five. Then five thirty. Then six. As it turned out, it was not until nearly seven o'clock that they were finally ushered into the president's office. Senator Dayton was furious, and Marcus braced himself for the tirade that was coming. But Aleksandr Ivanovich Luganov caught them all off guard by greeting them warmly and apologizing profusely for keeping them waiting. He explained that the crash of a Russian airliner near the border of Mongolia had kept him occupied for hours. He spoke only in Russian, while a fortyish woman standing at his side served as his interpreter.

Rather than sit behind his desk, Luganov met them in the center of the spacious, dark-paneled corner office. He was dressed in a charcoal-gray suit, a light-blue shirt, and a crimson silk tie, and he smiled broadly as he shook the senator's hand while official Kremlin photographers and videographers captured the moment. Standing just a few feet away at all times was Special Agent Pavel Kovalev, who Marcus knew was the chief of the president's security detail.

Luganov gave them a brief tour of the artifacts and framed power photographs that hung on several walls. There was Luganov standing with various American presidents. There he was at several G8 summits, back before the invasion of Ukraine, when Russia was still a member. There was Luganov with the premier of China, the dictator of North Korea, the supreme leader of Iran, and even the prime minister of Israel. On his shelves he had two crisscrossing scimitars, gifts from the king of Saudi Arabia. He had some ancient pottery from Egypt and an exquisitely painted ceramic bowl from India.

As the charm offensive continued, Marcus studied the man he had last seen at the German Chancellery in Berlin. Back then, Luganov's hair had been sandy blond and thinning with just a touch of gray about the temples. Now the gray was gone, and his hair was a dark brown. Marcus almost smiled at the notion that Luganov was coloring it, but he forced himself to remain impassive and inscrutable. Still, the hair aside, Luganov looked decidedly older and weathered to Marcus, with crow's-feet at the corners of his eyes and more wrinkles in his face and neck. The Russian had been only sixty-one when Marcus had seen him last and had seemed full of vim and vigor. Now he was approaching seventy, and Marcus couldn't help but notice that though he was still quite trim and broad-shouldered, he seemed somewhat stiff and was maneuvering about the room with a slight limp in his left leg.

When the tour was finished and they were about to take their seats, Luganov pressed a button to the right side of his desk. A door opened, and an aide walked in. Marcus recognized him instantly but maintained a poker face and said not a word.

"Senator Dayton, I'd like you to meet my son-in-law and most trusted counselor, Oleg Stefanovich Kraskin."

The two men shook hands; then Oleg greeted Pete and Annie in turn. When Oleg got to Marcus, he hesitated, if only for a moment. He said nothing, but Marcus registered the look of recognition in the man's eyes. They shook hands firmly, but that was it. Neither man acknowledged that they had met before.

Luganov sat down behind his desk and motioned for everyone to be seated. The interpreter retreated to a small wooden chair beside the desk. Oleg sat on the other side of the desk, his notebook and pen at the ready. The senator sat in an ornate cushioned chair directly across from the president, with Annie to his right and Pete to her right. Marcus took the last open chair, to Dayton's left, and the meeting got down to business.

It most certainly did not go as any of them expected.

58

Dayton wasted no time lighting into the president.

Diplomatically yet with fierce conviction, the senator charged Luganov with breaching the terms set forth in the Budapest Memorandum by violating the territorial integrity of eastern Ukraine and Crimea. Then he expressed outrage at what he called Russia's "war crimes" in Georgia and Syria before launching into a brief but aggressive closing argument.

"I urge you, Mr. President, not to take any action the people of Russia would regret in regard to the Baltics or any other member of the North Atlantic Treaty Organization. I am well aware that you have recently massed tens of thousands of troops, hundreds of battle tanks, and scores of bombers and fighters on the borders of Estonia, Latvia, and Lithuania, in addition to the hundred thousand troops you've put into Belarus and on the borders of Ukraine," Dayton said. "You say it's a series of military exercises, but that's what you said before you invaded Georgia in 2008 and before you invaded Ukraine in 2014. I have just spent several days in Kiev and the Baltics. I have met with their political leaders and their generals. I have reviewed their forces and seen their consummate professionalism and powerful commitment to freedom and their own sovereignty. Furthermore, I would remind you that the Baltic States are proud and loyal members of NATO, and they have the full backing of the rest of the alliance. And this is why I have come: to urge you not to gamble in this neighborhood. Stop attempting to intimidate the alliance. Give no more thought to acquiring territory that is not legally, morally, or in any way rightfully yours. Do not miscalculate here, Mr. President. The stakes are much too high."

Marcus found himself at once impressed and as tense as he'd ever been in a meeting between world leaders. He hadn't been certain this Iowan known for his "Midwestern nice" had the wherewithal to speak so directly to arguably the most dangerous man on the planet, and in his own office, no less. Only time would tell whether Dayton could prove to be a Churchill, but he certainly was no Chamberlain. Not today.

Marcus could see the anxiety in the translator's eyes, and at that moment he doubted she had ever been required to communicate such a statement to her boss before now. Marcus glanced at Oleg. The man's hand had stopped writing. An icy chill fell over the room as the senator looked the president directly in the eye. Marcus could see the man's jaw clenched as he waited for the translation.

"I did not invite you here to be lectured in my own home, Senator," Luganov began, eyes narrowing, when the translation was complete. "That said, I will give you credit for your candor. Believe me, I have heard you rage against me and against my government's decisions over the years from the safe confines of the Senate floor and the Senate Press Gallery and the Washington studios of CNN. I agreed to your request for a meeting because I wanted to see if you had the courage to say to my face what you routinely spout to the American people. Now I see you do, and I congratulate you, sir."

"Mr. President, with respect, I did not come here to lecture you," the senator replied. "And I most certainly did not come to be patronized by you. There is one purpose, and one purpose only, in my visit—to urge you to back your forces away from the borders of the Baltics and Ukraine and to warn you, if I may put it so indelicately, not to risk making a miscalculation that could plunge your country, mine, and the whole of Europe into a war that would surely spin rapidly out of control."

The senator paused, either for effect or for the translator to catch up. The Americans in the room braced for Luganov's reaction. But when the president spoke, he threw a curveball none of them had war-gamed.

"Message received, Senator," Luganov replied, his countenance softening and his body language relaxing. "I intend nothing threatening in these exercises. We conduct them all the time. We will continue to do so. Your country conducts such exercises. So does the rest of NATO. After all, I believe you attended a series of live-fire exercises in Estonia a few days ago. So I say again, these are nothing out of the ordinary, nor should they be construed as menacing in the slightest. Indeed, while they were scheduled to last through the month of October, my generals and I are so pleased with how they are going that I have decided to conclude them early."

Dayton was visibly astonished. "How early?" he asked, trying to regain his composure.

"They should be wrapped up in ten days' time, give or take a day."

"The exercises near the Baltics as well as those close to Ukraine?"

"Yes."

"I have your word on that."

"Don't be impertinent, Senator. I'm agreeing with you that we don't want anyone to miscalculate here. I'm agreeing to stand down my forces for the time being."

"Mr. President, please understand my country's hesitancy to count upon the word coming out of the Kremlin. How does the Russian proverb go? Trust, but verify."

"*Doveryai, no proveryai,*" Annie said almost under her breath.

At this, Luganov smiled. "Miss Stewart, you speak Russian?" he said in Russian.

"*Da,*" she replied.

Luganov asked, again in Russian, how much of his side of the conversation she had understood.

"All of it," she replied instantly, but in English.

Luganov looked impressed.

"And how precisely is my young translator here communicating my meaning?" he asked. It struck Marcus as an odd thing to say since the translator was almost certainly at or near the age of fifty, while Annie, Pete, and himself were in their late thirties.

"She is doing an excellent job," Annie said, looking at the woman in the corner and smiling warmly.

The woman looked simultaneously grateful and mortified. The thought of being a topic of the president's conversation had to be anathema to her. But Luganov abruptly changed the subject.

"There is more I will tell you, Senator," he said.

"By all means."

"I have not made this public yet, but I will tell you all because it will be news very soon," Luganov continued. "Tomorrow I am flying to Pyongyang to announce the conclusion of several months of secret negotiations."

"Regarding what?"

"The North Korean leader and I will sign a treaty," Luganov said. "The signing will be broadcast live around the world. I am creating a military alliance with Pyongyang. I will pledge to come to North Korea's defense should it ever be attacked by the South or by the U.S. or by any other force. In return, Pyongyang will completely abandon its nuclear program and turn all of its nuclear weapons, uranium, and additional nuclear materials over to me. Their nuclear reactors and laboratories will be dismantled or destroyed. What's more, I will invite international inspectors to observe and monitor the process."

Luganov stopped speaking, but the senator did not respond imme-diately. When he did, he congratulated the president on what he hoped would be a "significant move toward true peace on the Korean Peninsula."

Marcus's defenses were on full alert. He was certain Dayton was being played by the world's master manipulator, but even a blind man could see that Luganov's charms were casting their spell as intended. As surprised and impressed as Marcus had been with the senator when the meeting began, he now felt just as surprised and equally dispirited. If one of the leading Russia hawks in Washington could be so easily beguiled, then the people of the West were sitting ducks indeed.

Marcus brooded over his worries for the rest of the evening. Even the catered dinner with Ambassador Tyler Reed and DCM Nick Vinetti couldn't shake Marcus's genuine fear for the people of Europe and the fate of the NATO alliance. He was all but certain Luganov was prepar-ing to strike hard and strike soon. At which target—Ukraine or the Baltics—he could not say. Luganov's plan for a treaty with North Korea was almost certainly sheer disinformation and sleight of hand. Yet in the absence of proof, who would listen to an ex–Secret Service agent whose closest friends had diagnosed him as depressed?

59

THE HOTEL NATIONAL, MOSCOW—25 SEPTEMBER

The phone startled Marcus awake.

It was not his mobile ringing, nor the secure satellite phone he'd rented for the trip. This was the hotel phone on the nightstand beside the bed. Marcus was instantly awake and on his feet, the muscle memory reaction of years of training. He picked up the receiver even as he read the LED display on the clock radio. It was 3:37 in the morning.

"Hello?"

"Is this Agent Ryker?" asked a man's voice on the other end of the line.

"Who's asking?"

"Is this Special Agent Marcus Ryker?" the man asked again, stressing each word.

"I'm retired, but yeah, why?"

The line went dead. Then Marcus heard two light raps, not on the door to the hallway but on the one that connected to the adjacent suite.

"Who's there?" Marcus asked as he walked to the closed and locked door.

"Don't you recognize my voice?" the man said from the other side.

Marcus tried to place the voice but couldn't. It was definitely a native Russian speaker and a Muscovite. But the man was speaking too quietly for accurate identification.

"No, I don't."

"Agent Ryker, this is Oleg Kraskin. Please let me in. We must talk."

Oleg Kraskin? Why in the world would the son-in-law of the Russian president be staying in the suite next door?

Marcus wished he had one of the Sig Sauer pistols Nick had given to his team, but there was nothing he could do about that now. When he heard two more knocks, Marcus decided to take the bait. He unplugged the lamp on the nightstand, wielded it like a club, and unlocked and slowly opened the door. He was tense, suspicious, and ready for a fight.

To his astonishment, it really was Kraskin. He wore a black silk shirt, black jeans, and snakeskin boots, and he was alone—no handlers, no security.

"May I come in?" Oleg asked, his Russian accent thick, almost overpowering.

Marcus looked him over for a moment, then glanced behind him to see if there was anyone else in Oleg's room. Not seeing anyone, he finally nodded and stepped aside. Oleg was shorter than him—though not as diminutive as Luganov—and rail thin, almost gaunt. But he strode in with great purpose, through the bedroom and into the adjoining sitting room, and sat down on the couch.

Marcus closed and locked the door behind Oleg. He set down the lamp and followed the Russian into the sitting room.

"To what do I owe this early-morning honor, Mr. Kraskin?" Marcus asked, standing there in boxer shorts and a T-shirt.

"I don't have much time," Oleg said in a whisper. "So I'll get straight to the point."

Marcus opened his hands as if to say, *The floor is all yours.* Then he sat down in a chair opposite Oleg.

"Agent Ryker, you must promise me that whatever I share with you, you will tell no one that you heard it from me. Please, I must insist. I am putting my life in your hands by even coming to meet with you."

"I'll do my best," Marcus said. "But I have no idea what you're about to say."

"I can give you information critical to your national security and that of your allies. But I cannot do so unless I have your word that you will protect my identity."

Was this a trap? Marcus immediately asked himself. *Was he being set up? Recorded? Videotaped? How could he make such a promise without knowing answers to these and so many other questions?* Marcus glanced around the room, but Oleg quickly assured him that the rooms were no longer bugged.

"That all went out with the Cold War," he insisted.

"Fine," Marcus said. "But why come to me?"

"My motives are my own business."

"Yet you ask me to trust you."

"I do."

"I don't even know you."

"Believe me, Agent Ryker, you will want to hear what I have to say."

"Maybe so," said Marcus. "But let's be honest. I could be in danger—as could the senator—simply by you coming here."

"Not as much danger as I am in," Oleg replied. "Tomorrow or the next day, you all can leave. I cannot. But neither can I remain silent. I must tell someone, and I've chosen you. Perhaps you don't have reason to believe me. Fine. I ask you only to listen, and then go back to Washington and independently evaluate everything I tell you. If I speak the truth, perhaps you'll trust me to tell you more. But I need your word you will never betray my identity, and I need it now."

It was not an unreasonable request, Marcus concluded. Yes, taking the meeting was a risk, but perhaps it was worth it to spend a few minutes with a man so close to the Russian president. Even if the man had come to plant disinformation, simply hearing what he had to say might prove very valuable. So Marcus gave Oleg Kraskin his word.

"Perhaps you should write all this down," said Oleg.

"Say what you've come here to say; I will remember every word," Marcus assured him.

Oleg stared at Marcus for a moment, then closed his eyes. He seemed to be steeling his resolve for whatever task he had set for himself. Finally he reopened his eyes and looked directly at Marcus again. "Very well," he began. "You must understand that everything—or nearly everything—my father-in-law said to you and the senator and your team last night was a lie."

Marcus said nothing.

"He's not going to pull our forces back from the border of the Baltics," Oleg continued.

"Why not?" Marcus asked.

"Because twelve days from today—on or about October 7—he's going to invade the Baltic states."

"Which one?"

"All of them."

"You're serious?"

"I am," Oleg said. "He'll pull our forces off the border of Ukraine, as he promised, but your president must not be deceived. He will only do so to reinforce the units he's going to send into the Baltics."

"Let me get this straight," Marcus said, incredulous. "You're telling me your president has decided to invade not one but three NATO countries?"

"Yes."

"That's madness. Why would he do it?"

"Because he can," Oleg said. "My father-in-law is convinced no one will stop him, that these nations are his for the taking. He grabbed one-fifth of Georgia, and no one did anything. He took Crimea and eastern Ukraine, and what happened? Nothing."

"This is completely different," Marcus said.

"Because it's NATO."

"Of course."

"Nevertheless, he's gambling he can strike so fast and hard that no one can stop him, and once he's got what he wants, no one will want to risk nuclear war to take it back."

Marcus sat there trying to make sense of it all. It's not that what Oleg was saying was far-fetched. But it was surreal hearing it from the mouth of someone in the Kremlin inner circle.

"You say he's going to move on October 7?"

"Give or take a day or two, yes," Oleg said. "His original plan was to attack on October 25, the anniversary of the Russian Revolution. Now he's pushing the generals to be ready sooner, and my father-in-law is not a man to whom one says no."

"But I don't understand. This doesn't make sense. He's willing to risk nuclear war to seize three tiny states most people couldn't find on a map?"

"Perhaps most Americans cannot find them," said Oleg. "But I assure you that every Russian can."

"You believe they're yours."

"They *are* ours."

"That's why you want them back."

"Of course," Oleg said.

"Then why are you here telling me this? Why tip your hand? Why not let your father-in-law seize them in a surprise blitzkrieg?"

"The answer to that is very simple," Oleg said. "He is ready to risk nuclear war and the deaths of millions to get these three countries back. I am not."

60

The weight of that statement stunned Marcus into silence.

Glancing at his watch, Oleg continued. "Few people really know this man, Agent Ryker. I do. I married his daughter. I became part of his family. But I had no idea what I was stepping into. My parents revered him. My Marina worshiped him. What reason did I have to think of him any less highly? But now I have worked for him for years. I've traveled the world with him, been in most meetings with him, taken his dictation, handled his personal and professional correspondence, been sent on delicate diplomatic missions for him. I've spent more time with this man than with my own wife. And I'm telling you, I'm sickened by what I see. He uses people to gain whatever he wants, and then he destroys and discards them without another thought."

"And what does he want?"

"Power. Riches. Glory. Sexual pleasure. You name it. And not in moderation. His appetites are insatiable. When he has something, he craves more. When he does not have something, he will kill to get it and to stop others from getting it. He is a man without conscience and without remorse."

"Another Stalin?"

"No, I don't see him like a Stalin or a Khrushchev. He's not like any Soviet-era leader. Yes, he was shaped by those times, but he was never truly a Communist. He joined the party in order to advance his own ambitions, not the party's. When Communism died, he discarded it and moved on."

"A Hitler then?" Marcus asked. "Ready to grab the Rhineland, ready to show the Western powers that they didn't have the will to stop him, ready to kill millions—tens of millions—when they finally did try to stop him?"

Oleg shook his head slowly. "No, he's not a fascist or a national socialist."

"Then what?"

"He sees himself as a czar."

"Meaning what?"

"Meaning he sees himself as a visionary—an imperialist. He is determined to regain and restore the glory of Mother Russia by any means necessary. He believes Russia was humiliated by the Western powers in the previous century."

"And is that how you see him?"

"In part."

"But . . . ?"

"I believe the best way to think of him is as the head of a crime family."

"Like the Godfather?" Marcus asked. "You're saying he's Vito Corleone?"

"I'm saying he's Sonny," Oleg replied coldly. "Ambitious but rash, reckless—and he has a nuclear arsenal and the willingness to use it."

Marcus stood and walked over to the window.

"You do not believe me?" Oleg asked.

"No, I do believe you," Marcus replied, closing the drapes completely, then checking the hallway through the peephole to make sure no one was standing outside his door. "But I'm not sure who else will." He paced for a moment, then sat down again. "If you're telling the truth, you're committing treason by talking to me," Marcus said as much to himself as to Oleg.

"I *am* telling the truth, but I am *not* committing treason," Oleg retorted. "I am *not* betraying my country, Agent Ryker. The president is. The whole reason I have come to you—the whole reason I am telling you this—is because I want to *save* my country."

"How?" Marcus asked.

"You must tell Senator Dayton what I've told you—without telling him your source. The senator must then tell President Clarke, and Clarke must order his generals to send the necessary troops and tanks and planes to the Baltics to create a serious deterrent—a speed bump, as it were, large enough to cause my father-in-law to pause, to think twice, to back down before it's too late."

"Why not just go to the U.S. Embassy or to the media?"

"Because then I'd be found out and murdered for certain."

"And you think coming to me is safe?"

"Not safe, but perhaps safer."

"*Perhaps?*" Marcus asked.

"Agent Ryker, please listen to me. Ever since I first heard about this madness and saw the war plan, I've been trying to come up with a way to stop it. The only way I see is to get word to the White House of what is being planned. When the senator's request for a meeting came across my desk, I saw you were traveling with him. That's why I immediately recommended to my father-in-law that he take the meeting. It took some effort to persuade him, but in the end he accepted my logic and agreed to receive the senator and his delegation. I did not do it to meet Mr. Dayton. I did it to meet you, because I realized you might be the one person to whom I could plead my case. Do you recall that time in Berlin, when we first met?"

Marcus nodded.

"Do you remember what I called you?"

"No."

"I called you a hero."

"I'm not. I was just doing my job."

"You were willing to take a bullet to protect your president, your country, your country's government and way of life. And that wasn't the first time. I have read a great deal about you, Agent Ryker. I know that when your country was attacked on 9/11, you volunteered to join the Marines. I know you served in Afghanistan and Iraq. I know you are a patriot. I suspect you have not agreed with every decision made by every leader you protected. But you defended their legitimate right to make even poor decisions because they were chosen by the people and would be held accountable to the people. Well, I am no different, except that I don't have the luxury of living in a democracy. My leader is a thug, accountable to no one, and he is leading our nation—the country I was born in, the country I love—into disaster. I have come to you at great personal risk because I believe you can understand this better than any politician. And I'm asking you to help me, Agent Ryker. Because time is short, and I don't know who else can."

The praise made Marcus uncomfortable, but he sensed it wasn't flattery. Perhaps it was really what Oleg Kraskin believed. Then again, perhaps it was an effort to manipulate him. This could be a setup, another plot to deceive, maybe even masterminded by Luganov himself. But why would the Russian leader send his son-in-law here in the middle of the night to tip the Americans off to an invasion of three NATO countries? What advantage did that give the Kremlin?

"I can't take this story to the senator without proof," Marcus said. "And the senator certainly isn't going to President Clarke unless he has proof that an invasion is really coming. He would need evidence, something concrete and compelling."

"Don't worry," Oleg said. "I have all the proof you need and more."

61

It was nearly six in the morning when Oleg left.

Marcus waited as long as he could, which was about thirty-five min-utes. Then he called Nick Vinetti. He apologized for calling his friend so early, but Vinetti said he'd already been to the gym for an hour and was just about to head to the office.

"It was great to see you last night—all of you guys, but especially you and Pete," Vinetti said. "The ambassador found the whole conver-sation fascinating. He hasn't been invited to sit with Luganov since he arrived in the country. Don't tell him I said so, but I think he was a tad jealous."

"Thanks, Nick, but this is not a personal call," Marcus said.

"What's wrong?"

"Something's come up. I need to see you immediately."

"Sure, no problem," Vinetti replied. "My morning's full, but I've got time around two. How about then?"

"No, Nick—it has to be now. Clear your schedule."

"Why? What is it? What's wrong?"

"I can't say."

"Even on a secure satellite phone?"

"No—it's too sensitive. Can I come over now? I wouldn't ask if it wasn't critical and time sensitive."

"All of you?"

"No, just me."

"It's that serious?"

"Yeah."

"All right. It's—what—6:39 now? Can you get there by seven?"

"Yes."

"Fine. I'll give your name to the Marines at the front gate."

Marcus hung up the phone and headed to the elevator. Along the way, he told three of his men he was going out for a bit and if they needed anything to talk to Pete. Hailing a cab, he directed the driver to Bolshoy Deviatinsky Pereulok, Number Eight.

"Ah, the embassy?" the driver asked. "You *Amerikanski, da?*"

"*Da,*" Marcus said, handing him a wad of rubles. "And there's a lot more if you can get me there by seven."

The unshaven man didn't speak much English, but he understood enough. He hit the gas and raced through the streets of Moscow at high speeds. When he finally pulled up in front of the U.S. Embassy, they were late. It was twelve minutes past seven. But Marcus gave him the big tip anyway, knowing full well he'd never have gotten there any faster on his own. He showed his passport to the Marines in the front guard station. They immediately cleared him through and passed him off to a young aide who took Marcus straight to Nick's office.

"What's wrong, Marcus?" the deputy chief of mission asked when they were finally behind closed doors. "You okay?"

"I don't know," Marcus said. "I think so."

"So what is it? Why all the secrecy and urgency?"

"This room is secure, right?" Marcus asked, walking about the spacious corner office covered with power photos of Vinetti with all kinds of high-ranking American officials and a few Russian ones as well. "I mean, it's not bugged, is it?"

"No, of course not."

"You're sure?" Marcus pressed.

"Yeah, I'm sure. It was swept yesterday. Sit down, let me get you a cup of coffee, and then you can tell me what's got you on fire."

"No, no coffee—I'm fine," Marcus said.

"Well, I'm not," Nick said. "I was up late with a couple of old buddies and a few too many beers. As I recall, you were there too."

He walked over to his desk, pressed an intercom button, and asked his secretary to bring in a fresh pot of his favorite Brazilian blend and some blueberry muffins.

"Right away, sir," came the reply.

"Nick, I don't want a muffin."

"Too bad—I do. Now sit. Talk to me."

Marcus was pacing, but at Nick's insistence he took a seat across from his old friend.

"Last night was great," he began, trying to figure what exactly to say and how. "I mean, I completely disagree with the senator's analysis of the meeting with Luganov. But the time with the ambassador and you and your team was great. You put together a stellar evening with almost no notice, and I owe you one. Thanks."

"You got that right, and you're welcome."

"But something happened after we left."

"Tell me."

Marcus paused and took a deep breath, then lowered his voice and looked Nick square in the eye. "Someone came to see me in the middle of the night."

"Who?"

"I can't say."

"Can't or won't?"

"Just hear me out."

"Fine, but hurry it up. I don't have all day, even for you."

Marcus reached into his pocket, pulled out a black sapphire Samsung Galaxy phone, and handed it to Nick.

"Thanks, buddy, but I have my own."

"Turn it on," Marcus said.

Nick looked down and turned the phone on.

"Now enter 6653 and the pound sign."

Nick did.

"Open up the photo gallery."

Again Nick did as he was told and found fifty-three photos. Nick looked at Marcus, then back at the phone. It took a moment as he scrolled through the photos, but Nick could read enough Russian to understand what he was looking at. Marcus saw the blood drain from his friend's face. "One of these documents is a Russian war plan to invade the Baltics," Nick said. "And soon."

Marcus nodded.

"And this one is an internal memorandum from inside the Kremlin."

Again Marcus nodded.

"Where did you get this, Marcus?"

"Luganov has a mole."

"How high? How close?"

"I can't say."

"Why not?"

"It's too soon. They're nervous."

"They?"

"I don't want to say if it's a man or a woman."

"But it's a man."

"I don't want to say."

"Just one person?"

"Yes."

"And it's a man," Nick pressed. "At least tell me that much. Because if it's a woman that came to you in the middle of the night . . ."

"Fine, it was a man," Marcus confirmed.

"And he obviously has access to classified information at the highest levels."

Marcus said nothing.

"Is he a middle man?" Nick asked. "Or did he get these himself?"

"He says he has direct access to these and more."

"How much more?"

"Get out a pad and pen."

Suddenly there was a light rap on the door, and in came Nick's secretary, a pleasant, round woman in her late fifties, with a large pot of coffee, two U.S. Embassy Moscow mugs, a carafe of cream, a glass jar of brown sugar cubes, and two spoons.

"Thanks, Maggie—that'll be all for now," Nick said. "Hold my calls and all visitors until you hear otherwise. Oh, and one other thing."

"Yes, sir?"

"I need Morris to come up here immediately."

"Right away, sir," she replied, then left and shut the door behind her.

Nick pulled a yellow legal pad out of a drawer in his desk. Marcus poured them both steaming mugs of freshly brewed coffee even as he kept talking.

"Luganov is running a highly sophisticated disinformation campaign to keep the U.S. and the rest of NATO confused about his real intentions. That's why he accepted Dayton's invitation—to tell him he's going to end the war games early and pull his forces off the borders, when he's not."

"He's planning to invade. When, exactly?"

"On or about October 7," Marcus explained. "But there's more."

"I'm listening."

"You heard last night that Luganov is about to fly to Pyongyang to make a major announcement," Marcus continued. "But it's all bogus."

"Meaning what?"

"Meaning the treaty he's signing with North Korea in which Pyongyang will publicly agree to give up all of their nuclear weapons in return for a formal defensive alliance with Moscow is completely meaningless. There will be huge headlines in the next few days, and Luganov will win international acclaim for being a peacemaker both on his Western and Eastern flanks. But according to my mole, Moscow will actually replace North Korea's flawed and somewhat-unreliable nuclear weapons with far more powerful, accurate, and reliable Russian nuclear warheads and tactical nukes. See photo thirty-nine."

Nick did and began shaking his head.

"The Russians have been working for the past six years on an electromagnetic pulse bomb to fry our entire electrical grid and send us back to the Stone Age," Marcus continued. "According to the last document in the photos, the technology has been perfected, and the missiles are ready for launch. What's more, Luganov is fully prepared to detonate an EMP bomb over Chicago or somewhere in the Midwest if we fight him in the Baltics. But the mole and these documents say that the missile will be launched out of North Korea, not Russia, seriously complicating our response."

"Impossible," Nick protested. "The North Koreans don't have an ICBM capable of reaching Seattle or L.A., much less Chicago."

"Read to the end," Marcus replied. "Apparently they do."

62

There was another knock at the door.

Marcus looked up to see a pretty if somewhat-studious brunette with her hair pulled back in a bun, wearing a navy-blue pin-striped suit that would have blended in unnoticed on Wall Street or at the Commerce Department but was far more stylish than anything anyone else in the U.S. Embassy in Moscow was wearing.

Nick was still poring over the photos, but as Marcus rose to shake the newcomer's hand, he said, "This is Jennifer Morris. CIA chief of station for Moscow. Not only does she need to hear what you're telling me, but she's fluent in Russian and can do a better job than I can at figuring out whether these documents are the real thing."

Marcus was surprised. Morris couldn't have been much over thirty. This was the ranking Agency operative in Moscow?

Nick quickly briefed Morris on all that Marcus had said. He handed her the Samsung Galaxy and asked Marcus to continue explaining what he'd been told by his source.

Marcus waited a few beats for Morris to scroll through a dozen or so photographs, then picked up the narrative where he'd left off. "Obviously, I can't personally vouch for the authenticity of the documents in these photos," he conceded. "That's one of the reasons I'm bringing them to you. But if what this guy is telling me is true, they paint a pretty chilling picture."

Morris worked her way through the documents, reading and studying each one carefully before moving on to the next.

"Luganov is ordering his generals to launch an all-out invasion of Estonia and Latvia, and he's projecting they can fully control both in under sixty hours?" she asked.

"Yes," Marcus said. "And they think it will take another forty-eight hours to seize Lithuania as well."

"The objective being what?" she asked, still scrolling through the photos.

"Divide and destroy NATO, then dictate terms to the West," Marcus said.

"Because we won't fight back?"

"Because we *can't* fight back."

"Why not?"

"The moment Luganov moves, the plan calls for him to formally and very publicly annex all three countries," Marcus said. "Then he will declare that any counterstrike by NATO or the U.S will be considered a direct attack on the Russian Federation and will lead him immediately and without question to order the use of tactical nuclear weapons."

"It's a bluff," Nick said.

"If so, it's a good one," Morris conceded.

"Do you believe him, that he'd really use nuclear weapons?" Nick asked.

Morris didn't answer, but Marcus did. "Yes, actually I do, but that's not the point."

"And what is?"

"My guy believes it," Marcus said. "That's why he came to me. He's terrified. He claims to know Luganov well. Very well. He's worked with him for years. And he says Luganov wouldn't hesitate before ordering the generals to use nukes."

"This guy truly believes Luganov will start a nuclear apocalypse?" Nick asked. "I mean, come on. Luganov is a piece of work. I grant you that. But crazy enough to start an all-out nuclear conflagration? I don't buy it."

"Look, I'm only telling you what my source says. That's why he risked his life to come to me, to give us all this, so we'll pass it along to Clarke and the Pentagon."

"So how close is he?" Morris asked. "To Luganov, to the inner circle?"

"Close enough that he got all of this," Marcus responded. "How many people likely have code-word clearance for documents like these?"

"I doubt more than two dozen, if that," said the station chief. "Can you get more?"

"I'm not sure."

"Did he give you a way to contact him?"

"He doesn't want me to contact him, says it's too dangerous," Marcus said. "But I gave him my satphone and a number where he can reach me 24-7."

"You gave him an official U.S. government phone?" Nick asked.

"It's not a government phone. I rented some back in Washington for myself and each member of the security detail I recruited."

"And your source, he agreed to call you?"

"No, but he took the phone and said he'd call me if he needed to. But I'm not so sure he will."

"Why not? Didn't you ask for updates on the war planning?" Morris asked.

"Of course."

"Did you tell him to call you if the date of the invasion was either confirmed or changed?" she pressed.

Marcus leveled his gaze at her. "Look, Miss Morris, I don't know you, and you don't know me. But surely Nick here has given you a thumbnail sketch of my background. I know how to interview a witness and handle an informant. I get the stakes here, and the time crunch, too. So you're just going to have to believe me when I tell you I got everything out of him that I could. I set up a way that the two of us could talk securely. What else was I supposed to do?"

"Is he willing to meet you again?" she asked.

"He said no."

"Why not?"

"Because he doesn't want to be shot or hanged if he's found out. Besides, he said what he gave me ought to be more than enough to convince President Clarke and the North Atlantic Council to start moving forces into the Baltics."

"That's what he wants—NATO forces moving into the Baltics?"

"Absolutely—he must have repeated it at least five times. He said the only way he can see to stop Luganov from issuing the final invasion order is if there's a sufficient deterrent force in place or at least inbound."

Morris was hurriedly making notes. So was Nick. The coffee was getting cold. Morris said, "So you gave him a phone but you don't think he's going to call back, and he doesn't want to meet you again. Forgive me for saying so, but this guy doesn't exactly meet our usual standards for a reliable source."

"Maybe not," Marcus said. "But you've got to remember: this is a guy who took an enormous risk to reach out to me. It would be an even bigger risk to call or see me again. I don't think he's going to do it to give us more information, even if there's a change in the strike date. I already told you, he believes he's given us everything we need to make a decision and get moving. But I do think there's one thing that might make him call."

Morris leaned forward. "You think he'll ask for money? Because believe me, if we can verify what he's telling us is true, the Agency will give him whatever he wants."

"No, he doesn't want money," Marcus said. "He was emphatic about that."

"Then what?" Morris asked.

"I think he might want us to get him out of the country before the dam breaks."

"Did that come up in your meeting?"

"No, and that's been bothering me. I think he wanted to ask me but hesitated."

"Why?"

"Because he doesn't see himself as a traitor needing to flee his country," Marcus said. "He sees himself as a patriot needing to serve her."

"But you think he wants an escape hatch," Morris said.

"Wouldn't you?"

"I would," she agreed.

Nick nodded. "So would I."

"I think we need to come up with a plan to get him safely out of the country," Marcus continued. "A plan that's ready to go at a moment's notice."

"I think you're right," Nick said.

"There's just one problem," Marcus said.

"Just one?"

"Okay, more than one—but let's start here," Marcus explained. "If he does call, he's not going to want to work with anyone else. Just me."

"Why's that a problem?" Morris asked.

"Because I'm supposed to fly with Senator Dayton and his team to Vilnius tonight, then on to Brussels and London, then back to D.C."

"And if you don't leave, the Russians are going to notice," Morris said.

"And get suspicious," Marcus agreed. "And that's the last thing we need."

"So you need to be on that Learjet when it takes off," Nick said.

Marcus nodded. "Right. But then I'm going to have to get back into the country without the Russians knowing I've come back."

"And how exactly do you propose we do that?" Nick asked.

Marcus smiled for the first time. "Actually, I have an idea."

63

Marcus laid out his plan.

It wasn't just critical that he be able to slip across the Russian border and get back to Moscow without getting caught. There was another element he believed was vital to the success of the mission he was hatching: they had to get Senator Dayton back to Washington as quickly as possible.

"There's no time for him to go to Vilnius," he told them.

"Why not?"

"My source was explicit—he was giving the information to me, I'm supposed to give it to Dayton, and the senator is supposed to give it to the president."

"But why Dayton? What does it matter who gives it to Clarke?"

"This guy believes it will make a bigger impression on Clarke coming from a critic of his," Marcus explained. "Plus the president is more likely to order additional U.S. and NATO forces into the Baltics right away if he has bipartisan support in Congress. That makes Dayton's support essential."

"Okay," Nick said. "So what exactly are you asking me to do?"

"Find a way to convince Dayton to go back to D.C. and not Vilnius."

"And I suppose you have a plan to make that happen as well?"

"As a matter of fact, I do."

By nine Senator Dayton and Annie Stewart were back at the embassy.

They had been summoned by Ambassador Tyler Reed and now met in his seventh-floor office. Pete had not been invited. Nor had Dayton's chief of staff or press secretary. Those three were back at the hotel packing and grumbling about being left out of what everyone knew was an important meeting, given its last-minute and rushed nature.

"Thank you both for coming on such short notice," Reed said as he huddled with Dayton and Annie, along with Nick Vinetti, Jennifer Morris, and Marcus. "Senator, I realize you're planning to fly to Vilnius in a few hours. But something's come up. It's potentially very serious, and I wanted to brief you on it and ask you to consider changing your plans."

The ambassador turned the briefing over to Morris, who proceeded to give a summary of the war plan and other documents they had received and how seriously the Agency was taking a potentially imminent Russian invasion of the Baltics. The senator asked a flurry of questions. Morris gave as many details as she could but said there were certain items she was simply not at liberty to discuss. Chief among them was the identity of the source of the documents or how they had come to the Agency's attention.

"What do you need from me?" Dayton asked.

"Well, sir, as you know, Washington is seven hours behind Moscow," Morris noted. "So at the White House it's only 2:37 in the morning. The president is asleep. But I can guarantee you no one at Langley, the NSA, or the National Military Command Center at the Pentagon is. Everyone is poring over these documents from every conceivable angle to determine whether they are authentic and, if they are, whether they truly represent the credible threat of an imminent Russian invasion of three NATO countries. Once that determination is made, the national security advisor will brief the president."

"But we need to warn the Baltic leaders," Dayton said. "I can do that myself, starting tonight with the Lithuanian prime minister."

"Actually that's why I asked you to come back to the embassy," said the ambassador. "I need to ask you to leave that to the president and the secretary of state."

"But the prime minister is expecting me in Vilnius this evening," Dayton countered. "I've already had to reschedule once."

"I realize that, Senator, but please understand the sensitivity of the situation," Ambassador Reed replied. "We need to be careful not to rush to any final judgments. Our analysis is barely under way. But this has the potential of triggering war in Europe, and we need to keep the information tight until we're sure."

"It's not just the potential of war," Dayton noted. "We're talking *nuclear* war."

"Let's hope it doesn't get that far, but yes, we can't rule it out at the moment," Reed said. "And that's all the more reason to be careful of what we say and to whom we say it."

"You want me to hold back information about a potential nuclear conflict from our allies in the Baltics, less than two weeks out from a potential catastrophic invasion?"

"Correct. Until we know more, sharing this could inflame a situation that's already volatile enough. If and when we can confirm the documents and the threat are real, then rest assured that every NATO leader will be informed, the Baltic leaders first among them. But for now, I need you to call the Lithuanian prime minister from my office. Brief him on your meeting with Luganov. Tell him what he told you, and tell him you don't buy a word of it. Then head back to Washington immediately to give a personal briefing to President Clarke on your meeting with Luganov."

"Why?" Dayton asked. "Isn't the president going to be briefed by his national security advisor?"

The ambassador turned to Nick Vinetti.

"Sir, I've been on a secure call for the better part of the last hour with Bill McDermott, the deputy NSA, giving him the same briefing the ambassador just gave you. Bill assures me the White House wants a bipartisan response to this crisis, whichever way it unfolds. Having you there will be critical to gathering congressional support."

Marcus observed Senator Dayton as he processed the request. He wondered if he might pull Annie or himself aside to confer. But he did not. Instead, Dayton reluctantly but professionally accepted the ambassador's request and suggested they set up the call to Vilnius immediately. Marcus glanced at Nick and breathed a sigh of relief.

"Thank you, Senator," said Ambassador Reed.

"America first, eh?" Dayton said.

The ambassador smiled. "Not a phrase I would normally expect to hear from the lips of a progressive Democrat," he noted.

Dayton smiled back. "No comment."

Reed continued. "Normally, as you know, a U.S. senator wouldn't be in the loop regarding such a high-level mole at all, certainly not one in the Kremlin on the eve of a possible war. But given your leadership position and long years of service on the Intelligence Committee, you and Miss Stewart here are both cleared for all this. The rest of your staff is not. I trust you'll not share any of this with them."

"I'm fully aware of my oath, Mr. Ambassador, thank you. But what about Mr. Ryker? Technically, he's not on my staff, nor is he a federal employee anymore. Yet he's been with us the entire time."

The ambassador, looking suddenly uncomfortable, glanced at Morris and then at Nick Vinetti.

"You're absolutely right, Senator," Nick said. "But in this particular case, there's a simple explanation."

"And that is . . . ?"

"The mole came to him."

SEVEN

64

The Learjet was wheels up at 4:17 p.m. local time, and Marcus was on it.

But the pilots did not head straight for Washington. Instead they made a pit stop in Berlin, a mere three-hour flight from Moscow, and there Marcus said his good-byes. Senator Dayton and Annie thanked him profusely. Pete gave him a quick hug and two slaps on the back while Marcus whispered to him, "Good luck with the girl." Then Marcus shook hands with each member of the security detail, thanked them for a job well done, and asked if he could "borrow" one of their satphones.

Marcus never left the terminal. While he waited for the senator's plane to be refueled and take off for D.C., he rented a locker and stuffed his suitcase into it along with his wallet and American passport. Well after nightfall he linked up with a team of CIA officers dispatched by Morris, who led him to a Gulfstream business jet for the flight back to Moscow.

The name Marcus Ryker did not appear on the manifest, he knew. When the plane landed in Moscow, Marcus would not be getting off. He would be on the ground already.

They crossed into Polish airspace almost immediately, then flew over Belarus and entered Russian airspace around eleven thirty that evening. Marcus said nothing and talked to no one as he looked out the window at the lights of Smolensk, Yartsevo, Safonovo, and Vyazma in succession. When he felt the plane bank slightly to the north, Marcus checked his watch, waited ten more minutes, then unbuckled his seat belt, got up, walked over to the door, ripped it open, felt the blast of whipping winds and bone-chilling cold, and threw himself into the night air without saying good-bye.

There was no hesitation. In the Marines he'd done it hundreds of times, and it all came back quickly. Just after takeoff, the team from Langley had suited him up in a black military-grade jumpsuit and a black balaclava, Nomex flight gloves, an HGU 55/P ballistic helmet, night vision goggles, a rucksack of clothes, a sidearm, water, a handful of protein bars, and a small first aid kit—everything he might need to survive for the next twenty-four hours if his linkup were delayed for any reason.

Now, as he hurtled toward the ground from forty-five thousand feet, Marcus could not see a thing. The frigid late-September sky was thick with clouds, and there was no moon. There were no cities within fifty miles, no towns or hamlets or lights of any kind. Nor could he hear a sound, save the steady hiss of the oxygen flowing from the tank on his back, and his heart pounding wildly. If someone had told him twenty-four hours earlier he'd be jumping out of a plane anywhere in the world, he would have thought them mad. He'd certainly never imagined jumping into Russia, much less out of the side of a G4. Yet now he felt an exhilaration that had eluded him for far too long.

Marcus flashed back to the first time he'd ever jumped out of a plane. It had been summer. It had been a Cessna. It had been with Elena when they were only seventeen. They had done it without telling their parents and had even forged their parents' signatures on the permission forms—a move they both admitted had been wrong. Yet nothing the two of them had ever done to that point compared with the rush they'd felt that day.

But Marcus didn't have time to think about his wife just then. He checked his altimeter. He was already below four thousand feet. It was almost time. Seconds later, he passed below three thousand, then two thousand. Only then did he break through the clouds. Now he could see the clearing they'd chosen and the edges of the forest all around it. The moment he did, he pulled the rip cord and felt the chute eject. The harness tightened under his armpits and groin. The problem was, he was still coming in hard in a densely wooded section of pines. If he didn't change course, he would likely be impaled on one of the trees or get caught in the branches and find himself stuck four or five stories above the ground.

He did a series of S-turns, pivoting 180 degrees each time, then back again nearly but not quite another 180 degrees, into the wind. This helped him correct his course and aim for the clearing. But it was going to be close. He could see the tops of the pines rushing toward him, and he prayed there might be time for one or two more turns.

There was. When he cleared the edge of the forest, he was at four hundred feet, then three hundred. Through the night vision goggles, he could see the ground rushing up at him. It was grassy but also somewhat hillier than he'd expected. He made one more S-turn as he passed below a hundred feet. Now he was headed for one of the flatter sections of the field. As he reached fifteen feet, it was time to flare. Marcus pulled hard on the toggles above his head, both at the same time. He pulled them down to his waist, radically readjusting the shape of his canopy and thus dramatically slowing his rate of descent. The maneuver worked like a charm. Exactly like he'd been taught. Exactly like he'd done so many times. An instant before touching down, he lifted his feet and literally hit the ground running. His jumpmaster back at Parris Island would have been proud.

Marcus came to a complete stop, pulled off his helmet, and shut off the oxygen tank on his back. Scanning the horizon in every direction and seeing no one, he quickly gathered up his chute and stuffed it back into the pack. Then he powered up the satphone and sent a text to Nick Vinetti consisting simply of the letter X. A moment later came the reply—the letter Y. Satisfied, Marcus stripped off the Nomex flight suit and redressed in gray slacks, a black crewneck sweater, Rockport work shoes, and a black leather jacket he'd stuffed into the rucksack he'd strapped to his chest.

Fifteen minutes later, a midnight-blue Mercedes SUV pulled to the edge of the clearing and killed its lights. Marcus chambered a round in his automatic pistol, waited a moment, then approached the car cautiously. It was a formality, of course. If the driver or its occupants were FSB and had seen his highly illegal descent, he'd probably be dead already. When the driver's-side door opened, it wasn't an FSB agent who stepped out. It was Jenny Morris, bundled up in a navy peacoat and beige scarf, and she had news.

65

"Luganov's plane took off two hours ago," Morris said as she drove.

"Heading east?" Marcus asked as he sipped the coffee she'd brought him in a travel mug.

"Heading east. Pyongyang."

"Check," he said, nearly burning his tongue and deciding to wait until the coffee cooled a bit. "What else have you got?"

"Quite a bit," she said. "NSA has intercepts of communications between various Russian base commanders and logistics officers giving orders that match almost precisely some of the written orders the Raven provided."

"The Raven?"

"That's the code name the Agency gave your mole."

"Randomly generated?"

"Not exactly," Morris conceded. "When I sent back the eyes-only cable to the director with my write-up of your report, I gave your guy that moniker. Guess it stuck."

"So why the Raven?"

"Does it matter?" she asked.

"Don't we have like a two-and-a-half-hour drive to the safe house?"

"Yeah."

"Then I guess we have plenty of time, Agent Morris, don't we?"

After bouncing around over some rocky terrain, they turned onto a real road, and the ride smoothed out. Morris glanced at him and smiled. "I guess we do," she said. "But call me Jenny, okay?"

"Jenny—got it. So why the Raven?"

"It's a biblical reference, actually," she said, "but don't tell anyone at Langley. They probably think it has something to do with Edgar Allan Poe."

"What's the biblical connection?" Marcus asked.

"The Old Testament tells a story about this prophet named Elijah. He was on the run from a wicked king," she explained.

"Ahab," Marcus said.

Morris seemed surprised. "Exactly. Elijah had no food, no water. But God provided for him—led him to a small brook on the east side of the Jordan."

"And then commanded the ravens to bring him bread and meat each morning and evening," Marcus added.

"That's right," she said. "I guess you know the story."

"I do," Marcus said.

"My grandmother taught it to me when I was a little girl," Morris said as she blew down the desolate country road at more than eighty miles per hour. "She used to say, 'Jenny, God always knows what we need, and if we'll just trust him, he'll provide from the most unlikely of sources.'"

"Like a raven," said Marcus.

"Like a raven," she agreed.

Later, as they drove east toward Moscow on the M-9 highway, Marcus asked where she was from.

"I'm afraid that's classified, Mr. Ryker." She smiled.

"Call me Marcus, okay?"

"Okay, but it's still classified."

"So, you could tell me . . ."

"But then I'd have to kill you," she finished.

"I'm afraid you'll have to get in line."

They laughed. Marcus knew it was Agency protocol for field agents and certainly station chiefs not to reveal personal details. He thought it was probable that Jenny Morris wasn't even her real name. But whoever she was, and wherever she'd grown up, Marcus now knew she had a grandmother who'd taught her the Scriptures when she was little, and she'd liked those Bible stories. She'd remembered those stories. And all these years later, she was drawing on those stories in a time of great danger.

It was almost three in the morning when the Mercedes SUV pulled to a stop.

The rain had started nearly an hour ago. Thunder rumbled overhead and jagged sticks of lightning stabbed the moonless night sky. Marcus wiped the fog from his window and tried to get his bearings. To one side of the street, he saw a giant crater where an apartment building once stood. Morris pointed to the other side of the street.

"That's us," she said. "Ninth floor, apartment 9D. Grab your stuff and meet me in the lobby. I'll take you up, but I need to park in a garage around the corner."

"I'll go with you," Marcus said.

"No, you go inside and stay dry. I'll just be a minute."

There was no point arguing with the woman. She had the same air of authority Marcus remembered from some of the other CIA agents he'd worked with in the Service. So he opened the passenger door, grabbed his rucksack and parachute pack from the back, and dashed inside. As he did, he noticed the number on the side of the building—20 Guryanova Street—and in an instant he knew where he was.

From inside the dry lobby, he looked back at the crater and closed his eyes. He could envision the massive explosion emanating from the basement. He could see the nine-story building teetering at first, then collapsing so quickly that no one could have possibly gotten out in time, especially those who had been sleeping, which would have been nearly everyone.

He had studied the case years before during a Secret Service training class in Beltsville, Maryland. One of his instructors had spent an entire day discussing the series of apartment bombings in Moscow and around Russia that had occurred in the fall of 1999. They'd studied crime-scene photographs. They'd read forensic reports translated from Russian. They'd watched interviews with key participants and even a *Frontline* documentary on the bombings that had run on PBS. At first Marcus hadn't seen the crimes as relevant to his protection duties. But the instructor had argued that anyone doing advance work for the president, the VP, or a foreign leader had to consider every possible method of assassination, no matter how bizarre, no matter how unlikely. Sure, a would-be assassin might use poison or a sniper rifle or a suicide vest to take out his subject, if he—or she—could get close enough to the target. But might not the same sick mind choose to kill hundreds or thousands of people in a high-rise apartment building or an office building in order to take out their target?

"Ladies and gentlemen," the instructor had stressed over and over again, "you'll never play effective defense unless you truly understand how to play offense. The only way to properly guard your protectee is to think like an assassin. Until you do that—until you get into the mind of evil and see the world through the eyes of a killer—you'll never know how to counter all possible moves."

The apartment bombings had never been solved, Marcus recalled.

And apparently, at least one of the buildings had never been rebuilt—the one directly across this very street. Russian authorities had blamed the attacks on Chechen terrorists, but Marcus's instructor was unconvinced. "Look at the evidence," he'd said. "The bombs were made with military-grade explosives available only to the government. We know that not only from analysis of the bombs that exploded but also from the unexploded ordnance found by police in an apartment building in Ryazan."

Marcus remembered asking his instructor who else could have done it. In the fall of 1999, it had certainly seemed like the Chechens were to blame. Every Russian was already horrified by the atrocities going on in Chechnya. But looking back, the instructor had asked a simple but profound question: Who benefited from the bombings? Certainly not the Chechens. Grozny was carpet-bombed that very month. There was, however, someone who did benefit. Who was it who had stepped into the spotlight in the wake of the apartment bombings? Who went on TV to very publicly order the Russian invasion of Chechnya? Who saw his name ID soar, and his approval ratings with it? Who but Aleksandr Luganov, the Russian prime minister and former head of the FSB, a man who not only had access to the explosives used in the bombings but also clearly benefited in the aftermath.

Lo and behold, once Luganov had ordered the bombing of Chechen cities, the apartment bombings suddenly stopped. Luganov was elected president of Russia soon after. Was it really possible, Marcus had wondered so long ago, that Luganov had ordered some of his loyalists to blow up Russian apartment buildings so that innocent Russians would die and he could blame it on the Chechens, order retaliation against Chechnya, and see his approval ratings soar into the stratosphere so he could be elected the new czar of Russia? It had all seemed rather far-fetched at the time. Yet what would the people of eastern Georgia say now? Or those who lived in Crimea? Or eastern Ukraine or Syria?

Five minutes later they reached the ninth floor. Jenny Morris unlocked the door to the three-bedroom apartment and hung her soaking-wet coat in a shower stall. Marcus tossed his stuff in one of the bedrooms and headed back out into the hallway.

"Where are you going?" Morris asked as she dried her hair with a towel.

"The basement," he said. "I just want to check things out, make sure no one has left a present for us. Don't worry. I won't be long."

66

Morris let him sleep for four hours, but that was it.

There was work to be done. She told Marcus to join her at the kitchen table. Then she explained that she was going to administer a polygraph test and record the lengthy and critical conversation they were about to have. He was not happy, but she did not care.

"You know the stakes," she said matter-of-factly. "And you know the drill. So let's get this done."

Marcus didn't work for the government. He wasn't on the federal payroll anymore. They couldn't tell him what to do. But neither did he have anything to hide. He knew the polygraph test was the Agency's way of verifying that the information he had provided was genuine and that he didn't have any ulterior motives. So although he wasn't thrilled about the prospect, he shrugged and allowed her to continue.

Morris attached several sensors to Marcus's body that would track his heart rate, blood pressure, breathing rate, and temperature and feed the data to a laptop. She started with a few control questions designed to establish a benchmark of his honesty.

"Is your name Marcus Johannes Ryker?

"Yes."

"Do you currently live in Washington, D.C.?"

"Yes."

"Are you presently in the city of Moscow?"

"Yes."

She carefully watched the lines on the display showing data from the sensors. She had told Marcus to look straight ahead, not at her or the laptop's display, but he glanced over and saw that the lines were all flat. Next she asked Marcus to answer several questions untruthfully in order to see if the sensors would properly pick up the minute but distinct changes in his physiology indicating his body's unique response to lying. Once she was satisfied the machine was functioning as it should and that Marcus was cooperating appropriately, Morris moved on.

"Did this source take the initiative to make contact with you?"

"Yes."

"He reached out to you first?"

"Yes."

"You weren't the one to initiate contact?"

"No."

"Did you meet the source in your room at the Hotel National?"

"Yes."

"Did the source provide you with pictures of classified documents, purportedly from the Kremlin?"

"Yes."

"Did you look at all fifty-three of the photos on the phone?"

"Yes."

"Are the documents authentic?"

"I can't say."

"Please keep your answers to yes or no," Morris instructed. "Do the documents look authentic to you?"

"Yes."

"Did the source tell you he believes President Luganov is preparing to invade a NATO country?"

"Yes—well, no—actually three NATO countries."

"Just yes or no, please," Morris reminded him. "Is President Luganov preparing to invade three NATO countries?"

"Yes."

"Did you believe your source?"

Marcus paused. He wasn't sure how to answer that.

Morris tried again. "Did the source seem credible to you?"

"Yes."

"Do you believe he was sent to set a trap for the U.S. or NATO?"

"No."

"Do you believe anyone in the Russian government directed the source to reach out to you?"

Marcus paused again. It was a good question. He wasn't entirely sure, but he said, "No."

On the display, the lines jiggled. Morris looked up sharply and asked the question again. Marcus again answered no, and this time the lines stayed quiet.

"So you believe the source reached out to you of his own free will?" she continued.

"Yes."

"When the source left your presence, did you immediately contact the deputy chief of mission at the U.S. Embassy?"

"Yes."

"Did you give the Samsung phone containing the photos to Mr. Vinetti?"

"Yes."

"Did you show the phone or its contents to anyone else prior to meeting with Mr. Vinetti?"

"No."

"Did you inform anyone else—prior to contacting Mr. Vinetti—about the phone, its contents, or your meeting with the source?"

"No."

Marcus began to relax. This wasn't going too badly, he decided.

As it turned out, those questions were just the warm-up act.

Marcus had completely underestimated what he was in for. Over the next three hours—without so much as a break to visit the restroom—Jenny Morris probed every part of his life, his career, his finances, his part-time work at Lincoln Park Baptist Church, the details of his compensation from Senator Dayton, his relationship with Pete Hwang, how he had chosen each of the men on the security detail, why he'd said yes to going on the trip at all, given that he'd initially said no, and rather definitively at that.

Then the questions turned to his relationship to the Raven.

"Do you know the source?" she asked.

"I can't answer that."

"That's not an option," said Morris.

"Actually, it is," Marcus replied.

"At least answer this," Morris pressed. "Do you know his name?"

"I can't answer that either."

"Why not?"

"Because I gave my word to the source that I'm not going to discuss any details regarding his identity. You know he's a male. You know I trust him. You know he has access. That's it. That's all I'm going to say."

"Had you ever met him before?"

Marcus remained silent. He had nothing more to say if she was going to continue this line of questioning. He knew his credibility with his own government was on the line. A lie would not only go against his own code of ethics but could potentially cause President Clarke to disregard the urgent warning about imminent war in Europe. Better to just decline to answer.

"Do you believe he reached out to you, of all people, because he had met you previously?" Morris asked, trying from another angle.

Marcus felt deeply uncomfortable keeping information from his own government. He had, after all, spent most of his adult life protecting his country and his government. Now he was protecting a man deep inside an enemy's inner circle. Yet having given Oleg Kraskin his word to protect his identity, he had no choice. So again, he kept quiet.

So Morris changed topics, to one that made Marcus even more uncomfortable.

"Your wife, Elena, and son, Lars—were they killed in a robbery attempt?"

Marcus gritted his teeth. "Yes," he finally conceded.

"Shortly after their deaths, did you resign your position as special agent with the U.S. Secret Service?"

"Yes."

"One of the killers died at the scene. Was the surviving perpetrator of these murders ever caught and brought to justice?"

"No."

"Were *any* suspects ever arrested and charged in the case?"

"No."

"So the case remains open today?"

Marcus took a deep breath. "Yes."

"Any current leads?"

"Not that I'm aware of."

"Does that make you angry?"

Again he had to pause to steady his nerves. "Yes." There was no sense lying about that one.

"Do you want revenge against whoever was responsible?"

"No."

The lines on the display went crazy. Morris looked at him. He looked back and saw pity in her eyes. That only made the lines gyrate all the more.

"Would you ever take revenge if you had the chance?"

She was giving him a mulligan, and he was grateful for the small act of kindness.

"No," he said with every muscle in his body tensed.

The lines moved not at all.

The final area of questioning that created no small measure of discomfort pertained to his private life.

"Mr. Ryker, after the death of your wife, did you ever remarry?"

Marcus tensed again. "What does that have to do with anything?" he demanded.

"Just answer the question, please. We're almost done. Did you ever remarry?"

Marcus shook his head slowly.

"You need to give a verbal answer, Mr. Ryker."

"No," he said softly.

"Have you dated anyone in the last several years?"

"No." He suddenly felt very thirsty.

"Have any women expressed interest in dating you?"

Marcus couldn't imagine how this was relevant, but he answered anyway. "Yes."

"But you declined?"

"Yes."

"During your travels with Senator Dayton, were you ever propositioned by a woman?"

"*What?*" Marcus snapped.

"Were you?" Morris asked calmly.

"Never," he replied, then remembered to answer properly. "No."

"Not in the Baltic states?"

"No."

"Not in Moscow?"

"No."

"Were you in any environment, any situation, that could have been construed by you or by others as a honey trap?"

It had taken several questions, but Marcus finally understood her purpose. He was a widower, potentially vulnerable to the efforts of a foreign intelligence agency to seduce him with romantic affections or sexual favors, compromising his credibility as a witness. Marcus was the only person who had met with the Raven. Everyone else in the U.S. national security apparatus was depending on his credibility. So Morris had to ask. Spy agencies had been setting honey traps for needy, vulnerable men from time immemorial, and the head of the CIA's Moscow station would not have been doing her job if she hadn't asked every relevant question, no matter how uncomfortable it made her subject.

"No," he said at last.

68

In Washington the day was just beginning, and the president of the United States was fuming.

Andrew Clarke entered the Oval Office at precisely 7 a.m. As a steward brought him coffee, the chief executive pored over every story on the front pages of the *Washington Post* and the *New York Times*. They were all about Luganov, his surprise trip to Pyongyang, his extraordinary press conference announcing the denuclearization of the Korean Peninsula, and his announcement that he intended to deescalate tensions along the Baltic and Ukrainian borders. In a single day, the Russian leader had completely changed the media narrative about him. No longer was he regarded as a rapidly intensifying threat to global safety and security. Suddenly he was being hailed as a man of peace and a viable recipient of a Nobel Prize.

Disgusted, Clarke tossed the papers aside and informed his secretary that she could send in the guests who were waiting in the lobby of the West Wing for their 7:30 meeting.

The first to enter the Oval was Richard Stephens, the balding, sixty-four-year-old director of the CIA who had previously served as the senior senator from Arizona and chairman of the Senate Intelligence Committee. Following him in was Cal Foster, the silver-haired, seventy-one-year-old secretary of defense. A retired four-star general, Foster had served more than three decades in the U.S. Army and nearly five years as the supreme allied commander of NATO. Also joining them was Bill McDermott, recently appointed deputy national security advisor. The last man to enter the room was the White House chief of staff.

Director Stephens began the briefing by giving the president and each participant a black leather-bound notebook embossed in gold lettering with the seal of the Central Intelligence Agency and the words *The President's Daily Briefing*. Underneath that was the president's name. Below that were the words *TOP SECRET: Contains Sensitive Material*. Inside was an eight-page bullet-point summary of the most urgent and important intelligence information the commander in chief needed to know.

During the previous day's briefing, Stephens had introduced Clarke to the emergence of a possible high-level mole in Moscow code-named the Raven. He'd given the president an overview of the mole's allegations and the fifty-three photos of documents the source had passed to an American case officer. No specifics about either figure were given, but plenty of caveats were. Stephens had underscored to the president how raw and unconfirmed this intel was. He'd also drawn the president's attention to the section of the PDB mentioning the fact that Senator Dayton had met with President Luganov in the Kremlin, promising that more details of the meeting would be forthcoming.

Today they were.

"Mr. President, you'll find that the last five pages in today's PDB are a point-by-point account of Senator Dayton's conversation with President Luganov," the CIA director explained. "These are the verbatim notes taken by our station chief in Moscow, who met with the senator and his team when they briefed Ambassador Reed. I'd like to go over this with you rather carefully, because we expect the senator to be here by nine, and when he arrives, we want you to be fully versed on what was said in the meeting so we can focus our time with him on drawing some conclusions and seeing if we can come to a bipartisan agreement on where to go from here."

"Fine," Clarke said, leafing through the pages as he sat behind the *Resolute* desk.

"That said, Mr. President," Stephens continued, "the first two pages of your brief focus on what we're learning from the Raven and his case officer. Page 3 is a summary of Russian military activity over the last twenty-four hours. With your permission, I'll cover these. Then I've asked Secretary Foster to discuss options."

"What do we know about the Raven?" asked Clarke. "How close is he to Luganov? And how credible is the material he's passed on to us?"

"All excellent questions, and I will get to each one in turn," Stephens replied. "But if you'll allow me, sir, I want to start with the identity of the figure we described in yesterday's briefing as our 'case officer,' because to a certain degree, our level of confidence in the Raven is predicated on our level of confidence in the one bringing him to us."

"Very well," said the president. "Proceed."

"Thank you, sir. Now, keep in mind that the information we had regarding the Raven was only hours old when I briefed you yesterday. Therefore, I essentially gave you a mere abstract of what we'd received because we believed it could be enormously important. But I did not bring more detail at the time because there had been effectively no time to cross-check any of the information. Today I can tell you much more."

Clarke nodded and Stephens continued.

"This case officer—the person who made contact with the Raven— is not an actual case officer at all. He's neither an employee of nor a contractor for the Agency. Nor is he a Foreign Service officer or even an employee of the U.S. government. Not anymore."

"But he was?"

"He was never with the Agency in any capacity, but yes, he did work for the U.S. government in various capacities over the years."

"Do you believe he is credible?"

"We do, Mr. President. He served in the U.S. military and received a Purple Heart. Later he worked here at the White House for a time."

"So who is it?"

"Marcus Ryker."

"Ryker? You mean the Secret Service agent?"

"Yes, Mr. President," Stephens confirmed.

"The one who lost his wife and son a few years back?"

"Yes, sir."

"I thought he'd retired. What's he doing in Moscow, of all places?"

Stephens looked to Bill McDermott.

"I think I can explain that, sir," the deputy NSA said. "Marcus has known Senator Dayton since he and I both served on the senator's protection detail on his codel to Afghanistan back in '04. They have totally different political views, at least on domestic and social issues, but when Dayton decided to go to Europe to raise his profile for a presidential run, he hired Marcus to help him put together a security team. Though Marcus does not support the senator's presidential run, he agreed out of friendship and, you could say, out of a sense of loyalty to the man."

"Loyalty?" the president asked.

"It's a bit complicated."

"Give me the short version."

"Well, sir," said McDermott, "Marcus was under my command back in Afghanistan. So was a guy named Peter Hwang. During Senator Dayton's trip to Kabul, we came under attack by the Taliban. Two of our choppers were shot down. One was a total loss. The other—the one Dayton was in—had survivors. We had to make an emergency landing and found ourselves in a pretty serious firefight with a clan of jihadists. All of my men fought with tremendous distinction, but no one more so than Marcus. When it was all over, Dayton credited Marcus with saving his life. Every year on the anniversary of that attack, Senator Dayton either calls Marcus personally or sends him a handwritten note. I've heard them get into some rip-roaring fights on policy and politics. But they genuinely like and appreciate each other. Marcus believes he got into the Secret Service, in part, on the basis of a recommendation Dayton wrote for him."

"Loyalty," the president said. "Got it."

"So that's what put Marcus Ryker in Moscow," McDermott noted. "It's still not clear to us why this source—whom we're calling the Raven—came to Marcus. But Marcus says the Raven reached out to him, made the initial contact, and I believe him. Marcus believes the source is totally legit. Says he's wired in at the highest levels, though he won't give us a name or a title or even a hint at who he is, out of fear of putting the man's life in danger."

"We're sure it's a man?" asked Secretary Foster. "No possibility of a honey trap?"

"Marcus says it is, and I have no reason to doubt him," McDermott replied. "Ryker has served our country honorably. He took a bullet in the line of duty, Mr. President. I don't see any evidence that suggests he was compromised, nor do I believe he could be."

"Was Ryker subjected to a PDD?" asked the White House chief of staff.

"What's that?" the president asked.

"He's referring to a psychophysiological detection of deception test," McDermott said. "More commonly known as a polygraph."

"So was he?" the president asked.

McDermott looked back at Stephens.

"He was, sir," said the CIA director.

"And?"

"He passed with flying colors."

At that, Clarke pushed his chair back from the desk and stood. He walked over to the windows and looked out at the falling leaves and changing colors of autumn.

"So, bottom line, gentlemen, you believe this case officer—who is not a case officer at all—is credible. And by reading ahead in the PDB, I gather that the Raven's statements and the documents he's handed over to us have borne out so far. Correct?"

"Yes, Mr. President," Stephens confirmed.

"Meanwhile we have Russian fighter and bomber squadrons and tanks and ground forces being transferred in recent weeks from the Pacific theater to the borders of the Baltics and Ukraine."

"That's correct, sir."

"And the written orders the Raven turned over indicate that Luganov intends to use these forces to invade NATO allies?"

"Yes, sir."

"And both the CIA and DIA assess that unless we move a whole lot of men and matériel into the Baltics in the next few days, Luganov actually does have a credible capacity to seize Latvia and Estonia in less than sixty hours, followed by Lithuania in another forty-eight to ninety-six hours, give or take."

"We do, sir," Stephens confirmed.

"Moreover, the Raven claims that Luganov's trip to Pyongyang is nothing but a smokescreen."

"Correct."

"Yet Luganov has signed a strategic alliance with North Korea, and the North Koreans have promised to fully dismantle their nuclear program and turn all the components over to the Russians."

"Correct."

Clarke was now pacing around the Oval Office. "Not only that, but Luganov has just held a press conference in Pyongyang saying fears of a Russian invasion of Ukraine and/or the Baltics are preposterous. He says the Russian military is merely conducting exercises and that in the interest of international peace and harmony, he has ordered all or most of these forces to be withdrawn by next week at the latest."

No one said a word. It was all true.

"So those are the banner headlines we're waking up to," the

president continued. "Luganov defusing two regional crises in a single day. Looks like a genius. A man of peace. And what do I look like if I mobilize the Eighty-Second Airborne and the 101st and start moving battle tanks toward the borders of Russia?"

Every eye in the room turned to the secretary of defense.

"Mr. President," Foster said calmly, "I don't see that we have a choice. We have to move, and we have to move fast. You can announce that the moment Russia really does remove 150,000 troops off the borders of our allies, you'll be happy to consider redeploying our forces elsewhere in Europe. But until then, you have an obligation to ensure the NATO alliance is strong and that our capacity deterrence is unmistakable."

Clarke stopped pacing. "My only *obligation*, as you put it, is to the American people, who elected me in no small part to end our involvement in overseas conflicts, not exacerbate them and certainly not to potentially spark an international crisis by sending troops into a standoff with Russia. Until we have more information, until we have absolute proof that the war plan the Raven gave us is genuine, I will not send a single American soldier, tank, or plane into harm's way."

69

"I think we need a plan to assassinate Luganov," Marcus said.

Jennifer Morris was sitting at the kitchen table, reading a briefing on her Agency laptop. Marcus was standing at the sink, filling a kettle to make a pot of tea. He had just finished cleaning his Glock 9mm pistol, which lay on the table across from Morris along with a spare magazine. Beside them were bottles of cleaning solvent, gun oil, a soiled toothbrush, a cleaning rod, and a small box of Q-tips. It was clear from the stunned expression on Morris's face that he'd caught her completely off guard. But in his mind the conversation couldn't wait.

"Assassinate the president of Russia?" she whispered, standing and moving across the kitchen to have the conversation up close and as quietly as possible.

"Yes," said Marcus.

"Are you insane?" she replied. "We're trying to stop a war, Ryker, not start one."

"But what if Clarke refuses to order U.S. forces into the Baltics? Or what if he does, but he doesn't send enough? Or he can't persuade the rest of NATO to send forces to help us create a deterrent? What if Luganov simply moves up his timetable and invades earlier than the seventh? We can't base our entire plan on building up a big enough deterrent force in Estonia, Latvia, and Lithuania. We need a plan B."

"Maybe so," Morris said. "But it's sure not going to be an assassination."

"Why not?"

"First of all, it's illegal."

"Okay, there's that."

"Second of all, who's going to kill him—you?"

"I'd rather not, but . . ."

"*But what?*" Morris asked, incredulous. "Ryker, you really are mad. One, if you were actually to assassinate the leader of Russia, that's an act of war. And who's to say that would derail things? Why wouldn't Luganov's successor use the moment to invade anyway? Two, if you're unsuccessful—if you're killed or captured while trying to take out the leader of the Russian Federation—then you've given Luganov the ultimate pretext not just to seize the Baltics but to carry out any other crazy attack he's planning. Three, it's a completely stupid idea. And four, did I mention how stupid an idea it is?"

"So you're saying you'll keep an open mind—great," Marcus said as the water came to a boil. "Tea?"

Morris stood there staring at him for a moment, then smiled and said yes. Marcus made them each a cup, and they sat down at the kitchen table and pushed aside the Glock and the cleaning supplies.

"Look," he said, "the Raven was pretty clear that the invasion scenario is being driven entirely by Luganov."

"No, he said the FSB chief supports him too."

"Nimkov."

"Right."

"Fine," Marcus said. "But there's no indication that everyone else in the cabinet or even the war council does," Marcus noted. "Do you have a copy of the transcript the Raven gave us of the conversation between Luganov and the army chief of staff just before Luganov sacked him?"

Morris pulled up the document on her laptop, and they reviewed it together.

GENERAL: You are asking us to capture and occupy three NATO capitals?

PRESIDENT: And secure their annexation so that they might be rightfully reintegrated into Mother Russia.

GENERAL: But not Kiev.

PRESIDENT: Not right now.

GENERAL: Would it not be in our interest to seize all of Ukraine instead? The Ukrainians are very patriotic, and they're able fighters, but they are not members of NATO. Washington and Brussels will huff and puff, but in the end they will do nothing if we take Ukraine. I have war-gamed this with my staff. I'm convinced we could get it done in a month to six weeks.

PRESIDENT: But we can have the Baltics in four days.

GENERAL: How is it in Russia's interest, if I may ask, to provoke such a confrontation with NATO when Ukraine is ours for the taking with no risk of triggering Article 5?

"So your point is that the head of the Red Army was sacked because he told Luganov that going after the Baltics instead of Ukraine was a mistake," Morris said. "And you think maybe there are others around that table who harbor similar concerns?"

"What if there are?"

"Then wonderful, but what if there aren't?" Morris pushed back. "You don't have any proof, just a hunch. And how could you possibly justify a high-risk American operation to assassinate Luganov on a hunch?"

"Look, Jenny, the Raven made it perfectly clear to me that in Luganov we're dealing with a psychotic personality. The man thinks he's a czar. The Raven called him an old-guard imperialist willing to use any means necessary to take back lands he believes are rightfully his. Can we safely assume there are members of his war council that support him or at least won't risk countering him? Absolutely. I grant you that. But if Luganov is gone, if he's taken out of the picture, do the members of that cabinet still move forward with Luganov's plan, knowing full well that they risk a nuclear war with NATO in the process? You've got to admit that if Luganov was dead, their calculus would have to change. And that might give the West the time we need to avert a full-blown war in Europe."

Morris said nothing for several minutes. She slowly sipped her tea and stared at the Glock on the table in front of her while freezing rain pelted and rattled the windows.

"So—hypothetically speaking—how would you do it?" she asked finally, looking him in the eye once again. "How would you take him out? You're not an assassin, Ryker. And with all due respect, even if you were, you haven't fired a gun in years."

"You're right," Marcus replied. "But you're forgetting one thing."

"What?"

"I'm a Marine, and if there was one thing I was taught, it was this: Be polite, be professional, but have a plan to kill everybody you meet."

"Catchy," said Morris. "So you have a plan?"

"Not yet," he admitted. "But I'm working on it, and so should you."

70

Senator Bob Dayton wasn't sure which meeting worried him more.

The one he'd had with Luganov or the one he was about to have with Clarke.

True, Luganov was a modern czar, ruthless and throbbing with ambition. But he was not a figure unheard of in the history of Russian rulers. Andrew Hartford Clarke was something else altogether. Apparently willing to say anything and do anything to build his brand and advance his goals at all costs, Clarke was the most polarizing yet thoroughly original and entertaining political figure Dayton had ever met or even heard of. The man routinely, sometimes hourly, provoked surges of raging emotions both for *and* against him. He had single-handedly upended the Washington political establishment by winning first the Republican nomination and then the presidency when not a single pundit or pollster had given him a chance. Few members of

Congress, if any, had spent any time before the election actually considering what a Clarke presidency would look like, how it would operate, or how they would interact with it. Dayton himself had bitterly railed against Clarke in dozens of campaign speeches and hundreds of radio, television, print, and electronic interviews. In turn, he had seen his own approval ratings soar among the progressive base of the Democratic Party. Indeed, this was what had prompted him to think a run against Clarke for the presidency was becoming not just plausible but imperative.

As the leased Learjet touched down at Dulles International Airport and taxied to the Signature Flight Support Center for private aircraft, Dayton faced the most difficult decision of his political career. In less than an hour, he would be sitting in the Oval Office with a man he utterly despised, a man his supporters despised even more. To evince any hint of being ready to work together on the Russia crisis in a bipartisan manner with such a man could very well be political suicide. Yet not to work together, Dayton feared, could lead in short order to a nuclear disaster of incalculable magnitude.

If this weren't bad enough, Dayton could hardly expect to sidestep the media and hope his conversations with Clarke could somehow be kept confidential. Even before they'd left Moscow, Dayton had instructed his press secretary to pull out all the stops and line up every interview he could, and the young man had done his job. Tonight Dayton was scheduled to appear on *60 Minutes* to give an exclusive on his discussions with Luganov and the leaders in Eastern Europe who believed they were facing an imminent military showdown with Russia, and how the news out of North Korea could be dramatically changing the story line. The following morning he was set for back-to-back live interviews on ABC, CBS, NBC, CNN, and MSNBC on the same topics. Surely his meeting with Clarke would leak, and surely he would be asked about it in every interview. What would he say?

In many ways, this was a potential presidential candidate's dream scenario—a big media platform at a moment of global import. Yet

Luganov's moves were scrambling Dayton's playbook. The senator now had no idea what advice he wanted to give to Clarke or even how he wanted to characterize his meetings with Luganov or Clarke to the press, and he was quickly running out of time to figure it out.

The meeting did not go well.

For starters, President Clarke was not interested in being briefed by a man actively planning to run against him in the next national election. Twice he interrupted the senator to ask if this wasn't all a ploy for big ratings and fifteen minutes in the spotlight.

Dayton told the president it was his "moral and constitutional duty" to rapidly deploy tens of thousands of American and NATO forces to the Baltics and to supply the Ukrainians with arms, ammunition, and intelligence. "The only thing standing in the way is your own inexperience and hubris!" he shouted. When Clarke accused Dayton of using the crisis for political gain, the senator responded, "Mr. President, if you refuse or even hesitate to come to the aid of vulnerable NATO allies in a moment of peril, you will undermine the greatest military and political alliance in the history of freedom."

As McDermott would later relay to Nick Vinetti, the heated voices could be heard throughout the West Wing. Both men either were unable to control themselves or believed that when the high-profile dustup in the Oval Office inevitably leaked to the press, it would help them with their bases.

There was just one problem with such calculations, McDermott would tell his old friend. "Both men seem to have forgotten a nuclear war might bode poorly for either of their political fortunes."

MOSCOW—26 SEPTEMBER

Marcus knew Jenny Morris would be no help in taking out Luganov.

She'd humored him for a moment, but only because she believed he was kidding or yanking her chain. Pressed, however, she'd thrown Executive Order 12333 in his face, notably Part 2.11, which read, *"No person employed by or acting on behalf of the United States Government shall engage in, or conspire to engage in, assassination."*

Marcus was not only familiar with the order, he'd studied it quite carefully, as had all special agents, and he knew it wasn't quite as clear-cut as it might seem. Signed by Ronald Reagan back in 1981, the order never actually defined the term *assassination*, creating a significant gray area. Several later presidents and their attorneys general had, in fact, concluded that "targeted killings" of terrorist leaders—such as Osama bin Laden and the al Qaeda leadership—were not just legal but morally justified. The order had never been tested in the courts, and over the past few days Marcus had been asking himself whether an order inhibiting the nation's ability to act in self-defense was even constitutional.

It wasn't that Marcus supported killing foreign leaders in general. Still, he kept thinking of what might have happened if someone had taken out Hitler before he invaded Poland, before he set the Final Solution into motion. At least twenty-five attempts were made against the führer's life. Weren't men like Claus von Stauffenberg and his colleagues—who initiated the much-heralded, if unsuccessful, Operation Valkyrie—heroes for at least having tried to stop a madman from murdering millions?

What about Dietrich Bonhoeffer? His story cut closer to home. He was a German Christian, a Protestant pastor and theologian. When Hitler outlawed the preaching of the gospel and the teaching of the Bible and moved to take over the state church, Bonhoeffer first started an underground seminary, training young men to remain faithful to the teachings of Jesus instead of selling out to the Nazis. In the end, however, after much prayer and study, Bonhoeffer joined a conspiracy to assassinate the führer to prevent him from destroying the Germany he loved. Was something similar needed now?

Marcus wasn't entirely certain, but he was determined to have a plan, should an opportunity present itself. Of course, such a plan would hinge on his knowing exactly where Luganov was going to be at any given moment. Perhaps Oleg could get him the president's schedule. Right now he was probably in the air, on the way home from North Korea. And once he was back in Moscow, why would Luganov go anywhere public if he was counting down the hours to a full-on invasion of three NATO countries? More likely he would be holed up for the next few days in the Kremlin, huddling with his generals. Still, Marcus needed to be ready.

He got up and went into the kitchen. Morris was still sitting at the table, now sending an encrypted cable back to Langley, a pot of tea at her side.

"I need a weapon," Marcus said.

"No, you don't," she said, not bothering to look up from her work. "You're never going to get near him."

"You don't know that," he said. "But even if you're right, we still need an extraction plan for the Raven, don't we?"

Now she looked up. "Yes, but—"

"I think I may have one."

"You already have a weapon," she said, glancing at the Glock.

"You're telling me that if something goes down, you really want me defending myself with an American sidearm? No, I need something Russian, something untraceable. A Vul and a Vintorez would do nicely."

"A silent pistol and a sniper rifle?"

The MSS Vul had been the standard-issue pistol for the KGB, Spetsnaz, and other Russian and Eastern Bloc assassins and spies since the early 1980s. It could fire a 7.62mm round with impressive accuracy and make no more sound than a nearly inaudible metallic click. Even better, it emitted no smoke or flash.

The VSS Vintorez—"thread cutter" in English—was a highly effective Soviet-era sniper rifle used by Special Forces. Traditionally equipped with a high-end telescopic sight, when it was fitted with a night-vision scope, it became even deadlier.

For the next ten minutes, Marcus walked Morris through his idea to get the Raven out of the country. It was incredibly risky and somewhat complicated. It would require not just Morris's green light but her active cooperation. And there was one big problem: Russians were almost certainly going to have to die. Four of them, to be exact. Marcus didn't like it, and he said as much. But those were the facts. The Raven had a four-man security detail with him at all times, Marcus told her. He had given them the slip once, on the night he came to the Hotel National to meet with Marcus. It was too much to hope that the Raven would be alone again, especially in the lead-up to a major military operation. If Langley truly wanted this source in their hands, back in the U.S. or some place where they could debrief him to their hearts' content, to learn every secret they possibly could about Luganov and the inner workings of his regime, then this was the only way.

Morris was quiet. She asked a few questions, and he provided what he thought were reasonable answers. Then the two just looked at each other.

Finally Morris excused herself.

"Where are you going?" Marcus asked. "I need an answer."

"So do I," she said. "And this is above my pay grade."

71

NOVO-OGARYOVO, RUSSIA—28 SEPTEMBER

"Mr. President, we have a problem."

The tense voice on the other end of the phone belonged to FSB Chief Dmitri Nimkov.

"It had better be an emergency, Dmitri Dmitrovich—I've only recently returned from North Korea, and it's the middle of the night!" Luganov shouted into the receiver by his bed. "What's wrong?"

"It's Clarke, sir."

"What about him?"

"He just mobilized the Eighty-Second and the 101st Airborne Divisions."

One hour later, Luganov's chopper landed at the Kremlin.

He strode into the cabinet room with Oleg and Special Agent

Kovalev right behind him and found his senior military and intelligence officials nervously waiting to give him a more-detailed briefing.

Nimkov took the lead, as Oleg expected he would. In recent months, Oleg had watched as Luganov leaned more and more heavily on the FSB chief and less and less on Defense Minister Petrovsky. Oleg had first seen it on his trip to Vladivostok for the meeting with the North Korean leader. Nimkov had been the president's confidant, while Petrovsky was kept out of the loop on critical details of Luganov's meetings.

And Petrovsky hadn't even been invited to come to Pyongyang on the most recent trip. Nimkov had been, and Oleg had watched the fifty-four-year-old spymaster—operating in a role Luganov himself had once held—not only taking commands from the president but providing counsel that, from Oleg's vantage point, was being listened to and even heeded. Nimkov, more than any other cabinet member, was emerging as Luganov's right-hand man. Oleg had even begun to wonder if his father-in-law saw Nimkov as his heir apparent. Both men were ruthless and driven and supremely comfortable with the dark arts of statecraft. And Nimkov knew his place. He was careful to be—or at least appear to be—exceedingly loyal to Luganov. And Luganov always rewarded loyalty.

Nimkov began the briefing by explaining that while the news hadn't broken in the media yet, Russian intelligence had determined that the Pentagon was in the process of mobilizing and rapidly deploying more than forty thousand combat soldiers and Special Forces commandos along with hundreds of battle tanks, heavy artillery, antiaircraft batteries, and Patriot missile launchers. At the same time, at least a dozen fighter squadrons and four heavy bomber wings had been ordered to be prepared to leave American bases and head for Europe in the next forty-eight hours. Though it wasn't precisely clear where in Europe they were going, the FSB's operating presumption was that the squadrons were headed to the Baltics. Meanwhile, the Americans' Carrier Strike Group 10—with its flagship USS *Dwight D. Eisenhower*—had just been ordered to move out of the North Atlantic and into the Baltic Sea.

As best they could tell, Nimkov noted, the orders for the American ground forces were to deploy from bases across the American East Coast and Southwest to bases in Poland as part of NATO's ongoing Enhanced Forward Presence. They weren't deploying to the Baltics— yet—but twenty teams of American logistical officers had landed overnight in Estonia, Latvia, and Lithuania, strongly suggesting that the U.S. and other NATO forces would be arriving there within four to five days and certainly no more than a week.

Oleg Kraskin fought to keep his head down and his expression neutral. In fact, he was ecstatic. He'd taken a huge, potentially lethal risk, but it appeared to be paying off. He'd read wire service reports that Senator Dayton had canceled his trip to Vilnius and flown all night back to Washington. He'd seen the *60 Minutes* interview about Dayton's "knock-down, drag-out fight" with President Clarke in the Oval Office, in which he said he had urged the president not to be deceived by Luganov but to "send a clear message of solidarity with our Baltic brothers." He'd also read a *New York Times* interview with Dayton saying that despite the heated words he and the president had exchanged, he wanted to be crystal clear that he was offering the Clarke administration his full support if the president did come to the aid of NATO's most vulnerable members and promised to rally patriotic Democrats to make sure the effort was truly bipartisan.

Oleg's elation, however, was quickly extinguished. Before Nimkov had finished his briefing, Luganov erupted from his chair in a volcanic, profanity-laced tirade.

"One of you is a traitor, maybe more than one!" the president raged.

Stunned silence filled the room.

"Whichever one of you leaked word of my war plans to the Americans will be found and executed for treason."

A chill ran down Oleg's spine as the president ordered Nimkov to begin a mole hunt.

But Luganov wasn't finished.

"You think you have stopped me?" he thundered, scanning the faces

of everyone seated around the table. *"You haven't stopped me. I will go forward with the invasion. I will expose Clarke for the fool that he is. The Americans and the rest of NATO cannot possibly amass a force sufficient to deter us. There simply isn't time."*

Oleg was petrified. This could not be happening.

"Mikhail Borisovich, we will no longer strike on the seventh of October, as planned," Luganov continued. *"I now order you to be ready to move on the first."*

The defense minister looked ashen. "The first of October?" he said. "But, Aleksandr Ivanovich, this is not possible. That is only three days from now. My men will not be ready."

"They are not your men," Luganov bellowed. *"They are mine. And they will be ready—for the sake of Mother Russia, they will be ready, and they will bring us a great and glorious victory!"*

"Please, Your Excellency! The men can be ready by the sixth, maybe by the fifth, but I am not lying when I tell you that the first is simply too soon," Petrovsky insisted. "Even if we could be ready by the first, we have clearly lost the element of surprise. Moreover, we must now consider the possibility that the FSB has grossly underestimated President Clarke's ability to change course, to be unpredictable, and I must say this seriously complicates our plans."

It was astonishing to see the defense minister openly disagreeing with Luganov, especially in the midst of such a tirade. But even as he took dictation of every word being spoken, Oleg found himself secretly cheering for Petrovsky. Someone had to confront this madness. Someone had to move the president off of this catastrophic path.

Before Luganov could respond, Nimkov weighed in. "You are out of line, Mikhail Borisovich," the FSB chief said. "Your statements show hesitancy—perhaps even cowardice. The president has not made a suggestion. He has given you a direct order. He wants to invade the Baltics on 1 October, and none of us in this room have seen you salute and say yes, have we?"

"I certainly have not," Luganov fumed. *"And I am waiting."* The words

nearly vomited from his mouth. He was pacing about the room now, directly opposite Petrovsky but heading in his direction.

"Aleksandr Ivanovich, please," said his defense minister. "I have been with you on this plan every step of the way. But it was always premised on the element of surprise, on minimal American forces in the theater, on a lightning-fast strike and then holding these states knowing that neither the Americans nor anyone in NATO will risk a nuclear war to drive us out of the lands that are rightfully ours. These are your words, not mine. No one has been more supportive of you than have I. Indeed, I have worked night and day for months to make your plan a reality. But we must be honest with ourselves and concede that the strategic situation has just seriously and sweepingly changed, and not to our advantage."

"*I concede nothing,*" bellowed Luganov, still moving toward Petrovsky.

"But, sir, what if we invade now and the Americans decide to fight back? What if Clarke is stronger than the FSB tells us, more determined than we around this table have supposed? What if he does not blink? What if he actually invokes Article 5, and we find ourselves in a nuclear Armageddon with the Americans and all of Europe?"

This impassioned plea literally stopped Luganov in his tracks. The room was silent. Every eye shifted from Petrovsky to the president. Even Oleg forced himself to look up from his notebook to wait for the answer. The defense minister's logic was sound. His loyalties were unimpeachable. The man was risking not only his career but his very life out of a profound sense of duty and love of country. The contrast between Petrovsky and Nimkov had never been so clear.

Luganov was now gripping the backs of two chairs so hard his knuckles were white. His jaw was set. He was visibly controlling his breathing, and his voice became somber and filled with menace.

"Let me make myself perfectly clear: NATO is finished," he said quietly. "And if Clarke gets in my way, so is he."

With that, he ordered the defense minister to put all Russian strategic nuclear forces on full alert, to ready the air and ground forces for a 1 October invasion or resign immediately and be taken into custody on charges of treason and sedition.

Oleg felt physically ill. He turned cautiously to Petrovsky, hoping desperately for the man to take a stand. But he did not. The defense minister was trembling as he uttered the words "Very well, Your Excellency."

Luganov was going to war, regardless of what the generals said.

Oleg lit a cigarette, shuddering at the implications, and concluded he had to talk privately with Petrovsky, and soon. The defense minister might not be the only man of reason in the entire cabinet. But if there were others who believed their leader was foolish for playing a game of nuclear chicken with an American president who had never fought a war nor ever served in the military yet prided himself in being "unpredictable," they were keeping their counsel to themselves. Only Petrovsky had demonstrated the courage to speak his mind. The last cabinet member who had tried to do so was the army chief of staff, and he had been arrested and banished to the outer reaches of the empire.

If it was possible to dissuade Luganov from the disastrous path he was on, it had to happen fast, for they were rapidly running out of time. Perhaps together, Oleg thought, he and Petrovsky could devise a way to talk Luganov off the ledge. It was risky, but he resolved to find a pretext to call Petrovsky the moment the man returned to the

Defense Ministry. Maybe they could meet later in the day to consider their options, meager and dwindling though they were.

Yet as everyone gathered their papers and rushed out of the cabinet room, Luganov summoned Oleg to meet with him privately in his office. He was as angry as Oleg had ever seen him, but the volcanic eruption was over. Gone was the spewing molten lava, replaced by an icy discipline that unnerved Oleg even more.

"I may have to sack Petrovsky if he cannot do his job," the president said the moment Oleg shut the door behind them. "I will not abide disloyalty."

"Should I go speak to him?" Oleg asked, sensing an opening.

But Luganov slammed that door shut. "No," he said, walking over to the windows and looking out over the Kremlin grounds. "I made my expectations clear. If Petrovsky can't meet them, there's no use going to speak with him. Talk instead to his deputy, Shishkin. Make sure he understands his commander's intent, and make sure Shishkin is ready to step into his boss's shoes if a change must be made."

Oleg said he would do that and asked if that would be all. But there was more.

"We need the word to leak that the crisis has, in fact, been defused and that what I said in Pyongyang was the truth." Luganov turned back to Oleg and sat behind his desk. "Call the German foreign minister—what's his name?"

"Frankel."

"Right, you two are close, are you not?"

"Close enough," Oleg said.

"Fine—reach out to him. Take his temperature. Let him know that you've just come out of a meeting with me and heard me issue orders to cancel all exercises near the Baltics and Ukraine tomorrow. Tell him Russian troops should begin pulling out on the first. Also imply—but carefully—that Clarke may be in over his head and in danger of seriously misreading the situation. Then call that guy in Madrid, the one who was here last month."

"Galdós," Oleg recalled. "Carlos Ruiz Galdós, the speaker of their parliament."

"Right—call him," Luganov insisted. "We funneled money to their party through the Venezuelans last year, correct?"

"Yes, sir."

"Good. Don't bring that up, of course. But he should be helpful."

"Anyone else?"

"No, two should be enough. Coming directly from you, this will be given great weight. I guarantee the word will spread through the leadership of NATO before our heads hit the pillow tonight."

Oleg had his notebook open. He was taking careful notes of every assignment and becoming nauseated with each word he wrote.

"But first, I want you to call Marina," Luganov added. "Tell her everything is fine. Tell her war will not come. I don't want her to worry. Better yet, tell her you're taking her to Monaco next weekend, now that the threat of war has passed."

"Monaco?"

"Yes, yes, tell her that—she will be thrilled," Luganov continued. "Tell her I've been working you too hard. You're not getting enough time with her. Tell her to start booking flights and a hotel. She'll tell her girlfriends. I know my girl. Word will spread to all her friends and then to their parents that the clouds are lifting and the storm has passed. Her friends' parents are bankers, hedge fund managers, CEOs. They have many friends and contacts in the West, and they will spread the news even faster than the politicians. And the effect on our markets will be very positive. We will make money today, Oleg, you and I. We will make a great deal of money."

Oleg still could not believe how sanguine this man could be about taking the country into a completely unnecessary and highly risky war with NATO. Just then the intercom on the desk buzzed. Luganov's secretary said the FSB chief was waiting to see him. The president said he would be right with him.

"That is all, Oleg Stefanovich. Check back with me when you're done with all this. I will have more for you by then. There is still the matter of the traitor in my cabinet for us to deal with."

"Yes, Father, but . . ."

"What is it, my son? Dmtri Dmitrovich is waiting."

"I know, but . . . may I ask you a question?"

"Of course. What is on your mind?"

Oleg wasn't sure this was a good idea, but he knew he couldn't keep silent. This, after all, was very likely his last chance.

"I'm just wondering if, perhaps, you ever asked Dmitri Dmitrovich for . . ." He hesitated, almost certain he should not actually finish his sentence.

"For what?" Luganov pressed, a flash of irritation in his eyes.

"For an updated assessment of President Clarke," Oleg finally blurted out.

"Why?"

"Remember the other day I said I was worried, not about your plan to go to war but about whether you were getting the best advice on how the Americans will respond?" Oleg said, walking right up to the line and hoping he wasn't going over it. "What if the FSB is wrong?"

"They aren't," Luganov said flatly.

"But, Father, did Dmitri Dmitrovich tell you that Clarke was going to order forty thousand American troops to head for Poland and then possibly—even probably—into the Baltics in the next few days?"

Luganov said nothing.

"He did not, Father," Oleg continued. "Nor did he predict Clarke would send an aircraft carrier battle group into the Baltic Sea or deploy squadrons of B-52s and F-35s to the theater. In truth, the FSB predicted the exact opposite. Don't get me wrong, Father—I have great respect and admiration for Dmitri Dmitrovich and his entire operation. They are brave and courageous men doing a hard and thankless job for our country. But we must be honest—they have made some significant mistakes in recent days. What if they are reading Clarke wrong? It's true the man has shown little commitment to Article 5 of the NATO charter. He has called NATO obsolete and suggested he might not care if it folds. But what if he surprises us again? What if he is not the caricature we have in our heads, the buffoon the media portrays him to be? What if we play nuclear chicken with him and he *doesn't* blink?"

The room was silent. Oleg felt like he was going to vomit. He braced for the eruption.

Luganov abruptly rose from his chair and walked around the desk. Oleg stood frozen. Beads of perspiration formed on his forehead. His trembling hands grew clammy as he gripped his notebook and pen tightly and tried to steady his breathing. But then his father-in-law stunned him by putting his arm around Oleg's shoulders.

"You are a good and loyal son, Oleg Stefanovich, the son I never had," he said quietly. "I can see your concerns are genuine and that you speak what is in your heart. I admire this, and I value it more than you could possibly know. But in this case your fears are misplaced. NATO is compromised at its core, politically divided and militarily weaker than at any time since the Cold War. We have bought off more Western politicians than I have told you about. We have moles and sources everywhere—in Brussels, in Washington—I wish I could tell you all of it, but there simply isn't time. Not right now. Believe me. We know what we're doing. The American president is no match for me. I guarantee you he will not actually go to war over the Baltic states. And do you know why?"

Oleg shook his head.

"Because in the end he and everyone around him knows one thing— I *will* push the nuclear button. Indeed, I'm practically itching for the chance."

The darker the night, the brighter the stars;
The deeper the grief, the closer is God.

Marcus woke before dawn to the crash of thunder and pouring rain and a line from Dostoyevsky echoing in his head. Despite the miserable weather, he desperately needed some fresh air and some time alone with God. There was still no answer from Langley about his extraction plan. All he could do was wait. And pray.

So he dressed in sweats and running shoes, put on his wristwatch, and wrote a note to let Morris know where he was going and how long he'd be gone. Then he headed to the bathroom, intending to leave the note on the mirror for when she awoke. But there was already a note waiting for him. Morris had gone out for a run nearly thirty minutes earlier.

Marcus grabbed the satphone and stuffed it in his pocket, then headed downstairs and onto the street. The only illumination came from the streetlamps, but they would do. There was no traffic.

He decided to head north, making sure to carefully note landmarks along the way so he could find his way back when he was done. It was cold and getting colder. He could see his breath and soon felt the sting of the elements against his face. As the temperature dropped, this mess would become a freezing rain, and he fully expected snow flurries would be coming soon. He made a mental note to check the weather forecast when he got back and factor it into the contingency plans they were making. Then he cleared his thoughts, choosing to listen only to the sound of his feet pounding and splashing along the wet pavement and the gurgling of the rainwater flowing into the storm drains and sewers along the route.

It was time to start a new chapter, he told himself. He'd been stuck for too long. Maybe Pete was right. He'd been battling depression, and he'd been losing. How much longer could he go on like that? Elena was gone. Lars was gone. They weren't coming back. They'd loved the Lord. They were safe with him now. They weren't suffering. Only Marcus was. Years were going by. How much suffering was enough?

Marcus couldn't say why God had taken them. After much study of the Scriptures and many counseling sessions with Pastor Emerson, he no longer worried that God was punishing him for the years he'd let his work with the Secret Service dominate his life and distract him from his family. If he had sinned, he knew God had forgiven him. But the truth was he still struggled to forgive himself. He'd always thought there would be more time. He'd been wrong. He'd been dead wrong, and he was going to have to live with that regret in some shape or form for the rest of his days.

But he realized as he ran through the dark, rainy Moscow streets that he could no longer let his regrets paralyze him. The night had been dark, yet hadn't that made the stars all the brighter? His grief had been deep, but hadn't it driven him closer to the Lord? And though he couldn't have articulated it at that moment to anyone, Marcus couldn't shake the sense that he was being swept along by a plan known only by the Lord. It was time to stop resisting. He had no idea where the Good Shepherd was about to lead. But he was ready to follow.

Oleg walked down to his office, shut the door, and sat for several minutes.

He closed his eyes, trying to slow his swirling thoughts, trying to steady his churning emotions.

Suddenly he saw himself back in that pitch-black room, alone and disoriented.

The great hall—once so glorious and grand, so elegant, even opulent with its archways and paintings and chandeliers and circular staircase—now ablaze, shrouded in smoke. His eyes stinging. His lungs screaming for oxygen. His skin crackling in the blistering heat from the flames racing through the structure, greedily consuming everything in their path. Walls collapsing. Ceiling beams crashing to the floor. No path of escape. No sound but blood-curdling screams. And Marina, his beloved Marina. Suffocating. Burning. And nothing he could do to save her.

The same vision he had experienced so vividly the night before he had proposed, the night before he had been drafted into the president's service, now consumed him all over again. Only this time he understood it. The great hall was the great country in which he had been born and raised. Luganov was leading Mother Russia into a terrible and tragic fire from which neither he nor Marina could escape. How vast would be the cost in lives and fortunes. How powerless he felt, even here at the power center of all Russia.

Oleg opened his eyes. He knew what he had to do. It began with calling Marcus Ryker. But since that was impossible from inside the walls of the Kremlin, he steeled himself to do the work to which he had been assigned, to go through the day without anyone suspecting his thoughts or intents until the time was right to make his move.

Opening his notebook, Oleg stared at the page containing all the assignments his father-in-law had given him. He started working through them one by one.

His first call was home to Marina. No, he would not be coming home tonight. There was far too much to do, as there would be for the next few days. But there was good news, he assured her. The war clouds were lifting. The storm had passed. What's more, her father had insisted that they take a break and fly off to Monte Carlo that weekend.

Marina, as expected, was elated. She didn't have to be asked twice to make all the arrangements. She even suggested she take Vasily to stay with her mother, now living in exile, as it were, in a small dacha outside St. Petersburg.

"An excellent idea," Oleg said. "And your mother—how is she?"

"She is very scared," Marina confided. "She doesn't want to be so close to the Baltics if war is coming. She wants to come back to stay with us."

"When did you talk with her last?"

"Just yesterday."

"Call her the moment we get off the line," Oleg said. "Tell her everything's going to be fine. Tell her not to worry about the Baltics. Better yet, take Vasily and go see her tonight."

"Tonight? But what about you?"

"I told you, sweetheart, I am swamped with work," Oleg said. "Your father needs me at his side. But I will feel better—and so will he—if you and Vasily are safe with your mother, comforting her and letting her know everything will be all right."

The next call Oleg made was to his parents. He told them the exact opposite. The crisis with NATO could spin out of control at any moment, he told them. It might be best not to be in Moscow for the next few weeks.

"Are things really that bad?" his father asked.

"Let me put it this way," Oleg replied. "I just got off the phone with Marina and told her to book tickets to leave the country immediately.

She was beside herself, but what else can I do? I just want you all to be safe."

Oleg's mother began to cry. "Should I call Marina?" she asked.

"No—I told her not to take any calls right now from anyone but me. I told her to keep the lines open. I expect her and Vasily to be heading to the airport in the next few hours. I really think you should do the same."

"And go where?" asked his father.

"What about Hong Kong?" Oleg replied. "I'd join you myself if I could. Look, I've got to go. Things are very tense around here and moving fast. Please don't tell anyone I called. And definitely don't tell anyone where you're going. Just head to the airport and book your flight on the way. Don't worry about the house. I'll send someone over to keep an eye on things. In fact, if I get a chance, I'll go over there myself."

"You're a good son, Oleg Stefanovich," his father said, his voice trembling. "You'll let us know when it's safe to return?"

"Of course," Oleg replied. "Hopefully, it will not be long."

He told them he loved them and hung up. Then he opened the contact files on his computer and pulled up the personal mobile number of the German foreign minister.

74

It was almost noon when Dmitri Nimkov got back to Lubyanka.

The massive nine-story building once served as the headquarters for the KGB. Now it was home to the FSB. Waiting for him was his deputy, Nikolay Kropatkin.

"Sir, we may have a problem," Kropatkin said as he followed his boss into his spacious office in the northwest corner of the third floor.

"What kind of problem?" Nimkov asked as he dropped his briefcase on a small round conference table and then moved behind his desk, where he immediately unlocked his computer and began sifting through dozens of new emails.

"Dmitri Dmitrovich, please, I need your full attention," Kropatkin said a bit too loudly.

He hadn't meant to shout, but it worked. Nimkov looked up, startled. "Why?"

"Trust me."

"I trust no one," Nimkov said. "That's how I got this job."

"Very well," Kropatkin said. "I will tell it to you straight. We have a suspect, someone we believe very likely leaked President Luganov's war plan to the Americans."

"Who?" asked Nimkov.

"It will not be easy for you—or the president—to hear."

"Just tell me."

"Yes, sir—the person of interest is none other than Oleg Kraskin."

Nimkov blanched, then dropped into his chair. "That's not possible."

"I hope you're right," Kropatkin agreed. "But here's what we know."

For the next few minutes, the deputy chief of the FSB walked his boss through the evidence his team had gathered. First was a notation in the log kept by the head of Oleg's four-man protective detail. On Wednesday night, September 24, the log noted that Oleg had entered his bedroom for the night at 8:42 p.m. However, at 9:17 the following morning, Oleg had arrived at the front door, "looking rumpled and disheveled."

"How did he slip past his detail?" Nimkov asked.

"We don't know," Kropatkin said. "It was a serious breach of security and had never happened before. The supervisor told my investigators he thought the discrepancy was inconsequential since Oleg was uninjured. So he entered it into the log but did not report it to his superiors."

"Where did Oleg Stefanovich go?"

Kropatkin pulled a laptop out of his briefcase and placed it on Nimkov's desk. "It's taken us some time to figure that out, but this is what we've found."

A moment later Nimkov was watching excerpts of security camera footage.

"Oleg Stefanovich appears right there," the deputy noted.

"He's checking into the Hotel National," Nimkov said.

"Exactly. The clerk gives him a key. Here we see him getting into the elevator. There's a shot of him getting off the elevator and another of the hallway where he's letting himself into a room on the third floor, at the very end."

"And?"

"That room is right beside that of Marcus Ryker."

"Who is Marcus Ryker?"

"A member of Senator Dayton's delegation."

"Please tell me you're joking."

"I wish I were," Kropatkin said.

"You're saying Oleg Stefanovich gave the slip to his own security team, then checked into a hotel room directly next to a member of Senator Dayton's delegation—someone he would have met during the senator's meeting with the president earlier in the evening?"

"I'm afraid so, sir."

"Did Oleg communicate with Ryker after entering the room?"

"We can't say for certain. There's no video footage showing Oleg entering Ryker's room. But one of my men checked, and there's an internal door between the two rooms. And several hours later, there's this." Kropatkin played a video of Marcus Ryker emerging from his room and rushing for the elevators.

"In a bit of a hurry, I'd say," Nimkov observed.

"Yes, sir."

"Where is he going?"

"To the U.S. Embassy."

"Why?"

"Unscheduled meeting."

"How do you know?"

"A member of our surveillance team drove the cab that took him there," Kropatkin said. "Twenty minutes later, Oleg Stefanovich exits his room, leaves the hotel, drives his own car around the streets of Moscow for several hours, then returns to his apartment and walks through the front door to the astonishment of his detail."

"And then?"

"Showers, changes, and heads to the Kremlin for work."

Nimkov leaned back in his chair and rubbed his eyes. "What do we know about this Ryker fellow?"

"Former Marine, served in Afghanistan and Iraq, worked in law enforcement, then joined the American Secret Service. Decorated numerous times for bravery."

"And now he's working for Senator Dayton?"

"Not exactly. He's no longer in the Secret Service. His wife and son were shot dead a few years ago. Quit the Service soon after. Dayton hired him as a security consultant, but he's not a regular staff member."

"Could he have been recruited by the CIA?"

"It's possible," Kropatkin said. "He certainly fits the profile of someone the Agency would recruit."

Nimkov shook his head. "You can't really believe the president's son-in-law is a mole for the Americans, can you? Can I?"

"I'm not drawing any conclusions, sir. I'm just giving you the facts as we've ascertained them."

"And I concede they look bad." Nimkov got to his feet. "Could there be another explanation for him being at that hotel, in that room, at that time?"

"Perhaps." Kropatkin fast-forwarded the string of clips his investigators had assembled. "About ninety minutes after Oleg Stefanovich enters the hotel room, an unidentified woman comes to the same room," the deputy said, narrating the footage as it played. "That's her, with her face obscured by the headscarf. We have footage from several angles, but from none of them can we make a positive ID."

"Go on," Nimkov said.

"The woman remains in the room all night. Then, about two hours after Oleg Stefanovich leaves the hotel and checks out—paying cash— the woman also leaves the hotel, slips out a side door, and we lose track of her."

"So," Nimkov said, getting up and pouring himself a glass of vodka, "is Oleg having an affair? Is he cheating on the daughter of the president and simply got himself caught on video in the wrong place at the wrong time? Or is the woman working for the Americans, and Oleg Stefanovich is the highest-level mole in the history of the Russian government? I can't possibly take this to the president unless I have answers—solid and concrete and irrefutable ones at that."

"I understand, sir."

"Then what are you waiting for? Get me answers, and do it fast. We're running out of time. We're about to go to war, and we have to have this taken care of before we do."

75

Katya Slatsky was ecstatic.

The moment she hung up her phone and stashed it in her new Prada purse, another lavish gift from him, she excused herself from the party as quickly and discreetly as she could. Then she dashed out the door of the flat, burst into the stairwell, and ran down four flights, too impatient to wait for the elevator, as her thirtysomething friends giggled in her wake, exchanging knowing glances and catty grins over her "urgent business" that had "just come up."

They all knew whom she was seeing. Thus they all knew where she was going. From the beginning of the affair, Katya had sworn them to secrecy. None of them had been able to keep the secret, of course, and rumors had spread. At first Katya had been terrified, fearing the gossip would get back to Luganov and lead to a sudden end to the fling. But then the president had separated from his wife, Yulia, banishing her from Moscow to some dacha near St. Petersburg. Ever since, Katya had dreamt of the day her paramour would invite her to move in or, better yet, propose.

In her excitement, Katya raced out to the street and fumbled with her keys for a moment before finally finding the right one. She clicked open the driver's-side door to her brand-new silver BMW, another of his many gifts, buckled up, and roared off to Novo-Ogaryovo, her music blasting and her heart racing. She hadn't seen him in nearly a week—he was so consumed with his work—and she craved time alone with him.

Twenty minutes later she arrived at the first checkpoint on the outer perimeter of the presidential palace. She pulled to a stop and lowered her window. All the guards recognized her, of course, and she was on the list of expected and approved visitors. But she'd done this enough times to know the strict procedures that had to be followed. One guard asked her to look into a portable retinal scanning device. Another worked his way around the BMW with a mirror attached to a long pole, examining the underside of the chassis for possible explosive devices. Still several more agents carefully checked through the contents of her trunk and glove compartment and beneath the hood of her car, while the K-9 unit checked the sedan inside and out for any whiff of explosives.

Finally cleared with a smile and wave from all of the guards, who were completely dazzled by her stunning good looks, Katya winked back and drove on to her assigned parking spot even as she heard the roar of the presidential helicopter arriving at the landing pad on the north lawn. Now her heart was racing even faster. She was greeted and helped with her overnight bag by the chief steward, who led her to the next checkpoint. There she chatted up the security men, each of whom she knew by name, as she put her things through the X-ray machine and walked through the metal detector. Even after that, she was wanded down for good measure by a female uniformed guard. Katya knew family members weren't subjected to any of this. Yet she also knew all too well that she was not family. Not yet, anyway. So she didn't resent any of these measures. The agents were just doing their jobs. They were keeping her lover safe in unsafe times. Still, she looked forward to the day when she finally wore a diamond on her left hand and could come and go as she pleased without any of this hassle.

Not five minutes later, Katya was alone in the enormous bathroom off the master bedroom, changing into a new negligee and dabbing French perfume behind her ears and on her neck. *Would tonight be the night? Would he propose to her and sweep her off her feet?*

She was trembling with anticipation as she turned off the bathroom lights and slid beneath the silk sheets. Tonight, she felt sure, was going to be a night to remember.

It was well past 11 p.m. when Oleg was at last ready to leave the office.

He had made every call the president had demanded. He'd spun the man's lies to world leaders and their deputies. He'd conferred with the number-two man in the Russian defense ministry and made sure he knew he had the "president's deepest appreciation for his steadfast loyalty and dedication to excellence." He'd dutifully typed up the minutes of the morning meeting with the war cabinet and transmitted them to the classified distribution list, and he had been in and out of Luganov's office at least a dozen times in between, getting new call lists and assignments and providing the president hourly updates as the man relentlessly drove his government toward a war set to begin in scarcely more than forty-eight hours.

Now, with everything else on his list crossed off, he turned to a task he'd never written down. He plugged a thumb drive into his office computer, copied the hard drive's contents, and then shut the computer down for the night. Next he put all the classified documents spread out on his desk into his wall safe and locked them up. Then he donned his raincoat and cashmere flat cap, put the thumb drive in his briefcase, and locked the door to his office behind him.

Hardly anyone had gone home. The floor was still humming with activity, and Oleg had no doubt it would continue like that all night.

But Luganov had just choppered back to his palace in Novo-Ogaryovo. That meant Oleg was free to go, and he had other work to attend to that most certainly could not be done from inside the Kremlin's walls.

After his security detail drove him back to his empty house, he excused himself and said he was retiring for the night. Once inside his master bedroom, he locked the door behind him, lit a cigarette, and grabbed the satellite phone from the safe. When it was powered up, he walked over to the windows and pulled the drapes. At some point during the day the rain had turned to flurries, but none of the snow had stuck, and the precipitation had ended for the night. As he dialed the phone, though, he realized how much his hands were trembling, and it was not because of the cold or the wind. He turned and walked into the bathroom and locked the door.

After the fifth ring, someone picked up but said nothing.

"'A great disaster has befallen Russia,'" Oleg said, citing Solzhenitsyn.

"'Men have forgotten God,'" the voice at the other end replied. "'That's why all this has happened.'"

Then, per their predetermined verification plan, Oleg now cited Dostoyevsky from *The Brothers Karamazov*. "'Above all, don't lie to yourself.'"

"'The man who lies to himself and listens to his own lie comes to a point that he cannot distinguish the truth within him, or around him,'" the voice replied.

"'And he loses all respect for himself and for others—and having no respect he ceases to love,'" Oleg added with a sigh.

"It's good to hear your voice," Marcus said at last.

"It's good to hear yours," Oleg said. "We can speak freely? You're certain this is secure?"

"Absolutely."

"Where are you right now?"

"Closer than you might imagine."

"What does that mean?"

"I'm in Moscow."

"You're here? How? I thought—"

"I know. I did, but I came back. Don't ask me how. Suffice it to say your security services don't know I'm here, and for now I'd like to keep it that way."

"Of course. Do you have access to a car?"

"I do."

"Good—that's very good." Oleg quickly recalculated his options. "Listen carefully. I've got a gift for you."

"A gift?"

"Files."

"What kind of files?"

"Everything off my office hard drive."

"*Everything?*"

"War plans. Strategic memos. Transcripts of every conversation the . . ."

Oleg hesitated. He didn't want to use Luganov's name or title even though Marcus had assured him nothing they said could be intercepted. But he realized there was no reason to hold back now. If the FSB were on to him, if they could hear what he was saying, he was a dead man. Omitting a few key words here or there wasn't going to make any difference at all.

". . . the president has had with other world leaders and members of his cabinet," he continued. "Emails, voice messages, my private notes. I'm ready to give it all to you. I was calling to ask you how to do that, but maybe we can just meet."

Now it was Marcus who hesitated. Finally he said, "Of course, but I . . . I don't know what to say, except thank you."

"Don't thank me too soon," Oleg countered. "It's not going to be enough."

"What do you mean?"

"I'm giving you the mother lode, and it will give your people tremendous insights into everything Luganov is doing, thinking, ordering," Oleg said. "But it won't stop this thing. It can't. Events are unfolding too fast. He's going to war even faster than I'd thought, faster than he said." Oleg briefed Marcus on how accelerated the timetable had become.

"You're telling me the invasion is now set to begin in just forty-eight hours?" Marcus asked.

"Correct."

"Then we need to get you out now, before it's too late," Marcus said.

"No, that won't solve anything," Oleg replied.

"It's okay," Marcus responded. "I have a plan. We can get you out of the country and someplace safe, somewhere they'll never find you."

"No, please, that's not what I want," Oleg protested. "You don't understand. There's only one way to stop this war from happening, and it's not by me running."

"Then what?" Marcus asked.

Oleg paused, took a deep breath, and then said, "I need to kill the president."

"*I'm sorry. What did you just say?*"

It was a few minutes after midnight. Marcus had been out for a run—trying to burn off his anxieties—when his phone buzzed. Though the streets were empty, he'd ducked into the shadows of a bridge before answering.

"You heard me," Oleg shot back. "Someone needs to take him out. If NATO fights back, he's setting into motion a nuclear holocaust. If they don't, he'll have broken the back of the alliance, and then it will be open season on the West. With no one willing to stop him, he'll become the most powerful man in the world and the most ruthless. No one will be safe. He has to be stopped *before* he strikes. I don't see any other way. I wish I did. I've spent all day trying to come up with another scenario—any other—but this is it. I've concluded this is what I need to do. But I need your help."

Marcus swallowed hard. The logic was unassailable. It was the same conclusion he himself had come to. He'd just never considered Oleg might put himself forward to do the deed.

"What do you need?" Marcus asked.

"A plan," Oleg said. "I'm willing to do whatever's necessary, but I don't have a clue how to pull this thing off, and I'm running out of time."

"You're absolutely sure you want to do this?"

"Want to? No. But I must. There is no other option."

Marcus knew he was about to go where Jenny Morris never would, not in a million years. But he wasn't an employee of the U.S. government. Not anymore. Nor was he operating on the government's behalf. Not exactly. That's why Morris and the higher-ups above her could never know what he was about to say or do.

"Fair enough," he said, taking a deep breath. "There are three components in any successful assassination—the plan, the execution, and the escape. If you really want me to, I can walk you through each part, step-by-step. I'm going to have to ask you a lot of questions, and of course I'll answer all of yours that I can. But when we're done, I'm going to ask you one more time: do you really want to do this? Because if you pull this off, there's a very real chance you won't come out of it alive. You understand that, right?"

"I do."

"If you do beat the odds and survive and escape—and I'll do everything I possibly can to help you—you have to understand that you're going to be a marked man for the rest of your life. You'll have to disappear forever. Off the grid. No contact with family or friends. A new name. A new identity. Nothing will ever be the same. Understood?"

"Understood."

"Okay, first things first," Marcus said, pacing under the bridge and trying to gather his thoughts. "Where is the president going to be today? At the Kremlin?"

"No, he'll be at the residence."

"In Novo-Ogaryovo?"

"Yes."

"You're sure."

"Yes. He'll be there all day."

"Who else will be with him?"

"What do you mean? He'll have bodyguards and servants and—"

"I mean, will he be meeting with generals, the war council, key advisors?"

"Unlikely. Most of that will be done by secure phone calls and videoconferencing."

"Even forty-eight hours before a war?"

"Especially so," Oleg said. "The generals he needs to interact with are mostly at the Defense Ministry or on the front. There's nobody at the Kremlin he needs to see face-to-face. He prefers to think and strategize at the palace, not in his office. And of course, *she'll* be there as well."

"She who?"

"Katya Slatsky."

"I didn't realize she was still in the picture," Marcus said.

"Very much so, I'm afraid."

"Does she sleep there?"

"Sometimes, not always."

"Is she there right now?"

"I'd be surprised if she wasn't."

"Okay, that's good to know," Marcus said, processing it all. "Are you scheduled to be there today?"

"No, not that I know of."

"Can you get yourself invited, say for breakfast?"

"Well, maybe not for breakfast, given that it's already the middle of the night. But if I need to go, to bring him critical documents to sign, or whatever, then yes, I can certainly do that."

"Is that normal?"

"Fairly."

"How do you get there? Drive?"

"Usually they take me by helicopter."

"With your whole security detail?"

"No, usually just the head of the detail goes with me."

"Because there's plenty of security at the palace."

"Exactly."

"Are you ever searched when you get on the helicopter?"

"Never."

"When you arrive at the palace?"

"Not once."

"Do you have to walk through a metal detector?"

"No."

"What about putting your briefcase or other personal effects through a magnetometer?"

"What's that?"

"An X-ray machine."

"Oh no, never—I'm the son-in-law of the president. I have walk-in privileges. I don't even have a security badge. I'm family. They trust me completely. That's why I began thinking I might actually be able to pull this off. But how? We don't have much time, and you still haven't given me a plan."

"I'm working on it."

Oleg then surprised Marcus by asking about suicide bomber vests and ways of poisoning a man. Marcus ruled out both options. First, he said, he wanted Oleg to live, not die. Second, he had no access to polonium-210 at the moment, nor would he likely be able to scare up any on such short notice.

"We have to keep it simple," Marcus said. "There's no time—or need—for creativity. You're not a trained assassin. You're not trying to send a message. You're trying to stop a nuclear holocaust. Period. Which means you need to take out the man responsible for leading the world down that path. And you're uniquely positioned for the mission. Like you said, you're family. You're trusted. You have direct access to your target without being searched. So you need a small pistol, preferably one with a silencer. You can hide it in your briefcase or in your waistband under your suit jacket. You still with me?"

"Yes."

"Okay, so you smuggle the weapon into the place, and then you need to get him alone in a private area, just you and him. It doesn't really matter where—could be his office, his bedroom, whatever. It has to be somewhere there are no bodyguards present, no open windows where anyone could see you, and where this Slatsky woman can't suddenly walk in on you. Can you picture a place like that in the palace?"

"Yes," said Oleg. "Several."

"Do any of them have a restroom connected or nearby?"

"A few, why?"

"I'll get to that. But first, you have to be able to sit with the president and put him at ease. Give him whatever documents he needs to sign. Chat him up. Ask how the war preparations are coming along, and obviously get any additional intel you possibly can. But the key is, you have to make him feel comfortable, relaxed. You know what I'm saying?"

"I do."

"Then excuse yourself and go to the lavatory."

"Why?"

"Because that's when you're going to pull out the gun, click off the safety, steady your nerves, and prepare yourself for what you're about to do."

"Okay."

"Remember, he's not just the president; he's also the former head of the FSB," Marcus stressed. "He's a trained killer—far more trained than you. If he sees that gun coming out, you're a dead man. He can't suspect you for a moment. You go into that restroom, ready your weapon, ready yourself, and then reenter that room and come up to him—hopefully from behind, while his back is to you—aim, and pull the trigger immediately."

"Aiming where?"

"His head. You need to stop his brain functions," Marcus explained. "If you shoot him in the chest, even several times, he may still have the wherewithal to react, to attack you, to get the gun away from you."

There was a long silence as Oleg considered everything he was being told. Then he asked, "Won't all this be very loud? Won't everyone in the palace hear it—especially the guards—and rush in and kill me anyway?"

"Not if I can get you the right gun," Marcus responded. "If it's the one I'm thinking of, no one will hear a thing. Then you might actually have a chance at escaping."

For the next few minutes, Marcus walked the Russian through a step-by-step plan to get him out of the palace and to the airport, where a plane would be waiting to whisk him out of Moscow and hopefully out of the country altogether. It was a long shot, he readily admitted, yet it was worth trying.

Then Marcus had to bring up a very delicate matter. "I really need that thumb drive with all your files," he said without apology. "I'm sure you're right that having this information can't stop the war, but I need it anyway."

"Of course," Oleg said. "I'll bring it with me to the airport and give it to you on the plane."

"No," Marcus said. "I need to get it first."

There was another long pause.

"Because I may not ever get to the airport," Oleg said, his voice suddenly somber.

Marcus said nothing.

"I understand," Oleg said. Then he added, "Actually, I have an idea."

77

"Please hold for the president."

Dmitri Nimkov was still in his office, as was nearly every member of his staff. He was not surprised to receive another call from Luganov. They had spoken every few hours throughout the day as Nimkov provided his commander in chief continual updates on the movement of American troops pouring into Poland.

As of yet there was still no evidence that NATO members were working in concert. There was no announcement out of SHAPE headquarters in Brussels about positioning troops and supplies in the Baltics to create an adequately robust deterrent force. Indeed, most NATO sources were telling reporters, "No comment." But uncertainty about official decision making had not precluded individual nations from following the lead of the Clarke administration and coming to the defense of their Baltic brethren. Now, in response to an urgent request from the White House, at least four NATO member states were moving steadily despite Moscow's insistence that the West was "overreacting to normal and peaceful military maneuvers." In recent hours not only had Polish forces been fully mobilized for war, but British, Czech, and Hungarian Special Forces, attack helicopter squadrons, and fighter jets were arriving in each of the Baltic states as well.

Luganov had become more outraged with every update Nimkov had provided. But what had truly shaken the president was when Nimkov finally broke the news to him that there was circumstantial but compelling evidence that his son-in-law had had inappropriate contact with Senator Dayton's staff and might be the source of the leak of Luganov's war plans. Thus, while the FSB chief was by no means surprised by this latest call, he braced himself for another volcanic eruption.

"Dmitri Dmitrovich, are you there?" Luganov asked as he came on the line, his voice far more calm than Nimkov had expected.

"*Da*, Aleksandr Ivanovich—how can I help you?"

Nimkov could hear Katya Slatsky giggling in the background. He rolled his eyes and held his tongue. He didn't care what the president did in his private life, though he harbored concerns about Katya. She was too young and had far too many connections to the West from her years as an Olympic skater. The FSB closely monitored all her social media activity as well as her bank accounts and credit card usage. So far, Nimkov and an elite team of his most trusted men, led by Nikolay Kropatkin, had not found any evidence that Katya posed any direct threat.

"I still cannot get my mind off the suspicions your staff have against . . . you know," Luganov said after harshly telling his mistress to be silent when he was on the phone. Clearly he did not want to use Oleg's name in Katya's presence.

"We are doing all that you have asked of us, Your Excellency," Nimkov assured him. "My men have been interviewing employees at the Hotel National all day. We've also been digging deeper into Marcus Ryker, and I—"

"That's not what I mean," Luganov said, cutting him off. "I'm sure you're conducting an aggressive investigation, and I want you to brief me on everything you've learned at our 9 a.m. meeting. But that's not my point."

"Forgive me, Your Excellency. What are your concerns?"

"If the Americans are targeting him as a possible intelligence asset," Luganov said, "his life could be in danger, and then . . ." His voice trailed off.

"I'm sorry, Your Excellency. I'm not following."

At this, Luganov asked Nimkov to wait a moment. The FSB chief heard him excuse himself from Katya's presence. He heard several doors open and close. And then Luganov reengaged the conversation, presumably somewhere he felt freer to talk openly, probably in his personal study.

"Listen, Dmitri," the president began in a hushed voice. "Oleg Stefanovich has always been a good and loyal son. He has known and worked with me for years. I find it absolutely inconceivable that he would have willingly betrayed me. He certainly wouldn't have reached out to the Americans. But can I imagine a scenario in which Ryker and the Americans lured my son into a trap? I have been thinking about it for hours, ever since you first broached the subject, and I cannot rule it out. Oleg is brilliant, but he never worked for the FSB. He has no training in counterintelligence. And at times, despite all his worldliness, I have found him shockingly naive for a man operating at the highest levels of our government."

Luganov paused. Nimkov wasn't sure where this was going, yet rather than ask, he decided to wait. The president had not called to explore Nimkov's worries or his theories. He was a man of action. He had a plan, and if Nimkov was patient, he would find out soon enough what it was.

"Is Oleg at home with Marina?" Luganov asked.

"Well, he is at home, but Marina and Vasily went to stay with *her* for a few days." Nimkov was careful not to mention the name of the president's ex-wife.

"Does my daughter have security with her?"

"Yes, two female agents."

"That's not enough," Luganov said. "Increase her detail to a dozen. What about Oleg?"

"His usual detail is with him, sir."

"Four men?"

"Yes."

"Again, that's not enough," Luganov said. "He could be in real danger. Give Oleg a dozen agents as well. Then bring him to me by chopper in the morning."

"Of course, Your Excellency. What time would you like for him to arrive?"

"Have him here by eight. I'll meet with him after breakfast. Then you and I can meet at nine. He'll be safer here. Plus I want to confront him about this woman, find out who she really was, and ask him about any contact he's had with this Ryker fellow."

"Yes, Your Excellency," Nimkov said. "It will be as you wish."

"And one more thing, Dmitri Dmitrovich."

"Yes?"

"Bring the tape from the hotel."

78

"We need to go tonight," Marcus said when he got back to the safe house.

"What are you talking about?" Jenny Morris asked from the couch. She'd fallen asleep waiting for him to get back. "It's one in the morning."

Marcus pulled out a backpack and began filling it with the things they'd need as he explained that Luganov was planning to invade the Baltics in just forty-eight hours. He said nothing about the plot he and his source had cooked up to take out the president, only that the Raven had a treasure trove of material he urgently needed to get to the Agency.

"We don't have approval for your plan yet," she said, now completely alert and firing up her laptop.

The two had been developing and refining the extraction plan all day, trying to find a way to get Oleg out that didn't necessitate deadly force. They'd come up blank. Morris had lit a fire under her staff to make sure everything and everyone was in place—just in case they did get approval. But at this point, it seemed like a long shot.

"Even if we get the green light, I don't know if my team can move that fast," Morris added, entering the third of five nine-figure pass-codes to open a secure channel to the Magic Palace, the CIA's Global Operations Center in northern Virginia.

"I'm counting on you, Jenny," Marcus replied. "Make it happen."

The message moved with lightning speed up the chain of command.

Marcus dictated the report, and Jenny Morris sent it as an encrypted precise text to Langley. The twenty-line message landed in the hands of the shift supervisor of the CIA's Global Operations Center. From there it was transmitted to the director of Russian operations with a "FLASH TRAFFIC" priority. She ran it directly up to the seventh floor and put it in the hands of the deputy director of intelligence, who immediately asked for a meeting with the director. Twelve minutes later, Director Richard Stephens and the DDI were in a car headed for the White House.

When they arrived at the West Wing, they were taken to the Situation Room, where President Clarke and most of the National Security Council had been hastily assembled. No one knew what was coming, but all of them had been told to prepare for major developments, none of them good. The president convened the meeting of the NSC and gave the CIA director the floor.

"Mr. President, less than an hour ago, our case officer received a new message from Moscow," Stephens began. "The DDI is uploading an image, and it should be on the screens around you in a moment. But I'm going to read it in the meantime because it is, as you'll see, time sensitive.

"The Raven just made contact. Stop. Timetable for war changed. Stop. Invasion now planned for 0200 local time on 1 October. Stop. Luganov livid about POTUS decision to mobilize U.S. forces into Poland. Stop. Assumes forces headed for Baltics. Stop. Convinced there's a leak in his operation and has begun aggressive mole hunt. Stop. Told generals he will go to war no matter what. Stop. One senior official warned Luganov that Russian forces not yet ready, move could trigger a nuclear war with NATO. Stop. Luganov undeterred. Stop. Division in cabinet not enough to dissuade Luganov. Stop. War now all but certain. Stop. CRITICAL POINT: Luganov openly stated to his war council that he is fully prepared to go nuclear—even suggested he's looking for an excuse. Stop. Ordered all Russian strategic nuclear and conventional forces to highest state of readiness. Stop. Has been told by aides that element of surprise has been lost but moving forward anyway at full speed. Stop. Heading to meet the Raven for secret rendezvous. Stop. Preparing to execute OPERATION DAMASCUS BASKET on accelerated timetable. Stop. NEED IMMEDIATE GREEN LIGHT. Stop. Raven bringing with him 32 gigabytes of highly classified files. Stop. Will update when possible. Stop. YMM."

"What's *YMM*?" the president asked.

"*Your Man in Moscow*," Stephens said. "That's Marcus Ryker—our link to the Raven."

"And what's Operation Damascus Basket?"

"That's our extraction plan, sir."

"For Ryker?"

"No, sir—to get the Raven safely out of Russia."

"Such a plan is ready?"

"Almost, sir, but it is highly risky, and I haven't yet given my approval."

"Why not?"

"Mr. President, it involves our people taking out four Russian bodyguards who protect this particular official, the Raven."

"Isn't there any other way than using deadly force?"

"I've been asking the same question all day. But my people in the field say no. If we want this guy, it's the only way. I don't have to tell you the risks if our people are caught or killed in the process. But the upside would be enormous. It's your call, sir."

"Has the Raven asked us to set the plan into motion?"

"Yes, tonight."

"Does he understand what's at risk?"

"Ryker says he does. But Luganov has ordered a mole hunt, so they think it has to happen immediately."

"Are you guys ready?"

"Almost—we're finalizing everything as we speak, Mr. President."

"Do you want to walk me through the plan?" asked Clarke.

"Actually, sir, I've told you the most critical piece—I think the less you know the better," Stephens said. "But I can keep you apprised of developments throughout the night, if you'd like."

"Very well—coordinate through Colonel McDermott."

"So the mission is a go, Mr. President?"

"It's a go," Clarke said, then turned to Defense Secretary Foster. "Cal, the Agency is clearly doing what they can to get us the best intel possible. What do you and your men recommend we do with it?"

"Mr. President, in light of this new information—and working on the premise that it's all accurate—I have three recommendations."

"Lay them out."

"Yes, sir. First, I recommend we move to DEFCON 3 and stand by for a possible move to DEFCON 2. This will put all U.S. conventional and strategic nuclear forces on high alert. If nuclear war becomes imminent, we may have to move to DEFCON 1 for the first time in history. Second, you should direct the secretary of state to call an emergency videoconference of the North Atlantic Council to explain to NATO as much as we can of the latest intel and the imminence of a Russian invasion. Make it clear to our allies that any attack by Russia on the Baltic states or any other NATO member will trigger Article 5. And third, Mr. President, I recommend we get you on the hotline to talk with President Luganov directly and see if you can't head this thing off before the missiles start flying."

79

Everything he'd learned to protect our president, he was now using to take out theirs.

Given that he couldn't say a word to Morris or draw on any of her assets or expertise, Marcus rated the chances of success of assassinating Luganov at no more than one in five, if that. Still, that wasn't his main focus just at the moment. The plan for getting Oleg out was. This was one topic he could discuss with Morris, but it wasn't going well. They'd gotten the go-ahead from Washington only to learn one of the pilots they needed to fly them out was sick in bed with a 104-degree fever. The copilot was already doing all the preflight checks, but the flight plan hadn't been approved. And now a massive winter storm that no one had seen coming was moving in.

At least the weapons Marcus had asked for had come in. He had in his possession a Vul—a silent Russian pistol—and the Vintorez sniper rifle favored by Soviet Special Forces.

Marcus pulled off the main highway. He parked the white Volga GAZ-21 in the shadows behind a self-service Lukoil gas station that was open but deserted. Grabbing his satphone, weapons, and keys, he locked the beat-up old sedan and jumped into the brand-new Mercedes SUV that Jenny Morris was driving right behind him. Several hours from now they would leave the Mercedes here and proceed to the airport in the Volga, hopefully throwing off anyone who might observe them driving to or from their next destination.

As they drove the six miles to Rublyovka, home of Moscow's wealthiest and most powerful families, Marcus briefly considered telling Morris who his source really was, how they had met, and that they were actually going to meet him at his parents' house. The moment she saw him, after all, she would know exactly who he was. Still, he'd made a promise to the man, and he wasn't about to break it. If Oleg were killed in the house or taken down while trying to kill the president, Marcus might never need to tell her. If Oleg actually lived through the next several hours and made it to the plane, he could give them a proper introduction then.

The house should be deserted, Marcus knew. Oleg had assured him that his parents had left the country hours earlier and should be halfway across the continent by now. The Kraskin estate was nearly a kilometer away from the nearest neighbor. What's more, Oleg's childhood home was surrounded on three sides by dense woods, long manicured lawns, and even a pond in the backyard with a small island in its center. Oleg had given Marcus all the passcodes they would need to enter both the main gates to the community and the gates to his parents' property and to disarm the security system. And they had nearly a two-hour head start to get everything ready.

Neither Marcus nor Jenny Morris was prepared for the spectacular size of the secluded mansion or for the fantastic wealth Oleg's family had built up in the post-Soviet years. Marcus had understood they were successful but not that Oleg's father was an actual oligarch. Yet as they pulled through the iron gates along the half-moon drive up to the front door, they found themselves gaping at a sprawling, forty-room, Scottish-style baronial castle with steeped gables, ornate conical turrets, and even four black "witch's hat" roofs, one in each corner.

Marcus put on his gloves, pulled a black balaclava over his face, and donned night vision goggles as they approached. Morris did the same. The plan called for her to drop Marcus off in front of the huge house, then speed off down a service road, past the five-car garage and several stone outbuildings before pulling the Mercedes deep into the forest, cutting the lights, and parking a half klick from the house to begin setting up her equipment.

Marcus disarmed the security system and entered the house cautiously. There were no signs of life, no sounds but the ticking of an antique grandfather clock in the opulent vestibule, replete with Italian marble floors and seventeenth-century French artwork. The silenced pistol drawn—and the disassembled sniper rifle slung over his back— he stealthily moved from room to room, confirming that no one was inside, starting with the top floor and working his way down. Given the building's length and breadth, it took longer than Marcus had planned.

On the top floor, he found twelve bedrooms, including a master bedroom larger than any single room at the White House. Each bedroom had its own bathroom. There was a library and a study for Mr. Kraskin and another for his wife, as well as a workout room. On the main level, Marcus found a private movie theater with both a state-of-the-art digital projection system and a 35mm film projector. There was an indoor pool that could open to an outdoor pool overlooking the pond. A large screened porch adjoined a glassed-in breakfast room along with enormous living and dining rooms, a piano room, and a kitchen large enough to feed the Red Army. In the basement Marcus found three more guest rooms, a Jacuzzi room and sauna, a billiard room with a full bar, and laundry facilities.

He also found the panic room Oleg had told him about. He entered the code he'd been given and stepped inside. Fourteen feet by fourteen feet, with reinforced steel walls, ceiling, and floor, it was really more of a bomb shelter than a panic room. At one end was an independent oxygen system, several large drums of potable water, a chemical toilet, a small round table with four wooden chairs, and a television and shortwave radio. Bunk beds lined the side walls. At the near end of the room was a tiny kitchenette, a pantry with canned goods, and shelves lined with battery-operated lamps and flashlights. The room's systems operated from an independent power source that should remain up and running even if power went out in the rest of the house.

Marcus exited the safe room and reentered the code, closing the vault's steel door behind him. Then he found the utility closet Oleg had directed him to, the one containing two large water heaters, the HVAC system, the house's Internet routers, and an assortment of other panels controlling various systems within the house and throughout the grounds. He focused on the circuit box that regulated power coming in from the main electrical grid. Underneath it he magnetically attached a thin silver cylinder that could easily be mistaken for part of the original system if it wasn't studied carefully. Inside the cylinder were a remote detonator and enough plastic explosives to knock out power to the whole house.

His initial preparations complete, Marcus raced back upstairs, reactivated the master alarm system, and then—in the sixty seconds he had before the motion sensors kicked in—bounded up to the second floor and found the door leading to the attic. It was, as he'd been told, locked. But using the key he'd found in the drawer of the nightstand on the right side of the master bedroom, exactly where Oleg had said it would be, he quickly unlocked the door to the attic, then replaced the key in the drawer, headed back to the attic stairway, and closed and locked the door behind him.

Marcus activated his night vision goggles as he made his way into the unheated and thus chilly top-floor storage area and found himself next to a small window that looked out toward the private access road leading to the property. The window wasn't designed to be opened. He was tempted to cut out one or two of the glass panes to prepare for what was coming next, but he decided against it. The window was, for now, the only thing keeping out the rain and the wind, if not the cold. Instead, he removed and unzipped his backpack, pulled out the pieces of the sniper rifle, reassembled them, and settled in for the wait, though it wouldn't be long now.

"Razor to Keyhole, over," he said, lowering the volume on his earpiece slightly and adjusting the whisper microphone pressed against his right cheek.

"Keyhole to Razor, copy, reading you five by five—over," Morris replied.

"Status check."

"Good to go. And you? Over."

"Locked and loaded," said Marcus, "and ready for showtime."

80

Oleg padded out into the living room in his silk pajamas.

He intended to inform his detail that he couldn't sleep and order them to take him to his parents' house. But he was stunned to see so many additional agents.

"What's the meaning of this?" he demanded. "Who are all these people?"

The supervisor apologized for the surprise. He said the detail had been beefed up on direct orders from the president. Normally he would have informed Oleg immediately, but given all the stresses on him, he had thought it best to let him get his sleep.

As furious as he was terrified, Oleg stormed back into his bedroom and slammed the door, only to realize that he'd been so stunned by the presence of so many additional FSB agents that he hadn't said anything about going to Rublyovka. He picked up the phone by his bed and called the supervisor. Next he changed into blue jeans and a fisherman knit sweater and threw a change of clothes and a freshly pressed business suit and some toiletries in an overnight bag. Then he grabbed the satellite phone and took it into the bathroom.

Marcus felt the satphone buzzing in his pocket.

"What?" he whispered.

"We have a problem," Oleg said.

"Tell me."

"The president boosted my detail to a dozen agents."

"Why?"

"I have no idea."

"Has something happened?"

"I don't know."

"Has there been a threat made against you? Or do you think he suspects something?"

"I told you, I don't know," Oleg replied. "I just wanted you to be prepared."

With that, he hung up the phone.

Marcus closed his eyes. The calculus had changed. Now he knew he had to tell Morris whose house they were at and how high the stakes really were. How else was he going to explain all the extra company they were about to receive and all the firepower they were bringing with them? He just prayed she wouldn't call the whole mission off.

"Razor to Keyhole," he said. "I have new information for you."

McDermott huddled with Clarke in the Oval.

"Two things, Mr. President," he said as he stood beside the *Resolute* desk.

"Make it quick."

"Yes, sir. First, we're reaching out to the Kremlin to set up a hotline call for you and President Luganov. But we have to be realistic. It's the middle of the night in Moscow. I'd recommend we place the call at, say, 8 a.m. their time. That would be 1 a.m. here, if that's all right."

"That's fine; just make sure it happens."

"Absolutely, sir. The second thing is about the extraction of the Raven."

"What about it?"

"Well, sir, if our people can actually get him safely out of Russia, we need to make a decision about where to bring him."

"Here to the States, of course. Why?"

"We're talking about a very senior Russian official essentially defecting at a very delicate moment in U.S.–Russia relations," McDermott noted.

"And you don't think it's wise to bring him to the States?"

"It may be prudent not even to acknowledge that we have him, sir."

"Where else would you take him?"

"We're thinking Egypt, sir. We've set up a special facility outside Alexandria. Top secret. Completely off the radar. But safe."

"And deniable."

"Yes, sir."

"What does Director Stephens say?"

"He agrees."

"Then Egypt it is."

"Keyhole to Razor—they're coming," Morris said.

It was pouring again, a bitter, biting rain that was soon going to shift into snow. It was early, but it wasn't completely unheard of for the Moscow metropolitan area to get its first snow in early fall. Morris was shivering from waiting out in the elements for an hour and a half. But there was no point griping about it or even thinking about it. Through her high-powered night vision binoculars, she could see two black SUVs coming down the highway. They were less than two miles out.

Setting down the binoculars, Morris picked up the weapon at her side, attached its silencer, and peered through the night vision scope. Moments later, the entourage entered the gated community and pulled up in front of the estate. It was 4:01. The Raven, who she now knew was none other than Oleg Kraskin, and his newly enlarged security team were right on time.

Morris glanced at the Mercedes positioned about thirty yards to her right. She'd camouflaged it with branches and foliage. Now she worried the rains and wind might wash away enough of it to make the SUV visible if Kraskin's security detail did a thorough search of the woods. She felt in the darkness for her pistol and clicked off the safety. She took a long look to her right and to her left, then behind her. She didn't want anyone to catch her off guard. Satisfied she had the woods to herself—at least for the moment—she fought to slow and steady her breathing. She'd done two tours in Iraq with Army intelligence. She'd helped hunt down dozens of high-value targets before being recruited by the Agency and sent to language school to add Russian to her Arabic and Farsi. She'd done all sorts of crazy things for her government. But she'd never lain on her stomach in a Russian forest in the freezing rain, aiming a loaded weapon at a team of highly trained Russian FSB officers and Spetsnaz commandos.

She was seriously doubting herself for ever letting Marcus Ryker design this plan and run this operation. She didn't care if he was the only link to the Raven. He wasn't the CIA's top dog in Russia. He wasn't responsible for managing more than 120 officers and some three dozen Russian agents they'd recruited throughout the military, Duma, and executive branch. Yet somehow she'd let him dictate exactly what was going to happen and how. She hadn't even put up a fight. He spoke with a humility and yet an air of authority unlike any other civilian she'd come across. And given the amount of time they'd had, his plan was probably the best anyone could come up with. But it was risky. It was bad enough when they had to contend with four bodyguards, but twelve?

If this went badly, it was going to go very badly.

Marcus heard the vehicles pull up out front.

He turned his night vision goggles back on and glanced out the small attic window. He could see two large bodyguards emerging from the lead SUV. They were dressed in suits and raincoats and held submachine guns at the ready. One moved cautiously through the darkness around to the backyard; the other moved toward the front door. The rest of the detail remained dry and warm in their SUVs, which now turned around and parked facing the main gate and the road beyond it.

They had made their first mistake, Marcus realized. With a dozen men on the team, at least eight of them should have jumped out to set up a secure perimeter and thoroughly search the house—regardless of the weather—leaving behind only the two drivers keeping their engines running and two body men staying close to their principal, Oleg Stefanovich Kraskin.

"Keyhole to Razor," Jenny Morris whispered in his headset.

"What?" Marcus asked, annoyed by the sudden break of radio silence.

"Did you reset the alarm system? Over."

"Affirmative. Hold your position and wait for my command."

In theory, they were in an ideal tactical position. Morris had suggested that they could cut down the Russian security force with breathtaking speed, assuming that Marcus wasn't found by the lone agent sweeping the house. Once the "all clear" signal was radioed back to the head of the detail, the agents would prepare to whisk Oleg inside. As soon as the doors of both SUVs opened and all the agents—aside from the drivers—began to exit, it would be like shooting fish in a barrel. Marcus had the high ground from a fixed yet hidden position. He could open fire and likely take out four or five of the Russians before they even realized where the rounds were coming from. Simultaneously, he could give the order to Morris to begin firing from the woods at the agents emerging from the other side of the vehicles. If she was as proficient a marksman as she claimed, she could likely take out all or most of the Russians on her side in a matter of seconds.

But the windows of both SUVs were tinted. That meant neither Marcus nor Jenny knew which vehicle their subject was in. And they couldn't afford the possibility of Oleg being hit in the cross fire. It wasn't just the thumb drive Marcus needed. He needed Oleg alive to execute the next phase of the plan.

81

Don't die, and don't get arrested.

His mother's words rang in his ears as Marcus heard the front door open. He heard someone enter the code to disarm the security system. It seemed to take forever, but eventually he heard someone coming up the stairs from the first floor to the second. This was it. There was no turning back now.

He gripped the Russian-made pistol as he listened to doors opening and closing. Marcus could visualize every step the agent was taking. He'd cleared homes like this a thousand times and every time had forced himself to resist the temptation to believe everything was fine and the location was safe.

Marcus knew exactly what this agent was thinking. Oleg had announced the decision to come to his parents' home less than an hour before. He'd made the decision in the middle of the night. The agent would certainly have been told that the Kraskins had left the country earlier in the evening and would not be home. They had no servants or staff, no pets, nobody house-sitting, only a housekeeping crew that came on Monday mornings. Thus the agent believed no one could possibly have known that Oleg was going to be there that night. This—more than the rotten weather, which after all was a staple of a Russian bodyguard's existence—was the single most important reason the entire detail wasn't on highest alert. They simply could not foresee a realistic, immediate threat. Still, Marcus knew the agent was a professional. He would at least be looking for hidden weapons, explosives, listening devices, surveillance cameras, or anything that seemed odd or out of place.

The door handle to the attic rattled. The agent was checking to make sure it was locked. But rather than move on, as Marcus had fully hoped and expected he would, the agent slipped a key into the lock. Marcus froze as he heard the door open. He instinctively held his breath as a beam from the agent's flashlight shone up the stairs and swept from side to side, stopping finally on the small window. Marcus, hidden in a crawl space around the corner from the stairwell, was not immediately visible. But he was now grateful he hadn't removed any of the glass panes. That would have been a dead giveaway.

Marcus silently prayed the agent would be satisfied with a quick glance up the stairs and go on to finish his check of the rest of the house. But suddenly he heard the steps creaking. This guy was doing his job. He was doing it more thoroughly than Marcus had anticipated, and this radically changed the calculus.

Marcus quietly turned off his night vision goggles. He steadied the pistol in one hand. In his other he held the remote switch to the explosive charge in the basement. But he couldn't take out the power now. It would destroy his most important advantage: the element of surprise.

Marcus watched as the man's shadow came up the stairs, cast by the light from the second-floor hallway. He was moving slowly, too slowly, as if he suspected something. But how could he? Marcus had been careful to leave no trace of his presence. His backpack was at his feet, deep inside the crawl space. The sniper rifle was at his side. He hadn't left a flashlight or anything else on the stairs or at the base of the window. What was wrong? Why was the man moving so slowly?

Now why had he stopped?

Then Marcus saw what the agent saw. On the wall below the small window were smudges of dust. Marcus realized he must have made them when he was trying to maneuver in the cramped quarters. The man's flashlight was fixated on them. Surely he was evaluating whether they were fresh or had been left there by the owners or a workman or even Oleg in the past. Again he began making his way up the stairs. Time seemed to stand still. Marcus knew he couldn't shoot the man. To do so could blow his cover. Oleg was not yet out of the vehicle and in the house. If Marcus fired at this man and his whisper mic was on, he could alert a dozen Russian agents who could storm the house or speed off with Oleg and the computer files.

But if the agent found Marcus, he would likely shoot first and ask questions later. Either way the plan was blown.

Marcus had to make a decision. So he pulled the trigger four times in less than a second, firing blind through the crawl space wall. All four bullets pierced the drywall. Three hit their mark. The Russian collapsed and slid down the stairs.

Marcus bolted from the crawl space. He pivoted around the corner and saw the agent sprawled on the floor. It was possible he was already dead, but there was no margin for error. He fired two more shots, one into the man's heart, the other into his head. He knew he wasn't wrong about all the consequences that could unfold from his decision to take this guy out, but in the end the calculation had come down to one decision: kill or be killed.

82

Marcus immediately discharged the partially empty magazine from his pistol.

He pulled another mag from his belt and locked it in place. Given the Russian weapon's built-in silencer, no one outside the house could possibly have heard the shots. A quick peek out the window showed no movement, suggesting no one had heard the body fall down the stairs or heard the man's submachine gun drop to the floor.

"Razor to Keyhole, target down," he said. "Stand by to engage. Over."

"What target?" came the stunned reply devoid of all radio protocol. "What are you talking about? You shot someone already?"

"Wait one," Marcus replied as he shoved the pistol into his holster, grabbed the VSS rifle, and flicked a switch changing it from single-shot sniper mode to full-on automatic.

He inched halfway down the stairs, listening intently for any sounds of movement below. Hearing none, he double-checked the man's pulse and confirmed what he already knew, then scooped up the man's machine gun and stripped him of the rest of his weapons and ammo. There was blood all over the hallway carpet, but Marcus wasn't worried about that. One way or another, this would be over before any of the Russians made it to the second floor.

Marcus removed the man's whisper mic, earpiece, and battery-powered wireless radio and put them on himself. Now he had two—one connected to Morris and this one connected to the entire Russian detail. This would have been ideal if he spoke Russian, but he did not. Jenny did, and he briefly considered ways of patching her into the Russian feed. For the moment, however, it did not matter. Only one thing did.

"Razor to Keyhole—how do you say 'all clear' in Russian? Over."

"What in the world?" Morris shot back, a disturbing mix of confusion and fear in her voice, a mix that did not exactly bolster Marcus's confidence in her partnership at that moment.

"You heard me—'all clear'—*now.* Over."

"Vsay yasno, over," she replied.

"Vsay yasno? Confirm. Over."

"Correct. Why?"

Marcus wasn't happy. He wasn't conducting a Socratic dialogue. He was in the middle of leading an operation with by far the biggest stakes of their careers. Morris should know better than to question him or engage in any extraneous conversation. There was no way he was going to walk her through what he was doing. He'd be happy to explain all in their after-action report, if they got that far, but certainly not now.

"Stand by" was all he said in response.

Marcus turned off the light in the second-floor hallway. He powered his night vision goggles back up and moved to a bedroom with windows overlooking the front yard. Seeing no movement in the vehicles, he pressed the button to the Russian radio system and gave the all clear signal exactly as Jenny had said it and prayed it did the job. Then he waited.

Would they buy it or bolt?

A minute passed, then two, though it seemed like an hour. Finally he heard the radio crackle to life. The head of the detail, presumably, was giving the order. It was in Russian, but its meaning was plain enough. Doors began to open. The Russians began to exit their vehicles. They'd bought it. The mission was still on.

Marcus pinned himself against a wall on the second floor, next to the stairs but out of position for anyone to see him if they glanced upward. He was amazed at how calm he felt. His breathing was steady. His pulse was barely above normal. The initial rush of adrenaline he'd felt minutes before had drained out of his system. His equilibrium had settled. He was back in control. The odds of complete success were long, to be sure. But at this point he gambled that even if he died in a firefight inside the house, Morris could eliminate everyone outside and pick off the rest as they tried to rush Oleg back to one of the SUVs. Whether she'd live long enough to talk to him, much less grab the thumb drive and get it uploaded to Langley, he had no idea. But he now put the odds at fifty-fifty, and given the scenario, that really wasn't so bad.

He asked his partner for a head count.

"Seven bogeys out of their vehicles, heading for the front door," she said.

These, plus the agent he'd killed and the one in the backyard, made nine. But that was odd. That left only the drivers, both of whom were certain to stay in their vehicles, keeping them running and ready for a quick escape if necessary. Was only one agent going to walk Oleg inside? Sloppy, Marcus thought.

Morris radioed again. "Keyhole to Razor—the headlights of both trucks just went dark. Both drivers are getting out, along with what looks like the head of the detail. They're putting a tight cordon around the subject and moving him toward the front door."

Marcus was surprised and went to the window to make sure Jenny was right. Sure enough, she was. If the drivers were shutting down their vehicles and getting out, it must mean the detail saw no immediate threat inside or outside the house. That was good news. It meant he and Jenny still retained the advantage. Still, there were now ten highly trained Russian bodyguards in the house, and Marcus was going to have to take them on by himself.

"Eyes on? Over," he whispered, making sure his math was correct.

"Eyes on one—repeat, eyes on one—the one they left to guard the front door," Morris replied.

Marcus didn't like the fact that they had no eyes on the agent stationed out back. But it couldn't be helped now. He listened for the last group of agents to enter the house with Oleg. He could soon hear Oleg talking in Russian, and though he couldn't understand a word the man was saying, it was obvious what the Raven was doing—he was putting the men at ease. They were laughing now. He could hear someone opening the refrigerator, kitchen cabinets opening and closing. A microwave started running. A moment later, he heard some glasses clinking and the unmistakable sound of a wine cork popping. It seemed highly unlikely that the men assigned to Oleg's protection were going to start drinking. Luganov would have their heads. But Marcus wouldn't be surprised at all if Oleg started drinking. He was nervous. He would want to take the edge off.

Marcus hoped Oleg wouldn't drink too heavily. He would need his wits about him tonight. That was for certain.

83

The thunder had died off.

The lightning had stopped. A quick glance out the window proved the storm was not subsiding, but with the temperatures dropping, the rain had turned to a mixture of sleet and snow, and it was falling hard.

Marcus felt bad for his compadre. Jenny had been out in the elements for nearly two hours, and she had to be freezing. He liked this woman—professionally, anyway. He didn't really know her, of course. They hadn't trained together. He hadn't observed her in action. He had no idea what she was capable of or what her breaking point was. But he liked her moxie, if not her ability to maintain proper radio protocol.

"*On my mark,*" he whispered. "*Now.*"

Morris flexed her frozen fingers one last time and took a deep breath.

Then she fired twice in rapid succession.

The agent standing post on the front steps dropped to the walkway. She fired two more times just to make sure. She watched him closely, looking for any signs of life, either of his chest moving or the fog of the man's breath condensing in the frigid cold.

Nothing.

And the silencer had worked. She hadn't compromised her position at all.

"Target down," she said. "I repeat, target down. Over."

Marcus almost smiled under his balaclava. *Two down, ten to go.*

He double-clicked his radio to signal he'd received her message. No longer could he risk speaking, even in a whisper.

It was his turn now. He pushed the remote in his left hand. All the lights went out simultaneously as the power in the house went down. Marcus clicked on his night vision goggles and moved sure and fast.

He spotted one agent standing post inside the front door and fired a quick burst with the Vintorez, then realized to his horror he hadn't remembered to attach the silencer Jenny had given him. It was the first time he'd actually fired the Russian-built VSS, and it was far louder than he'd expected. The house erupted with confused men shouting at each other in the dark. They were not prepared with night vision equipment. This gave Marcus another advantage. Turning right, he saw an agent standing just inside the vestibule and fired again, dropping him to the marble floor. Dashing down the stairs and pivoting around the corner, he tossed a stun grenade into the living room and shut his eyes.

The explosion was deafening. The momentary burst of intense white light did its job, activating all the photoreceptors in his enemies' eyes and causing temporary disorientation and loss of hearing and balance. Marcus knew these men would recover quickly, given their training, so he had to make the most of what little time the M84 had bought him.

First he unleashed a burst of fire at an agent stationed by the door to the garage, taking him out immediately. Next he spun around and cut down another one by the back door. Running to the kitchen, Marcus expected to find at least one agent and Oleg but was caught off guard to find neither. He moved left, into the dining room, and saw an agent running right toward the piano room. The man opened fire—a scoot and shoot. Marcus dove for the floor, and fired the rest of his magazine at the man, clipping him with his last round and sending him sprawling across the Persian rug. Marcus quickly ejected the spent mag and replaced it with a full one, then spotted the man crawling across the floor, leaving a trail of blood in his wake. Marcus pulled the trigger, unleashing another short burst into the man until he stopped moving.

Seven down, five to go.

But where were the rest? And where was the Raven?

So far Marcus had seen no sign of Oleg. He hoped several agents had rushed him down to the panic room. That's what Oleg had told him his detail was supposed to do, but what if they instead tried to rush him out of the house and into one of the bulletproof SUVs? Could Jenny take them out in time without hitting Oleg?

Slowly, methodically, he worked his way back to the archway between the piano room and the dining room, sweeping his weapon from one side to the other. His ears were still ringing from the explosion and the gunfire, making it all but impossible to hear his enemies moving across broken glass and splintered furniture, though they almost certainly were at the same disadvantage.

The smell of fear in the room was rapidly overtaking the stench of the smoke from the flash bomb. Then Marcus saw two shadows moving in the distance. That's when the counteroffensive began.

Gunfire erupted from his right, from the backyard through the bay windows. Marcus instantly hit the deck but saw a grenade rolling past him. He scrambled to his feet and dove headfirst into the kitchen just before the grenade exploded, destroying everything in its blast radius. Marcus slid along the hardwood floor, winding up behind the kitchen island as more gunfire erupted all around him.

He raised the VSS rifle over his head and sprayed the room, hoping at least to buy himself a few seconds to reorient and retake the initiative. If he stayed where he was, he knew he was in very real danger of getting caught in a pincer movement. He had to make a break for it. Pulling the pin on a grenade of his own, he threw it the full length of the house. He heard it hit the far wall and roll into the vestibule, then heard men yelling furiously in Russian. The moment the grenade detonated, he sprinted forward. He didn't think he'd taken out anyone new. He just hoped he'd cleared himself a path.

Marcus didn't know the floor plan as well as Oleg's men, but he knew it well enough to navigate through the carnage to his target: the stairs leading to the basement. He tossed his last grenade down the stairs, then pivoted back and sprayed the vestibule with a full magazine. He bounded down the stairs, reloading as he moved, and came around the corner, gun blazing.

The explosion had bought him just the time and distraction he needed. Through the night vision goggles, he spotted an agent about ten yards to his right, standing guard in front of the panic room. The rounds hit their mark. But Marcus resisted the temptation to race to the end of the hallway, punch in the code, and see if his man was inside. Instead, he turned left, ducked inside the darkened billiard room, and made sure no one was in there. He waited.

It didn't take long. No more than ten seconds later, another grenade came down the stairs. The explosion shook the house yet again. Then came two sets of footsteps. The Russians were moving fast and no doubt worried that members of this attacking force, whoever they were, knew where their principal was and were heading there to abduct him.

Marcus considered popping out and shooting them both from behind. That would make ten. But something held him back.

84

For a few seconds it was silent.

Then Marcus heard the distinctive sound of pins being pulled on not one but four more grenades. Two went rolling down the hall away from his location, toward the other wing of the mansion. Two came his way. Before he could hit the deck, the successive explosions sent him hurtling through the air past the pool table and crashing against the wall on the far side.

The air grew thick with clouds of smoke and the fine dust of crushed Sheetrock. The floor was littered with shards of lumber, twisted metal, mangled light fixtures, and shattered glass. The ceiling had become a mess of scorched beams, melted HVAC ducts, and dangling wires.

Marcus had no idea where his rifle had fallen. It was somewhere in all this debris. He'd dropped it the moment he went airborne, but he couldn't search for it yet. Nor could he check to see if anything on him was broken or bleeding. He didn't have the luxury. He knew for certain these guys were coming for him. He'd be coming for them if the situation were reversed. If he made a sound, he would give away his position and make himself a target. But just because he was a sitting duck didn't mean he couldn't defend himself. Slowly he reached with his right hand for his pistol, drew it from its holster, raised it, and aimed it at what had been a door and was now a gaping hole in the wall. His ears were ringing even worse now. There was no way he was going to be able to hear someone coming around the corner. At least with his night-vision goggles he'd be able to see them coming before they saw him.

Then the goggles shorted out.

With his left hand he pulled them off and set them aside. As his eyes readjusted to the darkness, his mind tried to comprehend the new reality that he was no longer the hunter but the hunted.

He flexed his fingers. They were working. He wriggled his toes. They, too, were working. He turned his head from side to side, still never taking his eyes off the hole in the wall. His neck was in immense pain, but at least he hadn't broken it. As quietly as possible, he bent his right knee. He tried to bend his left knee, but a jolt of searing pain shot up his spinal cord. He pulled off a glove and dabbed the knee with his left hand. It was bleeding. No matter. He had to get up. He had to make sure his back was not broken. He had to get moving.

Four of the Russian bodyguards were still alive. Surely one of them had called for backup by now. Where would the reinforcements be coming from? How long would it take them to get there? How many would there be? He had no answers. But if he wanted to live—if he was going to complete this mission and get Oleg and his files out of here—he had to get on his feet.

His hearing was slowly coming back. Both eardrums might prove permanently damaged. Only time would tell. But at least he could hear something, and just then he heard the crunch of glass and wood in the hallway. Someone was coming. Without the night-vision equipment, the basement was pitch-black. He'd expected his eyes to adjust after a few moments, but there was nothing to adjust to. So Marcus actually closed his eyes and listened.

There were two of them, moving cautiously, surely as blind and maybe as deaf as he was. Marcus could see the men in his mind's eye, standing in the hallway now directly in front of him. He pulled the trigger.

Six shots in two seconds.

Left to right.

He heard both men collapse to the floor.

His eyes still closed, Marcus ejected the spent magazine and popped in a full one. Then, slowly, painfully, he forced himself to his feet.

Jenny Morris was covered in a blanket of snow, and it was coming down harder.

She was less worried about getting frostbite and losing a digit or two than losing her ability to react quickly when the moment arose. Her eyelashes were nearly frozen. Her fingers weren't numb but they were heading in that direction. She had no idea what was going on inside the house. Only the repeated bursts of gunfire and occasional explosions and flashes of orange light gave evidence that the fight was still on. That was a good sign—if someone was still shooting, hopefully Marcus was still alive.

Another fear haunted her, however. She hadn't seen the agent in the back of the house in a while. What if he had been alerted by his colleagues to a sniper in the woods? Could he have been ordered to outflank her and take her out from behind? She forced herself to resist the temptation to keep checking behind her. Marcus had left her with one simple order before going into the house: no one could get back to the SUVs alive.

She'd already fired at the tires of the SUV in the rear and flattened them all. Since then, she'd maintained her focus on the four-yard gap between the front door of the Kraskin home and the closed doors of the SUVs. The moment the front door opened, she'd have only a split second to open fire. She didn't necessarily need to hit or kill anyone. She did have to keep them from successfully getting into the vehicles and leaving the premises. Morris was determined to do her job, no matter how cold she was, regardless of how long she had to wait.

Her second radio crackled to life. Not the one that connected her to Marcus but her link to the Global Operations Center in Langley. They wanted an update. She had little to tell them. No, she had not heard from Razor. No, she could not confirm the Raven was alive. No, the package was not yet in their possession. No, she was not aware that the agents on-site had called for backup.

This last fact was a very serious development. Langley informed her that three choppers were spooling up on helipads behind Lubyanka. Heavily armed commandos were loading in. They would be airborne in less than two minutes and would arrive at her location in no more than fifteen.

"Copy that," she replied.

Before she decided whether to relay that critical last piece to Marcus, the front door burst open. She fired. No one came out the door. But now she had exposed her position. A sniper began firing back from, of all places, the little window in the attic.

Frozen stiff yet coursing with adrenaline, Morris rolled right, down a slight embankment, taking herself out of the shooter's direct line of sight. She doubted the guy had night-vision goggles. None of the others did. He was just firing at her muzzle flash. She continued rolling right until she could again see the window, the gun barrel poking through, and a shadow behind it. With her left hand she pulled the keys to the Mercedes from her pocket—it was still about twenty yards farther to her right—and clicked the lights on.

The instant the sniper saw the lights, he began firing in that direction. Morris cut the lights again, looked through the reticle of her scope, took a deep breath, and pulled the trigger twice. She saw the man's head jerk back violently and then disappear from view.

In those brief seconds, however, someone had gotten to the lead SUV. The engine roared to life. The headlights burst on. Jenny Morris opened fire with everything she had, but the vehicle took off into the night and she had no idea who was inside.

85

Marcus heard the words but couldn't believe them.

He'd given Morris one job, and she'd blown it. Not only had she allowed one of the SUVs to escape, she wasn't even sure who had driven it—an agent or Oleg. If it was an agent, that was bad enough. But if they'd lost Oleg and the files, then the situation was catastrophic, for reasons only Marcus could fully understand.

The possibility that there was still an ex-Spetsnaz soldier on the loose in this house seriously slowed Marcus's approach to the panic room. Worse, Morris had radioed him that helicopters filled with more men were heading their way.

Marcus pulled out his phone and turned on the flashlight app. He searched the floor of the billiard room for his rifle, and when he found it, he looked at his knee and saw blood dripping. He grimaced but put the injury out of his mind and turned his attention to the hallway. He'd heard no sounds, no movement whatsoever on the bottom level since he'd taken out the last guy. If someone was waiting in the shadows to pop him, so be it, he thought. He knew where he was going when he drew his last breath on this planet.

Moving as quickly as he could with a limp and in wicked pain, Marcus climbed over debris and the dead and finally made it to the panic room. He shone the flashlight up one hallway and down another but saw no one and heard nothing. So he entered the code into the touch pad. Nothing happened at first. Then the panic room's independent power source kicked in and the massive steel door slid open.

Oleg Kraskin sat on a wooden stool, looking fairly calm given the circumstances. Marcus lowered his weapon and pulled off his balaclava.

"Took you long enough," Oleg said.

"Sorry—hit some traffic," Marcus replied. "You okay?"

"I'll live, a little while longer, anyway," the Russian deadpanned.

Marcus took the gallows humor as a good sign. "Got something for me?" Marcus asked.

"Absolutely," Oleg said, producing the thumb drive. "And you?"

"Absolutely," Marcus said, reloading the pistol and handing it over.

He showed the Russian exactly how the silencing mechanism worked, where the safety was, and how close he would need to be to Luganov to maintain accuracy.

"Anything under five feet, you should be good. The closer the better, especially if you're behind him and he's not looking. But if you're facing him, then don't get too close or he could bat it away before you pull the trigger."

"Got it," Oleg said. "Is the plane ready?"

"It will be by the time you get there."

"And my ride—is it on the way?"

"Just lifted off from Lubyanka—ETA twelve minutes."

Oleg smiled grimly as he pulled a package of cigarettes and a lighter from his jacket pocket. He lit one and took a long drag. He closed his eyes and seemed to savor the taste and the moment.

"Before we forget, I need the passwords to get into all your files," Marcus said.

Oleg reopened his eyes. He reached into another pocket, retrieved a folded piece of paper, and handed it over. Marcus opened it and found it was a computer printout of at least twenty different passcodes. He took out his mobile phone, snapped several pictures of it, then borrowed Oleg's lighter and set it aflame.

Suddenly Morris's voice crackled over the radio.

"Keyhole to Razor—the choppers will be here in nine minutes. Over."

"Roger that," Marcus replied. "Get the car in position, and stand by."

He turned back to Oleg. "Since we have a moment, can I ask you a question?"

"Of course," Oleg said.

"You told me that Nimkov wants to proceed with the invasion but Petrovsky does not. Did I get that right?"

"You did."

"So if you succeed tonight and the president is out of the picture, do the war plans go forward without the full and active support of the defense minister?"

"Probably not."

"Are there others in the cabinet or in the war council pushing for war, others who really *want* to attack NATO?"

"No, I don't think so."

"Just your father-in-law?"

"And Nimkov."

"Right," Marcus said. "And if the president is gone and Nimkov is alone, could he persuade the others to proceed?"

"I don't know. I don't think so—no."

"What will Petrovsky do?"

Oleg considered that for a moment. "I think there's a real possibility he will arrest Nimkov for treason. And call off the war."

"Could he do that?"

"I believe so. The last public statement made by the president to Senator Dayton and the world was that he was going to pull all Russian forces back from the borders and deescalate the situation. Petrovsky could proceed on that basis while accusing Nimkov of trying to orchestrate a coup against Luganov. He could throw Nimkov in prison and announce that he was carrying out the express wishes of the late President Luganov. It just might work."

It had better, Marcus thought.

Again, Morris radioed in. "Seven minutes."

Marcus ignored her.

"So you remain convinced it all comes down to whether Luganov lives or dies?"

"Believe me, Mr. Ryker, I want there to be another way," Oleg said. "But I can't come up with one. Can you?"

"No, I can't," Marcus said. "And I'm sorry."

"Then may I ask you a question?" Oleg said.

"Of course."

"If you were in my place—if the situation were completely reversed—would you do it?"

Marcus paused. He hadn't thought about it in those terms. "It doesn't really matter what I'd do, Oleg," he finally said. "It's your life. Trust me, I won't judge you for a moment if you choose not to do this. You can leave with us right now, and we'll get you out of the country if you want. It's your choice."

Oleg looked thoughtful. "I keep thinking about what Solzhenitsyn wrote in *The Gulag Archipelago.* 'In keeping silent about evil, in burying it so deep within us that no sign of it appears on the surface, we are *implanting* it, and it will rise up a thousandfold in the future. When we neither punish nor reproach evildoers, we are not simply protecting their trivial old age, we are thereby ripping the foundations of justice from beneath new generations.' My father-in-law is attempting to perpetrate a terrible evil. I can't just save myself. That's the coward's way out, and I've been a coward for too long. I want to do something significant, something important with my life. I wouldn't have chosen this. I'd much rather have retired to the Riviera and tried my hand at writing a great Russian novel. But these are the cards I've been dealt. This is the hand I need to play."

"And your wife and son?" Marcus asked, wondering why he'd never once brought them up. "Don't you want to be with them?"

Oleg looked down at the smoldering cigarette in his hands. "Whom do you think I'm doing this for, Mr. Ryker? I may never see them again, but at least they won't be vaporized in a millisecond of brilliant light."

Again the radio crackled. The choppers would be there in less than four minutes. They were out of time.

86

"*Go, go, go!*" Marcus yelled as he bolted out of the house and into the Mercedes.

"*Where's Kraskin?*" Morris asked, visibly stunned to see her partner alone.

"*Never mind. Floor it, Jenny,*" Marcus ordered.

The CIA's top operative in Russia bristled, but with the choppers inbound she did as she was told.

Marcus reloaded his rifle and prayed for his crazy scheme to work as they blew through the front gates and tore down the slick back roads at dangerously high speeds.

It was still pitch-black. The clock on the dashboard said it was only 4:28. Few other cars were on the roads at such an hour, but the snow was coming down even harder now, and Morris had the windshield wipers on full blast. As blood continued oozing down his left leg, Marcus reached into the backseat, grabbed his backpack, and pulled out his first aid kit.

"I have the flash drive," he said at last as he fished through the kit until he found a hypodermic needle, loaded it with a painkiller, and jammed it into his left thigh.

"Good," Morris said. "But where is Oleg? Was he killed?"

"No, he's alive," Marcus said. He spread antibiotic ointment over the wound and wrapped it with gauze and tape. "He said he'd meet us at the airport. But first he has to go see Luganov."

"Why?"

"He said he had to see him about something critical that might help stop the war." Marcus stuffed the first aid kit back into his pack and tossed it behind him as he scanned the skies for the inbound hostage rescue team. At the same time, he was looking from side to side for the SUV that had gotten away, lest it was lurking in the shadows, waiting to ambush them. He knew full well he was edging close to a line. He wasn't lying to her, not quite. But he couldn't tell her a thing. Not now. Perhaps not ever.

"Ryker, that's not acceptable," Morris shot back. "We had orders from the president of the United States to bring the Raven out alive."

"Look, he knows the risks, especially with Luganov launching an all-out mole hunt. But he was adamant. He believes he has to go see the president one more time. There was nothing I could do."

"You could have grabbed him anyway."

"Kidnapped him?"

"Call it what you want, Ryker—the president gave us the green light to execute a plan *you* initiated. Not just to get the files but to get the Raven."

"And we will. I told you, he said he'd meet us at the airport."

"That wasn't the plan."

"It is now."

"Please don't tell me we just killed eleven Russians to retrieve a thumb drive Mr. Kraskin could have simply left on the kitchen table for us to grab."

It was a brutal accusation, tantamount to murder. Marcus would have none of it. He pushed back with a vengeance. "We're in the fog of war, Jenny. The situation changed. Oleg kept his word. He gave us what he promised. But he doesn't think it's enough. He thinks he can do more, something that could significantly change the course of the war or even derail it from the outset. You really think I should have kidnapped him? The son-in-law of the Russian president? What if I did? How would we get him to the airport? How would we get him onto the plane? Drug him? And then what? Take him to a black site? Beat the crap out of him to tell us everything he knows? And what after that? If we don't kill him, we have to release him. You want him to go public with all that? Are you insane?"

They continued racing through the frigid countryside in the dark of night, back to the Lukoil station to switch cars. Marcus began counting silently to fifty. *Panic is contagious. But so is calm. Stay calm. Do your work. Slow is smooth. Smooth is smart. Smart is straight. Straight is deadly.*

"So now what?" Morris asked after several minutes. "How exactly does this play out?"

"It's simple," Marcus replied. "The commandos arrive at the residence. They storm inside and find Oleg safe in the panic room and everyone else dead. They'll ask him what happened. He'll say he doesn't know. He'll tell them the moment the shooting began, his agents grabbed him and got him to safety, which is true. He'll say he heard all the explosions and gunfire but couldn't see a thing, which is also true. He'll ask that they take him to his father-in-law immediately to tell him what happened."

"And then?"

"Then he contacts us and makes his way to the airport, and we're out of here," Marcus said. "For now, you need to get in touch with your people. Let them know there'll only be two of us at first. Tell them to have a car waiting, something that won't draw attention, parked near the plane."

"Why?"

"So I can pick him up when he gets to the airport and get him to the plane as quickly as possible."

Suddenly they heard the sound of the choppers approaching. Marcus peered through the sunroof and through the front and side windows but could not see them. He lowered his window slightly. Snow started swirling into the interior of the car. But above the rushing of the wind, he could hear the choppers more clearly. They were off to their left. Marcus put their distance at least a half mile away.

Moments later they pulled into the gas station. But there at the first pump was something they had not planned for—the SUV that had gotten away, its tank being filled by a lone bodyguard. Morris slammed on the brakes, but it was too late. The agent had seen them. They were the only car on the road, in the middle of the night, coming from the direction of the deadly ambush this guy had escaped from. They were dressed in black and obviously looked suspicious. At the very least, the agent was going to check them out. When he saw their weapons, they would be finished.

The agent drew his sidearm and pointed it at Morris as he approached the Mercedes, shouting in Russian. Marcus knew he had to act. He bolted out of the car. Before the agent could redirect his aim and fire, Marcus pulled his rifle's trigger.

The shots went wide. Now the agent was firing back, first at Marcus, then at the Mercedes. The passenger-side window exploded. The rear windows were next. Morris peeled away. Marcus fired again. Bullets were crisscrossing through the frigid night air. Marcus hobbled right, still in immense pain, using the Russian's SUV to provide some cover. But at that moment he realized he'd made a serious mistake.

At first the bodyguard started coming around the back of the truck, firing nonstop. But now Marcus saw the agent change his mind and head back to open the driver's-side door. Once safely inside the bullet-proof vehicle, he would call for backup, and the area would be swarming with Russian soldiers within minutes. Marcus and Morris would never get away. Knowing he had only a split second to act, Marcus forced himself to ignore the pain in his knee. He raced around the front of the truck, firing everything he had. But Marcus wasn't firing at the Russian. He was firing at the SUV's gas tank and the nozzle that was still coursing with gallons of fresh fuel. As he fired, Marcus was rapidly backing away from the service island. With the gas flowing and fumes in the air, all he needed was to create a single spark. . . .

And then he did.

The massive explosion blew Marcus across the parking lot and flipped the SUV on its head. The fireball soared twenty, thirty feet in the air. Then came more explosions as the flames shot up the nozzle into the pump and the reserve tanks underground ignited.

Morris jumped out of the SUV and raced to Marcus. She grabbed him by his flak jacket, dragged him away from the flames, and helped him to his feet. *"We need to move—now!"* she yelled over the roar of the inferno.

Together they sprinted around behind the service building, which was completely demolished and ablaze. When they reached the Volga, Marcus found his keys, got in the driver's side, and reached over to unlock the door for Morris. Before she got in, however, he told her to go to the Mercedes, start the engine, put it into drive, aim it for the SUV, and then run for the road. He would meet her there.

This time she didn't ask questions. Nor did she hesitate in the slightest. She immediately got what he was saying and ran off to get it done. Meanwhile, Marcus shoved the key in the ignition and gave it a turn. Nothing happened. He tried it again while pumping the accelerator. The engine coughed and sputtered but refused to spring to life. Seconds later, Marcus both heard and felt the newest explosion. That was the SUV. Destroying the Mercedes would not only cover their tracks and destroy evidence but would add to the diversion and help them escape. Morris had done her job. But he had failed in his. Their getaway car was a bust.

The explosions had surely been spotted by the inbound Spetsnaz teams and no doubt by neighbors who were already calling the local fire department and the police. But Marcus stayed focused on the task at hand. Beside the Volga was a dark-green Lada, a pitifully bad Russian-made compact car that looked like a miniature version of a Fiat, if such a thing were possible. This one looked like a model from the early nineties. It had little power, possibly no heat, certainly no frills, but it was theirs for the taking.

Marcus wondered briefly whom the car belonged to. He had seen no one inside the service building or anywhere else in the deserted gas station. Perhaps a night clerk had gone running when the shooting started. But he didn't have time to worry about it now. So he ditched the Volga and hobbled over to the Lada. There was no need to dust off the snow. It had all melted away in the searing heat, and the car was dripping wet. It was also locked. Marcus smashed one of the rear windows, then reached inside and unlocked the driver's-side door. Reaching under the dashboard, he turned on his phone's flashlight app, pulled down a sheath of wires, and hot-wired the ignition. Within seconds the engine was purring. They were back in business.

The snow was coming down still harder. He flicked on the head-lights and cranked the windshield wipers up to the maximum, then maneuvered around the blazing wreckage and found Jenny Morris standing on the side of the road. The moment she got in, Marcus floored it. He told Morris to call her boss on the secure satellite phone and alert him to the changes in their plans before pulling out her laptop and uploading all the contents of the thumb drive to Langley. Time was of the essence, and they might soon have company.

87

Oleg Kraskin was terrified, unsure if he could go through with it.

It was almost five thirty in the morning when the helicopter carrying him touched down on the freshly plowed landing pad beside Luganov's much larger Mi-8 chopper. So far Marcus had been right every step of the way. From the moment the commandos had entered the panic room, he hadn't simply been questioned; he'd essentially been interrogated. The lines between the two had been badly blurred, but Oleg's story had held up.

No, he was not wounded, not seriously, though he'd banged up his knee in all the commotion. No, he had no idea who had attacked his parents' home. No, he hadn't seen a thing. Yes, the agents had done their jobs brilliantly and courageously. They'd immediately rushed him into the panic room and proceeded to fight bravely to save his life. In this, they had succeeded, and Oleg had gushed his profound gratitude for every single one of them. He'd literally wept when he'd seen the carnage and the destruction throughout the house. He'd bristled, even yelled back, when he'd felt treated like a suspect. In the end, there wasn't a shred of evidence that he'd been complicit in any way. To the contrary, he appeared to have been the target of a sophisticated and brazen assassination plot.

Thus, as Marcus had predicted, Oleg had been cleared and brought to the palace, to his father-in-law's side, both to recover and to assist with the war effort. All that had been the easy part. What was coming next would be infinitely more difficult, testing every ounce of discipline and cunning Oleg possessed.

Oleg grabbed his leather briefcase as six burly agents helped him out of the chopper. They created a tight cordon around him, and he limped inside the doors of the north portico. Waiting for them was another group of agents, manning a checkpoint Oleg had only seen used before for the staffs of foreign heads of state. Never for family. Never for him. This time, however, the checkpoint supervisor surprised Oleg by asking him to put his personal possessions—his watch, his wallet, briefcase, shoes, the change in his pocket, and anything else he had on him—through the X-ray machine.

"The president is expecting me," Oleg said indignantly.

The FSB officer nodded again. "Yes, sir. I understand, sir."

"I have urgent matters to discuss with the president."

"Of course—this will only take a moment," the officer assured him.

This was not going as planned. Oleg could feel beads of perspiration forming on the back of his neck.

"This is ridiculous," Oleg objected again. "I've never been subjected to such things."

"My apologies, Mr. Kraskin, but these are the president's orders for everyone entering the residence," the officer replied while his colleagues looked on. "Given all that's unfolding, we are operating under a heightened state of readiness. I'm sure you can understand. We cannot take any chances."

Feeling trapped, Oleg moved directly to the officer and got in his face. "Can't take any chances?" he asked. "Do you have *any* idea what I've just been through, what I've just survived?"

"I do, sir, and—"

"And yet you have the gall to speak this way to me?"

The tension in the air was thick. Several of the agents looked away. Still the supervisor humbly but firmly held his ground. "I mean no disrespect, Mr. Kraskin, but orders are orders."

The two men stood there for a moment, staring at one another. Then Oleg blinked. He untied his shoes and set them on the conveyor belt. He removed his belt and his cuff links and his watch and wallet and a fountain pen from his breast pocket and put them on the conveyor belt as well. The operator immediately moved the items through the machine.

"The briefcase, too, if you wouldn't mind," the supervisor said, noticing that Oleg had initially set the bag on the floor when he removed his shoes but hadn't placed it on the conveyor belt.

Oleg's heart was pounding. If he was stopped here, it would be disastrous. Not only would Marcus's plan be ruined and the war proceed, but Oleg would be going straight to the bowels of Lubyanka to face the torturers of the FSB and a fate far worse than death. He picked up the briefcase.

"Do you have a laptop?" the supervisor asked.

"I do," Oleg said.

"Please take it out and run it through separately."

Oleg did as he was asked.

Time seemed to stand still as the X-ray operator studied every square inch of every item. When each one was cleared and emerged on the other side, a different agent examined it manually. He removed the battery of the notebook computer, studied it closely, and then replaced it and turned the computer on. When it flickered to life, the officer was satisfied. He turned it off again, then turned his attention to the briefcase, thoroughly checking every section. When he found an unopened pack of cigarettes, he carefully tore the cellophane away, opened the pack, and dumped the contents on the counter. Convinced nothing was amiss, he put each cigarette back in its place and the pack back in the pocket of the briefcase where he'd found it.

Next he pulled out a small digital voice recorder. The officer opened up the back and removed the batteries. Then he opened a drawer in a desk behind him, fished out batteries of the same kind, and put these in the device. He turned the recorder on, but no sound emerged. The device was new. No messages had yet been recorded on it. Satisfied, the officer replaced the device in the briefcase and nodded. "You're all set."

Oleg began breathing again and was about to work his way around the magnetometer like he always did. However, the supervisor asked Oleg to take off his raincoat and his suit coat and put them through the X-ray machine as well.

"Then I'll need you to step through the metal detector," he said.

Oleg just stared at him.

"Again, my sincerest apologies, Mr. Kraskin, but the president's orders . . ."

Oleg paused, trying hard to look annoyed and not terrified. But terrified he was, and he could stall no longer. There was no way he was going to make it through the metal detector without setting it off. He would be immediately searched and quickly arrested when they found the gun.

Slowly, with a room full of agents watching him, he took off his coat and put it on the conveyor belt. Then he did the same with the jacket of his suit. When the operator turned on the belt and both items began moving through the X-ray machine, Oleg straightened his tie, wondering what to do next. There was no place to run, no place to hide. This was it, the end of the road.

Why hadn't he fled the country with Marcus Ryker?

88

Resolved to his fate, Oleg took a deep breath and limped forward.

The machine started beeping. He put out his hands, preparing to be wanded.

Just then Dmitri Nimkov came around the corner.

"That'll be all," Nimkov barked before any of the officers could begin the search. *"How dare you treat the president's own son-in-law like this, especially after all he's just been through! What's wrong with you men? Have you no respect for the family?"*

The men froze. Oleg was ashen. None of them moved, but Nimkov put his arm around Oleg and helped him gather his belongings. When Oleg was finished putting on his shoes and belt, he collected the rest of his things and put them in his briefcase along with his computer. Then he put his suit jacket back on, draped his raincoat over his arm, and as calmly as he could, thanked the FSB chief, surely the last man he'd expected to help him clear security.

"My pleasure, Oleg Stefanovich," Nimkov said. "Come. The president is waiting for you."

"Then by all means, lead on," Oleg replied, though he knew the route by heart.

When Nimkov saw Oleg moving so slowly, his left leg stiff as a board and pain streaked across his face, he asked what had happened. Oleg said it was nothing. He'd fallen during the rush to get to the panic room, inflaming an old hockey injury.

As they snaked through several hallways, Oleg noticed they were passing far more agents than were typically posted inside the residence. They were stationed every ten meters or so. Through the windows, Oleg couldn't help but notice K-9 units roaming the grounds. Sharpshooters in arctic combat wear were visible on the roofs of the outbuildings. With each step Oleg felt his fears rising and his resolve weakening.

Finally they turned a corner and arrived outside Luganov's private study. Stationed in that hallway were no fewer than six elite members of the presidential bodyguard division. None of Luganov's team was more trusted than these, and trusted most of all was Special Agent Kovalev, posted directly in front of the door. Kovalev nodded as Oleg and Nimkov approached. He knew them both well. Nevertheless, he asked both to present photo IDs. This was unheard of, yet neither man argued. Both dug their IDs out of their wallets. Kovalev studied them closely, then studied the men's faces. Oleg felt sure the man was going to see right through him, but he returned the IDs and stepped aside from the door to let them through.

The heavy, thick, steel-reinforced door opened into a short, carpeted, empty hallway—an additional security measure to make absolutely certain that no unauthorized person could approach the president. Nimkov, knowing his place, let Oleg enter first. When Oleg limped to the door at the other end of the hallway, he knocked twice. Only when he heard his father-in-law bid him enter did he open the door.

The president was sitting beside his desk in an overstuffed chair, gazing vacantly at walls lined with books of every kind, from esteemed Russian literature to military histories and biographies of great leaders to Western novels, especially political thrillers, for which Luganov had a weakness. He was dressed casually in blue jeans, a navy-blue V-neck sweater over a white T-shirt, and boots, and he was smoking a cigar. There was a roaring fire in the stone fireplace. There was also an open bottle of Stolichnaya and a half-empty glass. That didn't bode well so early in the morning, Oleg thought.

"Oleg Stefanovich, it's you—finally—you live and breathe," said Luganov, his speech slightly slurred, though that could have been as much from lack of sleep as an abundance of alcohol.

Oleg nodded but then turned on the FSB chief without warning. "I'm alive, but no thanks to the imbeciles this man assigned to me, Father. Dmitri Dmitrovich, how is it that you have such incompetents on my security detail? How is it that you have allowed my life to be put in such danger?"

Nimkov was completely caught off guard, and Oleg stayed on the attack. It was his father-in-law, after all, who had taught him the best defense was a good offense.

"Dmitri Dmitrovich, tell us, have you hunted down the filthy pigs who tried to kill me? Have you captured any of them? Have you killed any of them? Or is this too much for you and the sniveling, pathetic morons working for you?"

Nimkov tried to respond, but Luganov intervened. "Come, come; sit down, Oleg Stefanovich," the president said. "Set aside your coat and your briefcase and have a seat. You have been through a terrible ordeal. I know you are angry. I am as well. But there is no need to take out your frustrations on the FSB or its esteemed director. We are on the same team, are we not?"

Luganov motioned to an unoccupied chair to his left. Oleg reluctantly took it. Nimkov sat in the chair to the president's right. Then Luganov pushed a buzzer on his desk, and seconds later a steward entered.

"Bring some tea for my son and breakfast for us all," Luganov ordered. "It has been a long night. I think we all need some sustenance."

Luganov looked around the room. Neither Oleg nor Nimkov said a word.

"Yes, Your Excellency. Right away, sir."

When the steward stepped out of the room and closed the door behind him, Luganov gave the FSB director the floor.

"I deeply apologize, Oleg Stefanovich," Nimkov began. "This was a terrible breach in our security. I'm afraid we do not have any of the perpetrators in custody. But my men are thoroughly scouring the crime scene, and I guarantee we will make arrests sooner than you might think."

The way Nimkov uttered this last sentence worried Oleg. Was this a threat, delivered right here in the presence of the president himself? Oleg wondered what mistakes Marcus and his team had committed, what incriminating evidence they had left behind, and how quickly—if at all—it could be linked to him. Even more, however, Oleg wondered how long Nimkov was going to stay. The plan Marcus had given him hadn't factored in a second man in the room, least of all the head of Russia's security services.

"Dmitri Dmitrovich, what do you know so far?" Luganov asked.

"For starters, Your Excellency, we have recovered one of the getaway cars the attackers used," Nimkov explained. "Well, *recovered* probably isn't the correct term. *Located* is more like it. A Mercedes. An SUV. My men found it six miles away from the Kraskin estate."

"Where exactly?"

"At a Lukoil gas station the terrorists blew up to cover their tracks."

"Blew up?" the president asked.

"Completely demolished, and the fire's still raging," Nimkov confirmed. "It will take some time to sort out the damage. One of my agents was found dead at the scene. Shell casings everywhere. Seems there was quite a shoot-out. It all went down just as our hostage rescue team was arriving to get you, Oleg Stefanovich. As best we can tell at the moment, our man was in hot pursuit of the Mercedes. The two vehicles may have crashed into the gas station. It's not yet clear, but the roads were slippery in the snow."

Oleg was aghast at the news, suddenly wondering if Marcus was even still alive.

"What else have you found?" he asked, convinced it was in his best interest to stay on the offensive. "How many attacked the house, and who were they? Chechens?"

"I'm glad you asked, Oleg Stefanovich, because that's one of the strangest things about the attack," said Nimkov. "We haven't found the bodies of any of the terrorists in or around your family home."

"*None?*"

"Strange, isn't it? Twelve of my men are dead. Not a single perpetrator. Yet ballistics confirms all of them were firing their weapons."

"More evidence of their incompetence, if you ask me," Oleg fumed. He was trying to put on a good show, but he worried where this was going. He had no idea how many men Marcus had brought with him. He hadn't asked ahead of time because he didn't want to know. He hadn't asked afterward because there hadn't been time. But given the magnitude of the gun battle and the destruction caused to the house, surely there had been at least six or eight. That's what Oleg had assumed, anyway, and it was inconceivable the FSB agents hadn't taken out at least a few of them.

"Perhaps it was incompetence," said Nimkov, rising to his feet. "Or perhaps there's another explanation."

"Like what?" Oleg asked. He noticed that his father-in-law was being unusually quiet during the conversation.

"Perhaps they were set up."

"Set up? How?"

"Perhaps someone tipped them off, someone on the inside, someone trying to cover up a crime."

"Only your men knew where I was going to be tonight," Oleg shot back. "My own parents didn't know. Nor did Marina. Is there a mole inside the FSB?"

"There's a mole somewhere—that much seems clear," Nimkov said. The FSB chief turned to the president. "May I?"

Luganov assented, so Nimkov walked over to a television console that Oleg noticed was hooked up to a laptop computer.

"I have some surveillance video footage I brought for the president to see. Now that you're here, I'd like to show you as well, Oleg Stefanovich. And then, with the president's permission, I may have a few questions."

89

"Heard anything?" Morris asked.

"Not yet."

Five minutes from Domodedovo International Airport, Marcus pulled off the highway and turned onto Ilyushina Street. He parked the Lada in the rear lot of the Ramada. Morris checked the laptop. The files were done uploading. She pulled out the thumb drive and handed it back to Marcus. Then they quickly stuffed their weapons, ammo, radios, flak jackets, balaclavas, and other supplies into large duffel bags, shoved those in the trunk, locked the doors, and slipped into the building through a side door using a key card Morris had brought with her, per the extraction plan they'd jointly designed days earlier.

Once inside, the two headed directly for the restrooms off the lobby. There, each found a bag pre-positioned for them at the bottom of the trash bins. Each bag contained a change of clothes, a winter hat, coat, gloves, boots, a wig, glasses, a fake passport, and an airport

ID, and in Marcus's case, a fake mustache and goatee. Marcus washed the blood and sweat from his face and hands, then rewrapped his knee with fresh gauze and tape. He changed into the dark-blue coveralls and work boots, put on the rest of the disguise, and went back outside, where a Ramada shuttle bus, driven by one of Morris's men, pulled up.

The shuttle drove them directly to the private aviation terminal on the far side of the field, opposite the commercial passenger terminals. Once there, the two disembarked and proceeded through security as if they were members of the ground crew arriving for their morning shift. A bleary-eyed security guard paid scant attention to either of them as they passed through the metal detectors. They weren't carrying any weapons or explosives. They had no bags or other personal items to inspect. So they were waved through in fairly short order.

Heading to the flight line, they spotted the Gulfstream IV with the tail number they'd been given in advance, and climbed aboard, nodding to the actual ground crew members finishing their preflight preparations. Neither Marcus nor Morris drew any attention. As the early winter storm intensified, the crew was freezing and exhausted and eager to finish their shift and get home to their families.

On board, Morris stepped to the cockpit, knocked four times, and whispered a code word. A moment later the cockpit door opened, and two CIA officers dressed as pilots emerged and greeted them. Morris and the woman pilot headed to the two washrooms. Marcus and the man headed to the back of the plane, where they swapped clothes in the galley. Then the officer gave him a key to an airport security car parked near the door to the terminal.

"Is it covered in snow?" Marcus asked.

"Shouldn't be too bad," the officer replied. "We've brushed it down every fifteen minutes and turned over the engine twice. You should be good to go."

"And the weapons?"

The officer handed over a Russian-made pistol. It was a newer and larger model than the one Marcus had given to Oleg, and it was, as he'd insisted, equipped with a silencer. The officer said there was also a submachine gun in a canvas bag on the floor of the vehicle he'd set aside for them and two other automatic rifles and plenty of ammunition under the seats in the cockpit, just in case.

The swap was soon complete. The CIA officers were now dressed as members of the ground crew. Morris was dressed as the lead pilot, as she was the only one of the two actually licensed and rated to fly a Gulfstream, particularly in weather like this. Marcus was dressed as her copilot. He'd earned his private pilot license when he was younger, but on single-engine prop planes, not jets, and certainly not a G4. Morris thanked her colleagues, as did Marcus, and they deplaned. Marcus raised the steps and locked the cabin door while Morris went to the cockpit to review their preflight checklist.

There was still no word from Oleg, and Marcus was getting worried. He'd expected something by now. Unspoken between him and Morris—but very much up in the air—was the question for which Marcus didn't have an answer: How long would they wait before they had to cut Oleg loose and leave without him?

Oleg stared at the TV screen, his face pale and his hands trembling slightly.

He was no longer on offense.

Before Dmitri Nimkov could resume his questioning, the chief steward knocked twice. Luganov said he could enter, and soon they were being served cheese omelets, sweet rolls, fresh fruit, and steaming chai. The steward poured each man a cup. Luganov quickly grew impatient and waved him away, and he slipped out.

"Who was the girl?" Nimkov asked, standing over him.

At first Oleg was too shocked to respond.

"We're going to find out soon enough," Nimkov continued. "Don't presume to waste the president's patience or his goodwill."

Still, Oleg could not find the words, so shocked was he by the tape he'd just seen.

"Did you find her on your own?" the FSB chief went on. "Or did Marcus Ryker provide her for you?"

"You have no idea what you're talking about, Dmitri Dmitrovich," Oleg finally responded.

"Surely you cannot deny you gave the slip to your security detail last Wednesday night," Nimkov noted. "Surely you cannot deny you checked into the Hotel National. Or that you paid cash for your room and asked for a room that just happened to be next to a member of Senator Dayton's delegation, can you?"

Oleg couldn't bear to look at his father-in-law, but the contempt he had for Nimkov was reaching the boiling point.

"I believe you are actually acquainted with Special Agent Ryker, are you not?" Nimkov pressed, clearly relishing his role as interrogator. "You met him before, in Berlin."

Oleg said nothing. The plan was falling apart before his eyes.

"Surely you do not deny this, do you, Oleg Stefanovich?"

Oleg began to panic.

"How can you?" the FSB chief continued, his confidence increasing, his voice growing angrier. "You sit there next to your leader, so smug, with such hubris and contempt, refusing to answer my questions. But I already know the answers. I have sworn affidavits from no fewer than five witnesses that you interrupted a meeting in the German Chancellery to introduce yourself to Mr. Ryker when he was working for the U.S. Secret Service. What conclusion should the president draw from this?"

Oleg could feel the pistol, warm against his flesh. But he could not reach for it. Not yet.

"My staff retrieved your written report from that trip. You make no mention of unauthorized, personal contact with a member of the American government. Yet this just so happens to be the very same person whom you allowed into a meeting with President Luganov in the hours leading up to a war. And it just so happens to be the person in the room next to yours at the Hotel National. Is the president to conclude this is merely happenstance?"

Oleg felt physically ill.

"And the woman? Tell us who she is," Nimkov demanded. "It's all on video, Oleg Stefanovich. Enough of your silence and stonewalling. Are you really going to sit there and tell us you're not cheating on the daughter of His Excellency?"

Oleg was ready to respond, but Luganov—livid—cut him off. *"Oleg Stefanovich, give me the little tart's name and be done with it!"* the president demanded, rising to his feet, his face beet red.

Just then Nimkov's mobile phone rang. The FSB chief glanced at the president. The timing was terrible, but they were less than forty-eight hours from launching a war. Luganov nodded, and Nimkov answered it.

"Not now," he replied to the voice at the other end. "Of course I understand, but he's busy with a matter of national security. No, I will call you when I can."

"Who is it?" Luganov snapped.

"It's Agent Kovalev, sir," Nimkov replied. "Miss Slatsky needs to see you. She says it's urgent. What would you have him do?"

"She will wait," Luganov said, as angry as Oleg had ever seen him. "And tell Pavel I will not be interrupted again. I will let him know when I am finished. Until then, I am not to be disturbed. Do I make myself clear?"

"Perfectly, Your Excellency," Nimkov replied, and he passed the message on.

Both men were now towering over Oleg, and Oleg could bear it no longer. He would answer their questions. He would tell them what they wanted to know. He had to. What other choice did he have?

90

"Yes, Dmitri Dmitrovich, I deny it—I deny it all!"

Oleg, still sitting, leveled his icy gaze at the FSB chief. "I'm not having an affair, nor would I ever. How dare you imply that I would."

He shifted to the president and lowered his voice to be—or at least to appear to be—respectful of a father and a leader.

"Her name?" he said. "Her name is Marina Aleksandrovna Luganova. I have loved her from the day we met in college, and I have never been unfaithful. Not once. Not ever."

Now it was Luganov and Nimkov who were taken aback both by Oleg's defense and the ferocity and deep sense of conviction with which he made it.

"I'd been working too long," he said, his voice more subdued, regret thick in his voice. "I was never home. I missed Vasily, and I missed Marina even more. So I called her that evening from my office. Check the phone logs. I asked her to come down to the hotel and stay the night with me. I asked her to be discreet, to enter through a side door, to wear a scarf so no one could recognize her. The last thing I wanted to do was attract any attention to her or to you, Father."

Luganov was so stunned that he physically backed up several steps. Nimkov was clearly caught off guard as well. He followed the president's lead and stepped back from Oleg, though not quite as far.

"Is this true?" Luganov asked.

"It is," Oleg said. "All of it. Call Marina. Ask her yourself. She will tell you. I'm not a traitor, and I'm certainly not an adulterer. I love this country and I love your daughter more than life itself, and I would do anything to protect them."

The room was silent. The food and tea sat there cold and untouched. Nimkov picked up the phone on the desk, but Luganov grabbed the receiver from him. "I will do it myself. Sit down, Dmitri Dmitrovich. We will clear this up right now."

Nimkov sat as Luganov asked the palace operator to connect him to his ex-wife's home and get his daughter on the line.

Oleg winced and held his stomach. "Father, may I go to the restroom?"

Irritated, perhaps at the question, perhaps that Marina wasn't already on the line, Luganov grunted his approval. Oleg stood and limped for the door. There was a bathroom down the hall. But Nimkov put out his hand and blocked his path.

"Use this one," he said, pointing to the washroom connected to the study.

"It's reserved for the president," Oleg replied.

"Under the circumstances, I am sure he won't mind. We wouldn't want you to wander off."

Oleg looked to his father-in-law, who again grunted his assent after cursing the operators and demanding things move faster.

"Don't take too long," Nimkov instructed. "We're not finished."

Oleg said nothing but hobbled into the lavatory and closed and locked the door behind him. He glanced around. There were no windows. Nor would there be any hidden cameras. He turned on the faucet so the men outside would hear water running. Then he unbuckled his trousers. He had duct-taped the small pistol Marcus had given him to his inner left thigh, just below the groin. This was why he'd been limping. He'd never injured his knee. Oleg waited several moments, then reached over and flushed the toilet to mask the sound of tape tearing from his skin.

Setting the gun on the vanity, he pulled his trousers back up and buckled them again. As he pulled all the tape away and tossed it into the toilet, he stared at the pistol.

So this was it, Oleg thought. He'd done everything Marcus Ryker had told him. He'd actually made it onto the grounds of the presidential palace—past dozens of armed bodyguards, even past the head of the FSB—with a loaded gun.

The question was whether he could go any further. Oleg had never killed anyone. Yes, he'd done his time in the army. But after basic training, he'd served as a clerk in the office of the chief counsel. Was he really going to walk through these doors and shoot not just one but two men in cold blood? Neither he nor Marcus had war-gamed a scenario in which a second person would be in the room—certainly not Dmitri Nimkov. Nor had they considered the possibility that the FSB would have actually made the connection between Oleg and Ryker in the Hotel National. Such a development complicated matters enormously. Now there was a very real risk that Marcus—and thus the American government—could be linked to what Oleg was about to do.

He hadn't actually been sick to his stomach when he'd asked to be excused. Now he was. Was he really going to do this? Was he going to kill the father of his own wife, the grandfather of his only son? And even if he tried, would he be able to shoot the president before Nimkov could draw and fire back at him? Was it better to take out Nimkov first?

Doubts surged through him, but there was precious little time for indecision. Marcus had been clear—once he was alone in a room with Luganov, he should ask permission to use the restroom, retrieve the gun, and then come back into the room with the pistol drawn and fire immediately. Marcus had insisted he use the element of surprise to maximum advantage.

Oleg wanted to live. He wanted to see Marina and Vasily again. He wanted to hold them and grow old with them. But these were no longer options. Not if he went out of this room, gun blazing. For a moment he considered taking his own life right there in the lavatory. But that wouldn't stop the war. And it was the coward's way out.

Oleg thought again of Solzhenitsyn. How could he keep silent in the face of evil? How could he live with himself by burying the truth so deep or ignoring it so completely that it could "rise up a thousandfold in the future"? To do nothing might save his life, but did it not condemn millions of others? Only one thing would stop this terrible war from being set into motion and wreaking such mournful havoc on the whole of the Russian nation, to say nothing of the rest of the world. Oleg was the one man in a position to change the course of history. He knew that.

Yet, looking at himself in the mirror—at his exhausted, bloodshot eyes and the dark circles under them—he wondered. Could he pull the trigger? He wanted to, but was he fooling himself? Surely Marcus Ryker could do it. But could Oleg Kraskin?

91

Nimkov started pounding on the bathroom door.

"Oleg Stefanovich, that's enough. I have more questions, as does your father."

It was time to face his accusers and his fate. Oleg flushed the toilet one more time. He washed his hands and his face and dried them with a plush towel. Then he took off his tie, rebuttoned his suit coat, and opened the door.

Nimkov was standing there waiting for him.

"Before you say anything, Dmitri Dmitrovich, I am ready to talk," Oleg said, holding up his hand. "In fact, there is much I want to tell you. Perhaps you will call it a confession. I don't see it that way."

Nimkov said nothing but did step aside to let Oleg reenter the study. Oleg did so, careful to continue limping, then turned to look directly at his father-in-law.

"I am ready to talk, Father, and I am ready to face the consequences. I have not done what I have been accused of. I am not a traitor. But there are things I must say, and I will say them to you."

"Very well, Oleg Stefanovich," the president replied. "But first, let me say that I have spoken with Marina, and she confirms your story in every detail except one."

"What is that, Father?"

"She says at one point in the night in question, you asked her to step into the bathroom with her iPod and her headphones and to wait there—listening to music—until you told her it was safe to come out. She did not question you. But I must."

"I understand," Oleg said softly.

"Good." Luganov took his seat and ordered Oleg and Nimkov to take theirs as well.

Nimkov did. Oleg did not.

"If it's all right with you, Father, I would like to remain standing," Oleg replied, holding his sides. "I am very nervous—terrified, actually—and my stomach is weak, and honestly, I'm not sure I could remain still if I were sitting."

"Sit, stand—it makes no difference to me. But start talking," Luganov said. "Start with last Wednesday night at the Hotel National. What did you do from the moment you sent Marina into the restroom?"

Oleg could see both men were still angry. They'd taken a few steps back from the brink, but he had to calm them down, put them at ease. That might not be possible, but he had to try.

"If I may, I would like to begin with what I did not do," Oleg said. "I did not betray Mother Russia. I did not betray the Russian people. But there was business I had to attend to that night that could not wait, business of the highest order that related to the security—indeed, the very future—of our country."

"You made contact with Marcus Ryker," Nimkov interjected. "You knocked on his door. You woke him up. You made contact with the American, and you told him what the president—your own father-in-law—was planning. Admit it, Oleg Stefanovich. No more lies. We have neither the time nor the patience for—"

At this Oleg erupted. "*Silence, Dmitri Dmitrovich—silence.* I told you I would tell you my story, and I shall. But you don't even have the decency to hear me out. You've already been proven wrong once today. I was not having an affair. I was not being lured into a honey trap. I was not doing anything at that hotel for which I should feel guilty or ashamed. Now I'm ready to tell you more, but all you have are accusations, and slanderous ones at that."

Nimkov was turning red and about to rise out of his seat but Oleg exploded again. *"No, you will sit down, you will be quiet, and you will let me speak uninterrupted, Dmitri Dmitrovich!"*

There was a knock at the door. It was Agent Kovalev. "Is everything all right, Your Excellency?" the bodyguard asked through the door. "May I come in?"

"No—I said no interruptions," Luganov shouted back. *"Disregard me again and I'll have your head!"*

Kovalev apologized profusely. The door to the study remained closed, and after a moment, they heard the second door—the one to the hallway—close as well. With Kovalev back at his post, Luganov ordered Oleg to continue.

During the interruption, Oleg had turned away from the two men and was staring out the bulletproof window at the snow falling in the courtyard, all lit up by a series of outdoor lamps ringing the colonnade. He nodded to confirm that he would continue, but he needed a moment to catch his breath and quiet the blood pounding in his head. His eye landed on a birdbath in the center of the courtyard that had at least two or three inches of snow piled up on it already. During the rest of the year, there was typically patio furniture set up around the pool. Now the pool was drained and covered.

Oleg remembered happier times out there. How many summer days had he and Marina swum laps or played with Vasily in the shallow end? How many truly lovely meals had they shared with the first couple before all the tensions with Yulia had reached the tipping point, before Yulia had been sent away and Katya Slatsky had entered the picture permanently?

Oleg's life in this family had never been idyllic. He knew that all too well. There had been some moments he could cherish and wanted to hold on to, but they were far too few, and it was clear there could never be any more. Not where the president was taking Russia. The house was not yet burning, but the match was lit.

"Here I am, in your home, Father," Oleg said softly. "The home of your daughter, my wife, a home I once thought was mine as well."

He turned back around but could not bear to look at Nimkov. He looked only at Luganov, fighting to keep his voice calm and measured.

"I remember when the people elected you president. I remember standing at your side when you took the oath of office and swore to protect the people and lead us wisely—I remember every word. 'I swear in exercising the powers of the president of the Russian Federation to respect and protect the rights and freedoms of man and citizen, to respect and defend the Constitution of the Russian Federation, to protect the sovereignty and independence, security, and integrity of the state, to faithfully serve the people.' What happened to all that, Father? What happened to all that you promised us?"

The question hung in the air for a moment. Then Oleg unbuttoned his jacket, drew the pistol, and fired directly in Luganov's face. A puff of red mist filled the air. Then Oleg pivoted to Nimkov, whose eyes were wide with shock, and pulled the trigger a second time.

Blood was everywhere. Oleg was covered in it. He stared at the two bodies slumped in their overstuffed chairs. When he saw one of Luganov's legs twitch, he refused to be calmed by the possibility that this was merely a death spasm. Instead, Oleg stepped closer to the man who had believed himself a czar, placed the barrel of the pistol directly to his forehead, and fired again.

92

True to Ryker's word, the gun had made almost no noise.

Both Luganov and Nimkov had been so stunned by Oleg's attack—and had died so quickly—that neither of them had made a sound either. Thus neither Kovalev nor any of the agents stationed outside came bursting into the room. They'd been ordered not to enter the study until the president informed them he was ready. That, at least, bought Oleg some time.

Trembling slightly, yet far more calm than he would have imagined, Oleg walked over to Luganov's desk and picked up the blood-splattered phone. It was time to set the rest of Marcus's plan in motion.

"This is Oleg Stefanovich Kraskin," he said softly when the palace operator greeted him. "I'm here with the president, and he has several requests he'd like me to pass along. First, His Excellency and Mr. Nimkov need to head back to the Kremlin and would like to depart at precisely 8 a.m. Please advise the flight crew and his security detail to be ready at that time."

Oleg waited for her to get that down.

"Second, the president has ordered me to go to Brussels, so I need you to contact the head of flight operations and have a plane fueled up and waiting for me at Domodedovo Airport. Please inform the pilot of my helicopter that I need to get to the airport right away. I'll be at the helipad in three minutes. Once at Domodedovo, I'll need a secure lounge to place calls and make preparations for my trip. Got all that?"

Again he waited.

"There is one more thing," he concluded. "The president needs Miss Slatsky to meet him at the Kremlin, but please let her know that she will not be able to travel with him. Kindly inform her that she can fly with me. Once they drop me off at the airport, the pilot can take her the rest of the way. Is that clear? Good. If you need anything, text me. In the meantime, please continue holding all calls into the president's study and make sure all staff—*all* of them—know not to disturb His Excellency or Mr. Nimkov until it's time to leave for the Kremlin. . . . Right, you know the drill—war preparations, etc. . . . Yes, and you as well. Good day."

Hanging up the phone, Oleg walked back across the room and closed the drapes. Then he switched on several lamps around the study and went through his mental checklist. Ah, yes, the mobile phones. He turned to Luganov, searched around, and finally found his phone in his back pocket. He used it rarely, mostly when he wanted to have unrecorded conversations with Katya. Next he patted Nimkov down until he found his mobile phone in the right pocket of his suit jacket. He was tempted to steal them. Both phones—particularly the FSB chief's—had invaluable intelligence on them. But Marcus had been explicit. Silence them so they could not ring, but do not take them. Mobile phones could be tracked. Lifting one would trigger suspicion and a response.

Oleg checked his watch. He needed to get moving. He stepped back inside the restroom and calmly washed the blood off his hands and face. He wiped off his suit and his shoes, then dried his hands. Taking a fresh towel with him, he returned to the study. Now he retrieved his raincoat and put it on. This would cover the blood on his clothes. Then he grabbed his briefcase, wiped it down, and pulled out the digital recorder. He pushed Stop to end the recording and plugged earbuds in to listen in privacy. It took a moment of rewinding to find where he had exploded at the president and FSB chief. This part, and everything that followed, he erased. Then he rewound to the beginning, yanked out his earbuds, set the device on the desk, and pressed Play, turning up the volume so that it would sound—from the hallway, anyway—like people were still talking in the study.

He looked around one last time to make sure he hadn't left anything behind. He hadn't, but he suddenly remembered one more element of Marcus's instructions. He pulled out his personal mobile phone and sent a one-word text to a Russian mobile number Marcus had given him. *Хорошо.* "Kharasho" in Russian meant "good."

He put on his leather gloves and scarf and walked out the door of the study, through the short hallway, out the second door, and into the care of an armed escort ready to take him to his helicopter. No one hovering around the door struck Oleg as suspicious. But as they walked briskly to the helipad, his thoughts turned to Katya Slatsky. She was going to be furious to be leaving the palace with him and not her lover. He was going to need to say something to calm her down, and Marcus had given him nothing. He'd only insisted Oleg find a way to keep her away from Luganov, lest she find his body before his detail and scuttle any chance, however small, of a safe escape.

Yet Katya was the least of his problems. When he reached the north entrance, Oleg realized that he had completely forgotten about the fact that he would be assigned a new security detail. Apparently Marcus had too. Now six large and well-armed men were waiting to board the helicopter with him and Katya for the short hop to the airport.

"Commander, I need you and your team to meet me at the airport!" Oleg told the head of the detail over the whining rotors. *"The president has*

an important message he needs me to share with Miss Slatsky. I'm afraid it's of a very sensitive, personal nature, and we need to be alone."

"That would be highly irregular, sir, especially after what happened to you this morning," the agent shouted back.

"These are the express orders of the president," Oleg replied. *"But you'll never make it in time on the roads. Order another chopper, and I'll wait for you there. And don't worry. I'll be fine."*

Oleg did not wait for an answer. He pulled the side door of the helicopter shut, locked it, and ordered the pilot to take off for Domodedovo immediately. The pilot did as he was told. Katya, however, erupted with a torrent of profanity.

"Quiet, quiet, please, Katya. I have good news," Oleg told her. "I'm sorry you're feeling hurt and that we had to move so quickly. I truly am. Please know that. But the president cannot be disturbed by anyone right now, for reasons that you'll understand very soon, I promise."

"But I keep calling him, and he doesn't answer," she cried, her mascara running.

"He can't—not right now—but I have to tell you something very important."

"What?" she pressed. "What is it?"

Oleg took a deep breath, pulled off his gloves, and took her shivering hands in his own, leaning close to her ear. "The president—I can't believe I'm telling you this; he swore me to secrecy—but I just have to tell you."

"What is it, Oleg Stefanovich? Stop torturing me."

"Okay, I will," he said, and he leaned in even closer. "The president . . ."

He took a deep breath.

". . . is about to propose to you."

Katya's eyes went wide.

"It's true," Oleg assured her. "He showed me the engagement ring he bought for you. It's enormous, gorgeous."

"Are you serious? Aleksandr Ivanovich is really going to ask me to marry him?"

"I think it might even be tonight," Oleg added. "He didn't tell me where or how, but I got the impression it just might be tonight."

Katya squealed with delight.

"I beg of you, please don't tell him I told you," Oleg pleaded. "But I could see how upset you were. I didn't want you to think ill of the president. He has so many burdens on him right now, but he needs you to know he loves you and that you'll never be parted."

Katya couldn't speak. She was overwhelmed with emotion and collapsed into Oleg's arms, weeping with joy and tremendous relief.

93

The G4 had to be deiced again.

That took another twenty minutes. The temperature was dropping and visibility was poor and worsening with the driving snow. Then Oleg's text came in, and everything changed.

"It's him," Marcus said, staring at the screen of the mobile phone.

"And?" Morris asked, double-checking the gauges on the console one more time.

"He's on his way."

Morris looked up at her partner. She was still angry with him. He could only imagine what she'd be like if she knew the whole story.

"You'd better go," she said. "I'll make sure everything's ready."

"Thanks," he said to her, "for everything."

"We're not out of the woods yet, Ryker. Put on your headset and don't get caught."

She handed him a whisper mic and an earpiece, which he put on at once. She did the same. They tested them with a few sentences each. Then Marcus chambered a round in his pistol, put the gun in the holster under his jacket, and unlocked the cockpit door. He opened the cabin door and lowered the steps, and he was off.

Marcus headed straight across the tarmac for the airport security car the agents had left him. Only then did he remember that the car hadn't been brushed off since they'd boarded the plane. It took several minutes to wipe everything down, especially the headlights, and several more to chip a layer of ice off the driver's-side lock. It took longer for the engine to turn over and warm up. But once he had it running, he jacked up the heat and the windshield wipers and unzipped the canvas bag on the passenger-side floor.

"Operations to Post One, Operations to Post One, come in, over."

"Post One, copy, over," Special Agent Pavel Kovalev replied.

"We have a problem," said the watch officer in the operations command post located in the basement of the presidential palace. "Well, a possible problem."

"Roger that, Ops. What's wrong?"

"I just noticed that the drapes in the president's study are drawn."

"And?"

"Well, sir, I've never seen that done in the three years I've been doing this job," said the watch officer. "The drapes are supposed to remain open at all times so we can keep an eye on the president and make sure everything's all right."

"They're having a very private discussion, Ops," Kovalev replied. "The president doesn't want any disturbances or distractions until he leaves for the Kremlin."

"Affirmative, Post One, but the drapes are supposed to remain open for his protection."

"Are you saying there's a problem?"

"That's just it, sir—how would I know?"

"What was happening inside the study before the drapes were closed?"

"We're reracking that video now. The problem is with all the snow, the condensation on the window, and the glare, the images aren't clear. Everything's hazy."

"Switch to thermal."

"Doing that now."

"And?"

There was a long pause—too long for Kovalev.

"What is it, Ops?" he pressed. "What can you see?"

"*CODE RED, CODE RED!*" shouted the watch officer, the horror in his voice palpable, broadcasting on the emergency frequency for every agent in the compound to hear. "*GO IN NOW—I REPEAT—GO IN NOW!*"

The submachine gun was loaded and instantly accessible.

Relieved, Marcus flipped on the orange flashing safety light on the roof and began to proceed toward his target.

The airport maintenance team was doing a decent job keeping the runways plowed. This was Moscow, after all. They had plenty of experience with snow. Still, for whatever reason, the access lanes for baggage carts, fuel trucks, and other vehicles like his were taking longer. Fishtailing his way across the airport grounds, Marcus worried he might hit something or someone in the rapidly dropping visibility.

When he finally reached the helipad, it was empty. A ground crew was waiting. That was a hopeful sign, suggesting something was inbound. But there was no chopper visible, and Marcus's stomach tightened. He began counting to fifty but heard the roar. Then he saw it, descending rapidly from the thick cloud cover amid a swirling, billowing spray of snow and ice.

Marcus positioned the security car as close to the helipad as he safely could so Oleg wouldn't have to be exposed to the elements for a single second longer than necessary. He reached over and unlocked the passenger door. Then he stepped out of the car and into the bitter, whipping winds. As the chopper door opened, Marcus came around the car and stood by the passenger door, ready to open it the moment Oleg emerged. But Oleg didn't emerge. Not right away and not for several minutes.

"We may have a problem," he radioed Morris.

"What is it?"

"The chopper door is open, but the Raven has not emerged."

"How long?"

"Too long. I'm going to check it out."

"Copy that. What do you need from me?"

"Just make sure we're ready to get off the ground the second we get back."

Marcus strode to the door of the chopper, unbuttoning his overcoat as he did to make it easier to grab his pistol if he had to.

He had to.

Just before he reached the door, a gun went off inside the helicopter, blowing out a window. Marcus heard a woman screaming and a fight break out on board. Gun drawn, he raced up the steps only to find the copilot and Oleg wrestling in the tight confines of the cabin. Marcus didn't think twice. He double-tapped the copilot, then pivoted and double-tapped the pilot. A woman, wrapped in a black cashmere coat and furs, was screaming hysterically. Marcus had never seen her before, but she posed no threat. He grabbed Oleg by the collar and hauled him off the chopper without saying a word. Throwing him in the backseat of the waiting car, Marcus slammed the door shut, then got behind the wheel and peeled off across the tarmac.

"They know! They know!" Oleg began yelling the second they were alone. *"I don't know how, but they know!"*

94

Oleg was hyperventilating and risked going into shock.

But there was nothing Marcus could do about it. It didn't matter how the FSB knew or how Oleg had managed to avoid being hand-cuffed or shot inside that chopper. Their only chance of survival was to get back to Morris and off the ground. Even then, he doubted they had better than a one-in-ten chance of making it out of Russian airspace without being shot down by MiGs, assuming they could even could get away from Domodedovo in one piece.

As he radioed back to Morris that they were inbound, Marcus could hear sirens converging from the north and the west. Then he noted the police band radio set where the AM/FM system usually was. He switched it on and the radio crackled to life.

Marcus couldn't understand a word of Russian, but he instantly recognized both the fear and the urgency in their voices. "What are they saying?" he shouted to Oleg in the backseat.

"They just issued my death sentence," Oleg said.

"What?"

"The dispatcher is telling every police officer and security guard in or near the airport grounds that I'm responsible for assassinating the president of the Russian Federation and the head of the FSB," said Oleg. "The security services are unleashing everything they have to hunt me down along with anyone helping me. Shoot to kill. No mercy."

Marcus switched off the security car's flashing light and then for good measure cut the headlights, too. Given the dimness and swirling snow, he hoped that would lower their profile, making them nearly invisible. Whoever was hunting Oleg was headed to the helipad. The ground crew at the helipad had surely seen him pull Oleg off the chopper and into this car, but if the car was invisible, they still had a chance. It wasn't much to go on, but that measure of confusion might buy them the time they needed.

Just then Marcus spotted a police car—red-and-blue lights flashing, siren blaring—racing straight toward them. He slowed a bit and veered right, out of the patrol car's path, hoping it would blow right past them. Instead, the driver hit the brakes and tried to follow them but hit an ice patch and spun out of control.

Marcus accelerated, zigzagging dangerously through planes and food service trucks.

"They've spotted us," Oleg said, continuing to translate what he was hearing over the police band radio. "An officer is giving a description and our heading."

"What else?"

"Now they say I'm with one suspect, armed and dangerous, and that we're heading toward the private aviation terminal."

Well, they had that right, Marcus thought as he spotted the G4. Then Oleg pointed out two more patrol cars converging on them. The one behind them was coming up fast.

"We're going to be at the plane in about fifteen seconds," Marcus said calmly. "When we get there, I want you to bolt out the right side. You hear?"

"Yes."

"Get up the stairs and into the plane as fast as you can."

"What about you?" Oleg asked.

"I'll cover you. The second you get on that plane, hit the deck."

"What does that mean?"

"Get on the floor and stay there."

"Okay."

"Tell the pilot to pull up the stairs, taxi, and take off."

"What if you're not on board yet?"

"I'll be there."

"But if you're not?"

"Then I'm not coming."

Marcus tapped the brakes and skidded to a stop in front of the G4. Grabbing the machine gun and kicking open the driver's-side door, he looked back at Oleg and shouted, *"Run!"*

All three police cruisers tried to brake. One slid right past them and smashed into the side of the terminal. The others stopped more successfully, within twenty yards of them. Marcus pivoted into the snow and opened fire. Oleg watched him for a moment, then jumped out and raced up the steps of the Gulfstream while a hail of bullets erupted all around him. Marcus kept firing in short bursts as he moved around the hood of the car. When he saw he'd clipped the officer firing from beside the wrecked cruiser, he popped out a spent magazine and reloaded. Then he opened fire again—still in short bursts—as he crouched low and worked his way backward up the steps.

Rounds pinged off the metal stairs and the fuselage. Then someone opened fire from just over his right shoulder. He glanced around and saw Morris.

"Get in," she yelled. *"I've got you."*

Marcus turned and scrambled up the last few stairs as Morris hit the switch and the stairs folded into the plane. Together, they shut and locked the door behind them and headed for their respective seats in the cockpit.

"Take a seat and buckle in," Marcus shouted to Oleg as Morris revved the engines and began taxiing away from the terminal. *"Recline the seat all the way, and whatever you do, keep your head down and don't look out the window."*

Suddenly rounds began hitting the side of the plane again. From his vantage point, Marcus couldn't see who was firing, but he urged Morris to push the engines harder and stay out of the taxi lanes. This wasn't a normal takeoff. These were combat conditions, and they needed to get this thing in the air before more police cars arrived and blocked their exit or shot out their tires or their windows.

Morris did what he told her but said nothing.

Marcus craned his neck to one side and then the other, scanning for threats. When he turned back to her, he saw her wince, then saw blood all over her jacket and shirt.

95

"You're hit," he said calmly.

"I'm fine, Ryker," Morris replied just as calmly. "We'll deal with it in the air."

But she wasn't merely wincing now. She could barely sit upright.

"You're not fine," he said.

"Never . . . never mind . . . me," she gasped. "Do . . . your job."

She was having trouble breathing as well.

"You're not going to be able to get us off the ground," Marcus said.

"I have to."

"But you can't, so tell me what to do."

Morris tried to protest, but she couldn't get the words out.

"Conserve your energy," he told her. "Lean back. Point to things. Use as few words as possible. I'll get us up."

Finally she nodded, and Marcus took the controls. She walked him through everything even as she began coughing up blood.

Ground control was ordering them to stop. Marcus could see flashing lights coming from all directions. The G4 was approaching the first possible runway, but the ground lights were all red, indicating they had to stop for an aircraft either about to take off or land. Marcus looked to his left and saw no plane on the runway. He looked right and saw nothing on the ground, but there were lights in the sky at two o'clock. The sirens were getting louder, which meant they were getting closer. Oleg began shouting that the police cars heading toward them were being joined by armored personnel carriers with .50-caliber mounted machine guns.

That was it. They were out of time. He couldn't wait any longer. Marcus increased speed and eased the G4 out onto the runway, turning right, toward the approaching plane.

"No," Morris groaned. "You can't."

Marcus didn't respond.

"You're insane," she said almost in a whisper. *"Stop."*

But Marcus wasn't listening. He checked the flaps. They were at the zero position. Preparing for a short takeoff, he throttled forward to full power while pressing hard on the brakes. The high-pitched whine of the dual Rolls-Royce engines filled the cockpit. Then he released the brakes. They all snapped back in their seats as the Gulfstream began hurtling down the runway.

The Aeroflot jumbo jet was dead ahead of them, less than a mile out, on approach for the runway they were on and putting down its landing gear.

"You're gonna get us all killed," Oleg screamed, watching what was happening through the open cockpit door.

Marcus didn't respond. They were committed now. He was trying desperately to keep the plane centered on the runway with the rudder pedals, but with so little experience flying, and none in a business jet, they were veering to the right, then lurching back to the left. They were in danger of sliding off the icy runway, but they were picking up speed. There was a chain-link fence at the end of the ten-thousand-foot strip.

It was covered in snow and ice, but it was coming up fast. Panicked, Morris briefly took the pedals. She recentered the jet and ordered Marcus to increase flaps to takeoff position. The moment he did, they reached 150 miles an hour.

"*Now!*" she yelled.

Marcus pulled back on the yoke. The instant their wheels were off the ground, he abandoned gentility and pulled harder, creating a far steeper angle for takeoff. The ground controllers were cursing at him. They were heading straight into the Aeroflot, but Marcus refused to change course. Alarms sounded in the G4 cockpit.

"*Caution, obstacle. Caution, obstacle.*"

The Russian plane filled with hundreds of passengers was coming directly at them. Despite the storm, Marcus could actually see the pilots in their cockpit, frantically waving them off. He could hear them yelling at him over the radio. Yet he kept increasing speed. He was not going to divert. Too much was at stake. They had to gain speed and altitude if they had any chance of survival, even if that meant playing chicken with a jumbo jet.

At the last second, the Aeroflot banked hard to the right, retracted its landing gear, and boosted power. The G4 surged by, clearing the Russian jet by less than fifty yards. Marcus raised his landing gear and pulled the Gulfstream into the clouds and the freak storm bearing down on Moscow.

Morris was ashen, but both she and Oleg were quiet. The immediate danger had passed, but each of them knew what lay ahead.

"Where's the transponder?" Marcus asked as they passed two thousand feet.

"Why?" Morris asked, her voice thin and raspy.

"I'm going to turn it off," he said. "We've got to go dark."

Morris looked at him like he needed to be institutionalized. Marcus didn't care. He proceeded to turn off all the external lights and all the cabin and cockpit lights as well. Only the glow of the instrumentation remained. Relenting, Morris pointed to the transponder switch, in the lower right section of the center console, then used hand gestures to indicate he should turn it three clicks to the left.

Marcus did, and their digital signature—the communications system telling air traffic controllers precisely who they were and where they were at any given moment—shut down. The G4 would still show up as a blip on radar, of course, but now they were an unidentified blip. That certainly didn't make them impossible to track or intercept, but it made it harder.

Marcus asked Oleg to come up to the cockpit and help get Jenny into one of the seats in the back. Shaken but eager to assist, Oleg responded immediately.

"They teach you any first aid in the army?" Marcus asked.

"A little."

"Then take care of my friend. We need to get her home in one piece."

Oleg nodded and was about to leave when Marcus grabbed him by the arm.

"One more thing," he said. Marcus motioned for him to come in very close so Morris couldn't hear them. "She doesn't know what you just did, and she's in no shape to hear it now," he whispered. "Understood?"

Oleg nodded, a bit confused perhaps on how it was possible that Marcus's partner didn't know all the details. Nevertheless, while Marcus kept flying the plane, Oleg unbuckled Morris and carefully carried her out, apologizing profusely for the discomfort he was causing her.

Soon they reached a cruising altitude of forty-three thousand feet. They were racing for international airspace at a speed of nearly five hundred knots—about 575 miles per hour. Marcus engaged the autopilot. According to the extraction plan he and Morris had mapped out, they were headed for Helsinki. That was just 893 kilometers away. They'd already been in the air for twelve minutes. They had another fifty to go.

Marcus knew they'd never make it that far.

Defense Minister Mikhail Petrovsky was headed back to the war room when the call came.

He'd only gotten three hours of sleep, but at least he had been in his own bed. As his driver sped along Leninsky Avenue, parallel with the Moskva River, headed toward the center of the city, one of his bodyguards took a secure call from Nikolay Kropatkin, the deputy director of the FSB.

He handed the phone to his boss. "Kropatkin. He says it's urgent."

Petrovsky sighed and took another sip of black coffee from his travel mug before taking the call. When everything was urgent, was anything?

"Yes, Nikolay Vladimirovich, I have the revised estimates with me," he said in exasperation. "Tell the president I will transmit them the moment I get into the office."

"No, sir, that's not why I'm calling."

"Then why?"

"Where are you?"

"Four minutes out. Can it wait?"

"No, it cannot," Kropatkin said. "Brace yourself, Mikhail Borisovich."

"Whatever for?"

"The president, sir."

"What about him?"

"I'm afraid he's dead."

"What? That's impossible."

"I just got off the phone with the palace. Aleksandr Ivanovich is dead, as is Dmitri Dmitrovich."

"Both of them?" Petrovsky said, sitting bolt upright in the backseat of the bulletproof sedan, its flashing blue lights—and those of the security cars flanking them—illuminating his face in the stormy darkness. "When? How?"

"It was Oleg Stefanovich—he shot them both at point-blank range,"

Kropatkin replied breathlessly. "They were alone in the president's study. It all happened so quickly. But it appears that he had help. He got to the airport—Domededovo—where someone was waiting with a private plane."

"Tell me the police stopped him."

"There was a shoot-out, but Oleg was able to get on board a jet and take off. We were tracking it, but they've turned off their transponder, and for the moment we've lost it."

Petrovsky cursed and then ordered the deputy to scramble a dozen MiGs, find the jet, and take it down.

"Right away, sir," Kropatkin said. "I'll give you an update when you arrive. But that's not all."

"Go on."

"You need to convene the cabinet. We are about to go to war. The country does not have a president, but we desperately need one. And with all due respect, sir, it should be you."

96

"We have confirmation, Mr. President."

Bill McDermott handed Clarke a printout of a text he'd just received from the Magic Palace. The Gulfstream was safely off the ground. The Raven was on it. The Agency's people had the thumb drive in their possession, and its contents had been electronically uploaded to the CIA's mainframe computers. Their analysts were already starting to break down the data.

The president nodded approvingly. It was the first piece of good news he'd seen in days. But he was still furious with his NSC team. "Why hasn't the hotline call with Luganov been set up?" he demanded.

McDermott said he didn't know what the delay was. Officials in the National Military Command Center at the Pentagon said the problem wasn't on their end. Their counterparts in Moscow were dragging their feet, and it was not yet clear why.

Marcus unbuckled his seat belt and headed to the cabin.

His first priority was to check on Morris. She'd been hit in the right shoulder, Oleg said, and the wound was quite serious. Oleg was doing his best to patch her up. He'd put her in his own seat, which he had fully reclined. He'd managed to finally stanch the bleeding using every cloth he could find on board, from towels to pillowcases. He'd given her several shots of morphine to manage the pain. Then he'd covered her with a blanket and was now telling her stories of his childhood to distract her from how much trouble she was in.

"Not bad for a government lackey," Marcus said as he dabbed the perspiration off her face with a washcloth and wiped several strands of hair out of her eyes.

He leaned close to her cheek and whispered, "You're going to be okay. I'm going to make sure of it."

Morris tried to smile. It was more of a grimace, but it would do.

Marcus excused himself and went into the restroom. He was no longer wearing the disguise he'd put on at the Ramada. He'd taken that off when he'd changed into the copilot's uniform. Still, as he looked at his unshaven face in the mirror, he wasn't happy with what he saw. The disguise was gone. The pain was not.

He was suddenly hit with a wave of despair. He desperately missed Elena. Closing his eyes, he could still see her sitting in Mr. Grantham's English class back in the sixth grade. They'd only been eleven. They'd gotten married when in their early twenties. Now he was approaching his forties alone. His hair was going gray at the temples. He had crow's-feet around his bloodshot, exhausted eyes. He had scrapes and bruises all over his body—and for all his morning runs and evenings at the gym, he'd been surprised how quickly he'd been winded tonight.

Then again, this little team had made it farther than he'd really thought possible. It was only by the grace of God, he knew, not by any skill of his own. That said, what was next? Was the Lord really going to bring them this far only to let them be blown out of the sky? He reached into his pocket and pulled out the thumb drive Oleg had given him. He stared at it, wondering what treasures it contained. He hoped this had all been worth it. Only time would tell the full value to the American government, and perhaps to NATO, should the Clarke team choose to share any of the fruit of their classified labors. But the mission had cost more than Marcus had wanted to pay. He wasn't morally opposed to killing bad guys, especially to protect the people and country he loved. But killing anyone took its toll.

Would it stop the war? He prayed it would. Then again, he knew only too well that if his and Jenny's involvement with Oleg were discovered, that information alone could trigger a war with Russia anyway. And what if they did die tonight, shot down by an air-to-air missile? It was an ugly thought but a real and rapidly growing possibility, even probability. He wasn't scared. He knew where he was going when he died. He was pretty sure Jenny was a follower of Christ as well. He would have loved time to talk faith and so many other things with her. But what about Oleg? What would happen to him? Marcus suddenly realized that in everything that had transpired, he'd never thought once about Oleg's soul. Did the man know the Savior? Had he given his life to Christ? Were his sins forgiven? Had he ever even heard the gospel clearly explained to him?

Marcus couldn't remember thinking about such things in the Marines or the Secret Service. He'd done his job and done it to the best of his ability. He'd never second-guessed the morality of the mission. The Taliban were sheer evil. Al Qaeda was worse. Each person he took out had been a clean kill, casualties of a military conflict. Marcus was more than willing to give up his own life to protect his country and her leaders. But the deaths of his wife and son had changed everything. Studying with Pastor Emerson and the vets on Wednesdays back in Lincoln Park had changed him too. These days he thought a great deal about eternity. Why, then, had he not thought of Oleg's fate? He felt uncertain and ashamed.

Petrovsky got more bad news the moment he arrived at the Defense Ministry.

The air force had been scrambled, but the plane carrying Oleg Stefanovich still had not been found. There were just too many planes in the sky at the moment, too much clutter and confusion over Moscow and the western skies. It was like finding a needle in a haystack, he was told.

He went ballistic. "Get every plane on the ground—*now*," he ordered.

He turned on every TV in his office. Fortunately, news of the assassinations had not yet broken. A quick check of multiple channels confirmed that, but Petrovsky knew the story would not hold for long. He had already called Luganov's chief of staff and persuaded him to summon the entire cabinet for an emergency meeting at the Kremlin without giving any hint as to the reason. At the same time, he knew Kropatkin—now operating as acting director of the FSB—had made it crystal clear to his men that anyone who leaked this news would be guilty of treason and would be executed without a trial.

The one person he worried about most was Katya Slatsky, who had been taken to the Kremlin after the debacle at the airport. She had to be isolated indefinitely. If there was one person who could leak the whole thing prematurely and not care in the slightest about the implications, it was she. Petrovsky thus ordered Kropatkin to send someone to Luganov's private chambers at the Kremlin, drug her, and keep her drugged until they could figure out exactly what to do with her. Kropatkin didn't flinch but vowed to carry out the orders at once.

Meanwhile, Petrovsky issued written orders for all Russian military forces to cease their exercises and begin withdrawing from the borders of the Baltics and Ukraine. To the outside world, such actions would look entirely consistent with what Luganov had been saying publicly. The inner circle of high government officials, he knew, might believe

Petrovsky had orchestrated a coup d'état to stop a war they knew he did not support. He did it anyway. The hours ahead would be chaotic enough. There was no guarantee he would wind up at the top of the Kremlin's greasy pole, but if there was anything he could do while still alive and in power to defuse the prospect of nuclear war with NATO, he was bound and determined to do it.

97

"It's time," Marcus said.

He explained to Morris and Oleg exactly what was happening and how little time they had to decide their fate. As he did, the Gulfstream hit a bit of turbulence. The plane shook for a few moments—worrying an already-rattled Oleg—then stabilized again.

Just then, Marcus's satphone rang. He answered it, gave a nine-digit code proving his identity, listened carefully, acknowledged the message, and hung up. He raced back to the cockpit. Seconds later, a series of alarms started sounding and lights began flashing. These had nothing to do with the standard avionics package. The plane's sophisticated radar system had been installed by technicians at Langley. It was not unlike the ones used by American fighter jets and even Air Force One.

From the back, Oleg shouted a message from Jenny. "Turn off the autopilot."

Marcus did, then flicked a series of other switches and a new radar display flickered to life. Gone were the weather data and the images of the massive snowstorm hitting the northwestern provinces of Russia. Now he was staring at a display showing two blips forty miles back and gaining fast.

"What's that?" Oleg demanded, suddenly standing behind Marcus.

"Go finish getting her ready," Marcus replied. He didn't have time for explanations.

Reluctantly Oleg agreed. The moment he left, Marcus closed the cockpit door. The blips were MiGs. The Global Operations Center at Langley had just called to alert him that they'd intercepted a series of Russian civilian and military communications. On the civilian side, the Kremlin had issued a full ground stop on all flights preparing to take off throughout the Russian Federation. They were requiring all air traffic over the country to land immediately at the nearest airport. On the military side, Russian fighter squadrons throughout the Western Military District were being scrambled and directed to hunt and shoot down any Gulfstream business jets of any description. The Magic Palace had not indicated that the fighter pilots or their weapons systems officers had been given a specific tail number. They had, however, been authorized to use any means necessary to prevent any business jets from leaving Russian airspace.

Marcus was surprised the Russians had taken this long to issue such an order. He chalked it up to the fog of war and the interruption in the chain of command Oleg had created by taking out the president and the FSB chief. But none of that mattered. Whatever delay there had been, it was over now. The MiGs were up and in hot pursuit.

He turned the yoke, banking the plane to the north, off the flight plan and away from St. Petersburg and beyond it Helsinki. There was no way he was going to let the Russians force them to land. He and Morris had discussed this in depth when they'd been planning Oleg's extraction. If they were shot down, so be it. But under no circumstances could they let themselves or this plane and its contents be taken intact.

The fighter jets were now only thirty-two miles behind. No sooner had Marcus turned off and reset the alarms than they sounded again. He looked again to the enhanced radar screen and saw two more MiGs coming up from a base just south of St. Petersburg. These were only twenty miles out. When the alarms blared yet again, he spotted two more MiGs converging on them from the north, less than fifteen miles out. So that was that. They had no fewer than six fighter jets streaking toward them with orders to keep them from reaching international airspace at all costs. And then the radio began to squawk.

The first message came from St. Petersburg air traffic control. It was directed to all civilian flights, informing them that Russian airspace was now closed and ordering them to land immediately. Marcus was struck by the fact that Langley had gotten that message to them faster than the Russians themselves. Moments later came the second message, from the lead pilot of one of the Russian fighter jets. He spoke firmly in clear if heavily accented English: obey his orders and follow him to the nearest air force base, or be fired upon. Marcus didn't hesitate. He took the controls, picked up the intercom, and ordered Oleg and Jenny to cinch their seat belts as tight as they could.

Then he pushed the yoke forward and began a brutally steep dive. It took mere seconds to plunge from forty-three thousand feet to only twenty thousand feet, and Marcus found his stomach in his throat. The g-forces threatened to knock him out. But he hadn't lost the MiGs. They were screaming in from every direction, and as he leveled out the G4—now around eighteen thousand feet—he knew they were going to be fired on at any moment.

Marcus decreased speed and once again turned on the autopilot. Then he unbuckled himself and left the cockpit.

"You ready?" he asked.

They both nodded.

"As we'll ever be," Morris managed to say, brave to the last.

Bill McDermott sat in the Situation Room, next to the president.

Like his colleagues and Clarke himself, he had tried to hold out hope for his friend and the team he had with him, though he knew it was futile. Now that they'd been found—now that both the Kremlin and the White House were tracking the G4 in real time—there was no way Marcus, Morris, and the Raven were ever going to shake the MiGs. To the contrary, they were about to be blown to kingdom come. McDermott's eyes were glued to the flat-screen monitors, and he couldn't look away.

The largest monitor—the one mounted on the far wall, directly across from the commander in chief—showed the live radar tracking of six fighter planes converging on the Gulfstream. Various digital displays along the bottom of the screen provided rapidly changing data from each of the seven aircraft—altitude, airspeed, direction, and so forth. McDermott had been stunned by the G4's harrowing twenty-five-thousand-foot plunge, but he was even more disturbed by the bizarre decision to level off at eighteen thousand feet and slow down. Yes, the plane was smack-dab in the middle of a thick band of clouds. But it wasn't going to matter. It wasn't going to hide them or make them any less vulnerable. Marcus and Morris certainly knew that, so why weren't they still diving?

The Gulfstream wasn't a fighter jet. It wasn't built to withstand the extreme pressures of dogfighting. But by diving for St. Petersburg, not banking away from it, and flying low across the deck, they might buy enough time to figure out a way to get out into neutral territory over the Gulf of Finland. However crazy the Russians were, they certainly weren't going to shoot a G4 out of the sky over one of their most populous cities. Yet the radar track showed none of the moves McDermott would have made in Marcus's place. Then again, McDermott knew Marcus had never flown a jet. He'd flown Piper Cubs in his twenties. So he was at the mercy of the CIA's Moscow station chief.

Jennifer Morris was brilliant and highly respected throughout the intelligence community. And she'd helped Marcus pull off one of the greatest intelligence coups in the history of the Agency. Still, maybe she hadn't been ready for what came next. He couldn't say for sure, but one thing he knew: Jenny Morris was about to get his friend—and the best Marine he'd ever had the honor to command—killed.

The Situation Room was silent. The Pentagon wasn't feeding them live audio of the Russian pilots. Nor were they getting any communications from the G4. No one gathered around the conference table and staring at the screens spellbound was saying anything. Not the president. Not the generals. What was there to say?

Then McDermott saw it. He grabbed one of the remotes off the table in front of him and zoomed in on the image. American radar was picking up an air-to-air missile being fired by the lead MiG-29, followed almost instantaneously by a second one. It took only the blink of an eye, and the G4 disappeared from the screen.

Everyone knew what had happened. Yet McDermott couldn't believe it. He kept staring at the screen in silence as the MiGs turned in pairs, presumably returning to their base.

Then, out of nowhere, the Pentagon patched through the intercepted audio of the Russian pilots after all. They were whooping and hollering and congratulating one another, as were their base controllers and surely their superiors in Moscow.

And Bill McDermott just sat there, staring at the flickering screen, aghast.

The missiles had come quick.

The resulting fireball had been as blinding as it had been enormous. But as Marcus hurtled downward through the thick clouds and frigid night sky—free-falling at terminal velocity with an unopened parachute strapped to his back, Jenny Morris strapped to his front, and Oleg in a separate parachute a few yards to his right—he didn't feel scared. He wasn't thinking about the rest of the escape or the aftermath of the tensions between Russia and the West. Nor was he thinking about Elena or Lars, or about his mother or the Garcias or any of his Marine buddies, much less the rest of his life. There'd be plenty of time to think about such things soon enough.

Right now, in the silence, save the steady hiss of the oxygen flowing into his helmet, a single thought kept echoing in his brain. It wasn't from Dostoyevsky or Solzhenitsyn. It wasn't from his mom or even from the Scriptures. It was from Churchill, and for Marcus it captured the moment perfectly.

There truly was nothing more exhilarating than being shot at with no result.

EPILOGUE

THE WHITE HOUSE SITUATION ROOM,
WASHINGTON, D.C.—29 SEPTEMBER

McDermott's phone rang.

He instantly recognized the number. It was Nick Vinetti in Moscow. He took a deep breath and answered in a hushed tone so as not to distract the president, who was huddled in the corner with the defense secretary and the chairman of the joint chiefs, discussing their next moves.

Nick was calling from the operations center underneath the U.S. Embassy in Moscow. "You with the president?" he asked, his voice more stressed than sad.

"Yeah," McDermott said. "You calling about Marcus?"

"No, actually."

"No?"

"There's something else, something bigger," Vinetti said.

"What are you talking about?"

"Bill, something's about to break here, and you need to let the president know before he hears it from anyone else."

"Then spit it out," McDermott ordered. "What's wrong?"

"It's President Luganov."

"What about him?"

"He's been assassinated."

"What?"

"And not just him—Dmitri Nimkov, too."

"That's not possible," McDermott said.

"It's true, and there's more," Vinetti said.

"I'm listening."

"The guy you just put on that plane to whisk out of Moscow—the Raven—that's the guy the Russians say pulled the trigger."

McDermott felt the blood drain from his face. He didn't know if this meant the war was still coming or not. What he did know was that the world had just changed. Again. And he had to tell the president.

ACKNOWLEDGMENTS

After nearly sixteen years of writing thrillers about worst-case scenarios in the Middle East, it was time to shift gears and focus on new threats.

I am deeply grateful, therefore, to these and other experts on Russia, NATO, Europe, and U.S. national security and foreign policy who helped me make this pivot. They were exceedingly generous with their time, and while they may or may not agree with everything (or perhaps anything) in the finished novel, the book is far better for their insights.

- Hon. Stephen Harper, former prime minister of Canada
- Senator Lindsey Graham of South Carolina
- Porter Goss, former CIA director
- James Woolsey, former CIA director
- Rob Richer, former head of CIA operations in Russia
- Lt. General (ret.) Jerry Boykin, former Delta Force commander
- Jeff Gedmin, former director of Radio Free Europe/Radio Liberty
- Allen Roth, director of Secure America
- Andrei Illarionov, former chief economic advisor to Russian president Vladimir Putin (2000 to 2005)

I'm deeply grateful, as well, to our entire publishing team, without whom this book would never have made it to market.

Thank you, Scott Miller, for being my literary agent and my friend. You and your colleagues at Trident Media Group are the best in the business.

Thank you to the entire Tyndale House management team and staff—to Mark Taylor, Jeff Johnson, Ron Beers, Karen Watson, Jeremy Taylor, Jan Stob, Cheryl Kerwin, Dean Renninger, the entire sales force, and all the other remarkable professionals who work so hard to make Tyndale a publishing powerhouse.

Thank you to A. Larry Ross, Kristin Cole, Steve Yount, and Kerri Ridenour, who head up all of our public relations and media efforts. You did a wonderful job on *Without Warning*, and I'm so glad to be working with you on *The Kremlin Conspiracy* as well.

Thank you to June Meyers and Nancy Pierce, who work with me at November Communications, Inc. You both take care of everything I need from schedules to flights to finances and so much more, and you do it all with a heart of love and excellence. Bless you!

Thank you to my parents, Leonard and Mary Jo Rosenberg, and to all of my extended family and Lynn's. I am so grateful for you all.

Thank you to our four sons: Caleb, Jacob, Jonah, and Noah—and now to Caleb's wonderful fiancée, Rachel. I cherish all the joy and humor you bring into our lives.

Above all, thank you to my amazing wife, Lynn. You bless and inspire me more than I could have ever hoped for, dreamt of, or imagined, and I'm so astonished and humbled that the Lord brought you into my life!

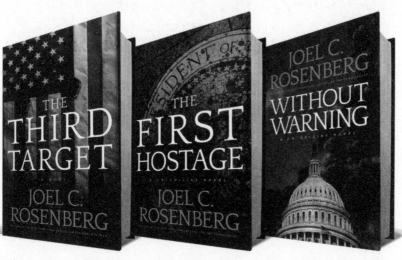